WHITE SPACES

Also by Elvin James Mensah

Small Joys

WHITE SPACES

ELVIN JAMES MENSAH

SCRIBNER

London · New York · Amsterdam/Antwerp · Sydney/Melbourne · Toronto · New Delhi

First published in Great Britain by Scribner, an imprint of
Simon & Schuster UK Ltd, 2026

SCRIBNER and design are registered trademarks of The Gale Group, Inc.,
used under licence by Simon & Schuster Inc.

1 3 5 7 9 10 8 6 4 2

Simon & Schuster UK Ltd, 1st Floor
222 Gray's Inn Road, London WC1X 8HB

Simon & Schuster Australia, Sydney
Simon & Schuster India, New Delhi

www.simonandschuster.co.uk
www.simonandschuster.com.au
www.simonandschuster.co.in

The authorised representative in the EEA is Simon & Schuster Netherlands BV,
Herculesplein 96, 3584 AA Utrecht, Netherlands. info@simonandschuster.nl

A CIP catalogue record for this book is available from the British Library

Hardback ISBN: 978-1-3985-1492-8
eBook ISBN: 978-1-3985-1494-2
Audio ISBN: 978-1-3985-2887-1

Printed and Bound in the UK using 100% Renewable Electricity at CPI Group (UK) Ltd

For Gulcan Akbal,

You make an imperfect world make perfect sense to me.

1

On the evening of my thirtieth birthday, Birch was sitting outside my doorway with two little ferrets running around his feet. It was after work and I was walking down the landing with my keys in my hand. Even before I reached the front door I pointed at him and said: 'No.'

He jumped to his feet with a ferret in each hand and yelled back: 'Yes.'

He was wearing shorts and one of my old hoodies. The ferrets were tugging at his curly brown hair, and he kept holding them away from his face, saying: 'Stop it, stop it,' as if they were misbehaving children. I tried not to laugh. I didn't want to encourage him. Eventually he tried to hug me but I leant backwards before he could embrace me. Then I pointed at the ferrets again and said: 'Seriously, no.'

He held them up at me and earnestly said: 'But Teddy, look at them.'

'I'm looking,' I said. 'And I don't care why you have them. Or where you got them from. I don't want them in my flat.'

'See, I thought you'd be this way,' he said. 'That's why we prepared this for you.' Dramatically he cleared his throat and started singing happy birthday to me, using the ferrets like a music conductors's baton as they jiggled around in his palms.

When he was done I stared at him a moment. He asked if this had convinced me to let them stay. I told him he'd convinced me of absolutely nothing.

'Don't you even wanna know their names?' he asked.

'What do you think?'

'Okay, great.' He held up one of them, the white one, and said: 'This one's called White Magnum. Or Whitey for short.' Then he held up the other one, which had brown fur. 'And this one's called Choc-Ice because—'

I put my hand up and nodded irritably like: *no, I get it.* He then pulled them both into his chest and said: 'Teddy, why are you so grouchy? It's your big three-oh.'

'Because I've had a long day,' I said. 'And I'm tired. And now there's this really annoying man trying to move two rats into my flat. Are any of these reasons doing it for you?' Birch and I had first met in secondary school; he had been living with me for the last five years. We had recently agreed that it was time for him to move out and he had pretended to be upset at the suggestion. But he always seemed to glide through life as if it were malleable and constantly contorting itself to accommodate his whimsies. So I knew he was secretly excited that I was pushing him out the proverbial nest. 'Why are you sitting outside anyway?' I asked now.

'To keep watch.'

'For what?'

'For you.'

'Why?'

'Nathan and Kain asked me to,' he said. 'Because apparently "I'm a nuisance" and "keep getting in the way". Can you believe that?' He used Whitey and Choc-Ice to gesture air quotes as he said this. 'They're both inside now.' I asked him what Nathan and Kain were doing and he replied: 'I'm not supposed to say.' Then I rolled my eyes and put the key in the lock.

When I opened the door the flat smelt rich and smoky. Nathan and Kain were placing plates of food on the dining table. They waved at me tiredly. They had a handyman business together and had finished a job that had lasted all day. They were still in their black polo shirts, cargo shorts and steel-toe work boots.

I'd known Nathan and Kain since secondary school too. Kain lived here with Birch and me. And Nathan lived about thirty minutes away in Deptford with his girlfriend and his son.

'What's all this?' I asked.

Nathan gestured at the food and wished me happy birthday. 'We tried, bruv,' he said. 'We got back late so we only cooked about half of what we wanted to.'

The table was topped with chicken skewers, mini beef patties, a big bowl of mac and cheese and several tall cans of beer. Kain took one can and opened it, then he raised it in a silent toast to me.

'We were supposed to be done at five,' said Kain. 'It was gonna be a surprise ting. And we were gonna put music on when you walked in, innit. But I forgot my keys so we had to wait in the van for—' he pointed dismissively at Birch, who waved at him with Whitey's paw. 'This silly paigan.'

'You know what, Kain,' said Birch. 'I'm not gonna engage with your little insults today, okay? And you wanna know why? Because I found love today. Yes, that's right. Ol' Birchy found love, while you lonely negroes roam around all on your ones.'

'I know you're not talking about me, cuz,' Nathan said.

'Not with my literal girlfriend and child at home. Who are also very real people and not two overgrown rats.'

Birch sighed. 'They're *ferrets* and they have names.'

'Which no one will be using,' I said. 'I'm serious. Take them back to wherever you found them.'

'And Teddy, what if I told you I found them all alone in a box, abandoned on the side of a motorway?'

'Then I'd say it's getting dark, so wear something reflective and look both ways.'

Kain and Nathan sat on the sofa. Kain downed his can of beer and Nathan removed the skullcap he had over his dreads. Then he stretched and yawned. Birch placed Whitey and Choc-Ice in an old shoebox. He then lay on his stomach and dangled his keychain in the air and made them jump and twirl around each other.

I looked at all the food on the dining table. Briefly I closed my eyes. Then I looked at the guys and said: 'This is wonderful. Thank you. But you really didn't have to go to the trouble.'

The three of them exchanged slightly nervous glances with each other. Then Nathan said: 'I know you're weird about birthdays, innit. But this is thirty, bruv.'

'Exactly,' added Birch. 'And now that you're basically ancient, who knows how long you've got to digest food without it being mashed into a fine paste first.'

Kain threw his can at Birch's head. And while Birch rubbed his forehead, I nodded approvingly and said: 'Thank you, Kain.'

Nathan and Kain both had quick showers and changed into vests and tracksuit bottoms. Birch and I were sitting at the table and he was making jokes about chewing my food for me. I told him he was allowed to only make one more of those jokes and he said: 'So that means I better make it a good one?'

'No,' I said. 'It means stop speaking.'

Then he told me I'd just 'grouched' myself out of my birthday present.

I chuckled and asked what he'd got me. And he said since this was the first smile he'd got out of me all day, he would give it to me. He got up and went over to the pullout sofa, which was also technically his bed. But sometimes he slept in my bed. From underneath the sofa he retrieved a white bag. When he handed it to me, I pulled out a framed photograph of us as kids. I looked up at him with an eyebrow raised like: where did you get this? He then told me my dad had uploaded this photo on Facebook yesterday and tagged us. I hadn't seen it yet. Ever since my dad had asked me to create an account for him, he'd become a serial spammer, posting about anything and everything. Even this morning he had wished me happy birthday over Facebook Messenger with a link to LMFAO's 'Sexy and I Know It' video, which he was currently obsessed with.

Birch and I were around twelve in the photo. Birch was lying on the floor in my parent's old house with a pained expression on his face. And I was kneeling beside him with my hands on his stomach, laughing hysterically. Birch spent a lot of time at my house back then. Especially after school and on weekends. He used to pretend to be sick so he wouldn't have to leave. I looked up at him again and smiled. He smiled back. Then I extended an arm out to him and we hugged each other. 'Thank you,' I said.

He kept his hands on my shoulders. Then, deeply, he looked at me with his bright brown eyes and said: 'I read somewhere once that old photos really help the geriatric when their minds start to—' I put my hand over his mouth and told him not to ruin the nice thing he just did.

When we were all seated around the dining table everyone piled food onto their plates. I left mine empty for as long as I could get away with. They then asked about work and I just shrugged and said it was still depressing. I was a senior editor at a magazine called *Rush!*. I'd worked there since I graduated university. Historically we'd been a pop music magazine. But recently we'd switched the focus of our coverage to indie, to a very muted reception.

To deflect the attention I asked Kain and Nathan about their own work. Recently it had been inconsistent, so they had to take bigger jobs that often overextended them, like roof replacements and large fencing work, for bigger payouts. Birch and I listened to them talk about clients from hell. Then Birch brought up the time he'd tried to help them. Once, without their knowledge, he downloaded a selection of shirtless gym-selfies Kain and Nathan had posted on Facebook and put them on a leaflet, along with their business number. He then gave them out to people in various clubs in Soho.

'You need to stop bringing that up, bruv,' said Nathan. 'I only just stopped being pissed about that.'

As Kain nodded in agreement, Birch said: 'Oh come on, boys. People love handymen. You swan about in people's houses with your calves out. And your big "strangle-me-please-I'm-begging-you" arms. And your slutty little shirts. You gotta use what you got to drum up business, guys. It's Business 101.'

'And what the fuck do you know about business, blud,' Kain said. 'You didn't drum up anything. The leaflet didn't even say we were handymen.'

'Yeah, that's what the number was on there for,' Birch said.

Then he tapped his temple with his finger repeatedly and said: 'We need to start using our brains, boys.'

It looked like one of Nathan's eyes was twitching. I laughed at Birch's continued attempts to justify the leaflet stunt with Kain.

I often thought of freedom when I thought of Birch. Even though I'd never really considered him any less black than Kain, Nathan and me, I also had a habit of conflating whiteness with freedom. His mother was a second-generation Jamaican. And both his biological dad and stepdad were from different parts of England. He didn't speak to any of them anymore.

Eventually I took a skewer and dragged off a cube of chicken with my teeth. I held it in my mouth for a moment, then I slid it into my cheek. As Nathan and Kain were yelling at Birch for trying to bring the ferrets over to the table, I retrieved a handkerchief from my pocket and unloaded the food into it. My heart raced as I looked around the table to see if anyone had noticed. But Birch was stood up now with a ferret in each hand, going on about how they were family and we needed to get used to it.

Later that evening, after Nathan went home and Birch had fallen asleep, Kain knocked on my door. I was sitting on my bed responding to a batch of birthday messages with the lights off. He had this sombre expression on his face when he opened the door and turned them on. He stood in the doorway and said: 'I know you didn't want a dinner. But Nate kept asking me questions and shit about why I didn't wanna do it. And it was starting to look like I didn't give a fuck about your birthday.'

I laughed assuringly. 'It's okay,' I said. 'Really.'

He came in and sat beside me on my bed. I glanced at our reflections in the mirror by my desk. The sight of us together made me look away; it invoked an irritation I didn't want to feel. Not irritation at him, but rather at the fact that I had any opinions about how we looked beside each other at all.

I asked him why Nathan had been so insistent that we do something, even though I'd expressed no interest in celebrating.

'He thinks you don't like restaurants,' he said. 'He thinks you don't like celebrating your birthday 'cause every year we're always asking if you wanna go out to eat.'

Casually I said: 'That's quite an assumption from him.'

Kain gave me a gentle shrugging gesture like: well, what's Nathan supposed to think. Then he said: 'He thought you'd like it if we just did shit here, where it was the four of us. So when I was like: nah, blud, just leave it. He thought I was being a massive hater, innit. So I just had to let it happen.'

'It was fine,' I said. 'I had a nice time.'

There was a brief pause. He looked at me with these doleful eyes. He then cleared his throat and told me he'd seen what I'd done with the piece of food earlier.

I looked down at my hands and then in a wounded tone of voice I said: 'Right, okay.'

There was another silence then which lasted a very long time. We'd been here before. And even then we never really knew what to say to each other. Or rather I didn't know what to say to him. So we simply said nothing.

From my periphery, I saw him begin the process of putting his hand on my shoulder. But something made him change his mind. He put his hand on his lap instead and stood up. He said he was going to clear the dining table and put some of the food in the fridge for the morning. He then asked if I needed anything. And without looking at him, I shook my head.

He let the door stay open when he left. I sat there still for a while. Then I got up and closed the door on the day.

2

After work the next afternoon, Birch met me at Passage, a drag bar in Soho where Nathan's girlfriend Mya worked as a bartender and was their resident drag king.

It was a summery afternoon. Birch was walking towards me in a navy hoodie and grey shorts. He had Whitey and Choc-Ice on leashes and was struggling to get them to walk in the same direction. When he stopped at the lights, people looked at him curiously. I shook my head at him as he crossed the road. 'Really?' I said. 'You've got the ferrets on leashes now?'

As he hugged me, he coughed. It was a deep raspy cough that made him rub his throat afterwards. I asked him if he was okay, and he just nodded, slightly teary-eyed, and said: 'The ferrets have names, Ted. You gotta start using 'em.'

I told him I'd call them whatever he wanted as long as I never saw them in my flat again. This made him drop to his knees and cup his hands over their ears. 'Oi,' he said. 'You're gonna fuck up their self-esteem with that kinda talk. And I swear to god, Teddy, if you make me walk around with a pair of anxious ferrets—'

I told him that people were staring and he said: 'So? Whitey and Choccy deserve respect, and they're gonna get it if it kills me.'

We sat at a table outside. We could hear Rizzle Kicks' 'Mama Do the Hump' playing from inside the bar and I noticed the Olympic rings had been painted onto the windows to celebrate the games starting next month. Birch asked me how my day had been. As he said this, he retrieved a Ziploc bag filled with little chunks of raw meat and started whistling to the ferrets. Whitey got on his hind legs and pawed at Birch's shin, while Choc-Ice twirled in a circle and licked his lips.

When I rolled my eyes, Birch said: 'What, Ted? They have to eat, don't they?'

A small dog raced up the path then, barking at Whitey and Choc-Ice. Birch yanked the leashes back, and the ferrets quickly cowered behind his legs as he yelled at the owner: 'Oi, keep your mutt away.'

I often pretended to find Birch's antics more exasperating than amusing. But the truth was most of the time I found his childishness endearing. I'd pretty much felt this way from the very first time I'd seen him in school. I was also intrigued by his eclectic approach to life. In the last two years alone, he had been a tour guide on one of those open top buses; a dog walker; he'd manned a hot dog stand in Trafalgar Square; and even worked in the mailing room at my office. Now he was housesitting for a rich white couple in Knightsbridge.

'Anyway,' Birch said now. 'How are you, man?' He looked at me and narrowed his eyes a little. 'This is, like, the second day in a row where you've looked fuckin' miserable. What's going on with you?'

'Miserable?' I said. 'Stop it. I'm fine.' I pulled the corners of my lips into an exaggerated smile.

He laughed and said: 'What? You don't believe me? Do you want a second and third opinion?' And then started reaching for Whitey and Choc-Ice.

'Birch, if you put them on the table and make them comment on whether I'm miserable or not, I'm gonna make you pay for your drinks.'

He put his hands up and said: 'Okay, fine. But what's wrong, man? Is it work? Are you beefing with Janice again?'

Janice was the editor-in-chief at *Rush!* She had spearheaded the magazine's transition from pop to indie music. She'd said that Britain's musical tastes were shifting and we needed to adapt. I'd argued that we would only alienate our readership and risk the substandard sales we were managing to muster up every month. And now we were struggling to find our feet.

I sighed. 'The sales of our last issue were crap,' I said. 'And I think it's done a bit of damage to morale. People just can't be bothered anymore. And Janice keeps acting like she can't see it.'

He smiled mischievously. 'Want me to fight her?'

'You think you'd win in a fight with Janice?'

'Well, I didn't say I'd win,' he said. 'I know she'd clobber me. But it's about the gesture, innit.'

I laughed. 'It really isn't,' I said. 'If you're gonna defend my honour, Birch, you better mean it.'

Birch had worked in the mailroom of my office for only a few weeks. He wasn't terrible at the job; he just got easily distracted. But in the end he was let go for having sex with someone in the stairwell. He didn't get caught – he just wouldn't stop telling people about it.

I told him now the last thing I wanted for my thirties was to worry about the security of my job, and that I didn't know what I'd do if I suddenly had to reevaluate and restructure my life. I felt like I had packed the different facets of my life in pristine glass boxes, and I was constantly trying to prevent cracks appearing in the casing.

Birch lifted Whitey and Choc-Ice onto his lap. They pawed

at his stomach and rubbed their faces in his chest. 'Well, man,' he said. 'If it all goes tits up, you can join me, Whitey and Choccy in our new digs.'

'New digs?' I repeated. 'You found somewhere to live?'

Birch nodded. He brushed his nose against the ferrets' fur and then in a high-pitched voice said: 'Yes, we have. Haven't we, my babies? Teddy tried to put us back out on the street but we landed on our feet, didn't we?'

I asked him where he was moving and he looked back up at me and said: 'Okay, Ted. I'll tell you. And I already know you'll have some opinions. But before you say anything, I just want you to remember that you're the one that kicked me out in the first place.'

'Well actually,' I said, 'we mutually agreed that it's been five years since you moved in with me. Now it's time to find some actual accommodation. And that you couldn't sleep on the pull-out couch forever.'

'You have your version of events,' he said. 'And I have mine.'

'Whatever,' I said. 'Where are you living now?'

'Okay, just remember, Ted, that I got a good deal out of this—'

I closed my eyes and pinched the bridge of my nose. 'A good deal out of what?'

'Lucy and Charlie are letting me move in with them.'

'The rich white couple?'

'My rich white couple, yes.'

'The ones you've been housesitting for?'

'The very same.'

I paused for a moment. 'I'm sorry, what?' I said. 'Lucy and Charlie, the rich white couple you're housesitting for, are letting you stay in their townhouse in Knightsbridge?' He nodded at me, so pleased with himself. 'How are you gonna make the rent?'

'You know,' he said casually. 'A little bit of this. A little bit of that. But anyway, man, you should see the house. It's fuckin' massive.' I told him he was making me nervous and then he said: 'Okay, T-Bear, I'll be honest with you. It's always been a bit more than just housesitting. And when I tell you what it is, you can't give me shit for it, alright? You gotta have an open mind.' I shrugged like: okay. 'Well, Lucy likes it when I fuck her while Charlie watches.'

I stared at him. Whitey and Choc-Ice pawed at his face while he watched me. 'Ted,' he said then. 'Your face isn't doing anything, man.'

'Sorry,' I said eventually. 'I'm just in the process of opening my mind.'

'How long d'you think that'll take?'

'I'll let you know.'

'Oh, I knew you'd be weird about this,' he said. 'That's why I didn't tell you.'

I raised an eyebrow. 'Because I'm the weird one in this situation? Is that what we're saying?'

I asked him then what the arrangement actually was, and he said Lucy was polyamorous and Charlie was into cuckolding, and that they were letting him stay rent-free out of the goodness of their little Caucasian hearts. And when I attempted to discuss the idea of using sex for rent and the various implications, he said the two things weren't related; that if anything Whitey and Choc-Ice were the trade-off.

'They gave you the ferrets?' I said.

'Yeah,' he said. 'They get a new pet, like, every month, man. So until I move in for real, it's like a shared-custody situation.'

*

Mya came outside to say hello then. She ran her fingers through mine and Birch's hair and said: 'Hello, my doves.' She was a couple hours into an eight-hour shift. I noticed her apron now had a pink 2012 logo embroidered beneath where it said PASSAGE. I pointed to it and said: 'Is Passage excited for the Olympics by any chance?'

She exhaled heavily. 'We have a whole new cocktail menu to learn,' she said. 'We're doing a Gold Medal cosmo.' I asked her what made it different from a regular cosmo and she replied: 'A bit of gold dust on the rim of the glass and a fifty percent price increase.'

Birch gasped and said: 'Fuckin' extortionate. I'll have three please.'

Mya kissed her teeth at him. When she noticed the ferrets tussling beneath the table she said: 'Birch, what the hell are those?' But before he could introduce them she said: 'Don't bring those rats here again. People eat here.'

'What?' he said. 'But there was a dog here earlier.'

'That's different.'

'Why?'

'It just is,' she said. Then she turned to me. 'Anyway, I'm sorry I missed your birthday yesterday. I feel awful. But I couldn't pass up the extra shift. You know I'm tryna catch these pennies.'

'Oh, don't worry about it,' I said. 'You can make it up to me by making one of those cosmos.'

'I probably should,' she said. 'I have to get the practice in.' She looked at Birch and said: 'You can have the ones that go wrong.'

Birch laughed. 'You say that like it's a threat,' he said. 'But I've had worse things inside me than a dodgy cosmo.'

She grimaced. 'I don't wanna think about what's been inside you, Birch.'

'You sure?'

She rolled her eyes and then sat down. 'Teddy, before I forget,' she said. 'You know how much Nathan and I love you?'

'Oh no,' I said. 'What do you want?'

She gasped. 'What?' she said. 'I can't tell you how much I love you on a random Friday afternoon?'

'You can tell me instead if you want,' Birch interjected.

Mya put her hand in his face then turned back to me. 'I need a favour,' she said. 'Would you be able to babysit Bakari next weekend please? I'm working a double and Nate's parents are flying out to Jamaica for the summer.'

'Of course,' Birch said. 'We can look after him for you.'

'No,' she said. 'I'm not asking you. I'm asking Teddy. You're not allowed to be left alone with my child ever again.'

'What?' said Birch. 'Why not?'

'Are you serious?' she said. 'The last time I let you babysit, you had him in a pub with a bunch of half-naked guys.'

'Is that what that little liar told you?' Birch said. 'We were in Wetherspoons! And there just happened to be a bunch of lads dressed like Adam Sandler from *You Don't Mess with the Zohan*. It was a stag-do! What was I supposed to do?'

'Oh, I don't know,' Mya said. 'Maybe keep your clothes on and not get arrested?'

'I didn't get arrested,' he said. 'Bakari and I watched an arrest *happen*. Massive difference.'

Mya shook her head. 'Birch, don't piss me off, yeah?'

'And the lads were all pretty lovely before the police came,' Birch continued, 'they were in blue swimming trunks and I was wearing Ted's blue boxers. We were all matching and they had a dance-off. I couldn't pass it up. What was I supposed to do?'

Mya narrowed her eyes. 'Birch, stop saying "What was I supposed to do?" Like you're not an actual thirty-year-old man.'

'Oi,' he said. 'Twenty-nine. Don't lump me in with the rest of these geriatrics. I've still got my whole life ahead of me. And also, Mya, they had Adam Sandler masks strapped to their faces. What was I supposed to—'

I looked at Birch and said: 'Please stop talking,' and then at Mya and said: 'Yeah, that's fine. I can do next weekend.'

She pinched my cheek. 'Thank you, Teddy,' she said. 'You can have Birch's dodgy cosmo instead.' She looked at Birch now. 'And you can stay parched.'

Birch looked at his phone then. He told us he'd just got a text from Lucy and Charlie. 'Jokes on you,' he said. 'I've got somewhere to be.' He picked up Whitey and Choc-Ice. 'Let's get you home, my babies.'

He hugged Mya, but only after she made him put down the ferrets. He then gave me a playful exaggerated kiss on the forehead.

As he left, he coughed again, a hard one that made him aggressively clear his throat after. I told him to see someone about that, but he just waved dismissively at me as he and the ferrets disappeared across the street.

Before Mya went back to work, she looked at my face and said: 'Why does your face look like that?'

I glanced up at her. 'I wish people would stop commenting on what my face looks like.'

She laughed. 'I just meant you were looking at Birch all longingly.'

'Oh,' I said. 'He just puts me on edge sometimes – did you hear that cough?'

'Yeah,' she said. 'It sounded bad. But why does that put

you on edge? And not those damn ferrets he's dragging around now?'

'Well, that too,' I said. 'But he had tuberculosis when he first started living with me.'

'Oh shit,' she said. 'Really?'

'Yeah, it was pretty bad,' I said. 'He was on this strict drug regimen and he had healthcare workers coming in and monitoring him and everything. He's been alright lately. But I've always had this fear of it coming back.'

'Oh, Teddy, look at you,' she said, grinning, yanking at my cheek again. 'It's so cute how much you worry about him. Just tell him to get it checked out?'

'Have you met him?' I said. 'You know how exasperating it is to get him to do anything.'

She nodded in agreement and then she said she better get back to work.

3

On Monday Nathan drove me to work in the white van he and Kain used every day. There were train strikes planned for the week and Nathan was heading into the city anyway.

He picked me up after a very early session at the gym. He was wearing a durag with the ends of his dreads sticking out and a damp grey vest, and he was still glistening with sweat. He had a piece of one of Mya's outfits – a floor-length cape – hanging inside a clear garment bag in the back of the van. It was for an upcoming show she had at Passage, and she'd asked Nathan to take it to another drag performer called Felicia Filth so they could reinforce the seams for her while she was working.

He had the radio turned to Capital FM and 'Black Heart' by Stooshe was playing. He was swaying his head side to side and gently tapping the wheel.

'You know I was thinking I should probably learn sewing or some shit,' he was saying. 'Or be on some garment construction ting, innit. Then I could just do this for her without driving around at the arse-crack of dawn.'

I looked at him curiously and said: 'I can't imagine you sat at a sewing machine making dresses.'

'Well imagine it, bruv,' he said. 'If there were enough hours in the day, yeah, I'd be right on that.'

When he hit a red light, he asked me to reach behind me and get his work shirt. It was crumpled up behind the seat. I unfolded it in front of me and saw the large patches of paint and dirt. I looked across to him with an eyebrow raised. He was taking off his vest then and spraying Lynx across his chest. He looked at my expression as he did it and said: 'Ted, I know. But we're installing some drywall this afternoon so it's only gonna get worse – it'll do for today, innit. I'll wash it after.'

I smelt it. 'But it stinks?'

He snatched it from me. 'Then stop fucking smelling it then,' he said. 'Who are you? Birch?'

'Birch smells your shirts?'

'No,' he said, 'but you know he would if he got the chance.' As he put the shirt on he said: 'Oh yeah, Mya said you'd babysit Bakari this weekend?'

'Yeah,' I said. 'Birch said he'd do it too. But after what happened at Wetherspoons that time she took that as more of a threat.'

Nathan shook his head and laughed. 'Bakari's excited, innit,' he said. 'He wants you to teach him to ride that bike you got him for his birthday last year.'

'You haven't showed him yet?'

'I've been busy, fam,' he said. 'It's fuckin' nonstop. Even though the money still ain't there like that. And now Mya wants to move out my parents,' so I gotta look for a second job so we can think about putting down a deposit. And even then—' I gave him a look that made him laugh and say: 'Nah, shut up, bruv.'

I laughed too. 'What?'

'If I want your help I'll ask for it,' he said. 'Just let me chat my shit, innit. And keep your wallet closed.'

Offering Nathan help was often a point of contention. It was difficult to gauge when to help. I'd bought Bakari a bike because Nathan regularly complained that Bakari kept asking for one, and he and Mya couldn't afford it. I'd got such an expensive model because I thought it would last Bakari so long that they wouldn't have to think about buying another one until Bakari was at least ten or something. But when I turned up at the flat with the bike, Nathan looked a little disappointed. Then he passive-aggressively implied that this was something he was taking care of.

'Well,' I said now. 'That was very presumptuous of you. I wasn't gonna offer to help anyway.'

'Then what was that look for, fam?'

'I was just trying to entice you with my eyes,' I said. 'You know I've always secretly wanted you.'

We laughed. Then he put his hand in my face and playfully pushed my head away. 'Speaking of that,' he said. 'Are your parents still talking to you about relationships and shit?'

'Not recently,' I said. 'I thought they might bring it up on my thirtieth. But my mum just said happy birthday and the next morning my dad randomly sent me a link to some lady doing that cinnamon challenge.'

He chuckled. 'Your dad's a joker.'

I agreed that he was. Then I said: 'I'm actually going up to Edinburgh to see them on Thursday. I bet they bring it up then.'

'Do you know what you're gonna tell them?' he asked. 'What is it? You keep saying you don't wanna be in a relationship and they don't believe you?'

'I think when I tell them that, what they hear is: I'm just waiting to be in one, which then makes them think I'm being lazy and not trying, which then makes them think I'm sad or depressed. I think it's just really difficult for them to believe that I could be happy without someone in my life in that way.'

As he drove over Vauxhall Bridge, I switched the radio station to Smooth Radio and 'Dreams' by Gabrielle came on. Nathan and I turned to each other and laughed.

'Oh god,' I said. 'Do you remember when we were, like, ten and Birch was obsessed with this?'

'Ah bruv,' he said. 'When he got your dad to record it off the radio on his little cassette—' He kissed his teeth. 'Nah. Turn it off, Ted. I swear, yeah, you couldn't beat or waterboard anything out of me. But play that song and I'm tellin' you everything, cuz. That nigga ruined that song for me.'

I laughed and turned the volume up. Nathan tended to dislike things Birch had been obsessed with. For me, however, Birch's grating enthusiasm gave sound to things that would've been otherwise mute.

Nathan asked me to turn down the music but I kept mouthing 'I can't hear you' at him.

At work our music editor, Monty, was waiting for me in my office. He had his ginger hair slicked back, and he was wearing a fitted polo shirt and beige chinos. He had his laptop opened up on my desk and he was grinning at a document on the screen.

'Monty,' I said as I sat down. 'You look pretty chirpy for a Monday morning. What's up?'

'Yeah, it's a good day, mate,' he said.

'Why?' I asked. 'Is there a positive sales report I've missed or something?'

'I dunno, mate,' he said. 'You've got that meeting with sales today, ain't you? Anyway, nah. I'm sat here smiling cause it's nearly party time, baby! And I'm in charge.'

Every year *Rush!* threw a themed summer party. They used to be big blowouts with hordes of fans and celebrities and a string of performers. But it had become increasingly intimate over the years. Initially it was to reflect our pivot from pop to indie music. But then our declining sales reports slashed the budget to nothing, so the minimalism became a necessity. Eventually our events planner was let go to cut costs and Monty was put in charge.

'Janice emailed me last night,' he said, beaming. 'I'm well excited, mate. I'm just putting some ideas together now.'

I asked him what theme he had planned and he said: 'Oh, I'm throwin' it back, Ted. Right back to the nineties, mate.'

On my desk I had a framed photo of Birch, Nathan, Kain and me at one of the last parties we threw before we downsized. The theme was Pimps and Hoes, and the four of us were wearing colourful suits and fedoras, smiling drunkenly at the camera. Throughout the evening we kept rotating who got to hold the silver cane. In the picture, it was Birch's turn and he was holding it above our heads triumphantly. I smiled at it and turned the photo around to Monty.

He took the picture off my desk and smiled at it too and said: 'How's ol' Birchy doing? I miss that guy.'

When Birch worked in our mailroom, he often slacked off with Monty. They seemed to revert back to children when they were together. Once they stuck a pad of white Post-it notes all over their faces and drew red circles on each other's cheeks so they looked like Jigsaw from *Saw*.

'He's alright,' I said. 'He's got ferrets now. We don't know why. Anyway, how are we doing on the materials for next month's issue?'

He unplugged a USB stick from his laptop and slid it towards me. 'It's all there, mate,' he said. 'Well, nearly. We've got our Q&A's finalised. The next batch of album reviews are sorted. We're still waiting on some features, so I'll see what's going on with those later.'

I flung my head back and swivelled in my chair. 'So we don't really have anything?'

He laughed. 'It's gonna be alright, mate,' he said. 'How many times have we been a few days out from the deadline and things just come together in the final hour?'

'Too many times,' I said. 'I don't like it, Monty. I wanna get the mock-up of the next issue to art by this afternoon. And then to Janice by close of business tomorrow. And hopefully we'll get her notes by Wednesday. So please talk to your team.'

Sarcastically he saluted me and said: 'Yes, sir.'

'I'm serious,' I said. 'The deadlines aren't suggestions. I don't want Janice on our backs again. You know she hates us.'

'No, I get you, mate,' he said. 'I'll have a word.'

Before he left my office, he clicked his fingers and said: 'Oh yeah, Ted, did you have a chat with the bird on reception like you said you would? I didn't wear this shirt for nothing, mate.'

I looked at his shirt and then up at his face. I asked him what was so special about it. Then he flexed one of his biceps and said: 'It makes me look like a fuckin' smoke show, don't it? And I want the new bird on reception to see the guns. I've been an absolute beast on the weights, mate.'

Monty was going through an acrimonious break-up with his girlfriend of eight years. He had been emotionally frag- ile for the last few weeks. There had been nights where I had stayed behind with him in my office because he didn't want to go back home to his empty flat. When he eventually showed interest in our building's new receptionist, I said I'd talk to her on his behalf. But I'd assumed he was only speaking out of sadness and desperation and was simply looking for a distraction, so I'd forgotten all about it.

'How are you doing by the way?' I asked him.

'I'm alright,' he said. 'But I'll feel even better if you keep your promise and have a word.' I didn't say anything. He'd told me he was notoriously bad at talking to women and that it was a wonder he'd even had a girlfriend in the first place. But despite the playfulness he displayed in our conversations, he still seemed so raw from the break-up that it felt strange to facilitate a meeting like that.

'Oh, come on, Ted,' he said now. 'You said you would, mate. Go on. Just ask her what her type is. And if it's sexy ginger blokes, I'll just come strollin' through to reception like—' he did a funny little walk as he went towards the door. 'And you've already spoken to her, so you've got a bit of a rapport now, ain't you?'

'Rapport?' I said. 'My ID card was broken and she was getting me a temporary one.'

He was standing in the doorway now. He paused a moment and looked away contemplatively. He then clicked his fingers again, pointed at me and said: 'Ah. You're making it a challenge.'

'Excuse me?'

'You're giving me clues, ain't you?'

'Monty, what are you talking about?'

'What you're saying is I need to pretend my ID card is broken so I have an excuse to talk to her.'

'I'm literally not saying anything.'

'Ah, this is classic stuff, Ted,' he said. 'Classic fuckin' stuff. I should've thought of that myself.' He gestured between us as if we were both in on a secret. He then took out his ID card and started bending it in half.

I glared at him. 'If your lack of professionalism gets us delayed further, I'm not gonna be very happy.'

He put his card back in his pocket. 'You're right,' he said. 'Give me yours instead.'

After the meeting with sales I sat in the toilets with my face in my hands. Every time my stomach started to rumble, I worked up some anxiety about someone coming in and hearing it. But I found that isolation was better than being around my colleagues, especially when I felt like this, like I was starting to lose control of something I thought I'd had such a firm grasp on.

I hadn't eaten in a while and the thought of doing so made me feel both embarrassed and sick. I liked how easy it was to ignore my afflictions at work. Even then, in the toilets, I could shift my attention from food to bad sales projections. I could exit the toilet and be confronted with the stress that came with that. Stress that would inevitably snowball and occupy even more space in my head. Feeling weak or ill could often be masked with the effort of feigning ignorance, as if I was laying a blanket over the mess in my mind and dusting off my hands.

After lunch I caught up with Janice in her office. She had short spiky blonde hair and one gold tooth. Her Jamaican accent also deepened when she was angry. When Monty and I had opposed her during *Rush!*'s transition from pop to indie and had argued that we would be alienating our readership, she had said: 'When are you two gonna stop being such pains in mi pum pum and get on board?'

She was sitting on her desk flicking through a binder when

I walked in. She hadn't been at the sales meeting so I thought she'd want to follow up. But when she saw me she stood and said: 'Why didn't you remind me it was your birthday last week?'

I sighed and told her that even on the brink of closure, this office was insufferable about birthdays and it was just something I wanted to avoid. She made a face and said: 'Oi. Mouth—'

'What?' I said. 'You know I don't like the attention.'

'Anyway,' she said. 'Come eat these cupcakes before they go stale. I had one of the work experience kids do a Tesco run. I've already had a few. You know, just a likkle taste test. But you can have the rest. Don't say I don't treat you nice.'

She stepped to the side. There was an almost empty plastic tray of red velvet cupcakes. I had no intention of taking them, let alone eating them. But the threat of Janice picking apart my disinterest in the cakes frightened me. In that moment, the only thing worse than eating them was the conversation that might happen if I didn't.

'Taste test?' I said. 'It was a pack of eight. There's only two left.'

'Take it as payment,' she said, 'for the grief you and Monty keep giving me.'

'You might as well have the rest,' I said. 'I really don't care.'

'No,' she said. 'I probably shouldn't. I mean, they were to celebrate your big three-oh.'

'And how many cupcakes deep were you before you remembered that?'

She narrowed her eyes at me. Then she said she hoped I did something fun for my birthday. Before I told her that I had, I ran my tongue across the top row of my teeth. I liked how smooth they felt now. A few months ago I got some composite bonding done to fix some of the enamel erosion that had amassed over the years from the vomiting. Before the fix, I'd started folding my lips over my teeth whenever I spoke to anyone. Increasingly I noticed people asking me to repeat things I'd said many times already. Once, during a conversation with Monty, he said: 'How about you just write it down, mate.'

Eventually Janice sat down and started talking about the disappointing sales reports and how she was struggling to get sponsors secured for our next few issues. 'We're gonna end up like fuckin' *Smash Hits!* did,' she said. I'd started to respond before she exhaled and said: 'I don't wanna hear it, Ted. It's too late for: "I told you so." I need solutions.' And I just shrugged and looked at her. As she continued to talk, I moved the cupcakes in front of me to create the illusion that I might eat them. At one point she put her palms on her face and pulled her skin down. I bit into a piece then and kept it on my tongue and eventually moved it into my cheek. When she did the same motion again I unloaded it into my palm and put the mushy chunks in my pocket.

As I was leaving she told me not to forget the cupcakes. Then as I went back for them, she tapped the table and said: 'Oh yeah. We got two passes for a gig. I'm forwarding you the tickets.'

'What band?'

'Fuck knows,' she said. 'But you and Monty should probably go. Get 'em interviewed. We need the material.'

The tickets were for a band called Alt-J. I forwarded them to Monty and he replied saying: 'Hell yeah, can't wait, mate!'

Before I went home that evening I sat in my office and scooped out the bits of cake from my pocket. It was really quiet. I felt tears glide down my face as I slid the grainy clumps into the bin beneath my desk. Sometimes I would wish that simply removing myself from a distressing situation was enough to grant me a kind of reprieve. But the hurdle wasn't just in the situation itself, but also in the aftermath. I hated how the anguish seemed to follow me and expose itself in various forms and suddenly I could see failure in everything, and not just in the inability to eat a simple cupcake. It was like I was unable to contain the darkness to one aspect of my life and I was being forced to sit back and watch it spread.

When I left the building, I got a text from Birch saying that Whitey and Choc-Ice had shat on my kitchen floor. I then got a similar text from Kain saying the house stank and that he couldn't wait for Birch and the ferrets to move out.

I smiled at my phone. I felt as if I were taking refuge in their antics, that their collective absurdities were scabbing over my maladies. And I felt grateful that I could manipulate my life this way, that I could temporarily exonerate myself from anguish in moments when it seemed impossible.

April 1993

Teddy spends his first few months of secondary school alone. The only people seemingly aware of his existence are the same people who have decided to prey on his loneliness.

That morning, after his father drops him off, Luke Williams, a tall, pale boy with dark blonde hair, meets Teddy outside the school gates. Luke is wearing a green parka, holding a bottle of Lucozade and is surrounded by a group of other boys; a following he rapidly amassed during those initial weeks of the school year. Almost in unison, they shout to Teddy: 'Oi oi, Skinny! How are ya?'

Teddy looks at the ground and doesn't respond. He is wearing jogging bottoms underneath his school trousers to make his legs look thicker, and two tops under his school shirt to make himself seem bulkier. He'd thought it would put a stop to all the 'skinny' comments. It's unseasonably warm for April and he can already feel a layer of sweat congealing across his stomach.

Luke steps towards Teddy and tells him that it's rude not to respond when he's being spoken to. He then looks back at his friends and says: 'I think I've got my feelings hurt a bit here, boys—'

Teddy mumbles something that Luke doesn't hear, so Luke

puts his hand over his ear, leans in closer to Teddy and says: 'What was that, mate?'

'I said I'm fine,' Teddy says meekly.

'Oh, you're fine, are ya?' Luke mocks in a high-pitched tone. 'Well I ain't, Skinny. Go on – ask me why?' Teddy stays silent for so long that Luke shakes him and repeats in a growl: 'Ask me why?'

And when Teddy finally asks, Luke shows him the back of his hand. The skin on his knuckles has crusted and scabbed over. 'See that?' Luke says. 'Not very nice, is it?'

The previous week, Teddy's father hadn't been able to pick him up from school. One of his colleagues at the post office had been sick, so he had to cover their route. Luke and his friends had followed Teddy on his way home. They tugged at his backpack and tried to etch their fingers through his little afro. When Teddy took off the backpack and handed it to them, they still pushed him to the ground and stamped on his chest. The pain had made him yell so loud that Luke and his friends screeched with laughter. It saddened Teddy to witness just how happy they were to see him squirm, to struggle, to beg. Eventually Luke straddled him and tried to get a clear shot at his face. But Teddy kept flinching and dodging his punches so frantically that Luke scraped his knuckles against the pavement.

Now, Luke opens the bottle of Lucozade. 'But I'm a forgiving person, mate,' he says. 'Go on. Have a drink on me. You never know, Skinny, it might even fatten you up a bit.' Dramatically, Luke clears his throat, spits inside the bottle and pushes it towards Teddy.

Teddy quietly retches and Luke and his friends snigger. When Teddy tilts his head away, the horror on his face only makes Luke laugh a louder, throatier laugh. Teddy retches again. Then Luke stops pretending as if this is a joke and barks: 'Down it!'

Teddy shakily reaches for the bottle. 'Oh my god,' someone says. 'He's actually gonna do it—'

'Oh, he is as well,' Luke confirms. 'See I told you, boys. Fuckin' vermin.'

After Teddy takes the bottle, he hears a loud Scottish accent from behind him. 'What are you all doin' out here then?' the voice says.

He turns around and sees his history teacher, Mr McAllister, standing at the gates with his arms crossed. He's a lanky man with dark, messy hair and an even messier beard. 'It's eight thirty,' he continues, tapping his watch. 'You should be in class, shouldn't you, boys? Makin' yourselves smarter. Puttin' those brain cells to use. Gettin' those gears turnin'.' He gestures towards the school gates. And as Luke and the rest of the boys filter through, he looks at Teddy and says: 'Eh, you know the rules—' He clicks his fingers and opens his palms, winking at him. 'Hand it over, son.' When Teddy gives him the bottle, Mr McAllister flings it over his shoulder and lands it directly in the bin behind him as the orange liquid projects itself into the air and trickles down like rain.

'You see that shot, lad?' he says. 'Magic Johnson ain't got nothing on me.'

Last Friday, Teddy had been watching the news with his parents. His mother had just finished gardening and his father, still in his postman uniform, was sat beside him on the sofa with his arm curled around him.

When the presenter announced that a teenager named Stephen Lawrence had been murdered in Eltham, Teddy's back stiffened and he felt his father hold him a little tighter.

As the presenter relayed details of the attack, it was as if the world was stripping itself of sound and colour, and everything that had once made it seem dynamic and vibrant was being rendered into something two-dimensional and flat. It was the first time he had been this hyperaware of his blackness. Although his father had routinely warned him about not looking suspicious in front of authority figures and to simply comply if he was ever stopped and searched, Teddy had always thought this advice had been more preventative than essential, the same way someone might've told him to look both ways before crossing the road.

When he went to sleep that night, and for many nights after, he couldn't get that image of Stephen out of his head: Stephen holding up his fist as he smiled at the camera. It had made him think about Luke Williams and his friends. He feared them, sure. But now his fear had suddenly undergone a kind of renovation. For as much as they'd targeted him, and for as much as he understood that his blackness was one of the reasons why – even though they had never explicitly said so – he'd never thought this kind of harassment was something that could cost him his life.

At lunchtime, Mr McAllister catches Teddy in the hallway. For weeks he's been skipping lunch and starving himself until dinner. On the first day of school he'd told himself that he couldn't eat because he was either too nervous or too embarrassed to sit alone in the canteen. Now he waits out the lunch hour in a secluded part of the field by the basketball cage.

Mr McAllister asks him if he has had lunch and he lies and nods his head.

'Great,' Mr McAllister says. 'Come with me.'

Teddy follows him down the hall and they stop at a class-room around the corner. Through the window he can see two students arm-wrestling. Mr McAllister opens the door and points at one of them: a husky boy with a mop of messy brown hair. His blazer is on the floor and his tie is undone around his neck. 'Alright, Teddy,' Mr McAllister says, 'this is Birch.' Birch looks up and enthusiastically waves with his free hand, and Teddy smiles and waves back. 'And this is Mr Nathan Lawrence.'

Birch makes a face and says: 'Oi, sir. Why does he get "Mr Nathan Lawrence" and I just get Birch?'

Nathan, who comparatively looks much neater, chuckles. 'Because I'm better than you.'

'Bullshit,' Birch says.

'Eh,' Mr McAllister snaps. 'Language, boys.'

'Sorry, sir,' they both drone.

Mr McAllister gestures Teddy to the empty chair between Birch and Nathan. Timidly, Teddy sits down and Mr McAllister says: 'This was supposed to be a kind of bad kids club. But now it's like a lonely boys club or something. I dunno, it sounds a lot better than detention, doesn't it?'

When Mr McAllister exits, Birch and Nathan watch the window intently until he disappears from view, and then they reach into their pockets and pile handfuls of sweets on the table. As Teddy watches granules of sugar from the fizzy cola bottles powder the table, he asks them why they're here.

Birch laughs and says: 'I'll tell you why I'm here, if you show me what you've got for lunch.'

Nathan kisses his teeth. 'You're such a tramp,' he says. 'You've already had your lunch.'

Birch tells him to shut up and Nathan rolls his eyes. He then tells Teddy to ignore Birch and enjoy his lunch.

Teddy thinks about telling them he's already eaten his lunch, but for some reason he says: 'I don't have any.'

Birch gasps and goes through his pockets. 'Ooh,' he says. 'I've got some cheese string. I was gonna have this during next period but you can have it, if you want?'

Teddy smiles at him. 'Oh no, that's fine.'

'I've never seen Birch share food before,' Nathan says. 'I'd take it.'

Birch tells him to shut up again. 'I share food all the time,' he insists. 'When we had pizza at yours last week – I let you have the last one.'

'Giving me the crust of your slice isn't the same thing.'

'Why not?' Birch says. 'Still pizza, innit?'

Nathan looks at Teddy and asks him if it is in fact still pizza. Birch looks at him too, giggling, and says: 'Teddy, of course it's still pizza – tell him!'

Teddy looks between them, amused. It's the first time he's felt like a definitive part of the student body, and not simply a cyst on its flesh, too benign to be removed. Grateful to be included in their camaraderie, he smiles and says: 'I'm not getting involved.'

Birch then puts his arm around him, leans his head against his, and looks at Nathan. 'He's on my side, really. He just doesn't wanna say it in front of you.'

Teddy laughs and pushes him away. He then asks them why they are in this 'club'.

'Well, my liege,' Birch begins, stripping down the cheese string and tilting his head back to guide it into his mouth. 'I'm what the teachers are calling a danger to my fellow class-mates. And thus cannot be trusted to—'

'He made us get into a fight with Luke Williams,' Nathan interrupts. 'Behind the bike shed and by the basketball cage.'

Birch asks if Teddy knows who Luke is. Teddy feels something tighten in his stomach as he nods. 'He's an arsehole, isn't he?' Birch says. 'I'm a bit of a hero, really. And I'd go up against him again if I hadn't promised Mr Mac two more weeks of good behaviour. But after that I'm taking him and his whole crew on. You watch.'

'He's a dreamer,' Nathan says to Teddy. 'They kicked his arse and he still got back up with his fists out, thinking he was gonna do something.'

'And I was,' says Birch. 'I just needed some time to catch my breath. Next time is gonna be different.'

'How?'

'Because I've seen the third *Karate Kid* now, haven't I?' Birch says, jabbing out his palms sharply in front of him. 'And now I'm all revved up and ready to go.'

Nathan tells him to stop it, that there won't be a next time.

But still Birch continues: 'Nah, because tell me this, right? How comes it's just us that got our lunches taken away, even though it was a six-man fight? It's an injustice, Nate. And I'm sick of it. And I've seen the third *Karate Kid*. And I'm gonna fuck 'em up next time.' He shoots a look at Teddy. 'Don't tell Mr Mac I said that or it'll be another week in here.'

Teddy makes a zipping motion on his lips and Birch winks at him, giving him a thumbs up.

Teddy asks then why they each have so many sweets on them. The question seems to trigger something in their heads and Birch and Nathan suddenly lock eyes and palms and start arm-wrestling again.

'You are weak, young Nathaniel,' Birch says theatrically, as if he's voicing a villain on a kids' show. 'Your puny arms are no match for my muscle, my brawn. Feel my power as I crush you and your little—'

Nathan slams Birch's hand on the table. 'You talk too much,' he says in a cool voice, sweeping all of Birch's sweets to his side of the table and offering a portion to Teddy.

After school, Teddy sees Birch and Nathan waiting for him by the gates. They're smiling and excitedly gesturing him over. He feels a deep melancholic pleasure wash over him then; he can't believe this is happening to him, and he's forcing himself not to question whether he deserves this. He smiles back and runs over, and they walk down to Deptford High Street together.

Birch throws an arm around Teddy and attempts to convince him of his plan to jump Luke Williams and his friends, while Nathan shakes his head in disappointment. As Teddy watches them bicker, he realises that this is the first time he has thought of loneliness as something curable, the first time he's felt that bad things don't necessarily come to an end but they can, at the very least, be placated; that friendship doesn't need to be declared for him to know that it simply is.

4

On Thursday I went to Edinburgh for a few days to visit my parents. They'd moved up there after I graduated from university. They lived on a quiet road in Craigentinny, in a little bungalow with a red roof. The driveway was only small, so the previous night my dad had moved his car onto the road so I could park there when I arrived.

That afternoon he met me outside as I pulled in. He was wearing a thick sleeveless fleece over a blue gingham shirt and a tweed flat cap, under which I could see tufts of bright silvery hair. When I got out of the car, he put his hands behind his head and started shaking his hips, doing the dance from the 'Sexy and I Know It' video, and then in his very thick Ghanaian accent yelled 'wiggle wiggle wiggle' at me. I closed my eyes and shook my head.

'He has returned,' he shouted. 'He has come back to us!' He clenched my arm and lowered himself onto one knee. He then flung his arms wide open and said: 'How may we serve you, my son?'

I laughed and told him to get up. He held my hand and he accused me of not appreciating his very warm welcome. When he stood back up, we hugged each other. Then I took off his hat and looked at it curiously for a moment. I asked him why he was dressed like a farmer.

He took it back. 'You think I look like a farmer?' he asked.

I nodded.

He downturned his lips and shrugged. 'If I look like a farmer, then maybe I was supposed to be a farmer in another life,' he said. 'You know your grandfather was a farmer in Ghana.'

'What happened to the tracksuits and football shirts?'

He put an arm around me. 'My son, you see,' he said. 'This is what happens when you visit your parents every five years. Your mind, it starts to, ehh—' He made a strange mumbling noise and then motioned in the air with his fingers.

My dad enjoyed pretending that I didn't visit him regularly, when in truth I did so every few months. I told him I was last here in March, so maybe it was his mind that was starting to go. He laughed and said we were too old to argue.

'But let me ask you this, son,' he then said. 'What would you do if, god forbid, your mother and I died. And the last time you saw us was all those months ago. And you never got to see me in my new threads.' He spun around dramatically. 'Theodore, my new threads! You see how quickly things can change.'

I rolled my eyes. 'Yeah, I guess that would've been tragic.'

He chuckled. 'You think you are funny?'

'Hilarious, in fact.'

We walked through the house and out into the garden. My mother was lying on her stomach by a colourful flower bed and I thought she'd collapsed or something. I yelled: 'Mum, are you alright?'

My dad held my shoulder and laughed. Then my mum

slowly raised her hand, gave me a thumbs up and shouted
that she was just weeding. My dad started to explain that
with perennial plants you had to get really close because of
their thick roots, and I promised him that I would visit more
if he spared me a lecture about botany.

Gardening was a passion my mother had rediscovered
since moving to Scotland. She was currently preparing to
enter a garden show competition this summer. I remembered
when I was younger, I would sit by the kitchen door on
summer afternoons and watch her plant new flowers in the
garden beds. But some of the kids in the area liked to jump
though the gardens and vandalise pretty things, so eventually she just stopped.

When she got up, she was holding two yellow flowers with
long roots dangling beneath. She high-fived my dad and
gleefully she said: 'I did it!'

We hugged then and she told me she missed me. My dad
encroached on our hug and wrapped his arms around the
both of us.

He looked at his watch, and said he was off to meet his
friend Jamie to go birdwatching in Holyrood Park, and that
he would be back in time for dinner tonight.

'Jamie?' I said. 'Mr McAllister? Since when do you guys go
birdwatching together?'

'Oprah,' he said. 'I don't have time for all these questions.
I already told you my best friend is waiting for me. We can
do this interview later.'

I knew my dad and my old history teacher had been
friends for years. But I also thought that the novelty of their
friendship would have worn off by now. I remembered at
parents evenings my dad would be so fascinated by Mr
McAllister's Glaswegian accent. And Mr McAllister would

be equally fascinated by my dad's job as a postman, and had even given him the nickname: Postman Theo.

My mother and I sat in the living room after my dad left. She was laughing at my confusion about my dad and Mr McAllister's relationship. We were sat beside the mantlepiece which had a collection of their photographs. Them on various holidays posing beside other couples, in necklaces made of flowers and holding cocktails; my dad sitting on the shoulders of a large bodybuilder, while my mother hooked her forefinger in the waist of the bodybuilder's speedos with a surprised expression and a hand over her mouth.

She gently placed the back of her hand on my face and said: 'Theodore, you're not looking well.' I made a face and told her I was fine. 'Are you eating?'

'Of course I'm eating,' I said.

I had decided to stop making my problems something my parents had to worry about. It was a decision I'd made out of a kind of twisted altruism. On the one hand, after being in and out of hospital when I was a teenager, I no longer wanted to burden them with something I believed I could manage on my own. And on the other, I felt a kind of humiliation that grew darker and more insidious the older I got, and had to acknowledge that this illness wasn't something I'd left in my adolescence, and that it had festered into my adulthood.

'If you are having problems again,' she said. 'You know you need to tell us.'

'Mum, I'm serious,' I said. 'I'm fine. Of course I'm not gonna look well. Work is stressful and I have three equally stressful friends.'

'What is happening at work?'

'Well, we're losing a lot of our readership,' I said. 'We've been doing so for a while now. But it's getting worse.'

She started to laugh and said: 'Ah – Theodore. Now who is still reading magazines? If people want news, they just go on their phones.'

'It's not a news magazine,' I said. 'It's a music magazine. You know this.'

Still laughing, she said: 'My point is still standing. News news. Music news. It's all on the phone. Don't you have a website?'

I lifted an eyebrow. 'What do you know about websites?'

She recoiled and said: 'What? You think I'm old and don't know about websites?'

I told her we did have a website but that it was very bare bones and our focus had been on keeping our printed media alive. She looked at me and laughed again as if its death was inevitable. 'Mum, why are you laughing?' I said. 'You were worried about how I was a few seconds ago. You know if I lose my job I'll have to move back up here with you and dad.'

'And what is wrong with that, eh?' she said. 'Your bedroom is still there.' She told me then that actually she wanted me to sort out the mess in my room before I went back home and get rid of all the things I didn't want anymore. 'I want a clean home,' she said, 'and your stuff is getting in my way.'

That evening we went for dinner at an Italian restaurant near Edinburgh Castle. At the table my parents asked how I celebrated my thirtieth and I told them that I just had dinner at my flat with the guys. They didn't seem very impressed with this. And I could feel in the way they looked at me that they had expected me to relay some extravagant stories, even though extravagance had never played much of a part in forming my personality.

To shift the focus off of me, I told them about Birch and

his ferrets. 'Two of them,' I said. 'Called White Magnum and Choc-Ice.'

'Ah!' My mum said. 'Now where did that boy get ferrets?' She laughed, kissing her teeth. 'That boy is always doing something.'

I told them he was living with a rich white couple now, who he was also sleeping with, and that they'd given him the ferrets as a gift or something.

'Sleeping with both of them?' My dad asked. 'The husband and the wife?'

'Apparently so,' I said. 'It's a polyamorous thing, I think.'

My dad laughed too then, throwing his head back. 'Eh!' he said. 'That boy. When you go back to London give him my love. I miss him.'

I said I would and then they asked what I'd been up to, how my own life had been. When I continued to talk about how badly things had been going at *Rush!* my dad stopped me and said: 'It cannot just be work work work. Look at Birch. Where are your ferrets? Where is your, eh, what did you call it? Where is your polyamorous?'

I made a face. 'Are you being serious?'

My mum hit him on his arm. 'What he means is you should have other things going on in your life,' she said. 'You should have more fun.'

'I am having fun,' I said.

They both stared at me and then my mum said: 'Teddy, you need a lover.'

'Right,' my dad added. 'Son, where is your *law-vah*? We are worried.'

Just then, our waiter brought over some water in a tall glass bottle. When they left, my dad asked me again where my *law-vah* was and lifted the bottle. He looked underneath it and said: 'I can't find it.'

My mum pulled back the tablecloth. 'I can't see it here either,' she said, giggling.

My dad then arched his hand over his eyes and looked around the restaurant.

I reached for his hand and put it back on the table. 'Okay, stop it,' I said. 'You've made your point. But I don't think I need to "find a lover". Why is it so hard to believe I'm happy?'

My dad told me it was because when he looked at me, he couldn't feel my happiness in his chest. He then angled his palm in the air and said: 'You are here.' Then he raised it higher. 'And you should be here.'

I sighed. 'I don't know what to tell you,' I said. 'I can't force you to believe I'm happy. But I am. Everything's fine.'

I forced a smile at them. Then I wondered why I was forcing the smile if everything was fine. The lie wasn't just for their benefit but for mine too. But since I was apparently so bad at disguising my distress, I thought maybe it was better for my parents to think that any sadness they could see in me was due to a lack of romance in my life.

'Son,' my dad said now. 'My dear Teddy. My lovely Theodore Jr.' I raised an eyebrow. There was a brief pause, then he took a deep breath and said: 'It doesn't matter if you are gay.'

We looked at each other in silence for a moment. Then eventually I said: 'Sorry?'

'I said it doesn't matter if you are—'

'No, I heard what you said,' I said. 'Who told you I was gay?'

My parents looked at each other, confused. And then my mum said: 'Well, you are thirty now. And we have never seen any girlfriend—'

'No women at all,' my dad added.

'And we thought maybe you were—' Her words trailed off

as if saying the word gay again might offend me. But my dad
made creaking sounds as if he were opening and shutting a
closet door to complete the sentence.

They told me then that they'd just started watching this
show and that the gay character, who had gone a few episodes denying they were gay, had finally come out to their
father, who had hugged him after an emotional conversation.
And that this had prompted them to think about me.

My dad clicked his fingers, trying to remember the name
of the show, saying: 'Have you seen it? It's the one where they
sing all the songs.'

I made a face. 'Glee?' I said. 'You guys have been
watching Glee?'

My mum nodded. 'It's very good.'

'Wait,' I said. 'You think I'm gay because you watched a
few episodes of Glee?' They nodded. 'And for the record, I
haven't brought any men around either, so—'

They said that if I was gay then I could tell them. And I told
them that if I was then I would've already. They still looked a
little confused, as if they'd thought they'd found the key that
unlocked who I was as a person, yet upon insertion, the key
simply wouldn't turn. But the truth was that I was a person
who had never desired to be in a romantic relationship. Or at
this point even desired to be sexually intimate with anyone.

I could articulate a lot to my parents. But they associated
singlehood with sadness and loneliness so much that I
couldn't bring myself to argue, so I just smiled at them and
asked if they were ready to order.

It had been evident to me from a young age that my extended
family didn't respect my father. I remember when we would
go over to their houses on Sunday afternoons after church, I

would see him get iced out of conversations. Once when I was eight they were huddled together talking about the footballer Justin Fashanu. One of my uncles was holding a newspaper with a picture of him and the front page said: £1M SOCCER STAR: I AM GAY. They called him an abomination and then one of my aunties said something about how his parents hadn't done enough to prevent this. 'It's just a cancer,' she'd said. 'Like any other illness. You catch it early. And then you cut it out.' I saw my dad's eyes spring open and then he said that Justin's sexuality didn't make him any less human or negate any of his accomplishments. Everyone looked at each other and laughed. And then another auntie looked at my mother and said: 'Look at him defending that degenerate. You need to watch out for Theo. He might surprise you one day.'

This blatant dismissal of my father's character confused me. Even back then there was so much I admired about him. I liked how he sobbed at sad movies and songs. I liked how expressive he was. I liked that he wasn't someone who withheld praise or was afraid to call something beautiful. And my mother loved this about him too. Whenever someone would attack or talk over him, she would pull him back into the fold and say something like: 'Uh, excuse me. Theo was speaking,' or 'Theo has a point.' And he would look at her like a whole ocean had risen in his chest and it was just everything he could do not to burst.

My parents always seemed like each other's anchors, pulling the other back to shore when they were adrift. I felt grateful to be witness to this kind of love; lucky even. But it was never something I felt compelled to seek for myself. At least not this version of it.

At the time I couldn't comprehend or even articulate why I felt that way. Then eventually I came to understand that, yes, I wanted love in my life, but that I also knew that love wouldn't necessarily come from anything sexual or romantic.

When we got home that evening, I started sorting all the stuff in my old room like my mother had asked. She had piled a stack of books and papers and pictures in the corner by the dresser. I sat on my bed and looked through them. I hadn't realised that I'd left so much stuff behind, especially the pictures, so I was surprised when I came across one photo in particular, of Birch, Nathan and me when we were younger. My dad had taken it. It was a candid shot of us in our school uniforms. Nathan was sitting on a low wall eating a box of chicken wings and chips. And Birch had hopped on my back. He was making me run while he pretended to be a flying superhero.

It reminded me to text Birch and ask how he was, if he was still coughing. While I waited for his reply, I continued looking through the stack. Eventually I came across a small selection of letters I'd written him over the course of a few years that I'd never sent. Near the end of secondary school we lost contact for a long time. His stepdad had kicked him out of their house but at the time, I was told he'd run away. In the hope that he would return, I wrote him letters and sent them to his house. I continued to do this even at university, telling him how much I missed him and about what was going on in my life. I even kept writing them when I moved to Edinburgh with my parents until I could afford my own place in London. In the end I wrote because I found it comforting. I accepted that wherever he was and whatever he was doing, for whatever reason, he didn't want to hear from me. And that perhaps I was a bit of a loser for trying to cling on to this old adolescent friendship so tightly.

Birch texted back saying he was fine, that he wasn't

coughing as much anymore. Then I asked him to book an appointment with the GP just in case. He ignored the message and replied with a selfie he'd taken of himself with Whitey and Choc-Ice instead. They were both sitting on his shoulders and he had his lips pursed, holding up a peace sign. Of course I really wanted him to take my concern seriously, but I just ended up smiling and laughing at the photo.

He was always belittling my concern in this way and I hated that just as much as I found it endearing.

In the early morning I went into the bathroom when I was sure my parents were asleep. I hadn't felt well since we'd got back from the restaurant. I'd managed to eat but I could feel the food sitting in the pit of my stomach and I couldn't stop thinking about it. Every time I opened my mouth I felt sick. I closed the door and knelt before the toilet and retched. I could sense the clumps of food in my chest, and their trajectory seemed to stop at the back of my throat, so I used my finger and then the back of my toothbrush to make myself vomit. The bathroom was at the back of the bungalow so I was happy my parents couldn't hear me.

Afterwards I lay on the cold tiles in the dark and looked up at the ceiling. In the silence I could hear how loudly I was breathing. My throat was burning and I felt exhausted. A few more moments passed before a square of harsh white light appeared beside me. Birch, who famously had an erratic sleep schedule, had sent me another selfie. I picked up my phone and held it above my head. It was a photo of Whitey and Choc-Ice sleeping in their dedicated play area in Lucy and Charlie's house. Birch had his head next to them, smiling softly at the camera as the flash spotlit his face.

5

That weekend Birch and I babysat Bakari. We took him to Deptford Park which was only down the road from where Nathan's parents lived. It was a very warm day but there was still a breeze that made the grass sway in small waves. On the way down to the park I held Bakari's hand while Birch rode his bike. He looked like one of those big circus bears on the tiny bicycles. When I said to this him he rode around in a little circle and sang that theme song you heard at the circus, which made us both laugh.

At the park I steadied the bike on the grass while Bakari climbed on. I put his helmet on him, and as I was about to tighten the straps, he giggled and said: 'I can do this part, Uncle Ted.'

I held up my hands and said: 'Oh really? Go ahead little man.'

He gave me a thumbs up when he was done. Then I held the bike as he started to cycle. Birch ran alongside us with his hands cupped around his mouth yelling things like: 'Look at you go,' and 'Okay, now do a wheelie. You can do it. I believe in you.'

Eventually I stopped holding the bike and watched him pedal gleefully across the grass. I didn't tell him I was letting go. And in the distance Birch and I saw him look to his side, then back at us. We were both dramatically cheering him on when Bakari started to panic. He began to wobble and then he toppled over. As we jogged up to him, Birch said: 'Shit. If he has any bruises Mya's gonna gut me.' I looked at him like: stop it. And then he said: 'No, Ted, she literally said she'd cut me to the white meat.'

Mya hadn't been serious about not letting Birch look after Bakari again. But Birch had been slightly offended that she had even suggested that he couldn't be trusted around him. When he expressed this offence to me, I said: 'Then you shouldn't have got arrested at Wetherspoons.' And he replied: 'Why won't anyone listen to me? Me and Bakari watched an arrest *happen*. It's different.'

Birch knelt by Bakari, who was sitting upright now, rubbing his face, saying 'Ow.' Birch put his hands on Bakari's shoulders and said: 'Okay, little man. Here's what we're gonna do. When we get home you're gonna tell your mum that—' He pointed up at me in this melodramatic accusatory way. 'Your Uncle Ted is a desperately irresponsible man and that this is all his fault.'

Bakari laughed his little high-pitched laugh and said: 'I'm fine, Uncle Birch.'

'I don't believe you,' Birch said. 'Because you told your mum that we nearly got arrested that one time. So lemme just make sure we're on the same page and check you for any cuts and bruises.'

Birch started to inspect Bakari's face with his hand and Bakari batted him away. 'But we did nearly get arrested,' he insisted. 'The police came.'

'Oi,' Birch said. 'Enough of that, you. We watched an arrest *happen*. It's a really massive difference that you should've told your mum about.'

'But Uncle Birch, they put handcuffs on you.'

'They did,' Birch said. 'But what you should've stressed to your mum was that they also took 'em off in the end.'

I told Birch to leave him alone. I then crouched before Bakari and asked him if he was okay and giddily he nodded and said he wanted to go again. I held the bike for longer this time, until I didn't have to anymore. Eventually Birch and I sat down on the grass and Bakari rode around us. Birch asked me how my visit to my parents was and I told him that it was fine, that my dad went birdwatching with our old history teacher now, is still obsessed with that LMFAO song and thinks I'm gay because he watched an episode of *Glee*.

He cackled and started poking me with his fingers, singing 'Don't Stop Believin''. 'Oh, I love your dad,' he said. 'Take me with you the next time you go up. I miss him.' I told him that my dad had said he'd missed him too, which made him smile. He asked then if my dad actually did the dance. I laughed and nodded. Then he said: 'Do you remember when we were little and me and Nate came over to yours that one time. And he made up a dance to "Buffalo Stance"'

'Yeah,' I said. 'And he put on Nate's gold puffer jacket and stretched it out.'

'Oh yeah,' he said. 'Nate was so pissed.'

'But then my dad bought him that Hornets jacket for his birthday to say sorry and suddenly he was the best guy in the world again.'

I asked him how it was living with Lucy and Charlie. And he said he was having fun, that they were even talking about going away for his birthday. 'I don't wanna toot my own horn,' he said. 'But I think I've saved their relationship, you know.'

'You think you'll still be there by November?' I said. 'You're like the most restless person I've ever known.'

'Nah,' he said. 'They love me, Ted. I can see myself there forever.'

Sometimes I wondered at what point in your adulthood you stopped inserting yourself into your friends' lives and accepted their decisions as valid in their own right. When did I stop objecting to questionable judgement, calling out naivety, attempting to understand someone like Birch's reasoning and simply say: yeah okay then, whatever works for you?

He looked across at me now. 'Ted,' he said. 'I know what you're thinking.'

I looked back at him and flatly I said: 'I can't imagine you do.'

'No, I do,' he said. 'You think just because I live in an expensive townie now, and get more than three meals a day, and that I'm generally ascending to the upper echelons of society, that I'm gonna leave you behind. But I promise you, T-Bear. I wouldn't dare leave you. Or those two other broke, no-money-havin', no-pennies-to-rub-together, not-even a-dime-to—'

'Birch, I beg you,' I said, trying not to laugh, 'shut the fuck up.'

A few hours later we went to the off-licence and bought some sandwiches, crisps and sweets. When we came back to the park, Bakari and I sat on the grass while Birch rode around in circles on the bike again. The sky had dimmed, now puffy with off-white clouds. We watched birds fly through them in long black ribbons. Bakari kept offering me bits of his food and I kept smiling and shaking my head. 'Don't tell your mum we let you have this many sweets,' I told him. He smiled mischievously and did a kind of happy dance with his shoulders as he unwrapped his second Mars Bar.

Eventually Birch stopped riding the bike and started to cough. He made a fist and pounded on his chest. Then he spat some phlegm into the grass. I felt relieved that the clump of phlegm wasn't coated in blood. Bakari screwed his face up and said: 'Uncle Birch, that's nasty.' And Birch just laughed and asked if he wanted to see it up close. Bakari yelled: 'No,' and turned away from him.

When Birch came to sit next to us, I asked him why he hadn't booked an appointment with the GP yet. But before he could reply Bakari looked up at us and said: 'What's wrong with Uncle B?'

Birch looked at him fixedly. 'Your Uncle Ted is just being overbearing.'

I looked at Bakari too. 'And your Uncle B is being neglectful of his health,' I said. 'Do you know what that means?' Bakari shook his head. 'It means he's getting sick again and he doesn't care.'

'Again?' Bakari said.

Birch looked at me now with his eyelids lowered. He then turned back to Bakari. 'A few years ago I didn't have a home and I got a little bit sick. That's all.'

I said: 'A little bit?' And he told me to shut up.

'You didn't have a home?' Bakari said, confused. 'Where did you sleep?'

Nonchalantly, Birch replied: 'You know, little man – alleyways, parks, under bridges. And I had this clever little trick, right. Whenever those bendy buses would come along, I'd get on through the back doors. And if you got on at the right stop you could stay on for like an hour. I had some of the best kips of my life on those buses.'

I lifted an eyebrow and said: 'How is fare evasion a clever trick?'

Bakari looked both horrified and intrigued. 'But what about your mum and dad?' he said. 'Why didn't you just go home to your bed?'

Birch laughed. Then he put his palm on Bakari's shoulder. 'You're a very lucky little man,' he said. 'Your parents are the best. They love you more than anything in the world. They would do anything for you. My folks were a little different.'

Bakari had this wounded expression on his face now. 'But why can't you be a very lucky big man?'

'Oi, calm down,' Birch said. 'I'm not that big.' Bakari giggled and gave Birch's stomach a little tap. Birch laughed too, then he said: 'I wouldn't say I wasn't lucky. I think some people just have different kinds of luck. And my luck was that your Uncle Ted here found me just when I really needed him to.' Birch nudged me. 'I mean, don't get me wrong, he did take his sweet time. But your Uncle Ted is a bit of a lifesaver.'

Bakari looked up at me now. He asked me where I'd found Birch and I told him that five years ago I'd found Birch on a train one day after work, that it was first time I'd seen him in nearly ten years. 'Then he came to live with me,' I said. 'And that was that.'

Bakari laughed then. 'Yeah,' he said, 'Dad says you and Birch should just get married already. But I don't think you're allowed because one of you isn't a woman.'

Birch chuckled and then cupped his hands under his chest as if he had breasts and said: 'Says who?'

On the way back to Nathan's parents' flat, Bakari rode the bike again while Birch steadied him. As we crossed over

Trundley's Road, Bakari glanced up at us and said: 'Oh yeah. What's a fag?'

Birch and I widened our eyes and looked at him. 'What?' I said. 'Bakari, where did you hear that word?'

'At school,' he said. 'I know it's a bad word but I don't know what it means.' Birch asked him who had called him that and Bakari replied: 'Oh, they didn't call me that. They called my dad that when he came to pick me up yesterday. What does it mean?'

Birch and I exchanged bewildered looks. Then Birch pulled out a packet of cigarettes from his pocket and shook them. 'They must've meant these,' he said. 'You know – fags.'

'But my dad doesn't smoke,' Bakari said. 'He says it's disgusting and you shouldn't do it.'

'Exactly,' said Birch. 'He's right, you shouldn't do it. It's a terrible habit.'

'Then why do you do it, Uncle Birch?'

'Because I don't have to listen your dad,' he said. 'He talks too much. Give me an earache.'

Birch put the cigarettes back in his pocket. Then I said to Bakari: 'It's just a bad word some people use to talk about gay people.'

'But my dad isn't gay,' he said. 'Because I know what gay is.'

'Oh yeah?' Birch said. 'Go on then—'

'It's when two men try to squeeze babies out of each other. And my dad hasn't done that yet.'

Birch looked across to me with a hand over his mouth. Then he looked back down at Bakari and said: 'Well to be fair, we don't know what your dad does, buddy. All those long nights away with your Uncle Kain – "working".'

He did air quotes around the word 'working' and I nudged him and said shut up. I remembered then that last week Mya had had a show at Passage. She was supposed to be picking Bakari up from school and she'd been running late, so she picked him up straight after her gig in her drag outfit. She was dressed like Ziggy Stardust in a ginger mullet wig, a light-blue suit and very pale makeup.

'I'll have a word with your dad about that kid,' I said to Bakari. 'I think they're just confused. People can be really cruel when they don't understand something.'

'Yeah,' Birch said. 'And I'll have a word too.'

'No the hell you won't,' I said.

Birch mouthed 'yes I will' at Bakari and they laughed. And I smiled, shaking my head at them.

6

On Monday morning I sat in the kitchen making edits on a few articles I'd requested from Monty's team. Kain was cooking breakfast for us. He was wearing a grey vest, black shorts, and a pair of sliders with white socks. He had the stereo on the counter beside the stove, listening to Dizzee Rascal's *Boy in da Corner* album, which had been his favourite since we'd received a review copy in the *Rush!* office when I first started working there.

I kept looking up from my screen and seeing him dance. At times he would turn around and rap some of the lyrics at me. And I'd nod along smilingly. Eventually I said: 'Are you this happy because Birch doesn't live here anymore?'

'Can't even lie, blud,' he said. 'It feels good, innit. I opened the fridge this morning and all my shit was still there. No one's taken my Babybels. I don't have to write notes anymore.' He picked up the tub of butter next to him and showed it to me. 'Look, Ted. It's been a week, fam, and it's still full. And no fucking breadcrumbs in the butter and that. I know that's your boy, yeah. But whatever crack house or hostel he's staying in, I hope it's permanent.'

'He's actually living in a townhouse in Knightsbridge.'

Kain raised an eyebrow. 'For real?'

I nodded. 'And also you say he's "my boy" like you're not friends with him too.'

'Eh,' he said. 'Me and Birch have never been that tight. Not even back in the day, you get me?'

Kain often said this but I didn't believe him. And although I didn't have much evidence to support this, I suspected that there were sections of his and Birch's relationship that I'd never been privy to. Admittedly, they seemed to get on better when Kain was drunk. But outside of that, I'd witnessed little glimpses of their camaraderie. A couple years ago, I'd got home from work and had seen them standing with their arms around each other, watching England v Slovenia during the World Cup, yelling at the television. When I closed the door, Kain quickly took his arm off of him and Birch laughed as if they'd been caught doing something sordid and Birch hadn't been ashamed of it.

'Whatever,' I said now. 'Are you sure you're not gonna miss him constantly talking about how big your muscles are?' He looked away and smirked. 'Ugh,' I groaned. 'I knew you loved it.' He tilted his head with a grin and shrugged like: maybe. 'Because you're definitely not gonna get that from me.'

He was using a spatula to fold over eggs in the pan now. 'Why not?' he said, and then he flexed one of his arms at me. I rolled my eyes and looked back at my screen.

The kitchen smelled like buttery eggs and smoky bacon. And as everything sizzled in the pan, he took some plates out of the cupboard. When he plated everything up, he asked me what was going on at work and I told him that Janice and I were still working on plans to revitalise our sales. 'She's sent me a list of bands she wants for our next issue,' I said. 'And I just know she's never even listened to half of them.'

'Who's on there?'

'Well, there's a band called Alt-J at the top,' I said. 'I think she only wants them because NME made a lot of noise about their album last month. I hadn't really been paying attention.'

'Nah, I know 'em,' he said.

'Really?'

'Yeah, blud,' he said. 'I got the album. *An Awesome Wave.* It's good.'

I raised an eyebrow. 'Since when do you like this stuff?' I asked. 'How did I not know this?'

He smiled. 'Man's expanding, innit.'

I laughed and then sighingly said: 'Everything was easier when we were just a pop magazine. I'm sure they're great, but I don't know what this is gonna do for our sales.'

'But who's still buying actual magazines anyway?' he said. 'It's 2012, fam. Unless you got Adele or fuckin' Beyoncé on there every month. What's the point?'

'Tell that to Janice.'

As he placed the food on the table, I asked him what his day looked like and he said that after midday he and Nathan were booked solid with different big jobs. He said they were regrouting tiles and refinishing hardwood floors and painting living rooms. I already knew his day was packed. I think I only asked because I thought it would momentarily soften my anticipation of eating the food. It didn't work. Even though I felt my stomach rumble and even start to hurt with hunger, I could already tell my body wouldn't let me finish the food. I started to feel a kind of pre-humiliation.

The plate was colourful with creamy scrambled eggs, mushrooms, streaks of bacon and sausages. 'This looks great,' I said. 'Thanks.'

He sat down opposite me and gave me a look that suggested he could already tell I was feeling some level of anxiety. 'You okay?' he asked.

I smiled at him tightly. I'd told him once that the way my parents used to help me when I was younger was to de-centre the food at the table. Kain liked doing this and often used it as an opportunity to discuss things he wouldn't ordinarily talk about openly. When Birch lived with us, he never joined Kain and I for breakfast because he had an erratic eating schedule and was often asleep late into the morning, so Kain wouldn't feel as if he had been compromised when he spoke to me. Kain used to be part of a rap collective called Element 23. Ten years ago, they were signed to a major record label and were pitched as rivals to So Solid Crew. At breakfasts and dinners like this, he would talk about his old music career, crushes he'd had on people, which would then segue into conversations about his sexuality, which would abruptly stop when I'd say something like: 'I really don't think Nate or Birchy would care if you told them you were bisexual.' And he'd shrug and say: 'Whatever, Ted.'

As he was eating now, he made a suspicious face at the table and then picked up a very long hair. He held it out in front of him and kissed his teeth. I looked at it too and laughed.

He lowered his eyelids and said: 'What the fuck are all these hairs?'

'Well, we've just come out of spring,' I said.

'And?'

'Ferrets shed twice a year,' I said. 'And this is one of those times.'

He made an exasperated noise. 'Why do you even know that fam?' he asked. 'And why did you even let that nigga keep those ferrets here for that long?'

'Well,' I said, 'first of all I thought if Whitey and Choc-Ice were gonna be here I might as well get clued up on them. And second – when has Birch ever responded rationally when one of his new obsessions was met with resistance?'

He rolled his eyes. 'Like when he painted himself silver and stood in Hyde Park pretending to be a statue. And kept tracking paint on your floors in the morning.'

'He made good money doing that,' I said. 'He was a proper tourist attraction for a while.'

'You're an enabler, innit.'

'I don't disagree,' I said. 'But he likes to stay employed. What was I supposed to do? Tell him: no, you can't do this job? It's not like I'm his parent.'

'You sure about that?'

'Well yeah,' I said. 'I guess it's a bit murky. But I'm not gonna control the decisions of a fully grown adult, am I? Despite the circumstances under which they came to be in my care.'

He laughed. 'I hate it when you talk like you're a lawyer or some shit,' he said. 'It's like you're his dad and he's a mis-behaved child. He's a brat, innit.'

'Oh, he's not that bad,' I said. 'And he used a water-based paint that time, so it was easy to get out of the floors.'

Kain stared at me blankly. 'Listen to yourself, blud.'

By the end of the discussion, I'd taken at least three or four bites of my food without noticing and Kain nodded at me with a smile as if to say: well done.

After breakfast Kain received a call. When he saw the caller, he answered it and turned away from me. I could see him still smiling in the reflection in the window he was facing as he spoke. The call was from a client who wanted to update him on the jobs their landlord needed done this afternoon. Kain kept on saying: 'Yeah, no worries, innit. That's cool.' And then eventually he ended the call and turned back to me.

We stared at each other for a moment until finally he said: 'What?'

I smiled. 'What do you mean: what?' I said. 'Why were you smiling so hard? Who was that?'

'It was just a client, blud,' he said. 'Leave it, yeah?'

I mimicked him. 'Leave it, yeah,' I said. 'Kain, you're literally still smiling. And you know you never smile for more than two seconds at a time. What's up?'

After another pause, he exhaled and told me then that there was a client that he and Nathan had done some garden work for a few days ago. He said the client had recognised him from when he was in Element 23 and even owned a copy of the only single they released. Kain had signed it, and when Nathan went to the hardware store to buy something, they'd had a conversation that had lasted the entire time Nathan was gone.

I couldn't stop grinning as he spoke. 'So is this a real appointment,' I said. 'Or is it just an excuse for you to see him again?'

He kissed his teeth. 'An excuse?' he said. 'Do you think I got time to be wasting like that, blud?' I lowered my eyelids at him, still smiling and he said: 'Okay, fine. A little bit, innit.'

'Was he flirting with you?' I asked. 'I thought you hated when clients did that?'

'Yeah, sometimes it's weird,' he said. 'But this was different, innit. He was nice. And he had this dope vinyl collection. And he just—' I could see him about to fade blissfully into a monologue when suddenly he stopped and said: 'Eh, Ted. Stop making me talk about this shit. I'm not

tryna express feelings or whatever the fuck. Being all emotional and that.'

Playfully, I said: 'Well is there something to potentially be
emotional about?'

'Ted—'

'What?'

'Shut up, fam.'

We laughed. And then he took our plates to the sink. As he
washed up, I asked him if he could at least tell me what this
person looked like or what their name was. But he just waved
me away and told me to leave it. I didn't really know how
Kain behaved when he liked someone beyond friendship. I'd
seen him actively try and resist crushes. And when they were
women, he'd pretend he only wanted to have sex with them.
And then make it seem as if anything else he might've felt
beyond that was a fiction I'd made up in my head and projected onto him. This was the first time I'd seen him embrace
liking someone this way. It was nice to see him so coy. It was
as if he was expanding emotionally before me, and different
facets of his personality were constructing themselves in real
time. Or rather these facets were finally coming into view.

'Fine,' I told him. 'I'll leave it. But I'm excited for you.'

I saw his reflection smile briefly and look back down at the
soapy dishes in the sink.

When he left to meet Nathan for work, he asked me how I was
feeling, and I told him I was fine. He then gave me a single
nod and closed the door behind him.

I didn't move from the table. I felt like the food I'd just eaten
was sitting in my chest. And the more I thought about the
food, the more this rancid taste began forming in my mouth.
Little puddles of saliva pooled in my cheeks. I became very

aware of my tongue and knew if I moved it that I'd probably vomit. I tried to think about something else and not how much better I'd feel if I did in fact vomit. I made a fist and punched my chest a few times, in some misguided hope that it would make the food settle inside me better.

I hadn't eaten properly in a while. And I'd felt so proud that I wanted the feeling to stay for as long as I could make it. When eventually I retched and felt some of the food come back up, I swallowed it back down and sat very still. In the silence, I looked at the empty wooden table, at the pristine countertop, at the light reflecting off the silver of the sink which Kain had wiped so thoroughly that there weren't even any droplets. And I felt somehow ugly and out of place. I thought perhaps feeling dirty was a sacrifice I had to make to feel like a normal perfectly-functioning person.

May 1993

Birch and Nathan are at Teddy's house for the first weekend of half-term. Teddy and Nathan are watching *Byker Grove* in the living room, while in another room, Birch and Teddy's dad, Theodore, are crouched by the radio. They're listening attentively to Mark Goodier host the *Chart Show* on BBC Radio 1.

A few days ago Birch heard a song called 'Dreams' by Gabrielle and hasn't stopped singing it since. He's been derailing conversations by singing the chorus, as well as interrupting class with other bits and pieces he remembers from the song. He even sang it as Theodore drove the three of them home on the last day of school; it wasn't even the song playing on the radio at the time but Birch couldn't help himself. Since he can't buy the song in stores yet – and even if he could he knows his mum and stepdad wouldn't give him the money anyway – he asks Theodore if he can record the song off the radio using Theodore's cassette recorder. When the song finally comes on, he finds it difficult to keep quiet as they record. And Theodore finds it difficult not to laugh as Birch rolls his body to the music.

When the song ends, Birch triumphantly holds up the cassette recorder and skips into the living room. He stands in front of the television and says: 'We did it! It's mine now!'

Nathan tells Birch to move out the way. But Teddy just looks up and smiles at him. He finds such a deep amusement in Birch's enthusiasm and feels very happy for him. And, in a way, it makes him feel happy too. He likes how Birch can be placated by the simplest of things: music and food and attention. He likes how he is only ever playfully annoyed at Birch rather than genuinely annoyed, like Nathan often is. Also, he likes how Birch inadvertently influences him. He'd heard the song many times too but hadn't thought much of it until Birch decided to sew it into their lives. And now he finds himself humming the chorus at random times too.

He finds that Birch's presence brings a kind of levity to his life, a lightness that balances out the bad things. When Birch is around it's easy not to think of the bad things. Bad things like what happened during lunch on the last day of school.

He smiles harder at Birch now and says: 'Good for you.'

At the beginning of May a new boy started in their year. He was a big bulky boy called Kain and looked a lot older than eleven or twelve. Teddy had noticed Kain because Kain had been welcomed into Luke Williams' group, which had surprised him. The only reason Teddy could think of for Luke and his friends picking on him so much was because they were different ethnicities. So he'd wondered if Kain's admission into the group had marked a shift in ideology or something. But then Teddy had overheard them making monkey noises at him and often referring to him as Lenny Henry. Teddy had seen Kain laughing along with them. It was the first time that the complexities of prejudice had even registered as something for Teddy to think about. It wasn't always about hatred, he'd discovered. Sometimes it was about humiliation. Life at this moment felt as if it were this vast landscape that was constantly unfolding in little pieces and showing him various shades of darkness.

During lunch on the last day of school, Teddy had been sitting on the field by the rusty basketball cage. Birch and Nathan had got detention again for fighting, so he was alone. He didn't like eating lunch in front of Birch and Nathan anyway, so he was happy to spend one lunchtime not explaining why he hadn't touched anything in his lunchbox. Eventually he saw Luke and Kain and the rest of their group moving in a cluster across the grass. Teddy made eye contact only briefly before he looked down at his food. But when he looked back up to see if they were gone, they were approaching him. They chanted at him, nonsensical sounds and yelled: 'Oi oi skinny,' repeatedly. They took his lunchbox and held it away from him. But he wasn't going to reach for it. Instead he braced himself. He had developed this process by which he would simply absorb the pain, and accept the total inevitability of it, and try as best he could to disassociate somehow. The pain was stripped of its potency if he deprived it of attention. He tried to think about what Birch might do or say if this were happening to him and it almost made him laugh. When it was all over and he settled back into reality, he would deal with the repercussions then.

After the punching and kicking and laughing finished, Teddy wrapped his arms around his knees and tucked his head into his chest. He stayed in this position for what felt like a very long time. When he looked up, Luke and his friends were gone. But Kain was still there, standing over him. Teddy instinctively tucked his head back down, as if this action alone would make Kain disappear too.

Eventually he felt Kain place a hand on his shoulder and say: 'Eh, you okay?'

Teddy was shaking, practically vibrating. He looked up again and gave Kain a narrow-eyed look like: what do you mean am I okay? What does it look like?

Kain took some tissues out of his pocket and started dabbing at Teddy's face. Teddy kept flinching as he did this and Kain kept steadying Teddy's face with his other hand and telling him to stay still and calm down. When he let go of Teddy's face, he asked him not to tell anyone about this, and said his face didn't even look that bad anyway, and that it wasn't worth making a big thing about and getting him and his friends in trouble.

Teddy looked around himself then. His sandwiches had been stamped into the grass and there was a tube of yogurt leaking into the dirt. Kain had been talking to him in this advisory way about not making himself such a target. And Teddy felt annoyed that this boy who had only been at the school a mere few weeks was giving him advice. But for reasons even Teddy himself couldn't clarify, he said: 'What should I do? It's not like I'm trying to make myself noticed.'

'They think you're gay, innit,' Kain said. Teddy raised an eyebrow and Kain continued: 'Yeah, you look like you're gay, so just stop it and they'll leave you alone.'

'Are you being serious?' Teddy said. Kain nodded at him as if Teddy should've felt enlightened at this information. 'How do I look like I'm gay?'

Kain shrugged. 'You just do, innit.'

He felt another piece of the landscape unfold. It didn't make sense to be targeted based entirely on assumptions someone else had made about who he might've been. And it didn't seem fair either. But the more life unveiled itself to him, the more illusory the concept of fairness seemed anyway. He had never actively thought about sexuality before. And it felt almost jarring that this was now a topic occupying space in his head. It made him question if gayness as he understood it wasn't something exclusively linked to sexuality; if there were other things that had made him gay and he just hadn't known it, which was clearly the case. He was suddenly more curious than angry with Kain. He wanted to know what specifically about himself seemed to inspire such vitriol. He wanted to know what to do to avoid further embarrassment. But in the end Teddy didn't say anything. He and Kain just looked at each other. Kain had this strange meditative expression as if he was trying to understand something about Teddy.

They then heard Luke shout: 'Oi Lenny – get a move on, will you?' Kain turned back to face him and then looked back at Teddy. He shoved Teddy back onto the grass and whispered an apology as he walked away.

It's obvious to Teddy that Birch doesn't want to go home this evening. Nathan leaves in the afternoon and Birch stays for dinner. Birch often doesn't want to go home when he comes over on the weekends. Teddy used to think this was Birch being strange and quirky, finding elaborate reasons to stay, long after Nathan had left. Once Birch had pretended to be so full from dinner that he couldn't walk, so he laid on the floor with his hands on his stomach, making loud groaning noises. This had made Teddy laugh and ask his parents if Birch could just sleep in his bed for the night.

This evening after dinner Birch convinces Theodore to record more songs off the radio onto the cassette. This makes Teddy happy because it means he can unload everything he's eaten into the toilet without fearing someone might walk in on him. He usually takes a moment and rests his head against the ceramic of the toilet afterwards and breathes very slowly in silence.

When Teddy comes back out of the bathroom, he stands at the dining room door and watches Birch and Theodore use the cassette recorder to record 'No Ordinary Love' by Sade on the radio, while Birch closes his eyes and sways his head and Theodore laughs at him. Teddy smiles at Birch then; he can't help it. He finds him so immeasurably adorable and sometimes wonders if this is why he's so immune to being irritated by his antics. He loves Birch's big curly messy hair and his mischievous smile and the little dimple in his chin. He loves how he always throws his arm around him as he explains yet another stupid plan to get back at the bullies at school. He loves how uncomplicated and practical he is. The bullying seems to spur Birch on instead of wearing him down and Teddy admires that. This admiration makes him feel a little pathetic that he hasn't even told Birch about what happened with Luke and Kain on the last day of school. Teddy knows he hides his anguish in his heart, and Birch seems to wrap his around his fists. He wishes he could articulate some of this to Birch, but he doesn't know how, short of putting his hands on Birch's shoulders and saying: 'I really like who you are as a person.'

In the end, Theodore asks Birch if he wants to sleep over again and Birch says: 'Well, if you really want me to stay the night, Mr Asiedu, I couldn't bear to disappoint you.' He runs over to Teddy then and throws his arms around him. 'Okay, Teddy Bear,' he says cheerily. 'Show me to your boudoir, good sir.'

*

Teddy and Birch are in bed together now. Teddy is on his side, his head laying on his hands, looking at the side of Birch's face. Birch, with his hands behind his head, is looking up at the ceiling. He's wearing an old set of Teddy's pyjamas which have a picture of Batman on the top, specifically from *Batman: The Animated Series,* and he keeps asking Teddy if he's watched it, and Teddy says no, he just thought it looked cool when he saw it in the store. Teddy enjoys the excitement in Birch's voice as he tells him how great the show is. And it seems to always be this way with Birch. He makes Teddy care about things that would otherwise simply pass through him. And he suspects Birch is unaware that this is a power he has. Everything becomes more alive, more electric, more attractive when they fall under the scope of Birch's obsession.

Nothing seems to be safe from this. One day in school, during lunch, Birch had become enamoured with a scurry of squirrels he'd seen on the field. Teddy and Nathan followed him around while he collected acorns from beneath the big oak tree and filled his blazer pockets, so he could become king of the squirrels or something. He thought it was funny, while Nathan kept tutting and saying: 'What are you doing? You're so weird. Let's go play football, man.' Now Teddy will randomly notice a squirrel run up the side of a tree and the moment will be imbued with significance for him. This is another thing he wishes he could tell him, but he just doesn't have the words.

In the dark now, Birch hums 'Glory of Love' by Peter Cetera. Teddy giggles and says: 'What song is that?'

Birch turns on to his side now and faces him. 'I think it's called 'Glory of Love,'' he says. 'I don't know who it's by though. But it's on at the end of *Karate Kid 2.* It's a really good song. I keep rewinding the video just to listen to it.'

When he asks Teddy if he's seen it, Teddy shakes his head. 'No way,' he says. 'You have to, man. It's the best!'

Teddy smiles. 'Maybe I can come over to yours one day and watch it?'

Birch doesn't say anything and turns back to face the ceiling. Teddy feels the atmosphere get a little tense.

'Or I can bring the video over here?' Birch says finally. 'You've got a better TV than me. And I think you should watch a masterpiece on a really good TV.'

Teddy laughs and says okay. And then Birch laughs too. Then they sit in the silence for a while, but the silence feels so heavy that it eventually prompts Teddy to ask: 'Birch, are you okay?'

Birch doesn't know how to answer this. The question makes him feel uncomfortable. But in a way that he can't cheerily navigate his way out of. But still he tries. He gently pulls Teddy into a headlock and ruffles his hair with his knuckles and says: 'Don't I sound okay, T-Bear, eh? Don't I sound okay?'

Teddy chuckles, trying, though not very hard, to get him to stop. When Birch eventually does, he doesn't let Teddy go and leaves his arm around him. And Teddy just lets it rest there.

Finally, Birch says: 'Yeah, man. I'm okay.'

And it's true, Birch thinks; in this very specific moment in time he is okay.

7

That weekend the four of us went to the tennis courts in Victoria Park. It was a slightly cold, overcast day, but we were all in polo shirts and shorts. Kain and Nathan were holding the rackets and Birch and I had the tennis balls as we walked onto the court. Birch was wearing a new hands-free leash that he'd fitted around his waist and had tied on to Whitey and Choc-Ice. They each had on a little pink harness as they energetically ran around each other.

We played doubles, and naturally Birch and I were one team and Nathan and Kain were the other. It was always this way; Birch and Kain couldn't work together in any capacity, especially as a team. Even if things started out cordial, Birch would inevitably do something to annoy Kain, who would then retaliate by yelling at him, to which Birch would retaliate by sabotaging the game: sometimes he would dive and catch in the ball with his hand. Or he would try and yank Kain's shorts down as Kain served. I knew how annoying this was but I would find it difficult to stifle my laughter and Nathan would shake his head at me and say: 'Stop encouraging him, bruv.'

That morning, after Birch tied Whitey and Choc-Ice to the fence, he excitedly hopped from one foot to the other, waving his racket around saying: 'Okay, boys, I want a good clean game.'

Nathan rolled his eyes. 'Tell that to yourself, cuz.'

Birch pointed the racket to Kain then and said: 'You – no funny business now. And no cheating.'

Kain gave him the middle finger and I asked Birch why he was trying to provoke Kain this early in the day.

He held his racket up to our faces as if he were telling me a secret, but he still spoke loudly. 'Don't ruin this for me T-Bear. You know he takes his shirt off when he gets annoyed. I'm not gonna be very happy if I don't see a sweaty six pack,' he said. 'It's the only reason I play, Ted.'

Kain then yelled: 'Eh, Birch shut the fuck up. Are we playing or what?'

Birch was mostly well behaved during the first set. When Kain stretched up, revealing his hard stomach, and served the ball, Birch wolf-whistled. And then, at the same time, Nathan and I glared at Birch and he just laughed and shrugged. I hadn't been particularly sporty when I was younger. And I still wasn't, really. But beyond the sport, what I liked was the camaraderie. There was something about these moments that reinforced how much I enjoyed sharing my life with them. As we rallied, sweating and darting all over the court, I felt deeply appreciative that this was the collection of people that had become my family. People from whom I could extract everything that made a life full and real: sadness and grief and frustration; joy and contentment and dependency. It was wonderful to watch them be so uninhibited in a world that often demanded from us fortification and vigilance.

After the game, Birch and I sat against the fence. I felt exhausted and a little lightheaded. Birch was playing with Whitey and Choc-Ice and kept lifting them up and wiggling them at me, and I kept gently batting them away. Nathan and Kain were standing by the net talking to each other. They'd both taken their shirts off now and had tucked them into the backs of their shorts. I tried looking everywhere but at them. But inevitably my eyes kept landing back on their bodies, their thick thighs and chiselled torsos.

'Oh, Ted,' Birch said. 'I knew you were a slut.'

I blinked rapidly and looked over at him. 'What?'

'When it's me lookin' at Kain and Nate, it's always: "oh Birch, stop pervin' on your friends – it's gross." But look at you. Just gawping away like it's nothing.'

I laughed. 'I'm not perving.'

'I was literally watching you perv, man.' He held up Whitey and Choc-Ice again. 'We all were.'

'I'm not perving,' I said. 'But even if I was, it's a completely different situation to when you sat cross-legged in front of them at the gym, eating a packet of crisps while they worked out.'

He shrugged. 'A show is a show, T-Bear,' he said. 'And I wish more people understood that. Was it something that security needed to be up my arse about?'

'Yes.'

'Oh, you're just like the rest of them,' he said. 'I guarantee if Whitey and Choccy could talk, they'd be on my side.'

I rolled my eyes. 'Anyway,' I said. 'I wasn't perving. I just—' I paused a moment. 'I just hate that I keep comparing.'

'Comparing?' Birch said. 'Oh! Because you're a rake and I've got a pot belly?'

'Don't call me that,' I said. 'I'm not a rake.'

Suddenly I felt insecure in my t-shirt and shorts, as if I were too thin to be wearing this attire. I hadn't thought much about what I looked like that morning, but now it felt like we weren't simply four men on a tennis court – instead we were three men whose arms and legs looked good in a sporty attire and one whose didn't. Kain drank from his water bottle and then poured some down his chest. Birch knocked his shoulder against mine and grinned stupidly at him. I looked too. I often tried not to feel envious and rationalised any jealousy with the idea that I too could look like that if I tried. But I knew that wasn't true. Everything always came back to diet, and even that morning I couldn't remember the last time I'd had a proper meal. Or even if I had, I couldn't remember the last time I was able to keep anything down.

'Are you alright?' Birch said. 'I'm only joking. You're not a rake. You're a sexy broom.'

I raised my eyebrows like: thanks.

'Good,' he said, lifting up his shirt. 'Now you say something nice about my body.'

We went to a coffee shop near Bethnal Green station after that. There was a little chalkboard menu outside with Olympic rings sketched on and various Olympic-inspired puns for the names of their coffee, like gold medal macchiato and silver spoon latte.

We sat at a table outside because of Whitey and Choc-Ice. They were unusually hyperactive that afternoon, climbing on top of each other and then pawing at Birch's shins. We all watched him lowering bits of meat from his little Ziploc bag into their mouths. When the waiter brought out our drinks, he almost tripped over them. He then gave Birch an icy look and told him that they didn't allow pets in here.

Birch looked up at him and said: 'Well, there's no sign. And we're not inside.'

He shrugged. 'Doesn't matter.'

They stared at each other for a moment. Then Birch moved his seat several feet away from the table, dragging Whitey and Choc-Ice along with him, until they were almost in front of the next shop over. Birch gestured at him like: is this better? Then the waiter rolled his eyes, put his tray under his arm and went back inside.

'I'm not bringing your drink over to you,' I said.

'That's fine,' Birch said. 'If me and my little lads aren't welcome then I'll stay here. I'll just chug some of the meat juice at the bottom of this bag.'

'Birch, if I actually have to say the words "don't drink the meat juice" to you, then I'm gonna drown Whitey and Choc-Ice in your sleep.'

'I'd like to see you try, man,' he said. 'I'm gonna sleep with them in a fucking death grip. I'm so sick of you guys threatening violence on them all the time. It's actually really racist.'

He picked them up onto his lap and glared at us.

'Why are you always so annoying, bruv?' Nathan said. 'Grow up.'

'Yeah, grow up and be all old and crusty like the rest of you,' he replied. 'I don't think so.'

'Aren't you thirty in a few months, bro?' Nathan said.

Kain put his hand on Nathan's shoulder and said: 'Blud, can you stop entertaining this foolishness so we can talk about the meeting with the council?'

'It's gonna be fine, fam,' Nathan said. 'Why are you so nervous for?'

Kain and Nathan had a meeting with Tower Hamlets Council to discuss a potential contract for their handyman business. If they were granted the contract, it would mean a steadier stream of work. They would be refurbishing public spaces and doing maintenance work in council houses in the borough, and no longer relying solely on word of mouth.

I looked at Kain. 'Yeah,' I said. 'You've got the references and experience and you do good work. What's the worry?'

Kain gave me a look that suggested I was maybe being a little optimistic. 'Yeah, I know,' he said. 'But my dad had all of that too, innit. And he still didn't get on with the council.'

I looked at him quizzically. 'Yeah, but didn't your dad also throw rocks at people's roofs to dislodge their tiles? And then knock on their door asking if they needed their tiles done?'

He laughed. 'He had his reasons, innit,' he said. 'No one would give the brudda a chance. He couldn't even get a meeting, blud.'

I laughed too. 'I imagine reputation counts for a lot in these meetings, so like I said: you'll be fine.'

'Listen to him, bruv,' Nathan said to Kain then. 'Stay positive, innit.'

Nathan and Kain had a job that afternoon refinishing some hardwood floors, so I'd assumed we wouldn't be staying long, that we would have some coffee and leave. But when the waiter came back with our drinks, Nathan asked for their food menu. I clenched my fists beneath the table unthinkingly and suddenly felt a little irritated at him.

Birch, who still hadn't moved his chair back to the table, yelled over to the waiter: 'Oh, can you get one for me too?'

Panic rippled through my chest. And I could already see, as if the scene had been projected before me, the three of them eating their pastries and sandwiches and mine sitting there barely touched, in front of me. I could already taste the piece I'd put in my mouth to create the illusion that I was eating, chewing and chewing until it didn't taste like anything anymore. I'd had such a nice morning that I didn't want to sour it by fending off questions from Nathan and Birch about why I hadn't ordered anything or abruptly excusing myself from the table.

When the waiter went back inside to get the menus, I looked around helplessly. Eventually my eyes met Kain's, who after a moment seemed to understand something about my silent panic. We looked at each other for a while, then he nodded at me. He glanced at his phone briefly and then knocked his shoulder against Nathan's and said: 'Nah. Fuck the food, cuz. We gotta go.'

'I'm just gonna get a sandwich, fam,' Nathan said. 'Chill.'

'Nah, let's go,' Kain insisted, standing up. 'We gotta pick up the floor sander from the store, innit. And you know boss-man likes to chat shit at the till.'

Nathan tutted. 'Yeah,' he said. 'We need to tell him to chill with the fuckin' stories, bruv. I don't even know what he's talking about half the time.'

Kain put his hands on Nathan's shoulders as they said goodbye to us and disappeared down the pavement.

Birch still wanted to order food. But I told him that I had a lot of work to do over the weekend for *Rush!*. So he agreed to just have something at home.

On the way home, Whitey and Choc-Ice seemed a lot calmer and Birch kept smiling at them. 'I was starting to get a bit worried, man,' he said. 'Apparently they're proper sensitive to new smells. And Lucy and Charlie've got me wearing these luxury fragrances and stuff.'

I made a face. 'Why?'

'Well, Lucy says I smell like cigarettes all the time,' he said. 'And Charlie likes it when I smell like her. And apparently she likes ... what was it? Dior J'adore.'

I laughed. 'Sounds expensive.'

'She has fuckin' shitloads of it, man,' he said. 'You want a bottle?'

'Birch, please stop trying to involve me in whatever this is,' I said. 'When you get arrested I want a chance at some plausible deniability.'

'T-Bear,' he said. 'I'm not doing anything criminal.' I lowered my eyelids at him. 'You know what? You should come over. It's totally legit. And they're great people.'

He started to cough then and I placed my hand on his back and asked if he was alright. And he nodded with his hand over his mouth.

'You never booked that appointment with the GP, did you?' I said.

He cleared his throat aggressively. 'I was gonna,' he said. 'But nah, man. I'm alright. I told you, it's just a cough. It's gonna be fine.'

I looked at him disappointedly. 'Birch,' I said. 'I don't like that I seem to care more about your health than you do. Book the appointment.'

'Fine,' he said. 'Fine – I'll do it. If it'll get you off my back.'

'Good.'

'Good,' he repeated abruptly. 'And stop looking at me like that, man. I'll be fine.'

8

On Monday the three of us went to visit Birch's new home in Knightsbridge. Kain and Nathan picked me up in their van after I finished work. They had just finished the last job of the day, fitting a fireplace in a house in Lambeth. Kain was driving, tapping his rough paint-stained fingers on the wheel while 'Next to Me' by Emeli Sandé played on Capital FM. And Nathan was on the phone to Mya.

I sat between them and then looked down and saw that in addition to the splashes of paint that they had on their calves and thighs, they also had these shiny rubbery patches on their shorts. I pointed to the patches with a curious expression and then Nathan laughed, putting his phone to his chest. He then pointed at Kain and said: 'This nigga is a barbarian, bruv.'

Kain kissed his teeth. 'Don't even start, bro.'

I laughed. 'Don't start what?'

Nathan animatedly threw his arms up. 'Who still uses nails to fix a fireplace to a wall?'

'Shut up,' Kain snipped. 'It works, innit.'

'Nah cuz,' Nathan said. 'You're on some ancient shit.' He looked at me. 'I had to go get some adhesive because the client was like: you're not gonna nail it on to the wall are ya? It's too bloody heavy. And Kain started arguing with him and shit.'

'Because why are we fucking around with adhesive,' Kain said, 'when you can just nail that shit to the wall and be done with it? It wasn't "too bloody heavy". I checked that shit. We're not amateurs, blud.'

'Anyway,' Nathan continued, 'when we were done, he squeezed some of the adhesive on me out of revenge. Just because he doesn't like being wrong. Got it all over my shorts and shit. So I did the same to him, innit.'

'It was an accident,' Kain said. 'Said I was sorry, didn't I?'

'Nah, don't lie, fam,' Nathan said. 'You were just vexed because the client had a point. I don't understand why you're always tryna pick a fight with these people. People want their shit the way they want it. You're gonna fuck up our reputation, bruv. With what? Two more days until that council meeting.'

There was a brief silence before Kain replied: 'It's just how my dad did it, innit. Why would I start changing shit now? He never had any problems.'

'Yeah, back in the nineties, cuz.'

I shook my head, still laughing. 'I can't believe these are the things that get you both so riled up,' I said. 'Fireplaces and adhesive.'

'That's discrimination, bruv,' Nathan said.

'Excuse me?'

'Nah, he's right,' added Kain. 'You can't believe we talk about fireplaces. But Birch runs around London with ferrets and leashes and raw meat and you don't say shit to him.'

'What?' I said. 'I think I've made my disapproval for Whitey and Choc-Ice pretty clear.' I saw them exchange knowing looks. 'What?' I said then. 'I have.'

We heard Mya's muffled voice leaking from Nathan's phone. He put it back to his ear and said: 'Oh shit, sorry. Yeah babe I'm still here.'

Lucy and Charlie lived on a quiet road lined with leafy plane trees. The house was tall and painted soft magnolia. It was fronted by high immaculately kept hedges and a black fence.

Birch opened the door about a minute after we'd knocked. We'd seen him peeking through the curtains as we walked up, so we knew he'd been stood behind the door probably sniggering to himself, in the name of drama or simply to be annoying, we weren't sure. He'd had his hair trimmed over the weekend and tied back into a neat ponytail. It was unusual seeing him so fresh-faced. You usually noticed all his long messy curly hair, before you saw his brown eyes or even the cute cleft in his chin.

'Boys!' he yelled, throwing his arms open. He was wearing a thick black robe with bright gold accents. And Whitey and Choc-Ice were perched on each of his shoulders. They were wiggling round and rubbing their noses against Birch's cheeks.

I looked at him curiously. 'How have you got them to stay up there?'

He sighed dramatically and said: 'A lot of fuckin' work, man.' Kain and Nathan both touched the fabric of his robe, making confused faces at each other, while Birch smugly nodded and said: 'It's Versace.'

Nathan, still rubbing the robe between his fingers said: 'They bought you a fucking Versace robe, bruv?'

'Well, not exactly,' Birch said. 'Charlie said what's his is mine, so it's pretty much the same thing. Anyway, come in, boys. Lemme give you the tour. Forewarning, it's massive.'

I'd felt anxious for Birch since he'd moved out. His entire life felt as if someone was constantly throwing him off a cliff, and he was always somehow finding his feet, however unconventionally. But despite this knowledge, the precarity of his life frightened me. Ever since Birch came back into my life, I'd felt as if I were walking behind him on a tightrope with my arms outstretched saying: 'Careful, Birch, careful.' I sometimes felt like I was the luggage that contained all the trepidation he should've felt, living his life with this degree of uncertainty.

Birch put Whitey and Choc-Ice on the ground and they both waddled after him as he walked down the wide hall-way. Nathan, Kain and I walked behind them. The hallway was all large mirrors and paintings and colourful flowers on high ledges protruding from the wall. Nathan kept look-ing around and nodding at everything and quietly saying: 'Woah.' Kain didn't seem too impressed and didn't really marvel at anything, and instead yelled to Birch: 'Eh, they got any drinks in here, blud?'

'Yeah,' said Birch cheerily. 'They got everything! Let's get some drinks in you, man.'

He led us into the main living room which had a high ceil-ing and pale-blue walls. In the middle of the room was a long grey sofa with white cushions and a sleek oval-shaped coffee table. The three of us stood at the door, while Birch walked inside gesturing dramatically at things: at the large television, at the stereo system and at the mini bar at the back of the room. There was also a corner that had been converted into a sort of playground with tunnels and ramps and platforms covered with chew toys and little colourful balls. Birch picked up Whitey and Choc-Ice and carefully placed them in there, and we watched them scurry up the ramps.

As he walked over to the mini bar now, he gestured at us to come in. I looked at Kain and Nathan and said: 'Do either of you get the feeling that we're about to be arrested for trespassing?'

'If we are,' Kain said, 'then they're gonna have to wait till I get a drink first. That mini bar is lookin' real nice, you know.' Nathan and I watched him head over. The mini bar was elaborately fancy: a black marble table decked with four bar stools. Racks and racks of bottles with brown and orange liquids. Wine glasses hanging upside down. A decorative arrangement of crystal whiskey decanters.

'Fuck it,' Nathan said, putting his arm around me. 'Might as well get arrested together.'

At the mini bar Kain had grabbed a bottle of wine and was inspecting the label. He then showed it to Birch with a raised eyebrow. 'You had this?' he asked him. 'Is it nice?'

Birch laughed. 'You think I'm reading labels, Kain?' He said. 'I don't read anything. I've just been chucking everything in my gullet. All I know is that it's all expensive stuff, so it's all good ... probably.'

Kain shrugged and asked for a corkscrew. Then Birch laughed again and said he hadn't seen the corkscrew in weeks. He took the bottle from Kain and went into the kitchen; we all followed. He turned on the stove to a high heat and then retrieved a saucepan from the cupboard. He then filled it with water and lowered it onto the hob. As he waited for the water to bubble we asked him what he was doing. He then dipped the bottle into the pan and the cork slowly started to squeeze itself out of the bottle. Then it projected itself into the air. He handed the bottle back to Kain, who took a swig and gave Birch a thumbs up, while Birch nodded with a self-satisfied grin.

*

After that Birch looked at us and said Kain and Nathan looked too scruffy and that I looked too corporate. When we asked him what he meant, a conspiratorial expression appeared on his face and then he ran upstairs. Kain got increasingly drunk while we waited for Birch on the sofa. Every time he took a swig, Nathan would put his hand on Kain's back and say: 'Eh, chill, bruv.' And then Kain would laugh and hold the bottle in front of Nathan's face, and Nathan would say: 'One of us has to drive us back.'

When Birch returned, he was holding three more of Charlie's robes, in yellow, white and pink. 'Okay boys,' he said. 'Get your kits off.'

'Are those more Versace robes?' I asked.

He held up two of them. 'These two are,' he said. 'And this one's just a normal one for you, Ted.'

'Why don't I get a Versace one?'

He folded the robes back over his arm. 'It wasn't up to me,' he said. 'Whitey and Choccy decided. They still don't really like you. I think they're still holding a grudge because you keep calling them rats. They're natural enemies, Ted. It's gonna take a while for them to get over it.'

I sighed and said whatever. And then he threw the robes at us. Kain stripped down first and Birch wolf-whistled. It was unusual seeing these little unstrained exchanges between them, and it made me want to smile. In Kain's inebriated state, Birch excitedly helped him into his robe and I felt a warmth settle in my chest as I watched them. Nathan put his on and looked at his reflection in the window behind the sofa.

Kain poured himself another drink from the bar. And then he joined Birch, who was sitting inside the play area as Whitey and Choc-Ice circled him frantically. Nathan and I switched on the television and flicked through the channels.

The sound had so much bass that Nathan suggested going on to the music channels. DJ Pied Piper & The Masters of Ceremonies' 'Do You Really Like It?' came on MTV Base. And while we sang along together, Birch and Kain were lying on their stomachs, using Whitey and Choc-Ice to play Pokémon, saying things like: 'Whitey, use Ice Beam!' and 'Choc-Ice, use Quick Attack,' while Whitey and Choc-Ice made chirpy dooking sounds and tussled aimlessly around each other.

Nathan and I looked down at them and laughed, and then he changed the channel again. He landed on Channel U. And then we saw the opening shots of 'Watch Ur Back' by Kain and his old rap group Element 23.

I gasped and then Nathan said: 'Holy shit, bruv.'

Birch, who was now as drunk as Kain, picked up Whitey and Choc-Ice and stood in front of the television and danced. I said I couldn't believe they still played Element 23 songs. It took Kain several attempts to steady himself on his feet. Then he looked at himself on the television, grinning. He looked so proud. In the video all seven members of the group were in dark, baggy clothing, rapping their verses in front of a large crowd on a street in New Cross, energetically shoving each other out of the way for screen time.

Nathan asked him to give us a performance and Kain actually did, enthusiastically. I really liked seeing him like this. It was as if we'd crept into the basement of what he presented as his personality and had shone a light and blown away dust from this secret, veiled, brighter aspect of it. When the song was over, Birch asked him if he missed this period of his life. And this question seemed to momentarily sober Kain. His smile disappeared. And he looked at us with this slightly bewildered expression on his face and just said: 'Nah, blud.'

*

Later in the evening, Nathan looked up from his phone and asked us if we were coming to Mya's show at Passage Friday night. We all said yes. Even Kain, who didn't like going to Passage because it was apparently too stuffy and crowded. But really it was because he thought the bar was too gay.

'I can't wait,' I said. 'She's hosting it, isn't she? Like, she's not just performing this time.'

Nathan sighed despondently. 'Yeah.'

Birch and I exchanged a look and then we both asked him what was wrong.

'Nothing,' Nathan said. 'It's gonna be fun, innit. She said it was gonna be divas night or something like that.' Birch and I looked at each other again, which made Nathan narrow his eyes. 'Fuck's going on? Why do you keep looking at each other like that?'

Upon further reflection, Birch and I had agreed not to tell Nathan about the comments Bakari had heard in school. Nathan could be very sensitive about Mya's career and we thought it might make it worse. But when Birch started to speak, I reflexively put my hand over his mouth. Kain, now too drunk to form a coherent sentence, laughed loudly at this. Birch licked my palm and as I dried it on my robe, he said to Nathan: 'Bakari told us that someone in his class called you a fag!' And then he turned to me and quietly said: 'I'm sorry, Ted. You know I'm not good at keeping secrets. It's something I'm working on, I promise.'

I glared at him. Then Nathan said: 'Someone called me a what?'

I sighed. 'Bakari said it was because Mya picked him up from school in drag,' I explained. 'I think it was when she did that Ziggy Stardust performance at Passage.'

'I was there that afternoon,' Birch added. 'She did "Starman" It was really fun. You shoulda seen it, man.'

Nathan had a blank expression on his face and we couldn't tell what he was thinking. In the silence, we heard Kain snoring. It sounded like someone was revving a chainsaw. It even made Whitey and Choc-Ice scurry up and get on their hind legs and place their paws on the little fence surrounding their play area.

Eventually Nathan said: 'What the fuck are people using that word around my boy for?'

Birch told him that they were kids and that they were probably just blindly repeating things they'd heard around. But what Nathan was actually feeling had suddenly clarified itself for me, especially when he could no longer maintain eye contact with us. He felt embarrassed. So when he didn't respond to Birch, I thought it best not to prod and dissect this feeling with him, and said nothing.

'And what's wrong with being a fag anyway,' said Birch. 'I'm pretty much a fag. And Teddy's dad thinks he's a fag. And with a bit of training Kain could be a proper fag too. And – don't tell him this because I don't think he's ready to hear it – I think Choc-Ice is showing signs of some faggotry too. It's cool, it's hip, get into it, Nate.'

I closed my eyes and tried not to laugh. When I opened them again I saw that Nathan was doing the same.

'It's getting late, innit,' Nathan said. 'We should go.'

We said goodbye to Birch at the front door. He was holding Whitey and Choc-Ice, using their paws to wave us off. In the van Kain fell back asleep and started snoring again. We drove for a while before Nathan turned on the radio to drown it out. 'Somebody That I Used to Know' by Gotye and Kimbra was on. As we crossed over Vauxhall Bridge the metallic skyscrapers looked majestic against the dark navy sky. Eventually I looked across to Nathan and asked if he was alright.

He didn't reply for a moment. Then he said: 'I feel like a prick, innit. Mya loves this shit. Performing and dressing up and that. And I can't just be here not feeling happy for her. I don't even like going to see her 'cause I'm just thinking about what people are thinking about me, innit. And now I'm getting called a fag by fucking kids. It's annoying, bruv. What am I supposed to do, Ted? And why does she have to wear that shit outside the club?'

'Is it just the name-calling that bothers you?' I asked.

'Nah, bro,' he said. 'There should be a separation, innit? What she does on stage and what she does in real life. Why was she even wearing that to pick up Bakari anyway?' I gave him a look which made him nervously say: 'What?'

I sighed. 'Nate,' I said. 'I don't think there's a reality in which you and Mya are in a relationship and you don't support her. I know how much these thoughts get to you and I know it hurts. But things are going to be said. And you might be embarrassed for a while or hurt. But we both know it's gonna pass. And you know how wonderful Mya is on stage, and I guess in an ideal world that should mean more to you than what someone might be thinking about you. What she does takes a lot of effort and dedication and creativity. And it's really impressive what she's able to come up with on basically no budget. You should be able to go and see her in her element without feeling so ashamed about it.' He looked away from me and back at the road. 'And remember? You were supposed to pick up Bakari but you and Kain got that job on short notice, so Mya had to quickly go get him?'

He was silent for a moment. Then he said: 'Well, damn, Ted. Are you tryna date my girl?' I laughed too. 'No, but I get you. And I do know how amazing she is, innit. I just wish I wasn't so . . . I dunno, bruv. Insecure? That's the word, innit?'

I smiled at him and nodded. 'You'll get there,' I said. 'In the meantime let's just think about what Birch said—' I moved my palm through the air as if Birch's words were written across the windshield: 'There's nothing wrong with being a fag.'

We laughed again. 'So your dad thinks you're gay, yeah?' Nathan said.

I chuckled. 'Apparently so,' I said. 'My parents watched an episode of *Glee* and thought they could see me in one of the characters.'

'What did you tell them?'

'I think I came across more defensive than I would've liked,' I said. 'Honestly, I think I would make a lot more sense to them if I was gay.'

'I know this is a weird question, yeah,' he said. 'And I don't even know why it is, bruv. But what do you think you are?'

I stayed quiet a moment. 'I know what I want,' I said eventually. 'In the sense that I know how I want to feel. What's pleasurable to me has just never had anything to do with sex or even being in a relationship with someone. And if it does, it just feels like I'm forcing it, you know? I feel fulfilled knowing I have people who care about me. And I genuinely don't know how to articulate that to my parents. It really bothers me that they don't think I'm happy with my life.'

'You know what, cuz,' he said. 'I always thought you wanted to smash Birchy Boy, innit. For years. Is that not what's going on?'

I shook my head, smiling. 'Obviously I love Birch,' I said.

'Even on like an aesthetic level, I think he's really cute. I've always thought that. I love his little chin butt. I love his perpetually messy hair. I love his weird little obsessions. I even love how allergic he is to maturity. But no, I've never wanted to have sex with him.'

'Ted,' he said. 'Does Birch know you feel that way about him?'

'I'm a little scared to imagine what Birch might or might not know,' I said. 'Let's be safe and not tell him.'

9

That Friday Monty and I went to lunch with Janice at her favourite Italian restaurant in Covent Garden. She'd been courting an Olympic-related sponsorship that'd fallen through. And instead of showing us what they'd said in the email, she wanted to discuss it in person away from the office. After we ordered she stared at us for a few seconds and then ran a tongue across her gold tooth.

'You two, right—' she said, wagging her finger between Monty and me; she had really long acrylic nails with white polka-dot patterns on them. 'You're both a pain in mi pum pum. You get me?'

Monty and I looked at each other and then back at her. Monty raised an eyebrow and we simultaneously said: 'What?'

She mimicked us and repeated 'whuhhh' in this really goofy voice. 'You're like a pair of Henry Hoovers, just sucking up all the shit.' Monty started to snigger and then I elbowed him. Then I asked Janice if she had any more insults in the chamber or if she was done. Then she said: 'I mean, is there anything you two won't do to embarrass me?'

'Janice,' Monty said. 'What are we supposed to have done?'

She took out her phone and opened an email which she

read out loud. The email said that after careful consideration they had decided not to sponsor the August issue of *Rush!*. They said that while they appreciated the creativity, it didn't align with their branding objectives. Janice put her phone down on the table and said: 'It's bollocks. It's all a bunch of bollocks.'

'Right,' I said. 'But you're the one that wrote the proposal, so why are you mad at us?'

'Because of the bad juju that's been following me around ever since we rebranded,' she started to fan herself as if this 'bad juju' had manifested as particles in the air.

Janice had hoped securing the sponsorship could tie *Rush!* into one of the biggest cultural moments of the decade. And the failure seemed to cement the idea that the magazine had fallen quite drastically from the standing it had ten years ago. Not only in sales, but also reputation.

'It's not lookin' good boys,' she said. Then she said all of this used to be so easy, that not too long ago sponsors used to clamour after us. 'That's why we're in my happy place today. Maybe it'll make all the bad juju go away while we think about where we go next.'

I'd seen Janice on television twice before I eventually met her in person. The first time was on a black entertainment show called *Stussh* on ITV when I was fifteen. She'd been telling the interviewer that she was making it her mission to put more black faces on the covers of mainstream pop mags in Britain. When the interviewer asked if this was a particularly prevalent issue, she said: 'Well, look at the band Damage. Wanna guess how many times it took 'em to get on the cover of *Smash Hits!*? Go on, have a guess. Now ask me how many times they had to ask to get on the cover of *Rush!*.' The second time I saw her was when Geri Halliwell left the Spice Girls. She was at the press conference being interviewed by CNN and she said: 'Nah, they haven't lost a thing. They've still got Mel B.'

Then, during my first year of university, she came to talk to all the journalism students about her job. I remembered thinking that she didn't look or sound like what I imagined an editor-in-chief at a major magazine would. There was something so anti-corporate about her that made a position under her wing seem attainable.

'Okay lads,' she said now, 'give me something to get my mind off this. I want at least fifteen minutes where I'm not thinking about this depressing shit.' She looked at Monty then and said: 'You – I heard you've been depressed 'cause you broke up with your missus—'

'Oi,' he said. 'I don't appreciate that. I'm not depressed. I'm just a little bit sad, okay? But since I ain't got anyone else to talk to, here goes—'

He told us that he'd tried to ask out the receptionist, but she'd told him that he wasn't her type. 'I was wearing that shirt that made my arms look proper hench 'n' all. Ted, you saw me that morning. Didn't I look well fit?'

I just shrugged and said: 'I guess.'

'Calm down, love,' Janice said to him. 'I got bigger arms than you. And anyway, maybe she doesn't like big guys. Maybe she likes 'em skinny like Ted.'

I felt something inside me constrict when she said that. And then awkwardly I smiled at her in this tight way that made me look constipated.

When our food arrived, Janice and Monty started to eat immediately. I'd ordered a risotto and they'd both got some lamb chops. At restaurants I liked ordering food that could aid in the illusion that I was eating my food more quickly than I was. Or that I was even eating at all. I found bowls of rice intimidating: for example, no matter how much I ate, it never seemed to disappear. But I could use my tongue to mush risotto into a soft paste, coat it with lots of saliva and swallow it as if I'd never even put anything in my mouth. I always found myself forming tricks to move through the moment more rapidly. Sometimes this worked and sometimes it didn't. I never seemed to have control over how my body would respond, even after I'd eaten as much as I thought was socially respectable. Janice and Monty finished eating quickly. And eventually Monty commented on how much food I had left on my plate. Facetiously I told him to mind his own business and he laughed. In the end I stuffed a few more spoonfuls into my mouth and then I excused myself to the toilet.

In the cubicle I let the food I'd stored in my cheeks roll down my tongue and into the toilet bowl. I'd only meant to unload what I had in my mouth. But then I ended up retching so violently that the food I'd already swallowed came out too. Even when it was over I knelt by the bowl with strands of spit hanging from my lips and tears in my eyes. I breathed slowly in the silence, looking at the dark-brown mess clumped under the surface of the water.

I tried not to think about anything. I was desperate to let this moment live in a vacuum. Nothing could tether me here if I just pretended that outside of the toilet, everything was okay.

When we left the restaurant Janice said goodbye and headed to Covent Garden station. And Monty was off to get some soundbites from a new band rehearsing for a gig that night. I stood outside the restaurant with my eyes closed as the air washed over my face. When I opened them back up I saw Monty walking back to me. I wiped my palm over my face and smiled at him.

'You alright, mate?' he said.

'Yeah,' I said. 'What's up?'

'Before I forget,' he said. 'I wanted to ask what you were up to tonight.'

I felt very flushed and kept blinking. 'Um, I'm just going to Passage to see my friend perform,' I said. 'Why?'

He asked me who I was going with. I made a face and asked him why again. Then he said: 'I just wanted to know if I could come with.'

'Why?'

'Ted, is that all you can say, mate?'

I laughed. 'No,' I said, 'I just mean that we don't really hang out outside work. What's brought this on?'

He placed his hand over his mouth and gasped. 'Ted,' he said, throwing an arm around me, 'think of this concept, mate: we could be best buds outside of work.'

Flatly, I said: 'I don't know, Monty. That kind of messes with the original meaning. And anyway, why are you so sure we're best work buds? How do you know I don't like Janice more than you?'

'Cause you're a pain in her fuckin' pum pum, mate,' he said. 'Didn't you hear her? But you're not a pain in mine.' I stared at him a moment. 'C'mon mate. Once I go see this band and type everything up, I won't have anything going on. I don't want any more Friday nights where I haven't got shit to do. It ain't right.'

I laughed. 'Fine,' I said. 'I think Birch would probably be really happy to see you again anyway.'

That evening Birch and Nathan were already drunk by the time Monty and I arrived at Passage. They were stood outside facing each other, doing the dance to DJ Casper's 'Cha Cha

Slide,' which was playing from inside the bar, while Kain stood looking at them shaking his head.

When Monty saw Birch, he pointed at him and yelled: 'Oi oi – Stairwell Shagger! That you, mate?'

Birch curtseyed and said: 'Tis I, good sir.' They hugged each other and then turned to look at me. 'Teddy Bear,' Birch said, 'you didn't say you were bringing this massive hunk down.'

Nathan and Kain walked up to me and asked about the Stairwell Shagger thing. 'When Birch worked in my office he had sex with someone in the stairwell,' I said. 'He could've got away with it but he wouldn't shut up about it.'

Nathan looked ready to probe this story further. But then he just looked at my face and said: 'You alright, bruv?'

'Yeah,' I said. 'Why?'

'You sure?' He said. 'You look – you look pale. Do you know how hard it is for a nigga to look pale, fam?'

He went to touch my face but I batted his hand away and said: 'No, stop it, Nate. I'm fine.'

'Then why do you look all grey and shit, bruv?'

Birch and Monty were walking through to the bar with their arms around each other. I could hear Birch telling him about living at Lucy and Charlie's and about Whitey and Choc-Ice. Monty kept knocking his head against Birch's and laughing with his hand on his chest and saying: 'Ah, I've missed you, mate.' Kain was trailing behind them with his hands in his pockets, nodding his head to the music.

I looked at Nathan. 'Look – I'm fine,' I said sternly. 'It's been a long day. I just need a drink.' And then with an awkward laugh I said: 'You know, to get the colour back in my face.'

He looked slightly bewildered. He squinted his eyes at me like: okay then.

*

The club was downstairs below the bar and was dimly lit, whirring with colourful strobe lights. 'Red Alert' by Basement Jaxx was blaring from the speakers. Every time I moved, my shoes tore off the floor like Velcro. At the back of the club were a stage and rainbow-coloured fringe curtains. Birch and Nathan immediately seized Monty and they disappeared into the crowd.

Kain and I headed to the little bar. We sat on the tall stools and I ordered us some drinks. But before the bartender went away to prepare them, Kain called him back and ordered a plate of fries and chicken tenders. He didn't look at me. And when the bartender asked us to pay, he gave him his card before I could. I knew what he was doing and I started to feel annoyed. The feeling materialised like a spiky clump in the back of my throat, and I suddenly didn't want to speak to him. But I still wanted this to be a nice night and I wanted to feel good, so to suppress my annoyance I asked him how things were going with the guy he'd told me about. He finally looked at me and even flashed a smile.

'It's going good, innit,' he said.

I smiled too. 'Well, it looks like he makes you really happy.'

He nodded and then smiled bashfully at the table. I asked when I could meet him and he just shrugged and kind of shook his head aimlessly. 'Well,' I said. 'I'd be happy to have him round the flat whenever you're ready.'

He still didn't comment but his smile did grow wider.

We turned around then and saw that Birch had assimilated into another group of people, some guys in DIY crop tops with their bodies sparkling with glitter. Birch was rolling his hips and flailing his arms. He then took off his hoodie and circled it over his head, shaking his stomach, while everyone laughed and cheered him on. Kain and I laughed too.

The food and drinks arrived then. I'd ordered a cosmo for me and a whisky sour for Kain. When I took a sip, it hit me like a freight train. I felt this heavy debilitating sensation in my body. And I saw my vision greying around the edges slightly. The chicken and fries were on a sheet of oil-soaked tissue folded into a little blue tray. He ate a few fries himself and then pushed the tray towards me, shaking it without saying anything. I took one. But then he shook the tray again, harder. I felt the annoyance surging through me again. I grabbed a few more fries and looked at them clamped between my fingers, at the salt on my fingertips, at the little streaks of oil dripping down my nails. I hated how precarious my mind was, how delicate. I hated how it exacerbated small and simple things and made them so aggressively mountain-ous that it seemed to trigger this weakness in me. I could feel tears emerging in my eyes as I put the fries in my mouth. I chewed with my eyes closed. I couldn't remember the last time I'd actually digested any food properly. When I opened my eyes Kain was looking at me now and he asked if I was okay. I nodded and smiled so hard that my cheeks pushed my eyes closed again. I felt him tap me on the back in a sort of 'well done champ' way. He then asked me if I wanted to dance and I shook my head.

He looked at my face for a moment too long. He might've challenged me on this but the song 'I Know Where It's At' by All Saints came on then, which he and Nathan had loved when we were teenagers. Once at a school disco they had even done an impromptu dance routine to it. So when Nathan came over to grab him I knew I wouldn't have to explain my discomfort. When he left I sat there very still with my jaw clenched.

*

Later in the evening I saw Birch coming out the toilets with a random guy following closely behind him. The guy went in the other direction and Birch wiped the back of his hand against his mouth. When he saw me at the bar he came over. I looked at him with an eyebrow raised like: I know what you've been up to. Then I asked him if he wanted a glass of water or something. He made a repulsed face and said: 'Ted, do you know why people are so angry these days? Everyone's so tense and frustrated.'

'What the hell are you talking about?'

He then repeatedly smacked his tongue against the roof of his mouth and said: 'I swear you can even taste it in the cum.'

My curious expression dropped into something blanker. 'So is that a yes on the water or—?'

He nodded. As the bartender poured him a glass, I said: 'Aren't Lucy and Charlie gonna mind you running around, sucking cocks?'

'Well, it wouldn't be fair if they did, Ted,' he said. 'They fuck each other regardless of whether I'm around or not. So why can't I run around sucking cocks? You know what? I'm gonna find another one right now.'

He started to walk away but I pulled him back towards me. 'I think the one is enough for tonight.'

He was about to say something when he looked at me fixedly. 'Have you been crying, T-Bear?'

I made a face and then quickly twisted my palms in my eyes. 'No,' I said, forcing a laugh. 'Why?'

'Your eyes are all shiny,' he said. 'Like sad shiny. What's up, man?'

I laughed again. 'I don't know what you're talking about Birch,' I said. 'I'm fine.'

*

The music died down and then in a low gravelly tone, a voice announced over the speakers: 'Kings and *Queens*, please welcome: Miss Mya.' Everybody cheered and then the club brightened up in an intense kaleidoscope of colours. Mya appeared on stage from behind the rainbow curtains, looking resplendent beneath the spotlight. She had a bright blonde wig on that cascaded in massive curls down her back.

Birch and I looked at each other with confused expressions and then back at Mya. We'd never seen her look so glamorous on stage before. It was usually very masculine suits and leo-tards and jumpsuits. Now she had on an extravagant silver headpiece, a red corset, elbow-length gloves and knee-high platform boots. Birch cupped his hands around his mouth and yelled that she looked sexy. She danced and lip-synced to a mashup of Lovestation's 'Teardrops' and 'Horny '98' by Mousse T. She was wonderful. There was a point where she dropped down into splits that made the crowd scream and clap. I had my hands on Birch's shoulders as he bounced up and down shouting her name. I could see Kain, Nathan and Monty in the crowd marvelling at her too. Nathan seemed especially excited. His enthusiasm seemed to outpace even Birch's, which I'd never seen before. He was circling his fist in the air and blowing kisses. I was suspicious of this sudden adoration, which then made me suspicious of why Mya had changed her act so drastically.

After the performance, we all met Mya in the alleyway by the backdoor of the club. She had her wig and outfit in a large shopping bag and she was now wearing a blue tracksuit. Nathan had his arm around her repeatedly saying: 'That's my girl.' And we all stood around them telling Mya how amazing she had been. At one point Birch said to her: 'Do you think I'd make a good drag queen?' And then everybody laughed as if he'd just asked a simple, innocuous question. And then Birch looked around with a mildly confused expression like: what's funny? I didn't laugh. I knew nothing Birch ever said was innocuous. Something always seemed to come of his quips and offhand remarks.

'Get me in a wig and some nipple tassels,' he said, 'and I'll rock the house down like you just did.'

Mya laughed him off again and pinched his cheek. 'Oh, bless you, babe.'

Monty introduced himself to Mya then. Mya shook his hand and asked if he enjoyed the show. He nodded enthusiastically and said: 'So why ain't you got a proper stage name then? You drag lot tend to have all these silly little names, don't you?'

Mya put her hand across her chest and said: 'Silly?'

Monty looked startled suddenly. 'No I don't mean silly,' he said. 'Sorry, I just meant like—'

She laughed and shook her head like: no, it's fine. Then she said: 'I thought about it at first. But I put so much of myself into all the things I make that I just thought: why should I go by another name, you know? When people talk about how fabulous I am, I want them to be talking about me.'

'Yeah, no,' Monty said. 'I get that. You were great. When you hit the splits, love, I fuckin' lost it.'

Mya glanced down at her bag. 'But this was a bit different for me though,' she said. 'Maybe I should've had a new name tonight. I'm usually more suited up.'

'Nah, you gotta keep this,' Nathan said, kissing her on the cheek. 'You need to keep this look.'

She glanced up at Nathan. She looked disappointed but he didn't seem to notice.

I was standing behind everyone taking slow and quiet

breaths now. I felt dizzy and kept shaking my head in an attempt to settle myself. I started to feel limp then and stumbled backwards, hitting the wall. Everyone blurred in front of me. But I could still make out Birch and Kain looking and mouthing things at me. Then I couldn't see them at all. I felt myself falling. On my way to the ground I felt this acute sense of disappointment; disappointment that I was letting myself be exposed like this, to an audience, that I was no longer able to hold the pieces of my life together.

I didn't know if I would ever recover from this kind of failure. And as I smashed onto the concrete and the world pulled itself away from me, I thought about how much harder I would have to work to repair the blanket of normality, if I somehow survived this. And I already felt exhausted at the prospect of the task.

August 1993

Teddy and Theodore sit in the reception area at the GP's office in New Cross. Teddy is staring blankly at the sea-blue walls while Theodore irritably flips through a stack of pamphlets he's picked up off the coffee table.

'Is this all they have?' Theodore asks.

Teddy snaps out of thought and looks up at him. 'What?'

His dad fans out all the pamphlets. 'I said is this all they have?'

Teddy shrugs and looks back at the wall and tries to keep his hands from shaking. The only way he knows how to steady his nervousness is to stay quiet and still, so he feels slightly annoyed when his dad says he's going to ask the receptionist if they have any pamphlets on eating disorders. When Theodore gets up, Teddy puts his hand on his arm and pleadingly shakes his head. Theodore looks at him and sighs and sits back down. After a while, Theodore notices that 'What Is Love' by Haddaway is playing on the radio by the receptionist's desk and tries to get Teddy's attention by dancing to it with his arms and then, with a goofy face, shuffling his hips from side to side in the chair. Teddy smiles but only briefly, which Theodore takes as a win: he's made his son smile.

Lately, Theodore's been spending a lot of time in their local library. Since making the appointment with the GP, he's been retrieving books about eating disorders, literally anything they have available, which isn't very much. It's as if he's been training for a game show or something, reading detailed summaries about things that sound scary, like bulimia and anorexia nervosa, and wondering what this could mean for his son.

Last Friday, Theodore found Teddy in their bathroom after dinner, hunched over the toilet with his eyes stained a dark red and tears running down his cheeks. The panic that filled his chest then was so intense he almost slipped on the bathroom mat as he dropped to Teddy's side.

Theodore had noticed that Teddy, even before that evening, had been struggling to finish his food and that there seemed to be a kind of pained desperation with every mouthful. Initially, he had considered whether Teddy's taste in food was changing, or if he was simply bored with what he was being fed and didn't feel as if he could tell them. But then he decided that, no, there was something genuinely wrong with his son. When he would ask Teddy if he was okay, Teddy would smile with an agonised expression and nod. But Teddy often did this whenever he was asked if he was okay, so at some point Theodore had stopped taking Teddy's responses at face value.

Before Theodore entered the bathroom, Teddy had flushed away his sick, but there were still large dark chunks left floating in the bowl.

Holding him tight, Theodore said: 'Son, what is this?' He understood, albeit on the vaguest level, what might've been happening, so he didn't want Teddy to feel as if he had to overexplain himself. In fact, he would've preferred if he could completely understand the situation without as much as a word from him. When Teddy didn't reply, Theodore said: 'Because this doesn't look like shit. Unless you are an alien.' Teddy smiled at this; Teddy's smiles were always like little accomplishments for Theodore, like checkpoints that dictated how successful he was on the way to his destination. 'Because if you are an alien,' Theodore continued, 'then you need to tell me now so I can call the government or a scientist, or the Queen herself, and make some cash money.'

Teddy's smile turned into a laugh. Theodore tore off some squares of tissue and wiped at the sludge around Teddy's mouth.

'Dad, I'm sorry,' Teddy said.

Theodore kissed his teeth. 'Ah, don't be sorry, son,' he said. 'Just tell me why you did this. Do you think your mother's food is disgusting?'

Teddy laughed again and shook his head. With his voice shaking slightly, he said: 'Dad, I don't know what's wrong with me. I can't eat properly.'

Theodore took Teddy's hand then and pulled him up to sit on the edge of the bathtub. He asked Teddy what he meant by not eating properly and Teddy looked down at his hands and told Theodore that he didn't know. They sat in silence for a while. Theodore then put his hand on Teddy's back and gently moved his palm back and forth. Eventually Teddy admitted that he wished he was bigger, that he wasn't so thin. He told Theodore that he wanted to fill himself with so much food that people wouldn't call him skinny anymore; he even held out his arm and said: 'Look at me, dad. I'm like a stick and people laugh at me.' When Theodore said: 'Who? Who laughs at you?' Teddy wept and replied: 'Everyone.'

Eventually Teddy explained to Theodore that he was just trying to eat more, but lately food repulsed him, even when he was hungry.

They're in the room with the GP now. The doctor is a stout brown-haired woman with a disgruntled way about her, which unnerves Teddy. But for Theodore, her coldness is like a large sheet of ice that he can melt with the warmth of his personality. When, without making any eye contact, she asks what's brought them here today, Theodore informs her about all the research he's been doing about eating disorders. He tells her some of the titles of the books he's got from the library, and all the possible diagnoses that Teddy could have, and the list goes on for so long that he thinks it'll make her laugh. But it doesn't. And she just looks down at Teddy and says: 'Is that true? You're having trouble eating?' And when Teddy nods, she delivers a litany of things that could be wrong with him. She says he could be stressed by academic pressure, or that he might have digestion issues, that he might just be a picky eater, that he's just simply going through puberty.

Theodore, somewhat offended that she hasn't warmed to him, says: 'Okay? So what do we do? Why can't my son eat?'

'Well in my opinion,' she says, 'I think it's all about discipline, isn't it? Just a little bit goes a long away. Loads of people manage it, don't they? I mean, look at me. I've been on the turn for the last couple days. But I had a ham and cheese bap a few minutes ago; it was quite lovely actually.'

Teddy and Theodore stare at her. Then she sighs hard and says: 'But we do get people like you comin' in—'

Theodore raises an eyebrow. 'People like us?'

'Yeah,' she says, 'people who just need to roll their sleeves up and get stuck in, you know? Like I said, a bit of discipline, it does wonders.'

'I don't understand what you're saying,' Theodore says. 'How can I help my son?'

'Well,' she says, chewing on the lid of her pen now. 'I suppose we could get him on some vitamins or supplements, if it came to that. But that's a bit extreme, isn't it? It's what we give some of the lasses that come down here.' She looks down at Teddy now and says: 'But don't be embarrassed about that. You see, I pride myself on being quite forward-thinking, which is a lot more than what you usually get 'round here, I'll tell you that for free. I'm quite switched on in that way. And I know even little lads like yourself need a bit of help sometimes. But you're throwing around words like "eating disorders". And if I'm being completely honest, it's not even worth thinking about, really. You look perfectly capable of bucking your ideas up and gettin' a bit of grub down you.' She giggles to herself now and nudges Teddy's arm. 'Unless there's a little lass you've got tucked away that's makin' you do this. Trying to cheat the system and get their hands on a couple free pills, eh? Eh?'

This whole session confirms something Teddy was beginning to suspect anyway: that the world at large prioritises the illusion of normality above anything else. He understands now that it's something to not only strive for but to cling to desperately; that there are things worth sacrificing for this. The world might not care if he's being devoured by his turmoil. But they will care if he stops smiling while he's being eaten alive.

In the end the GP tells them to come back if things get any worse. And they do. And eventually Teddy is prescribed medication that makes it hard for him to sleep and constantly leaves his mouth feeling dry. Eventually he develops various gastrointestinal issues that often make him feel nauseous and bloated. But he doesn't tell his parents much of this. Or at the very least he minimises the extent of his discomfort. His parents are relieved when Teddy is prescribed the medication. It feels like an accomplishment. They think it will not only help but cure him entirely. And Teddy feels deeply grateful for their lack of understanding. It makes it easier to lie and pretend. Theodore in particular is so happy that he has identified a problem – one he barely understood at that – and has helped his son find a practical solution. And Teddy doesn't want to destroy that sense of triumph.

Sometimes Teddy thinks the GP was right. Maybe he did just need to try harder. Maybe this was something to push through. He could stuff himself with food, clean his plate, swallow without vomiting. Like she had said, it was all in the discipline.

10

After I collapsed at Passage I found myself in Monty's flat. He lived near Euston station. It was very late now and I was laying on his sofa while everyone else was scattered around the room. I didn't remember much about the journey over there, only that Monty and Kain had been holding me up as we walked down Southampton Row. And Nathan and Birch had been talking about calling an ambulance, with me vehemently resisting the idea. When we got to his flat Monty offered me a glass of water and two tablets of paracetamol.

I looked around as I took the tablets. His flat felt cramped but only because he seemed to have gone for an extended period without cleaning it. He had strings of empty beer cans lined up on the ledge of his living-room window. There were little mounds of dirty washing piled around the room. And the place smelt like he hadn't opened up a window in a while. Even Birch, who had his own tenuous relationship with home cleanliness, looked around and said: 'Damn Montgomery, are you alright?' And Monty just laughed and replied: 'Yeah, I know. This place could use a bit of a spritz.'

Nathan made a face and said: 'A bit?'

'I've had a tough few weeks, alright?' Monty said. 'I'll get to cleaning at some point.' Kain asked him what had happened and Monty told everyone about his break-up. Birch nodded at him curiously, making 'mhmm, mhmm' noises while Monty spoke, and then eventually Birch said: 'So what did you do to her then, man?'

'Oi,' Monty said, 'what makes you think I did something? It was amicable, mate.'

'Then why does your flat look like this?' Birch asked. 'I'm not even joking – I've literally slept under bridges cleaner than this.'

Monty narrowed his eyes. 'Enough of that,' he said. 'Your mate nearly dropped dead tonight. Let's focus on that, shall we?'

Everybody looked at me. I smiled at them in this tired nonchalant way that I hoped would pacify their concern. But Nathan glared at me and said: 'What's going on with you, fam? I knew there was something up with you tonight. I told you, innit – you looked sick.'

There was a seriousness in his voice that shocked me. I could sense that if I matched this seriousness then something about this exchange could escalate, so casually I said to him: 'I'm fine. I promise. I've just felt so swamped lately. And I don't need a doctor to tell me that I'm suffering from work-related stress.'

Kain looked at me, tilting his head slightly, as if to communicate that he understood what had happened to me and that the two of us could go home and he could make me something to eat. But as I smiled at him, communicating that I was considering this exit, Birch grabbed one of Monty's shirts from one of the piles. He balled it up and threw it at Monty. 'Eh, Monty,' he said. 'Are you stressin' out our boy? Are you the reason he's collapsing in the club? Oh, you fuckin' journalists. You won't rest until we're all pulling out our hair like the rest of you.'

Monty laughed and threw the shirt back. It landed on Birch's face. 'I'll have you know, mate,' Monty said. 'I'm an exemplary colleague. Teddy, tell 'em—'

I laughed. 'Those late deadlines would probably have something to say about that.'

Dramatically Birch pointed at him. 'I fucking knew it.'

Monty, still laughing, shook his head and then said: 'I know it's nearly midnight. But I bet the Chinese round the corner is still open.'

Reflexively, I told him I wasn't hungry. Nathan's eyebrows shot up and he said: 'Really, bruv?' Then Monty added that he hadn't seen me eat much today. He even reminded me how much food I'd left on my plate when we were at that restaurant with Janice earlier. I understood then that my collapsing had fundamentally shifted something. And that it would take a different kind of tact to move peaceably through my life now. It felt as if I was no longer able to close the door on a part of myself I'd previously kept locked, and now that they could see glimpses of rot. It was no longer effective to be evasive and hope people would stop prodding me so I said: 'Yeah, you're right. I should probably eat something.'

I heard Birch clap and say: 'Yay, free food.' And then Monty turned around to him and said: 'Fuck off, mate. We're splitting it five ways.'

When the food arrived Monty went through his record collection and pulled out Massive Attack's *Blue Lines*. He lowered the vinyl onto his record player. Nathan and Birch were sitting together, cross-legged on the floor. I was sitting upright on the sofa now with a plateful of rice on my lap. I watched Nathan and Birch twist some chow mein around their forks and cheers their tines before eating. Monty and Kain were sitting on another sofa together and they were talking about how much they loved the album. And by the time 'Unfinished Sympathy' came on, they both had their eyes closed, singing 'you really hurt me baby' with their hands on their chests. I looked around the room then and smiled. I felt such a gentle almost nostalgic warmth in this moment. It made me want to climb inside it as if it were something physical and cavernous I could suspend myself inside.

Birch twisted more chow mein around his fork and held it towards me, smiling. I smiled back. Then I walked over and ate it off his fork. Eventually, Birch asked Monty if he had any beers and Monty said he had some wine in the fridge.

'No beer?' Birch said.

Monty shook his head. 'Ran out. But it's fine. Wine blacks me out a lot quicker than beer does anyway.'

Birch turned to me and Nathan and sincerely said: 'Well that's concerning.'

Nathan and I looked at Birch curiously. Then I reminded him of the time he said he'd have a vodka IV drop hooked into his veins if he could.

'Yeah,' Birch said. 'But I was young and stupid back then.'

'You said that shit last week, bruv,' Nathan said.

'Exactly,' Birch said.

While Monty and Kain were still talking, we poured ourselves some red wine into tall plastic cups we had to wash beforehand, and looked through the rest of Monty's record collection. I always knew he had eclectic taste in music but I was surprised that it was to this extent. We flipped through records from the Pet Shop Boys to Metallica to the Sugababes. Eventually I happened upon Gabrielle's album *Rise*. I took it out and showed Birch. He gasped and took it from me. He then held it up and said: 'Yes.' Nathan put his face in his hands and said: 'No.' Birch interrupted Monty and Kain then and asked if we could put it on. Monty turned around and said: 'Yeah sure thing, mate,' and switched out the records.

While the album played we talked about how, when we were younger, Birch used to get my dad to record songs off the radio onto my dad's cassette. Monty laughed and said he used to do that too. But only so that he could pretend to be the radio presenter Bruno Brookes and do his own count-down of the singles chart. By the time 'Out of Reach' came on, the atmosphere had turned slightly sombre and Monty was talking about how much his ex-girlfriend's mother had loved this song. 'I actually took 'em to see Gabrielle at the Hammersmith Apollo a couple years back,' he said. I remem-bered this. Monty and I were editorial assistants at the time and it was the first time we'd received free concert tickets.

I asked him how he was feeling now and he gestured to the various piles of mess around the room and said: 'Well, look around mate. It's been ages now and I still can't be arsed to do anything.'

'Well, if you want we can help clean up?'

I felt Birch, Nathan and Kain all looking at me like: what do you mean we?

Frustrated, Monty shook his head and said: 'It's not about the mess—'

Birch put his hand on Monty's shoulder and sincerely said: 'But maybe it should be?'

Monty laughed and pushed his hand away. 'No, what I mean is,' he began, 'I just miss havin' people around, you know? All my friends were her friends. And I just fuckin' hate comin' home after work and hearin' my bloody footsteps echo. There used to be so much life in here. Now it's all just quiet and sad and lonely.' Nathan asked him how long they had been together. And Monty said: 'About eight years.' He looked at us now with this mournful expression in his eyes. 'You guys are lucky. You're always movin' about in a pack. No wonder Ted doesn't wanna share.'

Birch raised an eyebrow and said: 'What do you mean?'

Monty laughed. 'I had to beg him to let me hang out with you guys tonight,' he said.

Birch looked at me and gasped. 'T-Bear, you selfish bastard.'

'No,' I said. 'It wasn't like that. I didn't say he couldn't hang out with us. I was just asking him why because we never really hang out outside of work.'

Nathan looked at me too and said: 'Teddy, you selfish bastard.' Then Kain laughed and added: 'What Nate and Birch said.'

'Well excuse me for thinking we were a bit closer,' Monty argued. He looked at the guys now. 'Did he tell you that he used to stay behind at work just so I could bawl my eyes out after my break-up? But no, I get it, Ted. Making new friends in your thirties is hard bloody work so I understand why you'd wanna be a – what is it everyone's calling you these days, mate?'

'A selfish bastard,' Birch said.

'Birch, shut up,' I said. I looked at Monty. 'Fine – Monty we're officially out-of-work friends now. Happy?'

Later that night Monty had a few more cups of wine and talked more music with Kain. Eventually he looked at Kain in this really curious way and said: 'Hang on a minute, mate. Why do I know your face?'

Confused, Kain laughed and shrugged and told Monty

he didn't know. Drunkenly, Monty reached for Kain's face as if to study it. Kain was drunk too so he didn't bat Monty's hand away. He didn't like being touched by people he didn't really know. Monty kept saying: 'No, I swear I've seen your face before.'

Birch and Nathan, who were starting to doze off against the sofa, heard Monty say this and perked back up. Birch started to say something but Nathan and I simultaneously put our hands over his mouth. Monty looked at us and said: 'What? Am I onto something here?'

'Yeah, you're nearly there,' I said. 'Have a guess.'

Monty looked at Kain again and then he widened his eyes. 'Oh my god, mate—' he said. 'You were a—' Sloppily, he made a fist and placed it at his mouth like a microphone. We all laughed while Kain bashfully nodded. When Kain explained that he used to be in the band Element 23, Monty snapped his fingers and said: 'No fuckin' way.' Hurriedly, he stood up and opened up one of the cabinets beneath his television. He retrieved a big CD wallet and started flicking through the sleeves. Then he showed Kain and said: 'I bought this back in 2001. The same week So Solid Crew came out. I thought it was such a fuckin' tune, mate. I was proper rooting for you and everything. Sorry how it all turned out.'

Kain shrugged and just said: 'Yeah, it is what it is, innit.' And thanked him for even buying a copy.

Monty asked him why Element 23 had never released a second song, that he'd seen loads of artists have their debut singles underperform and still get to put out another one, and that some even managed to get an album out. Kain shook his head and chuckled slightly. He then said: 'They wanted me to go solo, innit. But – but the industry is just fuckin' weird, bro. People chat shit. And then they do weird shit. And

I weren't tryna get involved in that – you get me? I still love music obviously. But I don't wanna be under no contract. I don't wanna owe anyone anything.'

'No, I hear you, mate,' Monty said. 'I've interviewed a bunch of people in my time and I could tell you some fuckin' wild stories.' He pulled out the cover from the sleeve. It was a shot of Kain and the rest of the group wearing all black, standing on a glossy white soundstage beside a pair of comically large speakers. 'I couldn't get you to give this a little sign, could I?' Monty asked. Kain took the cover and held it for a moment. It seemed to sober him and he looked a little despondent. But eventually he smiled at Monty and said: 'Sure.'

In the morning Kain and Nathan went to get some coffee for their hangovers and headed to their first job of the day. Birch went back to Lucy and Charlie's. And Monty was sitting at his dining table in boxers drinking a mug full of wine. I sat with him. Then as he was about to take another drink I gently took the mug from his hand. He rested his head in his palms and sighed. Then he looked at me and said: 'You probably can't tell from lookin' at me but I *am* embarrassed, drinking in front of you at bloody seven in the morning. But I have to start the day this way or I think too much. And it's never a good thing when I do that.'

I smiled at him. 'You don't have to be embarrassed around me,' I said.

'Yeah, you say that, mate—' he said. 'But I know what you're thinking – what a fuckin' ugly mess.'

I laughed and said: 'Well, I don't think you're a *mess*.' He laughed too and gently nudged my arm. Then I said: 'I'm also thinking we should probably clean your place up a bit. If anything I think it'll make you feel a bit better.'

He laughed flippantly. 'You think so?'

'I do.'

We cleaned. He collected all the beer cans and I washed the dishes. Birch and Nathan had made a mess of his CD collection last night; they were trying to count how many *Now That's What I Call Music!* compilations Monty owned. Monty inserted one of the discs into his CD player now and 'Lady (Hear Me Tonight)' by Modjo started playing. He started dancing in this goofy way with his shoulders that made me laugh. I told him I applauded the fact he still had lots of physical media. 'I don't remember the last time I bought a CD,' I said. 'But I've had an immaculately kept iTunes library since, like, 2007.'

'Nah mate,' he said. 'It's the best. I've still got every album and, even every single, since my mum started giving me pocket money.' I asked him what his first was. He threw the bin bag full of cans over his shoulder and stood in front of a glass case of CD's by his television, staring at them for a moment. 'Ah,' he said finally. 'Now, mate, I'm not embarrassed about it anymore. But at the time my mates took the piss out of me for ages.'

'What was it?'

'Do you remember "Cleopatra's Theme"?'

I laughed. 'Of course,' I said. He started singing a bit of it. 'You were into Cleopatra?' I asked.

'Fuck yeah, mate,' he said. 'I used to get on my mum's wick, jumping on my bed trying to do the dance routine from the video. I swear to you – they were on the Smash Hits Poll Winners Party once, and that was like the highlight of my year.'

He asked me what my first was and I said it was 'Dreams' by Gabrielle. He clicked his fingers and said: 'Classic.' I then told him it was because Birch was into it. 'Like *really* into it,' I said. 'Actually a lot of the music I purchased back then with my pocket money was just songs Birch developed obsessions with. I think that same year I got "Moving on Up" by M People. I actually used to keep a list of songs he loved. Every time he was into something, he'd make sure it got under your skin too.'

When we were finished we sat on the sofa. He looked around and exhaled like he'd just drank a refreshing glass of water. 'You were right,' he said. 'I do feel a bit better. Maybe today might be the first day in ages where I don't think about my ex.'

'Woah,' I said. 'If you can pull that off then good for you.'

He laughed. I tapped him on his thigh and said I should get going. As I stood up he held my arm and asked me how I was feeling after last night. For some reason I pretended to not know what he was talking about. Then I said: 'Oh. Oh yeah. I'm fine.'

'You sure, mate?'

I nodded. He lifted an eyebrow and looked like he didn't believe me. I insisted that I was and then suspiciously he said: 'Okay.' And as I went to put on my shoes he said: 'Make sure you have a big meal today, yeah? I'd let you take home some leftovers but unfortunately I'm a bit of a greedy bastard.'

'Noted,' I said.

11

One morning a few days later Kain and I went for a brisk walk. We only did this together occasionally. But I was feeling a lot better since I'd collapsed and wanted to prove to myself that I could still appear healthy.

We had our earphones in as we walked through Limehouse. We went down narrow roads and passed industrial units and warehouses. We then paced along Regent's Canal, past all these dilapidated buildings all colourful with graffiti, and then through Mile End Park. Eventually we arrived in the vastness of Victoria Park where we sat on a bench by the lake and drank from our water bottles. We looked at the sprinklers erupting into the sky in various configurations, at the Chinese Pagoda, and at the narrowboats idling by the bank.

We sat in silence for a while. Kain took out his earphones and I heard 'Novacane' by Frank Ocean playing through the buds. I looked at him watching the water contemplatively now and eventually I asked him if he was okay. He flashed me a nervous smile.

Confused, I said: 'What?'

'I think I need some advice,' he said. I looked at him like: what do you mean? And he continued: 'I saw that guy again, innit.'

'The client?'

'Is that what we're calling him, yeah?'

'You haven't told me a name yet, remember?' I said. 'Can you at least show me what he looks like?'

He laughed and then showed me a photo they had taken together on his phone. He said the guy's name was Harley and that he was twenty-eight and lived in Bermondsey. I looked at the photo and it was such a surprisingly sweet photo from Kain that it jarred me slightly. 'You're smiling,' I said. He laughed at this. 'You're actually smiling for a photo.'

Bashfully he looked away from me. I dramatically put a hand on my chest in exaggerated affection. Then I told him it was like Harley was softening him up. He smiled again and nudged his shoulder against mine. I looked at the photo again and focused almost forensically on Harley this time. He was a slim guy with a cheerful face and cornrows. I told Kain he was cute.

'Anyway,' I said, 'why do you need advice?'

He put his phone back in his pocket. He then crossed his arms and stared out at the lake. He told me that Harley had asked him out on a date and he wasn't sure what to do. 'Okay,' I said. 'I mean, that's really nice. What's wrong?'

He made a face and gestured at me like I should've known what was wrong. I made the same face and gestured back. Then he said: 'Harley wants a proper date-date. Outside and shit.'

'Yeah,' I said, 'a lot of dates tend to happen outside, Kain.'

'Ted,' he said. 'Stop taking the piss, blud.'

'I'm not,' I said. 'I just don't see what the issue is. You like him and he likes you. And he's asked you out on a date. Why are you so frustrated?'

He sighed. 'Nah Ted,' he said. 'You ain't hearin' me, fam. He wants a date. Outside. Holding hands and shit. He's gonna think I don't like him, innit. Because I'm not about to do any of that shit. You think I'm just gonna go to a restaurant and sit at a table with another brudda and what? Feed him strawberries and that.'

'Hm,' I said. 'I feel like you have a very warped idea of what a date is. Why would you have to do any of that?'

'I dunno, blud,' he said. 'But it's what he probably expects, innit.'

I told him that when people went on dates for the first time they generally didn't do anything they didn't feel comfortable doing. I'd said this in a slightly sarcastic and patronising way, hoping he'd find the humour in his panic. But then he said that behind closed doors he had been very affectionate with Harley, more affectionate than he'd ever been with anyone else. But this was something he wouldn't be able to replicate outside, and that he was scared that he had presented himself to Harley as someone he wasn't. And ultimately he didn't want Harley to hate him.

'Well, I think you've got it the wrong way round,' I said. 'I think the person you're so fearful of other people seeing is who you really are. You haven't deceived anyone. So don't worry about that.' I smiled at him. 'And you've been on dates with women just fine, haven't you?'

'That was different, innit,' he said.

'It doesn't have to be.'

He exhaled then and rubbed his face in his hands. And then, accusingly, he asked if I was about to call him bisexual again.

I laughed. 'When are you going to stop saying bisexual like it's some kind of slur?' I said. 'You can exist very uncomplicatedly as a bisexual man. Look – you're even doing it right now.'

He started to laugh. But then he hardened his face and said: 'Nah Ted, you don't get it. No one's gonna see it like that though. They're just gonna see a gay nigga, innit. They're not gonna see that spectrum shit you're always chattin' about. It's like, I could fuck a hundred girls, yeah? And it wouldn't mean shit, 'cause I fucked one guy.'

'Well, okay,' I said. 'But don't you think, if everything that made you who you are was determined exclusively through the eyes of random people who don't know you, and have no reason to care about you, then you wouldn't really be anyone?' He didn't say anything. 'Or at most you'd just be this big unsightly sci-fi-like creature, constantly phasing into all these ungodly configurations as you moved past all these people deciding who you should be.' He chuckled at this. 'And by all accounts you're quite attractive, so this should be a no-go for you anyway.'

He half-heartedly flexed one of his arms. Then I said: 'It's a shame Birch isn't here. He would've loved that.'

We got up and started to walk back. He took his phone back out and clicked from that Frank Ocean song to something by Bon Iver. He was still looking a little despondent. Before he put his earphones back in, he said: 'I might cancel you know. He's gonna drop me afterwards anyway.'

'Well, before you do that,' I said, 'I think you have to give yourself the opportunity to find out what you're like when you're on a date with someone you're really into.'

On the walk back we talked about the meeting Kain and Nathan had had with the council. He said that Nathan thought it went well. But he wasn't so sure they were actually going to get the contract. I asked him why and he said: 'It's just a feeling, innit. It was kinda weird, fam. They kept asking questions like they were tryna trip us up or something.'

'How do you mean?'

'They looked through our proposal and the first thing they asked was how many full-time staff we employ. I looked at them like: what do you mean, cuz? It's just the two of us. And you know that. The vibe was just dead. Then they asked for ten years of audited financial statements, when they already knew we've only been operating for three. They just kept asking shit I couldn't answer without them thinking I was getting vexed. And at the end they were like: "We really appreciate your enthusiasm." I know what that means, innit. It means they're not tryna consider us. And Nate was all: "Why do you look pissed, bruv? They said they appreciate our enthusiasm."' Kain kissed his teeth.

'Well, obviously I'm gonna join in with Nate and his optimism. It's not over till it's over and even you can try again.' He just shrugged like: okay.

Later on he asked me how I was feeling these days. When I told him I was fine, he said: 'That was bare scary, innit, what happened at the club. I'm still thinking about it.'

I just shrugged and smiled anxiously at him. I could feel myself becoming very evasive. I didn't like being this way, especially around Kain. It didn't make sense to hide from the one person who had glimpsed the parts of myself I didn't like putting words to. But despite this I could already feel myself raising some kind of fortress. Kain didn't have the words to put to it either. And we'd never actually spoken about disordered eating or anything related to it before. Everything he had come to know about me and my intimacies had been conducted wordlessly.

There had been one evening a few years ago where we'd gone to dinner to celebrate Nathan's twenty-sixth birthday. We went to a tapas restaurant in Soho. We shared all the dishes and I came close to eliminating the pressure I felt to clear my plate. It was a pleasant evening and we all ate and laughed a lot. But when we got home and Birch and Kain went to sleep, I went to the bathroom and vomited so violently that I woke up Kain. I remembered being panicked and thinking about all the ways in which I could clean up and leave the bathroom before he walked down the hall. But I felt too weak to move. He opened the door and stared at me. The embarrassment I felt then had sprung on me so aggressively, it was as if someone had thrown a brick at my face. I started to cry. And Kain felt too awkward to do or say anything. But I supposed it also felt too mean to leave me, so he just stood there.

We never spoke about that night. And he didn't say anything to Birch either. But over the next few days, every time we were in the same room together he seemed to watch me with an attentiveness that made it difficult to pretend I was fine. And it became ridiculous to maintain the fiction that I was. So I accepted that even though the specifics of my disorder hadn't been discussed, he still knew. And our relationship quietly adjusted accordingly. One morning he even surprised me with breakfast. There were only a few bits on my plate: one single piece of toast, a small portion of scrambled eggs, a sausage. He didn't say anything to me. He just ate his own food and watched me intermittently while I tried to eat mine. From then on it felt as if he could see me, but only in blurs and outlines and indistinct shapes.

*

Now as we crossed the road towards Limehouse station, he asked if I needed to see someone and I told him I didn't. This was usually the extent of our discussions about this. But this time he said: 'Are you sure?' And I said I was. 'But what if it happens again?'

'It won't.'

'How do you know?'

I tensed up. 'I think I know myself well enough to know if I need to see someone,' I said. 'I messed up my diet. That's all.'

'But you don't really have a diet, innit,' he said. 'And before you give me that look—'

I raised an eyebrow. 'What look?'

'That look you do when you think I'm about to make you uncomfortable by talking about this shit.' I asked him what he meant and he said: 'Like when we were at Passage and I made you eat them fries. And you looked like you were gonna shank me, cuz.'

'What?' I said. 'No I didn't.'

He laughed. 'Yes you did, fam,' he said. 'You looked at me like: if this brudda makes me eat these fuckin' fries I'm gonna go sick on him.' I laughed and rolled my eyes. 'I'm only bringing it up because Nate said something about it, innit.'

'What did he say?'

'On our last job, he was just like: what's up with Ted? And I had to be like: I don't know what you're talking about, cuz. There's nothing wrong with him. But I don't think he believed me.'

I could already tell that whatever I said from here on would be filtered through a kind of delusion, that I was firmly placing myself in a world entirely different from theirs. 'But there isn't anything wrong with me,' I said.

'He's not stupid, fam,' said Kain. 'He thinks you're keepin' secrets and shit. And then he's lookin' at me crazy like: what kinda friend am I, not seeing that there's something up with you.' We stopped walking suddenly and then he put his hand on my shoulder. He looked at me carefully and said: 'Teddy, my nigga, you're making me look like a bad friend. And I don't like that shit.'

I took his hand off me and said: 'Well like I said, there's nothing up with me. So your status as a good friend is still intact.'

He tightened his lips. 'Ted,' he said. 'You're bare frustrating, you know that? It's *me* you're talking to. Why are you acting like we both don't know what's going on? I'm tellin' you, blud, when you collapsed it was proper scary. Your eyes went white and you just flopped to the ground. And then you didn't even wanna go to the hospital.'

'I know,' I said. 'I'm sorry. And I appreciate your concern. I always do. But I just need you to back off.'

He held his hands up as if surrendering. 'Fine,' he said. 'But when Nate talks to you, you're gonna have to come up with something better than: I'm fine. Or I don't even know, fam. He might get violent.'

I laughed. 'Violent?' I said. 'When's Nate ever been violent?'

'He has his moments, innit.'

'I don't think I've even seen him make a fist before,' I said. 'You on the other hand. Need I remind you of the time you nearly broke my nose back in school?'

'Eh,' he said. 'We don't talk about that.'

'See,' I said. 'There's lots of things we don't talk about that have no bearing on our relationship.'

He narrowed his eyes at me. 'You think I'm dumb, innit,' he said. 'I know you're just tryna twist shit so you don't have to talk about anything. You're manipulating me, fam.'

'It's not manipulation,' I said. 'I'm just saying we both have things we'd prefer not to talk about. And that should be okay. Like I keep telling you – I'm gonna be fine. And I'll tell Nate the same thing when he asks.'

12

That weekend I received a text from Birch asking me to meet him in Knightsbridge. When I asked him why, he said Lucy and Charlie were holding Whitey and Choc-Ice hostage and he needed help getting them back. I was with Mya at Passage at the time. She was having her lunch and I was having a cocktail. When I showed her the text, she kissed her teeth and rolled her eyes. Then I laughed, taking another sip of my drink.

'Is he being serious?' Mya asked. I lowered my eyelids at her and then she said: 'Yeah, sorry, stupid question.'

I called him. When he answered, I asked: 'Birch, what do you mean Whitey and Choc-Ice are being held hostage?'

'Lucy and Charlie took 'em back,' he said. 'But we already bonded. I even fuckin' named them, Ted. They can't just do that. I'm not havin' it. I want my fuckin' ferrets back.'

'Well, why did they take them back?'

'Ted, it's a long story, okay,' he said. 'If I give you the details, we'll be here all day. I just need you here to keep watch.'

'Keep watch?' I said. 'Are you trying to break into their house or something?'

Mya reached over and snatched my phone. 'See, this is what I mean, Birch,' she said. 'Why are you always doin' shit that attracts police attention? First you try and get my six-year-old son arrested, and now this? Aren't you tired? When does it end?'

Even though my phone wasn't on speaker, I could still hear Birch yelling about him and Bakari not actually being arrested and only being witnesses to an arrest.

I gestured for my phone back. 'Birch,' I said. 'I'm not going to help you break into their house.'

'Why not?'

'Have you considered the optics?'

'Yes, I've looked at the optics,' he said. 'And they're saying: you'd feel better about breaking into this house if Lucy and Charlie were black and poor. There's a name for people like you, Ted. And it's not nice. You're actually being really racist right now. But, like, in the opposite direction—'

'What the hell are you talking about, Birch?'

'T-Bear, please,' he said. 'I don't have time to explain the intricacies of your own racism to you right now.' He sighed. 'Look, we won't even have to break in. I have a key. I just need you to look out for nosey neighbours. And then help me carry out all of Whitey and Choccy's stuff, like their cages and toys; you know they're used to living in luxury.'

'And take it all where exactly?'

'Well, that's another thing I needed to talk to you about.'

'You're not moving back into my flat.'

'See,' he said. 'This is why I texted you. Now I have to beg you for shelter over the phone. This is all very embarrassing, Ted.'

In the end, I went to Knightsbridge; not to be an accessory, but to help de-escalate Birch. Mya came along because she didn't have a shift that afternoon and was curious how everything would play out. When we arrived Birch was on his hands and knees behind the black fence, digging through the dirt in the large flowerpots that housed roses and hydrangeas.

'Birch, what the fuck are you doing?' Mya asked, leaning against the gate.

He looked up at us. 'Why did you bring Mya? This is a two-man job. We don't need her.'

'I have the afternoon off and wanted to see the mess,' she said. 'And also because you're a massive, massive idiot.'

Birch looked at me. 'And there she goes chattin' shit about my weight again,' he said, clawing a clump of dirt from the pot and throwing it up at her. She flinched, blocking her face. And then in retaliation she opened the gate and placed her foot on his back, nudging him over onto his side.

'You're lucky I'm not in heels, you little bitch,' she said. 'Seriously, what are you doing?'

He went back to digging through the flowerpots. 'What does it look like?' he said. 'I'm looking for the spare key.'

'In the dirt?' I asked.

'Yes,' he said. 'In the dirt. I got drunk a few nights ago and I think I left it in one of these pots.'

'Why?'

'Because I'm smart, Ted,' he said. 'When I'm trolleyed I like to move about, don't I? And I can't be jumpin' around with my valuables in my pockets. So when me, Lucy and Charlie left for the clubs that night after pre-drinks, I remember dropping the key in here somewhere.' He looked at me and Mya. 'You know what, you two – get down, pick a pot and help me look. And if you find any money, it's mine.'

'I'm not getting on my knees for you,' Mya said.

'See?' he said. 'You've never been a team-player, Mya. And you've always had it out for me.' He reached up for my arm and pulled me over to him. 'If we can't find it then I'm putting a brick through that fuckin' window. I'm getting my ferrets back.'

I joined him on the floor but I didn't dig. 'I thought you already had a key and that we wouldn't have to break in?'

'Well, if I told you about the flowerpots I didn't think you'd come.'

'Oh, you think?' I said.

Eventually we found the key. It was caught between the pot and the bottom of the fence. Mya had spotted it when Birch picked up a stray brick and had started to aim at the window, and I'd been pulling on his forearm, trying to get it out of his hand.

When we entered the house, I saw Mya glancing up at the high ceilings, shimmering chandeliers and expansive windows. 'Shit, this is nice,' she said, grabbing Birch's shoulder. 'Birch, you lived here?'

Birch nodded at her happily. And then as if suddenly remembering that he didn't live here anymore, he took her hand off his shoulder and continued leading us into the living room.

In the living room, Whitey and Choc-Ice's play area was empty. Birch ran up to it and looked around frantically.

'Where are they?' I asked. 'I thought you said they left them behind.'

He was still looking around, confused. 'I thought they did,' he said. 'Lucy and Charlie went to Italy yesterday.'

'So?'

'Well, you can't just take a pair of ferrets to Italy, can you?'

'Why not?'

'I dunno,' he said, 'because of plane regulations or

some shit.' He turned around to face us. 'Teddy why are you making me explain air law to you, when Whitey and Choccy are missing? No, kidnapped. Probably scared, waddling about in Cinque fuckin' Terre, when they should be here with me.'

Mya looked at me and said: 'What the fuck is air law?'

I put my hand on her shoulder and silently shook my head. Then Birch told us to help him remove some of the things in the play area. He climbed into it and started disassembling some of the climbing structures and tossed chew toys and the material from the hammocks over to Mya and me. But we just watched him. Eventually, Mya looked across to me as more toys landed at our feet and said: 'There's something really wrong with that man, Ted.'

I sighed and then said: 'Birch, would you stop. Please.'

'Yeah, this is silly,' added Mya. 'Just get new pets, innit.'

He turned around and glared at her. And then asked how she'd feel if Bakari went missing and someone had said that to her. And when she'd replied that it wasn't the same, he turned around again and yelled: 'It's exactly the fuckin' same.'

I joined him in the play area now. I put my hands over his, just as he was about grab something else. We looked at each other. 'Ted,' he said, his voice soft, less frantic now. 'They said they were mine. They can't just go back on their word.'

'We'll figure something out,' I said. 'Don't worry about it. I mean, you know they're safe, don't you? They're just on holiday.'

Mya wanted to look around the house after that. She said if we'd gone to the trouble of breaking in, she might as well. Birch and I stayed in the living room, sat on the sofa, listening to her footsteps upstairs, going from room to room. In one of the rooms we heard her scream and Birch looked across to me and said: 'I think she's found Lucy's closet. It's like another little house in there.'

When Mya came back down she said: 'Lucy has a lot of cool shit. I think I saw a diamond bra.' She looked at Birch. 'What does she even do?'

Birch shrugged. 'Um, they go to bars and on lots of holidays and lots of restaurants—'

'But what do they actually do?'

'I just told you,' he said. 'Bars and restaurants and holidays.'

Mya rolled her eyes. 'Anyway, I feel like Nate would love it if I wore some of that stuff on stage.'

I looked at her contemplatively. 'Is Nate the reason your last show was so different?'

'Why?' she said. 'You didn't like it?'

'Oh no,' I said. 'We loved it. We thought you looked phenomenal. I just thought you seemed a little disappointed afterwards.'

Birch looked at me with a confused expression and said: 'Did she?'

'Well you were drunk and running around sucking cocks in the toilet, so you probably wouldn't have noticed.'

He laughed. 'Oh yeah.'

Mya sat down between us. 'He still talks about that show, you know,' she said. 'He never talks about my shows like that. It's always like: "Oh, that was good, innit." But nah. This time that man was *sprung*. He even asked about the next one and what I was gonna wear for that. But it's like, what do I do now? Getting all glammed up was fun for a night. But that's not really what I'm about, is it? What's he gonna do when I get my suits back out and put my tits away?' She paused for a moment. 'I'm just a bit pissed off because it felt like he was relieved. It's been years and I keep feeling like he's embarrassed by this big part of my life, and I hate it.'

Birch laid his head on her shoulder and she idly ran her fingers through his hair. I asked her if Nathan had spoken to her about what Bakari had heard at school.

She nodded. 'Yeah, that was shit,' she said. 'And we even had a meeting with his teacher and that kid's parents. But I don't think Nate even really cared that Bakari had been exposed to that kinda language. He just didn't like that someone thought he was married to a man. Sometimes he makes it seem like even when I'm out of drag, I'm walking around in his handyman gear and a fucking strap-on.'

Birch put his arm around her. 'If you were my girlfriend I wouldn't mind you walking around in Nate's uniform and a strap-on.'

She smiled at him. 'Birchy, my love, shut up.' She then looked at me and said: 'Has he said anything to you?'

I sighed. 'He has,' I said. 'I think he feels embarrassed that he feels the way he does. But I think he'll come around. He loves you and he knows how much drag means to you.'

'I hope you're right,' she said. 'Because my next show I'm doing Prince *and* Lenny Kravitz.'

'Both?'

'Yup,' she said. 'One side of my hair is gonna be dreaded and the other is gonna be an afro.'

Mya went back upstairs. Birch rearranged himself on the sofa and laid his head in my lap, looking up at the ceiling. I could sense he was tired, so we just sat in silence for a while. I didn't realise I'd been looking at him for as long as I had, because eventually I saw his eyes slide upwards and then he said: 'T-Bear, if you think I'm one of the most beautiful men you've ever seen, I'd rather you just told me.'

I shook my head a little. 'What?'

He giggled. 'You keep staring at me, man.'

'Oh,' I said. 'Sorry.' We sat in silence again for a while, and then finally I said: 'Birch, what happened with Lucy and Charlie?'

He exhaled really hard and then looked up at me again. There was this real melancholic look in his eyes now, which suggested I should probably take what he had to say seriously. I looked down at him and stroked his hair, delicately gliding my fingers through its long curly strands.

'They wanted me to do something,' he said. 'And I wasn't into it. And that was that.'

'What did they want you to do?'

He stopped looking at me and went quiet for a second. 'I don't wanna say,' he said.

'Why not?'

'Because it's embarrassing.'

I laughed. 'Birch you were digging through dirt and yelling about "air law" an hour ago.'

'It's not that kind of embarrassing, Ted,' he said. He didn't laugh back, which made the smile on my face disappear. I heard him audibly swallow. 'A while ago there was this guy—'

'What guy?' I said.

'Oh, this was years ago,' he said, 'when I was still on the streets. Way before I met you on that train. There was this guy I'd see. Or he would always come and see me. And basically he'd make me do things so I'd have a bit of money on me for food and stuff.'

'What kind of things?'

He just shrugged and then I felt him start to shake, only slightly. But eventually he stopped. I asked him if he was okay and he nodded. 'Just things,' he continued. 'Bad things that really hurt. Anyway, Lucy and Charlie wanted to do something that made me feel how I felt back then, when I'd see that guy. I mean, obviously I never told them about him, so they didn't know. But it just scared me a bit, so I said no and they didn't like that. And then the whole vibe changed, I guess.'

I felt as if my heart was trying to accommodate pain it didn't have the capacity to harbour. We didn't often talk about that period of Birch's life. As someone who routinely handled difficult conversations with humour, he didn't even make offhand jokes about it.

'Who was this guy?' I asked.

He shrugged again. 'I dunno,' he said. 'Just some guy that wore this super fancy suit. That's all I really know about him. That and he had a proper mean sense of humour.'

He raised his palms to his eyes then, and when he pulled them away his eyes were red and his hands were slightly wet. I didn't say anything. And neither did he. And we sat in the silence again for a really long time. I continued to casually play with his hair as he looked up at the ceiling.

Eventually, Mya came back downstairs. She was wearing a pink wide-brimmed hat, adorned with all these ribbon-like decorations. She posed at the door as if she was being photographed and said: 'Do you think Lucy will mind if I borrow this? I have an outfit I'm working on that would pair so well with this.'

'Don't you think we've had enough criminal activity for one day?' I said.

Birch sat up. His eyes were still a little damp. 'Yeah, you don't know what you're talking about, Ted,' he said, getting up and walking towards Mya, gesturing for her hand. 'Let's commit more crimes, my darlin',' he said. 'If they're gonna take my babies away, then I'm gonna take Charlie's Versace robes.'

I sighed. 'Birch, please don't take his Versace robes.'

'I'm taking his Versace robes, Ted.'

April 1997

Teddy sits at the table in Kain's kitchen while he cooks. It's after school and Teddy is still in his uniform, but he's taken off his blazer and hung it on the back of the chair. The bridge of his nose is slightly swollen and he keeps periodically touching the lump to see if it still hurts.

Kain is wearing a white vest and grey shorts, standing by the stove squeezing tomato paste into a cup filled with a pepper-tomato blend.

'Your dad makes you cook even when you're sick?' Teddy asks.

Kain's nose is blocked and his throat is sore, so when he replies, his voice sounds an octave lower. 'Yeah,' he says. 'He has to work, innit.'

There's a radio on the window ledge playing 'Sweetness' by Michelle Gayle, and Teddy can see Kain's hips moving slightly. But in a very soft, hesitant way that suggests Kain is actively preventing himself from falling into its rhythm. As Kain pours a bag of rice into a pot, Teddy looks around the kitchen and then out the door and down into the corridor. He thinks about how hollow Kain's house feels compared to his. It's something he wouldn't feel so much if the pictures hanging on the walls didn't have four family members in them. It's just Kain and his father that live here.

Eventually he turns back to Kain and says: 'That smells really nice.' Kain turns around too, smiles and says thanks.

It's Teddy's first time in Kain's home. He's only here to hand Kain his maths homework. Kain has been off sick for a week and Mr McAllister, who now also teaches maths in addition to history because of the school's recent staff shortages, has asked Teddy to do him a favour and drop it off for him. Teddy feels deeply indebted to Mr McAllister. Students during the spring and summer months are prohibited from spending their lunches sitting inside classrooms. But Mr McAllister lets him stay with him for the entire hour break. Birch and Nathan are at a rock-climbing facility in Tunbridge Wells and without their societal protection from Luke Williams and his friends, Teddy doesn't feel safe sitting in the field or standing on the playground or even being alone in a cubicle in the toilets.

After Kain turns the stove on and puts a lid on the pot, he joins Teddy at the table. 'Your nose looks better,' he says. He laughs then, hoping Teddy will laugh back.

Instead Teddy narrows his eyes and says: 'I'm not ready to laugh about it yet.'

'I've been trying to say sorry, innit,' Kain says. 'But you've been ignoring me.'

'I haven't been ignoring you,' Teddy says. 'You want me to say I forgive you so you can feel better. But I don't want to. And I don't believe you. I've been lying to my parents about why my nose is swollen so no one gets in trouble. You didn't even really say you're sorry, you just kept pulling me into corners and saying: "Teddy, we good, yeah?"'

Kain laughs at Teddy's mimicking of him, which makes Teddy laugh too, even though he doesn't want to.

'Why did you even do that?' Teddy asks.

Kain shrugs. 'Fine,' he says. 'I'm sorry for what I did to you. We good now?'

This is the thing Kain did. One morning last week Teddy arrived at school at seven a.m. He had been doing this ever since Birch and Nathan went away so he wouldn't have to meet Luke Williams and his friends at the gates. He sat in Mr McAllister's empty classroom and half-heartedly read a textbook to appear busy and studious. But that morning someone had followed him into the room. He flinched when he heard the door open again and saw Kain standing there with his backpack thrown over one shoulder. Teddy felt like a rodent that'd been spotlit in the dark doing something debasing, even though he was literally just sitting there pretending to read.

He watched Kain walk into the room, hoist himself up on the table in front of his and stare at him. Kain asked him if he was always this early to school and timidly Teddy replied: 'Sometimes.'

Recently Kain had amassed a kind of celebrity status in the school. A few weeks ago, at the end of last term their English teachers took them to see *Romeo + Juliet* in the cinema. On the coach on the way back to school, Kain recited Quindon Tarver's rendition of 'Everybody's Free' that had featured in the film, to a round of applause, even from the supervising teachers who up until then had been somewhat indifferent about Kain's general existence. Kain was always doing things like this now – in the school playground, by the school gates, on the field – delivering impromptu performances that drew little crowds. Teddy and Birch would often watch him from afar and talk about how talented he was, and then remind themselves that they actually hated him because of his association with Luke Williams. Nathan, now, rarely offers his own disparaging remarks on Kain. He and Kain have been on the school's football team for the last two years. And over the course of numerous training sessions and away matches, they have bonded over various songs they like and women they find attractive and athletes they admire.

Kain asked Teddy why he was here so early then and Teddy, without looking up from the textbook, just said he liked the quiet. Without being asked, Kain told Teddy that he was early because of football training. He then landed one of his trainers on Teddy's desk with a loud thud and little clumps of dirt tumbled off of it. He told Teddy that they were Adidas Predators. And Teddy, still without looking up, just raised his eyebrows like: good for you.

Kain sarcastically mimicked the motion of Teddy's eyebrows and said: 'They were two hundred pounds, bro. Do you know how long I had to save up for these?' Teddy didn't respond. 'David Beckham wears them, fam.'

'Okay?'

'What – you don't care about football?'

'Not really, no.'

Kain looked at Teddy curiously then. Frustrated, he took the textbook from Teddy. It was just a random book about the Second World War Teddy had in his bag from his last history lesson. Kain flicked through the pages and a piece of paper fell out. He caught it before it drifted to the ground and said: 'What's this?'

There was a list of songs on it. Whenever Birch developed a new obsession with a song, Teddy would write it down. It'd happened so frequently over the years that it had bloomed into a whole list. The most recent addition had been 'You Got the Love' by the Source and Candi Staton. He'd heard Birch humming it during their last lesson together before Birch went on the trip. After he wrote the song down, he folded the piece of paper into the back of the textbook and forgot about it. He had been finding that Birch's little obsessions have been shaping his own taste in music. That year in particular, he even enjoyed predicting what might occupy Birch's attention if he happened to hear it on the radio before Birch did.

He tried to snatch the list back from Kain, but Kain lifted it higher, so Teddy had to stand up to successfully retrieve it. Annoyed, he folded it back up and slid it into his pocket.

He sat back down then and said: 'Kain, what do you want?'

Kain made a face. 'I just wanna talk, innit,' he said.

'About what?'

Kain looked away for a moment. Then eventually he said: 'Oh, do you know Lynn?' Teddy nodded. 'She's buff, innit? You like her?'

Teddy just shrugged like: I guess.

Lynn was a tall mixed-race girl with long brown hair in their year that all the boys seemed to like. It often amused Teddy that her shade of light-brown skin held so much currency that sometimes it was even affixed to her name and people referred to her as: Light Skin Lynn.

Kain asked Teddy what he thought of her and irritated, Teddy replied: 'I don't think about her. What are you even talking about?'

'Oh, come on,' Kain said. 'I'm tryna help you out.'

'Help me how?'

'Everyone still thinks you're gay, innit,' he said. 'I'm just giving you some advice, bruv. You gotta talk about girls more, so you can be a cool guy. And I promise you people are gonna stop giving you shit. It's easy. You just have to link up with someone and no one's gonna think that shit about you any-more. Not with Lynn though. She's out of your league. She's out of everyone's league. So who do you like?'

Teddy looked at him for a moment. 'No one,' he said.

'Really?' Kain said. 'How can you like no one? This is why people think you're weird, innit. You know Luke hates you. He said he'd kill you if he had the chance.'

Teddy stiffened then and his hands went numb. 'He wants to kill me?' he asked meekly.

'Yeah,' Kain said. 'I'm telling you, fam, he don't like people like you.'

A cold abrasive sensation settled in Teddy's chest. Kain was still talking but Teddy could barely hear him now. There was a new clarity to Luke's hatred of him that was loudly occupying his thoughts. It felt like scaffolding had been erected around his mind and various tools were now drilling and hammering his brain, abruptly re-aligning his percep-tion of his immediate world. Eventually, he heard Kain say: 'There has to be *someone* you like.' And bluntly Teddy replied: 'I don't need your help.'

'Aren't you scared of dying?' Kain said.

'Well, what does it matter to you?' Teddy snapped, raising his voice. Kain recoiled then and looked at him with his mouth slightly open. 'Why do you care if Luke wants to kill me or not?' Teddy continued. 'Why are you trying to give me advice when you're just as much a part of it? We're not friends. We're not anything. Nobody asked you to help me. So why don't you just leave me alone and—'

Before Teddy could finish speaking, Kain kissed him, hard, bashing his lips into Teddy's and nudging Teddy's head back a little. Teddy's eyes widened and he froze. Kain's eyes were closed and he was breathing very hard. The only thing surfacing in Teddy's mind now was how much he didn't want this. And the longer Kain rested his lips on his own, the more he started to feel as if pieces of his autonomy were being taken away from him.

After a few seconds, Kain pulled away suddenly and looked out the window, into the corridor. A petrified look appeared on his face as he caught a glimpse of someone in the window. But before Teddy could turn to look too, he felt Kain clutch the back of his head and slam his face against the table. He felt his nose cracking down on the wood. Sharp lines of pain burned through to his eyes and then to his head. For a moment everything existed in a wall of blurry noise.

Then, as everything slowly clarified itself again, he saw little puddles of blood on the table. And when everything settled into place, he saw that Kain was gone. And so was whoever had seen them in the corridor.

Now, in Kain's kitchen, the radio is playing 'Back to Life' by Soul II Soul.

'Why did you kiss me?' Teddy asks Kain. Teddy has been in two minds about asking Kain this question. On the one hand, he's not entirely sure if he cares why Kain kissed him; he just really hates that he did it. But on the other, it was such a dramatic and impulsive thing to do that Teddy can't help but feel curious about Kain's reasoning. But in the end Kain doesn't answer the question. He's no longer making eye contact with Teddy and he has this tense almost painful expression on his face now. It makes Teddy feel a little guilty for even asking. Clearly, Teddy thinks, it's something that hurts Kain to talk about. And he supposes he could rational-ise the situation for Kain on his behalf, though he doesn't want to. He sees tears glisten in Kain's eyes now. He can tell

Kain's trying very hard not to blink so the tears don't seep out. At this, Teddy feels immeasurably uncomfortable. He's never seen Kain cry before; it's like he's preparing to see Kain phase into an entirely different person before his eyes.

Eventually the silence becomes so heavy that Teddy changes the question and says: 'Why do you still hang out with Luke and his friends?' Kain looks back at him now and Teddy continues: 'You told me that they hate me. But they also kind of hate you too, no? They make monkey noises at you. And they've been calling you Lenny Henry for years. And you just laugh along with them like it's nothing.'

Kain's tears begin to fall now. He wipes his face with his palm in one swoop. But his expression doesn't change; it's still stoic, like he's trying not to acknowledge that he's crying. 'It's just a joke, innit,' he says solemnly, looking down at the table.

'I don't get it,' Teddy says. 'Everyone at school really likes you. They all think you're really talented. Why do you have to go around bullying people? Do you enjoy it or something?'

Kain tells him that he doesn't bully people, that it's mostly just Luke and that he can't control what Luke says or does. This frightens Teddy to the point of questioning his own sanity. It feels as if they're both looking at one specific object and calling that object wildly different things. Teddy reminds him that just a few weeks ago Luke had instructed Kain to yank Birch's sandwiches out of his hands and throw them across the field. And he did it, excitedly. Birch had ran after them desperately yelling: 'Five second rule! Five second rule!'

Kain wipes his hand over his face again. He tells Teddy that when he first came to the school, Luke was nice to him.

And Teddy says: 'He wasn't being nice. He was just making fun of you.' But Kain just shrugs and says it was nice to have friends, friends that were respected and feared, and that it was better to be degraded within the circle than outside it. 'I'd see what they would do to you,' he says. 'And I didn't want that to be me.' He sighs then and looks at Teddy carefully. 'I shouldn't have done that to you,' he says. 'I shouldn't have put my hands on you like that. That was fucked up, innit. I just got scared that someone saw us. And that they were gonna think I was a – whatever. But I'm sorry.'

They sit in silence for a moment. Teddy can sense that this is as far as Kain will go, that there will be no further elaboration or clarification of his actions. Teddy even suspects that Kain is more upset at the idea of someone seeing him and making assumptions about his sexuality, than he is about actually hurting Teddy. But Teddy understands now that there's something here that cannot be discussed, not even casually. Something that cuts so deep that it can only exist between them in silence. Teddy has never wanted to discuss his own sexuality, so he'll forfeit his quest for answers by not forcing Kain to discuss his. Teddy doesn't know why his forgiveness is so important to Kain, but he'll accept his apologies. But not without various stipulations.

He looks at Kain now and says: 'Can you tell your friends to leave me and Birch alone?' And Kain nods, okay. Then Teddy says: 'And now you know that I'm not mad at you, can you leave me alone too, please? I'm a really easy person to ignore. So it shouldn't be too hard.'

He can't understand why but Kain looks wounded by this request, confused even. But still he nods.

'Good,' Teddy says. 'Thank you. We have no reason to talk to each other again.'

Before Teddy leaves, Kain asks if he wants to stay for dinner. 'It's jollof rice,' he says. 'I made too much. It's supposed to be for me and my dad.'

But Teddy shakes his head and says goodbye.

13

During the Jubilee weekend, Nathan and I went to see Coldplay at the Emirates Stadium. Monty had been given two tickets to do a feature on their show for next month's issue of *Rush!*. But he was travelling down to Kent to see family that week, so he gave them to me instead.

That afternoon, Nathan and I took the Piccadilly to Holloway Road. Kain and Birch were looking after Bakari while Mya was at work. On our way out of the station I asked Nathan how he'd managed to get Kain and Birch to agree to babysit Bakari together. He laughed and said: 'Birch is just happy Mya still lets him babysit after that whole thing with the police at Wetherspoons. And I think Kain's on strike after that shit with the council. So he ain't got anything to do right now, innit.'

That week, Nathan and Kain found out that the council had rejected their application for a contract with their business. They were told it was because of insufficient experience and other vague explanations that they couldn't really make sense of. When Kain got the news, he called me at work and nonchalantly said: 'It is what it is.' But at home that evening he was so quiet, and even went to bed early without eating. Nathan, however, seemed to be in better spirits about it at the time. He'd even said they would just have to work harder and expand their business on their own. But as we approached the stadium that afternoon I asked him how he was really feeling about everything, and he said: 'I ain't even gonna lie, bruv. I was really looking forward to steppin' up that income so I could move us out of my parents'. I don't know what I'm gonna do. I was tryna be all brave and that. Because obviously we can't have both me and Kain being all withdrawn and shit.'

'There has to be a way to appeal the decision, surely,' I said.

Nathan shrugged. 'Would we even get another meeting though?' he said. 'Look how long it took them to even see us the first time. And look how long it took them to give us an answer.' He paused a moment and then gave me a very exhausted sounding sigh, and said: 'Nah, bruv. I don't even wanna think about it or it'll put me in a shit mood, innit. I just wanna have a good day.' He put his hand on my shoulder. 'Thanks for inviting me. I know you only do this kinda shit with Birch, innit.'

I laughed. 'That's not true.'

'Nah, it's calm,' he said. 'This is a you and Birch ting and I respect that. So it's nice to be included, innit.'

The stadium was already packed. We got our passes from the media check-in table, as well as these yellow wristbands that were supposed to light up later on in the evening. Then we went up to the bars to queue for some beers. Eventually we went to our section, a box with other journalists that housed around twenty or so seats. As I said hello to a few faces I recognised from other events from previous years, Nathan walked to the edge of the section. I joined him a few moments later. We looked down into the belly of the stadium, at all the people moving across the white panels on the grass like ants. Robyn was the opener and she was on stage at the time. A small crowd had gathered around the stage and everyone waved their cups in the air as she sang 'With Every Heartbeat'.

Nathan wasn't a big Coldplay fan. He only knew a handful of songs. I'd invited him because he was an Arsenal fan and he'd always wanted to visit the stadium. And I'd also thought it would cheer him up after the whole thing with the council. He'd even worn his Arsenal shirt. And at different points walking around the stadium he'd asked me to take pictures of him standing smilingly next to various Arsenal memorabilia.

I usually didn't enjoy stadium shows. I often found them detached and impersonal. But there was an electricity here I could feel reverberating through me. Watching the crowd move up and down in these massive waves, the fireworks, Chris Martin jumping around the stage in his turquoise shirt, the bright green and pink confetti exploding into the air, I felt as if there was a significance here that seemed to extend beyond the band and the concert itself. I felt aloft with the sensation that being in this exact place, at this exact moment in time, with this exact person meant something. I'd never been somebody who moved through the world pondering how much significance underpinned various moments of my life. But when Nathan threw his arm around me during 'Viva La Vida' and sang along so loud his voice started to crack, I felt overcome with this intense energy, almost threatening in its magnitude, as if the world had started rotating in the opposite direction.

I stopped taking notes on my phone and put it back in my pocket. Then I put my arm around Nathan and sang too.

*

On our way home Nathan drunkenly sang Coldplay songs. People came up to him, throwing their arms around him and joined in. I laughed at this but eventually Nathan could no longer walk straight so I had to carry some of his weight on my shoulders.

I'd received several messages during the concert. Birch had sent me a few selfies he'd taken with Bakari and some photos he'd taken of Kain, who was shielding his face and giving the camera a middle finger. There was one selfie of Birch trying to kiss Kain on the cheek and Kain looking at Birch through the sides of his eyes with this annoyed narrow-eyed expression. I showed Nathan and he laughed so loudly it made people turn back to look at us. Mya had sent me some pictures too. She was working on her outfits for her next show at Passage. She was re-creating a Lenny Kravitz look from the nineties and had used metallic fabric spray on a plain jumpsuit. Now she was halfway through making the accompanying wig.

I felt Nathan look at my phone as I swiped through the pictures. I looked at him and he had this sobering expression now. 'You okay?' I said.

'Yeah,' he said. 'Course, bruv.' He went quiet for a few seconds. Then he said: 'So she's going back to dressing like mandem now?'

'What do you mean?' I said. 'This has always been her thing. You know that.' He didn't say anything. 'You know she thinks you were only excited about her last show because of how drastically she changed it up. She told me and Birch that she had fun with it. But I'm pretty sure she only did it because she thought it would please you.'

'And I was pleased, innit.'

'So you don't want her to ever go back to the drag she loves doing?'

'Nah, don't say it like that, bruv.'

I laughed. 'Say it like what?' I said. 'It's what you're saying isn't it? Let's call a spade a spade. You thought because she put on a corset and a blonde wig – she'd love it so much that she'd never look back.'

He looked at me with his eyelids dropped like: come on, and said: 'Why ain't you on my side, bro?'

'Because unfortunately her side makes a lot more sense than yours,' I said. 'Imagine if I said to you now: yeah Nate, fuck everything that brings your girlfriend joy, and makes her feel seen, and makes her feel as if her place in the world means something. Fuck all that. You feel insecure about the type of drag she does, so she needs to just cut that shit out and put on a dress.'

He laughed. 'Not even gonna lie, Ted,' he said. 'I know that was a joke. But even you just saying that got me kinda vexed.'

I laughed too. 'See? And what would you say if I said that's what you sound like to me?'

'I know,' he said. 'I already told you, innit. I know I sound like a dickhead. But I can't help it. When we had that meeting with Bakari's teacher, even she was looking at us all weird. This lady basically looked at us and said: yeah, people are calling you a fag but can you blame them – look at your girl.'

I widened my eyes. 'She said that?'

'Nah,' he said. 'But that was the vibe, innit.'

As we entered the station I told him that every time he met aspects of Mya's drag with resentment, it probably reminded her of how her father used to treat her. I'd first encountered Mya at university during freshers week. It was the first time I ever drank socially. I overdid it and she helped sober me up. She was on the fashion course and I was studying journalism. I told Nathan then that when we graduated, she tried to get her father to come down for the ceremony. 'It was the most bizarre thing,' I said. 'He just laid into her over the phone and told her that she'd wasted the last few years of her life.'

'Shit,' he said. 'For real?'

'She never told you?' I said. 'Yeah, apparently he never really liked her doing fashion or anything like that. In the end my dad stayed after my ceremony, so she would have someone there. She had friends that really loved her and everything. But obviously they all came with their own families.'

'You know,' he said. 'I knew I was being a dickhead. But I think I've surprised myself with how much. I don't want her to feel like I don't support her. I love her, innit.'

I forwarded the pictures of Mya to his phone. I figured she hadn't sent them to him because she was convinced she wouldn't like his response. He swiped through the pictures.

'Tell her you think her outfit looks great so far,' I said, 'and how you can't wait to see how it comes together in the end.'

He started to type and laughed. 'I mean, it does look pretty bangin' to be fair.'

On the underground I realised I'd gone the whole day without worrying if Nathan was going to ask me whether I'd eaten or not. When the thought occurred to me, it was as if I'd successfully navigated a complex obstacle course without even thinking about it. I was feeling as if, since my collapsing at Passage, I'd developed something new within my personality that protected me from such probing, even if I had no idea what that something actually was. As Nathan continued to sober up there was a levity that remained in our conversation that surprised me. When we boarded the DLR at Bank he even joked that since Kain, in his depression, was either ignoring or declining prospective jobs from clients, I didn't need to buy him a new work shirt anymore.

Jokingly I held up my hands and said: 'I've learned my lesson, Nate. I'm not buying you anything anymore.' We even laughed about a time when, just after Bakari was born, I'd bought him an expensive crib as a present. At the time, it hadn't been a laughing matter at all.

We managed to get the front seats in the first carriage of the DLR, the ones that made it seem as if you were driving the train yourself. I looked across at him and asked if he was going to be alright taking on the brunt of the jobs while Kain sorted himself out.

He shrugged. 'Yeah, I guess,' he said. He then paused and glanced out at the little squares of orange light dotted on the sequences of tall flats. He looked back at me and said: 'You know, I think he's got a secret girl or something.'

I made a face. 'What makes you say that?'

'Because, yeah, he's pissed at the council thing,' he said. 'But not like normal Kain pissed. Like one minute he'll be all mad, chattin' about how unfair the world is and shit. But then the next he'll get a text and he'll be smiling like a fuckin' idiot at his screen. He's got a secret girl – I'm telling you, Ted. And I think she's called Hayley.'

'Hayley?'

'Yeah,' he said. 'Yesterday we were in the van talking about what we were gonna do. And he thought I weren't looking, innit. But I saw some gyal called Hayley messaging him. He got all quiet. He just sat there, cheesin' at his phone, bruv. And I was like: Kain, you good? Who's that? Then he just said: nothing, blud. Then he put his phone away. I swear he's linking up with some white girl called Hayley on a hush-hush ting.'

A part of me wanted to laugh. But instead I said: 'That's a lot of conjecture to glean from a smile and a name.'

'Conjecture?' he said. 'Nah, bro. That's facts, innit. You know that nigga don't smile. You didn't see him. He was basically giggling and kicking his feet, bruv. But what I don't get is why he's being all secretive and that. What? He thinks I'm not gonna like that she's white? I like white girls as much as the next guy, innit.'

'Why are you so sure they're white?'

''Cause I ain't never met no gyal-dem called Hayley.'

I looked at him for a moment and sighed. 'I suppose there's a certain charm to your ignorance.'

'I'm not ignorant, bruv,' he said. 'I'm a realist.'

'Okay, realist,' I said. 'Maybe you should just bring it up with him, if being out of the loop is bothering you so much?'

'Eh,' he said. 'I didn't say it bothered me. I'm just curious, innit. But, still, what's the point? None of you niggas tell me shit anyway. You lot like your secrets, don't you?'

I thought there was something quietly targeted about his use of 'you lot' but I didn't say anything, not even to ask what that was supposed to mean. I just casually lifted my eyebrows like: okay. And then he looked out the window again. Oddly, it didn't feel awkward even though it so easily could've been. Before we pulled into Limehouse station, Birch messaged Nathan and asked him how the concert was. Nathan showed me the message and then he put his arm around me and we took a very smiley picture together.

As we went down the stairs and exited the station, Nathan talked about how he was a Coldplay fan now. We hugged each other outside. I watched him walk down to the bus stop and then I made my way to my flat. It was dark and unseasonably cold now. During the walk it dawned on me that as much as we cherished each other's friendship, none of us seemed to believe in it enough to let ourselves be cared for by the other. It was like we were plants sharing the same patch of soil, and as we grew, we folded and twisted around each other, ensuring not to touch each other with our various afflictions and traumas and worries. Sometimes it felt as if what we called friendship could only sustain a certain amount of weight before it transformed into something else entirely.

But I supposed, deep down, beneath the soil, in our roots, we knew it was capable of so much more.

14

The following week we sent the next issue of *Rush!* to print. That afternoon Monty and I were in Janice's office. I was sitting on the sofa beside a wall that had a selection of our past magazine covers on. And Monty was sitting on Janice's desk, next to a bottle of really disgusting brandy she liked to celebrate each publication with. She usually poured us a glass each, which Monty and I would then discreetly unload into the dirt in the plant pots as she drank hers.

That morning Janice had pre-empted a rumour that *Rush!* would be ceasing publication. One of our editors had a contact at the tabloid running the story. They had been told that our recent sales reports had been leaked and this had given some credibility to the rumour. Janice had emailed the contact, not to discredit the leak but to assure them there were no plans to stop operations in light of it. The rumour had reached our team and now she was on the main office floor talking to everyone, trying to forge a sense of morale. Monty and I could hear her congratulating everyone on the publication of the recent issue. Monty got up and walked over to me with his hands in pockets. He looked up at the magazine wall and said: 'Say we were shutting down, what would you do?'

'I don't know,' I said.

He looked down at me. 'Fuck me, mate,' he said. 'We ain't even shutting down and you already look proper deflated.' He clipped his palm on my shoulder and shook it. 'It's just rumours, Ted.'

I laughed. 'If we're being honest,' I said, 'I've felt pretty deflated ever since we started pretending to be an indie mag five years ago. But I know no one wants to hear me relay that point again.' He laughed too and then said he'd grown to like it. And I replied: 'Are you joking?' And then reminded him of what had pretty much been our only major argument at that point. When we were a pop magazine he'd had free rein to write any kind of album reviews he wanted. But after the transition I had to tell him to stop writing negative reviews. In one instance he was almost fired for upsetting one of our biggest advertisers. Back then Monty and I were more professional with each other. In the end we had a meeting where he accused us of being puppets. And I said as long as we had these advertisers that was exactly what we were.

'Yeah,' Monty said now. 'But I'm a lot more chill about that now. I don't care if my team has to pretend the last MGMT album was a masterpiece.'

I stood up and joined him, looking up at the magazine wall. It was overwhelming seeing our evolution sprawled out like that – all the pinks and blues and yellows, covers with Mis-Teeq and the Sugababes, gradually merging into the more subdued colour palette we'd used to signal our transition.

'I feel like we're both resigned in different ways,' I said. I looked across at him then and asked what he would do if we were shutting down. He said he would think about getting back into drumming.

'Drumming?'

'Yeah, mate,' he said. 'I was a hired gun for a bunch of bands in my early twenties. I've gigged all round the country with like five different ones.' He told me then that when he'd visited his parents earlier in the month, he had re-discovered his old drum kit. I said I never knew that about him. Then he said: 'Yeah, well, these are the kinda juicy details you get when you become more than just work mates.'

Just then Janice came back into the room. She ran her fingers through her spiky hair, looking frustrated. 'Right,' she said. 'Who wants a glass of brandy then?'

Monty and I exchanged revolted expressions. Then Monty said: 'Janice, don't you think we should sink a bit of money into our website? It's pretty shit. And everything's online now, isn't it?'

After she poured our glasses she said: 'Montgomery, it's too late for websites and it's too late for the internet. So stop asking me useless questions and pick up this raasclart glass, yeah?'

She drank hers quickly, squeezing her eyes shut and throwing her head back. Monty and I looked at other each again as she clenched her jaw and sharply sucked air through her teeth. I asked her if we should be worried. Then, in the weird American accent she used whenever she felt flustered, she said: 'Ain't nobody worried. Do I look worried?'

I could tell Monty wanted to say: 'A little bit, yeah.' But decided against it.

After work Monty and I walked through Soho looking for a pub. But it was Friday night and many of them, even Passage, were so packed people were spilling onto the street. So eventually Monty asked if I wanted to come round to his for a drink. I said yes. Ever since we decided to be actual friends instead of just work friends – and ever since the boys and I had spent that night at his flat – I'd started to care very much about what his life looked like when he went home in the evenings. The thought of him sitting alone and drinking only to numb himself to loneliness made me feel as if I needed to be there for him in a way that mattered.

Monty talked extensively about his ex. It seemed as if he was no longer mourning but was now eternally nostalgic about the relationship. Once in my office he spoke about her so much I said to him: 'I think you might need a therapist or something.' And he laughed and said: 'See, mate. I love this. Your little sarcastic quips, takin' the piss outta me.' Then he proceeded to reference a time he'd heard Birch say something stupid to me and what my response was and said: 'I want that. Fuck, I miss banter so much.'

We took the long way to Euston. Walking along Embankment we saw the giant Olympic rings floating on the Thames. Eventually we passed several coffee shops, all of which were full. Walking past the windows, the panels seemed to frame people like something out of an art gallery: a woman on her laptop, a man reading a book, someone else on their phone. This made Monty turn to me and talk about how lonely a city London could feel.

'You think?' I said. I'd never experienced the feeling of loneliness as something indigenous to a place, especially London. I'd always thought of loneliness as exclusively internal.

'Yeah,' he said. 'I didn't realise how lucky I was when I was with my ex. I had everything laid out for me. I had mates. I always had plans. There was always someone around, you know? I never stopped and thought: wow, this is actually pretty fuckin' sweet. Look at me walking through Oxford Street with a bird on my arm, looking at the bloody

Christmas lights. Look at me in the pub with a bunch of lads havin' a pint.'

'What happened?' I asked. 'Surely everyone can't have abandoned you.'

'Maybe abandoned ain't the right word,' he said. 'It's just different now. Everyone's just really cautious about hanging out with me 'cause they were all her mates, weren't they? It's not like how it is with you and your boys. Now when I ask to hang out, they're all like: oh, I can do coffee for about twenty minutes in August if that's alright.'

I asked him what his social life had been like before. He didn't say anything for a moment. Then eventually he sighed and said: 'I guess I've always been a bit of a lonely bloke. I think everything good that happened in that period of my life was a bit of a detour. And now I'm back where I'm supposed to be.'

'I don't think loneliness is somewhere anyone is supposed to be, Monty.'

'Yeah, well,' Monty said. 'Here I am.'

Monty's flat was a lot cleaner than the last time I was here. In fact it was almost immaculate, with only bits of gym equipment littered around the place. He poured us two glasses of white wine and I sat on the sofa while he flicked through his record collection. Eventually he pulled out a little 7-inch vinyl that featured the song 'Flowers' by Sweet Female Attitude and lowered it onto his turntable.

He took off his coat and sat next to me on the sofa. He then downed a mouthful of wine and exhaled, nodding his head to the song. He asked me then how I was feeling these days, if I'd had any more episodes like my collapse at Passage. And in a casual tone of voice I said I hadn't. I'd been clinging on to a lot of safety behaviours lately, which basically meant I was trying not to feel guilty with how desperately I was avoiding public eating, even with the likes of Kain. For lunch that day I'd had a few bites of an egg-and-cress sandwich, on a walk I'd taken because people kept coming in and out of my office.

I then asked him if part of the reason his flat was looking nicer was because he'd decided to put himself back out there. He looked away from me, embarrassed. 'What?' I said.

He groaned. 'Yeah I have, mate.'

'Oh,' I said. 'And how was it?'

'I'm not gonna lie,' he said. 'It is fuckin' embarrassing. And I will be offended if you laugh at me.'

'Then I won't laugh.'

Playfully he traced a smile onto my face with the tip of his forefinger and said: 'Nah, Ted. I can already see you grinnin', mate.'

I looked at him like: Monty, come on.

'Fine,' he said. 'So – went out last week. Pulled. Dunno how. I was half-cut so the chat was probably diabolical. But I brought her back here and things started getting a bit hot, you know, a bit raunchy. Started takin' each other's clothes off. But when it got down to it, mate, I just weren't into it.'

'No?'

He shook his head. 'So I sort of pulled her off me and said: eh, look. I think you're really fit but I don't think I'm looking for a shag tonight. I just want a good cuddle. I just want someone to hold me for a bit.' I asked him what she said to that and he made a kind of exasperated expression. 'She burst into hysterics, didn't she? Literally couldn't stop fuckin' laughing. But I don't even blame her. Imagine a bloke takes you back to his gaff and you're expecting a proper rammin'. And he says actually fuck that, lets cuddle.' Speechlessly, we just looked at each other. 'See, mate,' he said. 'Embarrassing.'

I smiled at him and took another sip of wine. Jestingly I said I was sure there was a woman out there waiting to be cuddled by him. He finished off his glass and laughed, re-arranging himself on the sofa and said: 'Yeah, I'm gonna stalk the pubs at night, asking unsuspecting women if they wanna come back to mine for a cheeky hug.'

I laughed too. 'Well, we don't have to make it dark.'

He then said that it was already difficult making friends in your thirties. But it was equally hard replicating the kind of intimacy you had in sexual relationships without the sex. This thought made me blink rapidly and look at him. He looked back at me and said: 'What?'

'No, nothing,' I said. 'I just really understand what you're saying.'

'Really?'

'Yeah.'

There was a brief silence. He looked at me a moment. Then eventually he said: 'Do you think it'd be weird if I asked you to hold me?'

'If I was slightly more sober then maybe,' I said. 'But luckily for you—' I shook my wine glass at him.

He laughed and then he laid his head on my chest. I put my arm around him and we laid there in the quiet as his record player drew to a stop. He asked me then how I went about this whole dating thing and I said: 'Dating is not really my thing. I'm happy with the people I have in my life.'

I was expecting him to prod and poke at this assertion. Or at last say something like: 'Really? Why not?' But instead he just said: 'That's fuckin' awesome, mate. I wish I had that.'

15

In July I went to Passage to watch the Olympic opening ceremony. Mya wasn't performing that night, just working the
bar. She was also in charge of the playlist. She really didn't
like that Muse song that was sponsoring the Olympics, so
she left it off. Instead she filled the playlist with Olympic-
related songs she preferred like Heather Small's 'Proud.' She
even put on ones that were only tenuously related. So when
'On a Night Like This' by Kylie Minogue came on, I lifted an
eyebrow at her and she said: 'The Sydney Olympics? Twelve
years ago? Duh?'

I laughed and asked for another cocktail. The bar was
packed. Kain was joining us later and he was bringing Harley
to meet us for the first time. Apparently Harley had asked
Kain if he could meet his friends. And since Mya and I were
the only ones who knew Kain was bisexual, Kain thought he
could appease Harley's desire for public affection this way.
Birch and Monty were seeing Duran Duran at Hyde Park that
evening. And Nathan had taken up a temporary position as a
machine operator at a warehouse in Croydon to supplement
his income.

Even though Mya wasn't performing, before Kain and
Harley arrived she changed outfits. She re-emerged from

behind the bar wearing an elaborate Elton John-inspired ensemble: feathered sleeves abloom in Union Jack colours and bright exaggerated makeup. When they arrived, Mya saw them before I did. She got someone to cover her on the bar, then she took me over to a booth she'd reserved for us near the back. I felt this excitement in the pit of stomach. I'd never seen Kain with anyone before. He had been seeing a woman when he moved into my flat after Element 23 had broken up. But I'd never actually seen her, just various evidence of her existence, like her underwear on his bedroom floor as I walked by.

Harley was a short smiley guy with cornrows; he came up to about Kain's shoulder. He was wearing a white t-shirt with a picture of Rihanna on it, the one from her *Loud* album, and a pair of khaki chinos. As Kain was introducing us, Harley was looking up at him with this relieved expression, as if he had been terribly nervous beforehand and now that nervousness was evaporating. If anything Kain looked a lot more uneasy than Harley. Before they sat down Harley looked at Mya and complimented her outfit. 'I'm obsessed with the feathers,' he said, running his fingers through them. Mya beamed and told Kain that she loved him already.

Mya and I led a lot of the conversation while Kain seemed to be constantly trying to get comfortable. Harley told us that he was originally from Kent. But about six years ago he'd moved to London to study journalism and just ended up staying. Now he did both freelance writing about pop culture and an administrative office job he didn't really care about to make his rent. When I told him that I'd studied journalism too and that I was a senior editor at *Rush!*, he widened his eyes and said: 'Oh shit, really?'

Mya and Kain laughed. And I smiled at him. I

couldn't remember the last time anyone had been this visibly excited about my job. To maintain this sense of celebrity, and his sense of wonder, I didn't talk about the various difficulties the magazine was having. Jokingly I asked him why I'd never seen a pitch from him in my inbox . And he said: 'I just thought those kinds of magazines were too much of a long shot, to be honest. I might have been optimistic when I was twenty-one. But I'm twenty-eight now and I need a sure thing.'

'Well,' I said, 'I'll be your sure thing. Send over any pieces you've got and I'll make something happen.'

He furrowed his eyebrows. 'Are you being serious?' He looked at Kain: 'Is he being serious?'

Kain nodded and said: 'He's serious. He doesn't chat shit.'

Harley looked back at me. 'You don't even know if I'm a good writer or not—'

I laughed. 'I guess I'll find out when you send over some material,' I said. 'I'll give you my email.'

'Okay,' Mya said. 'This is cute and everything. But I just wanna know how this—' she gestured at Harley and Kain '—happened. Kain, I don't even remember the last time I saw you with someone.'

Harley turned to smile at him and then he said: 'Well, I was sick and my landlord asked if I could keep an ear out for the handymen coming to do the garden because all my housemates were out. So when Kain and his friend were doing the work in the garden I was, and sorry if I sound like a creep, looking at them through my bedroom window. And yeah, at first it was just because I thought they were really fit. But then I was like: where have I seen the tall one before?' He told us then that a friend of his had actually given him a few of her old CDs for an article he was writing on the decline of physical media. And that Element 23 single happened to be one of them. Then eventually he and Kain got to talking and it was Kain that ended up asking him out.

'You know what's mad, yeah?' Kain said. 'I didn't even think that many people had it. It was supposed to be this massive flop ting. And now look—'

Harley and Kain briefly smiled at each other.

'Yeah,' Harley said to us. 'I'm actually trying to convince him to go back to music. Don't you guys think he's too talented to give up completely?'

He then tried to put his hand over Kain's on the table. I could tell he was doing this in a partly playful, partly sincere way. But Kain quickly withdrew his hand. The motion was so abrupt that it made us all go silent for a moment. And nobody acknowledged it. Mya and I exchanged an incredulous look. Then we saw Harley silently look down into his lap. In a flimsy attempt to ease the tension, I put my hand over Mya's and mischievously smiled at her. I was thankful she seemed to understand what I was doing. She removed her hand and dramatically said to me: 'Uh, Ted, my love, I'm a taken woman. I have a family. This could never be. I know how devastating this must be for you.'

This made Harley lift his head back up and chuckle. He wagged his finger between Mya and me and said: 'Aren't you two, uh—?'

Mya and I looked at each other and laughed. 'Oh no,' Mya said. 'I literally have a six-year-old son with a whole other, very sexy, man. He would've been the other guy you saw in the garden with Kain. And Teddy's in love with someone who's fucking two people in a relationship and runs around London with a pair of ferrets for no particular reason.'

'Wow,' said Harley. 'That sounds exhausting.'

'First of all,' I said, 'I'm not in love with him. And second: he's actually not in that relationship anymore. And he's living with me again. Don't you remember, Mya? The breaking and entering? Digging through the plant pots? Air law?'

Harley looked at all of us, laughing with a faux nervous-ness, and said: 'I can't tell if you guys are joking or not.'

'That's completely understandable,' I said. 'I think it's best to assume everything we're saying is true unless someone says otherwise.'

Harley giggled. 'Got it,' he said. 'But now I have a ton of questions. Like what the hell is air law?'

'I promise there's no explanation that would make any sense to you.'

'I wanna meet this person,' he said and then looked at Kain. He looked irritated and a little withdrawn now. 'Do you know him too?'

'Nah,' Kain said. 'I've never met that brudda in my life.'

I could tell he was trying to be teasing while still being annoyed with himself for being unable to bypass his insecur-ities. In the end, Mya went back behind the bar and ordered a round of drinks to our table. I decided then that it was more important that Harley was comfortable than it was to try and lift Kain out of his irritation. So Harley and I continued to talk while Kain sank deeper into silence. But eventually everyone started to clap and cheer when the opening ceremony began. There were two large televisions mounted at either end of the bar. The drunken applause continued as we watched molten metal forge the Olympic emblem, and then as the large steel rings were raised into the air and sparks cascaded down like fiery rain.

When the drinks were brought to our table Harley told us that he didn't drink, so he had several fountain Pepsis throughout the evening. I felt nostalgic when he said this. I never used to drink either. It took me a while to calibrate how much I could handle during university, but I discovered it was an effective way to avoid questions about my diet. Socially, no one asked me about food if I was always seen drinking.

There was a sequence of framed photographs on the wall above our booth that we casually looked at. They were pictures of drag kings and queens and various performances on the little Passage stage, going as far back as the mid-eighties. I noticed that Mya's recent performance was featured, the one where she wore the bright-blonde wig that Nathan loved so much. The image made Harley giddy and he took a picture of it. Eventually Kain, who had been sipping at his drink and occasionally nodding at various points in mine and Harley's conversation, excused himself to the toilet.

Harley looked at his phone then. When he placed it back on the table, the screen lit up. I noticed that his background image wasn't of him and Kain, but of him and someone else, a tall husky guy with long brown hair and pair of binoculars around his neck. They had their arms around each other. I asked him who that was and he said: 'Oh, that's Muddy. He's my best friend.'

I smiled at him. 'I'm sorry things feel very frosty tonight,' I said. 'Kain just finds it very difficult to be himself in public spaces.'

He shrugged in this disappointed way that made me feel sad for him. 'No, I get it,' he said. 'He kept putting off our first date because of that. But I've just never seen this side of him before. When he comes over he's usually really talkative and *he's* the one trying to hold my hand. Like, I'm usually the one pulling him off me.'

'Yeah,' I said. 'I'm familiar.'

He looked at me quizzically and said: 'Oh, did you guys used to date?'

I laughed. 'Oh no,' I said. 'We've just known each other since we were kids.'

He asked if I thought Kain would eventually find this easier. And I told him this was his first relationship with a man that he'd told anyone about. 'I think he'll settle into it,' I said. 'It might not have gone perfectly but he was willing to take the step. But don't worry Harley, we're still gonna make sure you have a good time tonight.'

He smiled. 'Thank you,' he said. 'I think I'm gonna go and ask Mya for a selfie before I forget.'

November 2000

Mya knows almost everyone at the party. She's proud of this because it's only a few months into her first year at university and she feels like she's befriended almost everyone on her course. And other courses too. It's only now that she's been able to put a name to the various facets that make up her personality. Since starting university, she's been called an extrovert so many times that she now feels like a circuit board that's had all its channels of energy lit up as if to say: this is who you are.

She likes knowing that people not only pay attention to her but that they like her. She likes hearing evidence of their admiration. For the last few months she has been shapeshifting through various iterations of herself, in a way that she couldn't when she was living at home. Last week she had dreadlocks that hung just above her shoulders. Now she has a platinum-blonde buzz cut. She's wearing a long leather jacket and a blue tube top that she repurposed from an old pair of leggings. People keep telling her that she's dressed like the singer Sonique in the 'It Feels So Good' video, which is exactly what she was going for. The DJ even played the song for her twice and shouted her out. Now she's watching people swaying their bodies in euphoric clusters around her

while she dances. She feels so completely ethereal beneath
the stuttering strobe lights.

When she told her father she was going to pursue a degree
in fashion he didn't say anything. But she knew he was disappointed. It was a disappointment she couldn't make sense of.
And how could she? Her father didn't talk to her, not really.
He had never expressed to her any plans for her future. In
childhood, there'd never been any impassioned speeches
about potential marriage or a career in law or medicine or
anything like that. There was just this insidious sense that
whatever she was supposed to amount to, she simply hadn't
done it. She may not have known the specifics of her father's
disappointment in her but, in general, she knew why it
existed. And she had accepted the reason: her mother, Alice,
had passed away when she was ten. And since then her
father had retreated into himself. Before Alice passed away,
Mya would perform little concerts in their living room for
her. Spinning around on the carpet in one of Alice's purple
jackets and wearing one of her curly black wigs and using
the kitchen broom as a guitar so she looked like Prince in
Purple Rain. Or erratically rubbing every bit of Alice's makeup
collection on her face so she could emulate Grace Jones for an
evening. Alice would radiate with joy and say: 'My daughter
is a star.'

Even though her father had enjoyed these performances
for what they were – he was always smiling and singing
along and even cheering – Mya suspected that he had hoped
she would grow out of them. And perhaps apply to life the
same seriousness that, at sixteen years old, she was applying
to making costumes and assuming various identities. The
more elaborate and polished and, eventually, masculine her
costumes got, the more uninterested her dad seemed to be

in her. She didn't know exactly why she preferred to emulate male singers; it was just thrilling for her. One year she
had bound her breasts for the first time, to emulate a Lenny
Kravitz look that she liked. When she showed her father, he
said nothing, barely even looked at her and left the room.
When she heard him praying intensely in his bedroom that
night she realised that the years of silence had festered into
a kind of resentment towards her. This was the first time
she had tried to put words to his silence, as if she was trying
to assemble pieces of a jigsaw that had no images on them.
Maybe, she thought, what her father wanted for her was a
future filled with marriage and kids and a job that needed no
further elaboration beyond its title, that would make people
say: Look at her. She's normal. She's done so well since her
mother died.

But in the end she felt closest to her mother when she
was happy. And happiness was at its most potent when
she was creatively expressing herself in any way in which
she felt moved to.

She's outside now. Standing beside the large green bins, she
lights up a cigarette. She leans against the wall and exhales,
watching the smoke plume into the air in a dense grey cloud.
From the other side of the bins she hears somebody retching.
It's a deep, guttural retching that makes her visibly wince. She
makes a face then and without peering over to look she says:
'You alright over there?' But the person doesn't respond and
continues to vomit. Eventually she walks around and sees a
man crouched down, leaning against the wall with his eyes
closed and long bands of saliva dripping from his chin. He's
wearing a black-and-blue Avirex jacket and jeans. 'Oh my
god,' she says. 'Are you okay?'

The man opens his eyes and surprisingly he attempts to smile. 'I think I just had too much to drink,' he says. 'I didn't really drink that much before uni. Everyone here is like a professional or something.'

'Fucking hell,' she says, 'let me get you a glass of water or something. Jesus Christ, babe.'

She holds out her hand and he says thank you as he grabs hold of it. Inside the club 'Holler' by the Spice Girls is playing now. They manoeuvre through the crowd and sit on stools at the bar. Mya asks the man where his friends are and he glances around the club and shrugs. After Mya asks the bartender for some water, she wipes at his mouth with some tissue and says: 'I'm Mya by the way.'

The man smiles faintly. 'I'm Teddy.' She tells him that she's never seen anyone have that kind of reaction to alcohol before. And he says: 'I was just drinking anything people put in front of me. I got really caught in the moment. Everything's still so new, you know?'

'Well, Teddy,' she says. 'First rule: eat before you drink, babes. Didn't you have lunch?'

Teddy doesn't answer her question. And as if someone has suddenly tapped him on the shoulder and asked him to comment on the music, he says instead: 'This is the Spice Girls, isn't it? I think it might be the first song of theirs I've actually been into for a while.'

Confused, Mya recoils a little. And Teddy sees her do this but he doesn't react to that either. She can see that his eyes are a little strained and widened, as if trying to clumsily communicate how uncomfortable he feels with this line of questioning. So she says: 'Yeah, it's cool. But it's not my favourite.' She almost physically feels him relax then. When he asks her what is in fact her favourite, she gives him a whole list and he beams. And then proceeds to tell her about a friend he'd had once who was always singing their songs.

When the bartender comes back with the water, Teddy takes a huge gulp and Mya's phone starts to beep. From her purse she retrieves a little navy Nokia and looks at the screen. It says: NATHAN, which makes her smile. When Teddy notices her smile he asks her what's got her grinning and coyly she responds: 'Oh, no one.' Of course, this 'no one' is someone she's currently getting to know. She met him at a local bar in Soho that lets her perform on weekends for free drinks and where Nathan regularly bartends. Nathan has never seen her perform. His shift always ends about an hour before she gets on stage, after which he dashes to Croydon where he begins a ten-hour shift as a warehouse operative. But they talk a lot beforehand. Nathan often calls her beautiful and has a penchant for remembering small things she says in passing, like the name of the specific module she's studying or a song she'd mentioned liking, and the reason she liked it. It gives her this fluttery tingling sensation in the pit of her stomach. Often she'll say: 'You really remembered that?' And cheekily he'll respond in his deep voice: 'I know you, innit.'

Teasingly, Teddy says: 'Oh, come on.' But it's her turn to deflect now, so she asks Teddy what he's studying and he says journalism. She tells him she's doing fashion design. She asks him then if he's enjoying journalism and he says: 'Yeah, it's alright. This morning we had an editor from *Rush!* magazine come in to talk to us. She was fun, if a little unhinged. Afterwards I asked her what I had to do to work somewhere like *Rush!*. And she said if I could find a microwave to warm up her Pot Noodle, then I could have whatever I wanted.'

'Was she being serious?'

He laughs. 'I genuinely have no idea.'

They talk a little more after that, about how nervous Teddy still feels being away from home, and how happy she feels to be away from hers. She puts her hand on Teddy's shoulder and says: 'You'll be fine, babe.' At one point Teddy compliments her outfit and she gets up and twirls dramatically, the hem of her leather jacket flailing upward, and says thank you. Eventually Teddy says he's going to go home now.

'Are you alright getting back to halls?' she asks.

He nods smilingly. 'Like you said, I'll be fine.' And then with a very sincere expression he says: 'Thank you.'

She returns to the dancefloor now. The DJ has chosen 'Pure Shores' by All Saints as the evening's comedown song. Life, she thinks, rarely feels this good. She's moving her body now in this soft fluid way, with her eyes closed and her hands above her head, gliding hypnotically side to side. She feels like she's encased in a glass sphere floating above the centre of the dancefloor. And the people around her are looking up at this bright circle of light, marvelling at all this joy she's exuding.

She wants to capture this moment of unrefined happiness, almost as if it's the most significant artefact of her life.

16

In early August everyone came round to the flat to watch Usain Bolt run the hundred-metre sprint. Birch had said he'd be in charge of snacks and had spent that afternoon in the kitchen. He was attempting to recreate a hummus recipe that he'd got from his mother. Birch no longer had a relationship with her. But he associated the recipe with the few happy memories he'd had with his mother, one of them being watching Olympic events on the TV together. I asked him how he was going to recreate a recipe he hadn't had since the early nineties. And he laughed and said: 'Ted, come on. It's just hummus.'

That evening Kain was sitting shirtless on the sofa texting. And I was sitting at the dining table reading through some samples of writing Harley had sent me. He had a blog where he regularly reviewed albums across various genres and every time I read one I'd say to Kain: 'He's really good.' And he would smile to himself like: I know. His talent made me feel really giddy and excited. Since that night at Passage, Kain had apologised to Harley and had scheduled another date during which he promised to be less guarded.

Mya, Nathan and Bakari arrived later. Birch had emerged from the kitchen now and was sat next to Kain, drinking a beer. Bakari ran inside and leapt onto Birch's lap. Birch smiled and ruffled Bakari's hair. Without looking away from his phone, Kain raised his hand towards Bakari and they bumped fists. Bakari then reached for Birch's beer with both hands while Birch giggled, shaking his head, holding it away from him. Bakari's nostrils started to flare then and he started smelling Birch's shirt.

'Uncle B,' Bakari said. 'Why do you smell so weird?'

Birch sniffed his shirt too. 'Oh,' he said. 'Your Uncle Birchy's been cooking, hasn't he?'

'Cooking what?'

'Hummus.'

'What's that?'

'It's something you dip things in.'

'Dip?' Bakari said, laughing. 'That's not cooking.'

Birch shook Bakari off his lap, while I said: 'Careful.'

'You're eating your pita bread dry because of that,' Birch said. 'In fact—' Birch turned to Mya and Nathan and said: 'Your kid's gonna go hungry tonight.'

Bakari laughed on the floor while Mya came to take off his jacket and hang it up.

Nathan was standing beside me at the dining table now, nudging me, quietly gesturing at Kain, saying: 'He's probably still chattin' to his secret gyal. You see how that nigga didn't even say hello to me.'

I looked up at him. 'Nate,' I said. 'Just ask him.'

'Nah, bruv,' he said. 'Do I look like I care that much to be askin' about shit he don't wanna tell me?'

I rolled my eyes. 'Is this a trick question?' I said. 'If I didn't know any better I'd say you were jealous.'

He shoved me and laughed, kissing his teeth.

Monty arrived a few moments later with a bottle of wine.

He was wearing a green bomber jacket and tapered chinos. Birch hugged him. And when Monty sat down Kain did another absent-minded fist bump with him. Then Monty looked at him and said: 'Fuck me – look at the pecs on you, mate.' Birch whipped his head around and said: 'Right?' And Kain laughed to himself.

Later Birch brought out the bowl of hummus and a plate with a spread of pita bread, breadsticks and grilled vegetables. We were all in the middle of the living room now with the TV on. Nathan asked Birch if he'd made this and he nodded proudly. Mya asked me if I'd been in the kitchen while Birch was making it. And I said I'd only been there to grill the vegetables. She looked at Kain with an eyebrow raised and he returned the same cautious expression. Monty grabbed one of the red peppers and drenched it in the dip, while the rest of us exchanged nervous glances. Eventually we all dipped something in the hummus. Birch rubbed his hands together and asked us how it was.

'Birchy, my love,' Mya said. 'I'm not tryna be mean because I know you were just tryna do a nice thing. But haven't you ever heard of portion control with ingredients and stuff?'

'What do you mean?' Birch said.

She put her hand over her mouth. 'There's too much vinegar, babe.'

My face soured at the taste. 'Yeah Birch,' I said. 'Why've you put so much vinegar in this?'

'What are you talking about?' he said. 'I didn't even use vinegar.'

Nathan started to cough. 'Then why is it all I can fucking taste, bruv?'

Kain and Mya had embittered expressions on their faces and spat mouthfuls out into their palms. Monty flashed a stiff smile and gave Birch a thumbs up as his eyes watered slightly. Bakari smacked his tongue against the roof of his mouth with a repulsed look and said: 'Uncle B, this is nasty.'

'What?' Birch said. 'No it's not – it's my mum's recipe.'

'Did your mum not like you, cuz?' said Kain.

Birch stood up then and said: 'I'm so sick of you Neezes and your constant negativity.'

Monty leant over to me and whispered: 'What are Neezes?'

'Oh,' I said. 'No one likes Birch saying the N word. So we agreed every time he said it he'd lose a letter. And now he's down to the N and the I.'

'You know what guys,' Birch said. 'You've done it. You've pushed me to the edge.' We asked him what he was talking about and he said: 'I think I'm gonna become a racist. I've been thinking about it for a while now, and yeah, I think it's time. I'm gonna do it. The white side won.' He went to high-five Monty. But as Monty raised his hand, I put my hand on his arm and wordlessly shook my head. 'I'm gonna find Nigel Farage and have his babies.'

'Yeah, 'cause that's what he wants,' Mya said. 'Little mixed-race babies running around.'

'Anyway,' Birch said. 'I hope Bolt loses tonight.'

I sighed. Birch seemed more erratic and emotionally volatile than usual. Even as recently as this morning I'd heard him talking in his sleep and occasionally waking up to pace around the living room. 'Well, instead of getting Nigel Farage to impregnate you,' I said. 'Taste it yourself.'

'Fine,' he said. 'I will.' He scooped a huge blob of it in his palm and slathered it on his tongue. 'See—' he said. 'Tasty.' Bakari chuckled and told him his eyes were watering. And Birch with his mouth still full said: 'Because I love it so much.'

*

During the race everyone stood up in front of the TV, yelling and clapping. Bakari waved around a blue foam finger Birch and Monty had brought back from the Duran Duran concert a few weeks ago. After the race, we had a few drinks and talked about the *Rush!* party in a few weeks.

'Remember guys,' Monty said. 'The theme is nineties.' He parted his hands like the word 'nineties' was written in the air. We talked about outfits we'd worn in the past, like when we'd worn the colourful suits and fedoras when the theme was Pimps and Hoes. And when we'd had on long black leather jackets for a Y2K-themed one. At one point, Birch said he wanted to go as Tupac so he wouldn't have to wear any clothes, and I said: 'What happened to being a racist?'

He scoffed and said: 'That was about four beers ago, T-Bear. Keep up.'

Kain suggested we pick a band and Nathan said Blackstreet. But Mya suggested we do Boyz II Men instead. 'I've got some spare material I can make some cardigans out of.'

Birch made a face. 'Cardigans?' He said. 'That's not sexy. I wanna be sexy.'

'Cardigans can be sexy,' insisted Mya.

'No they can't,' Birch said. 'You just wanna get rid of some old tat. And you're using us to do it. I wanna have my arse out.' He looked around at us and said: 'Boys, don't stand for it.'

I laughed and said: 'Boyz II Men it is.'

Later in the evening Mya remade Birch's hummus. In the kitchen, he told her how he'd made it the first time and then they argued over whether Birch had used too much lemon juice or not. Mya was holding a wooden spoon and every time Birch tried to say she was wrong about something, she hit him over the head with it. Monty and I were standing by the fridge and Birch kept turning around and saying to us: 'Guys, this is abuse. Tell her to stop.' And we would just shrug at him, laughing.

Bakari wandered into the kitchen then with his foam finger. He looked up at Mya and Birch and said: 'Mum, why are you hitting Uncle Birch on the head?'

'Because your Uncle B is a very foolish man,' she said. 'And now I have to make everything from scratch so we don't starve tonight.' Monty asked her why we couldn't just get a takeaway and Mya said: 'Then ol' Birchy wouldn't learn anything.'

Birch crouched down to Bakari and said: 'You see, that's why I love your mum. She knows how to make something out of nothing. I mean, look at that cheap wig—'

Mya turned around and placed her foot on Birch's back and rolled him over onto the floor. He stayed there on his back and said: 'Why do you keep pushing me over with your foot?'

'Because you're a little—' Mya looked at Bakari and told him to put his hands over his ears. And he did so, giggling with his eyes closed. 'A little bitch. And for some reason you're always crouching when you're chatting shit.'

Birch glared at her. 'Okay, Bakari,' he said, 'roll me back into the living room please, we haven't annoyed Nate and Kain in a while.'

Casually Mya said: 'Birch, stop traumatising my child with your arrested-development please.'

Birch told Bakari to cover his eyes. And again with a little giggle he did so. Birch then stuck his middle finger up at her. We all then watched Bakari trying to roll Birch away, shaking our heads.

*

That evening after everyone had gone home and Kain had gone to bed, Birch came into my room. He stood at the door and asked if he could sleep in my room tonight. I said only if he apologised for trying to kill everyone with his hummus. But he didn't laugh. So I smiled at him and lifted up the sheets, tapping the other side of the bed. He positioned himself next to me and clung to my body, resting his cheek on my chest. I put my arm around him and said: 'What's up?'

'I keep having these nightmares,' he said. There was silence as I waited for him to continue. But he didn't say anything else. Eventually I asked him what kind of nightmares. He exhaled and said: 'It won't make any sense to you, Ted. So when I tell you you're gonna ask me a bunch of questions. And I don't wanna talk about it. But at the same time I do wanna talk about it. Does that make any sense?'

'Yeah,' I said. 'But when have you ever worried about making sense?'

He laughed. 'So there's this guy that's always looking for me,' he said. 'You know, in the dream. I can feel him following me and he won't leave me alone. And I know it's my fault.'

'Why is that?'

'Because eventually he does stop following me,' he said. 'And when he does, and even though I know he's not a nice person, I have this feeling in my chest like I've been abandoned. And I really hate that this very unkind man doesn't want anything to do with me anymore. So I end up going to find him. And when I find him it's always as bad as I think it's going to be, Ted. Like so bad that I feel my mind fighting with itself. It wants me to wake up so I don't have to experience the things that this man's doing. But then there's another part of my mind that wants me to stay asleep because, I dunno, it thinks I deserve it? It's really weird.'

Gently, I ran my fingers through his hair. He started to shake and I tried to steady him with my other hand. There were moments in our friendship when I didn't know how to disentangle the parts of him I was supposed to take seriously, and the parts which I was supposed to laugh at. But at moments like these, where he'd handed me such a vivid piece of his pain, I didn't know what to do. He made it very difficult to have complete access to his anguish. It was always encased in tinted glass. For example, I said: 'This wouldn't have anything to do with the man in the suit? The one you were trying to tell me about a while back?'

And he replied: 'Now, T-Bear. What did we say about questions?'

I smiled. But it was a very tight melancholic smile. 'Sorry,' I said.

He sat up now. 'But I think I know why I'm getting these nightmares, Ted.' I lifted an eyebrow. 'It's 'cause I need new ferrets.'

'What?'

'Well, Whitey and Choc-Ice abandoned me,' he said. 'So I just need to get new ferrets. And then my mind won't be so desperate to remind me that I'm someone people – and ferrets – like to abandon.'

'But Birch, there's clearly a lot more going on than whether you need new ferrets or not.'

'I'm not sure what you heard, Teddy Bear,' he said. 'But I definitely need new ferrets.'

'But what about the man?'

'What man?'

I tutted. 'The one in your nightmare?'

In a playful and patronising tone he said: 'Ted, are you still drunk? I'm talking about being a ferret dad again and you're talking about some imaginary man. I didn't wanna say anything, but I think you might need to lay off the—' He made a drinking motion with his hand.

I rolled my eyes. 'This is all I'm getting from you tonight, isn't it?'

'Yeah, pretty much, man,' he said. 'Goodnight.'

Dramatically he fell back onto the bed and pretended to snore. He was facing away from me now. I shook him and said: 'I know you said no questions. But just give me one. Or, actually, two.'

He was silent a moment. Then eventually he said: 'I'll take them on a case-by-case basis.'

I asked him how long he had been having these night-mares and he just shrugged and said: 'A while.'

'How long is a while?'

'Is this the second question?'

'No,' I said, 'the second question was how would you feel about me trying to get you to see someone about these nightmares?'

More silence. 'I guess I would feel as if that was a question too many,' he said. 'I probably shouldn't have said anything. I know you're a little worrier. You see how I don't even have that cough anymore? I think I just wanted an excuse to sleep in your bed tonight.'

17

A few weeks later I met Harley at a coffee shop in Dulwich. Kain had taken tentative steps to revisit the music industry. An old friend of his, who had been instrumental in securing Element 23 a record deal, had set up a home studio. He had asked Kain to lay some vocals on a new demo he'd produced, and Kain had invited Harley and I to the session. He didn't know if anything would come of it, but he was excited to be in proximity to music in this way again.

Harley and I sat at a table waiting for Kain to arrive, drinking coffees. He was driving down from a job in Elephant and Castle that afternoon. I was on my phone looking at pictures Mya had sent of the cardigans she was sewing; she'd decided to embroider our names on the chest. She'd done the first few letters of mine and I told her they looked wonderful. Harley was reading a book by Stephen Kelman called *Pigeon English*. I remembered reading about it in the *Metro* on the way to work last year after it was shortlisted for the Man Booker Prize. The review had mentioned that the premise was inspired by the murder of Damilola Taylor. Harley was about halfway through it. I asked him what he thought, and he grinned at me conspiratorially and said: 'I'll let you know.'

I'd told Harley that afternoon that *Rush!* would be

publishing one of his reviews. I'd also told him how impressed I'd been by his writing. I couldn't remember the last time the topic of writing alone had invigorated me so much. I'd sent him a selection of early album releases we'd received and asked him to pick one and email me about five-hundred words on it. Even though I'd once told Monty that we were puppets for our advertisers and therefore negative reviews were essentially prohibited, I told Harley he could be honest, that I only cared if the piece was engaging. He looked excited at the news, though not as excited as I'd thought he'd be. It turned out his prospective relationship with Kain was still weighing on him.

'Did you know he's saved me in his phone as Hayley?' he said. 'At first I thought it was funny. But now, I don't know. It's starting to feel like he's embarrassed of me on more levels than I thought.'

I was irritated at Kain's inability to communicate to Harley how much he liked him. It made me think of the love I had for, say, Birch, and how that love looked the same regardless of what space we were in. Harley looked so disheartened that I wanted to do something dramatic like hug him. Instead I assured him that Kain wasn't embarrassed. And I wasn't surprised when he looked like he didn't believe me.

'Maybe at another time in my life I might've accepted a relationship like this,' he said. 'But I'm not twenty anymore. I feel like if he had it his way our entire relationship would be confined to text messages and my bedroom. And sometimes I genuinely think that would be enough for him and he would be happy.' He looked at me now with these sincere eyes and said: 'Was he always this way?'

'Well, we weren't always friends,' I said. 'In school he was actually one of the people that made life really difficult for me. But eventually I came to understand him and the things he was going through, which made forgiving him a lot easier.' He asked me what things Kain had done. But I wasn't prepared to be as forthcoming as he wanted, so lightly I chuckled and said: 'You know, just typical bully things.'

'How did you end up living together?' he asked then.

'We weren't friends, but we were cordial,' I said. 'Then after we left school we lost contact. Then he had his moment in the sun with Element 23. And after they broke up, we found each other again. We were older then. Things were different. He needed a place to stay so he rented my spare room.'

Harley sighed and then said: 'What would you do? If you were in my position.' I gave him an expression that said: I really wish I knew what to say. Then he said: 'Sorry – are you gay too? If you don't mind me asking.'

I laughed. 'I'm not,' I said. 'I mean, my parents think I am.'

'How comes?'

'Because they watched an episode of *Glee*.'

He arched an eyebrow. 'You're doing that thing again where I can't tell if you're joking or not.'

I laughed again. 'And I told you to assume it's all true unless stated otherwise,' I said. 'And also it's because I turned thirty this year and they've never seen me with anyone.' He asked me then if I was straight and I said no. I told him I didn't date or do relationships and that a lot of my fulfilment came from my friends. He made a curious 'huh' sound and said: 'I have a friend like that.'

'Who?' I said. 'Your friend Muddy?'

He nodded. 'When we were younger he didn't know what being asexual meant and he thought there was something wrong with him. Thankfully he knows better now.'

I smiled. 'I've never felt as if there was something wrong

with me,' I said. 'It's more not knowing how to tell my parents that something exists other than gay and straight that frustrates me.'

'You think they won't be accepting?'

'My parents are very accepting,' I said. 'Almost to a fault actually. But the whole point of their obsession with my love life is that they think I'm sad and lonely. If I "come out" to them as asexual, and aromantic I suppose, it needs to signify that I'm still fulfilled and happy.'

'So you just need to find a parent-proof way to communicate that?'

'Exactly.'

He laughed. 'Teddy,' he said. 'No offence, but that's a pretty nice parental problem to have.'

Kain arrived wearing a white t-shirt that seemed to suck itself against his biceps and brown overalls with patches of dry paint on them. He said: 'What's good?' and wrapped one arm around Harley, briefly nestling his face in his hair. I could feel Harley's disposition soften as he gently brushed his cheek against Kain's forearm and looked up at him, smiling. Kain really was attractively imposing. I'd stopped seeing him this way through sheer familiarity. Outside of Birch's comments about his physique and my own insecure comparisons of our bodies, I rarely saw him as an object of attraction, though he clearly was.

Kain left his arm around Harley as we walked down to the studio. He talked about how invasive and talkative the person he was working for today had been. Then he asked about our days. Harley and I kept exchanging quiet glances with each other, which made Kain cock an eyebrow like: what's going on?

*

The studio was in the basement of someone's house. When Kain knocked on the door, a tall thin man with a moustache opened it. He and Kain bumped fists, then Kain introduced him to me and Harley as Jeb. We waved at him. Then cheerily he said: 'Nah, any friend of Kain's a friend of mine, let's hug it out.' And we did.

We walked down into the basement. It was a small space that smelt faintly of weed. There was a single bulb in the centre of the ceiling hanging off a thin wire. And there was a two-seater sofa in the corner with its leather ripped to shreds. There were plaques on the wall. Encased in some of them were various gold and silver discs and a selection of magazine editorials. One of them featured Kain and the rest of Element 23 on an issue of *The Face* magazine from 2001. I remembered buying this issue. It was one of the group's most high-profile piece of promotion, and where I'd read that they had formed through various impromptu performances in Covent Garden.

Harley and I sat on the sofa, and Kain went into the booth. He stood behind a tall microphone and put on a pair of bulky headphones. Jeb pressed several buttons on the mixing desk and then a production of heavy skittering beats buzzed through the room. The song sounded dated in the sense that I could envision Tinie Tempah releasing it two years ago. But I kept this opinion to myself. I wondered if Harley was thinking the same thing as we nodded along, smiling. Kain was rapping in this deep and gruff way I'd never heard from him before. It was delightful seeing the wall he'd raised around himself become increasingly transparent. He was in his element. He looked visibly looser, freer, as if in that moment the world in its entirety made total sense to him.

Before the song was over, a man appeared in the room. He was standing by the door, holding a bottle of beer in one hand and a joint in the other. At a glance he had a very unfriendly, mousy face. He didn't say or do anything. He just leant on the wall and occasionally made eye contact with Jeb, and then with Harley and me. Eventually Harley nudged me and said: 'Do you know that guy?' I looked at him properly, narrowing my eyes slightly. Initially I only recognised him vaguely. But then it clicked; his name was Quentin but he called himself Q. He looked a lot older now. When Element 23 disbanded, a few of the members decided to continue under a different name. Then, without Kain, they recruited new members to make up the numbers. Quentin had been enlisted because he'd had a humiliatingly disastrous audition for the first series of *Pop Idol* that year, the kind they relentlessly lampooned on *Harry Hill's TV Burp*. And the group thought they could use his infamy for publicity. But no one had made Quentin aware of that.

When Kain finished, Jeb pressed a button and yelled: 'Hell yeah. That was really awesome, man. We're still gonna go for another take though. Just gonna go for a slash.' Then he looked at Harley and me as if to say: wasn't that great, and we nodded approvingly. On his way out he manoeuvred around Quentin, ducking his head at him casually. Quentin stopped him and said: 'Eh, when you gonna get me in there? I've been here all day, bruv.' And Jeb gestured at him with both hands like: chill out. We couldn't work out why he was there. But we had been left alone with him and felt compelled to acknowledge his presence.

Kain and Harley made eye contact with each other. Jokingly Harley blew him a kiss. Kain, who hadn't seen Quentin in the room, caught it and smiled affectionately.

Quentin watched this transaction happen and then yelled: 'Eh, look at the battyman. Who let you in here then?'

We looked at him. 'Excuse me?' I said.

He downed the last bit of beer in his bottle and said: 'Not talking to you. I'm talking to that little Mary next you, blowing kisses and shit.'

He was doing a kind of forced hard laugh now. A wounded expression appeared on Harley's face as Kain exited the booth. I felt this intense rigidity settle over me and I stood up and glared at Quentin. 'What the fuck's your problem?' I said.

I felt Harley tug at my shirt and say: 'No, Teddy, it's fine. It's really not a big deal. I'll just leave.'

I looked at him and said: 'What? You shouldn't have to leave.' I gave Quentin a levelling glance and said: 'Apologise to him.'

I noticed Kain wasn't saying anything. I gave him a prompting look to chime in but he looked frozen. He didn't even speak when Quentin said: 'Are you mad? As if I'm gonna apologise. Do you know who I am?'

Harley kept trying to leave but I kept stopping him and, in an increasingly aggravated manner, kept asking Quentin to apologise. Eventually the confrontation got so heated that he shoved me. I shoved him back. Finally, as Quentin came to shove me again, Kain walked over and stood between us with his hands outstretched and asked Quentin to calm down. We heard Jeb's footsteps then and he appeared in the doorway, asking what was going on. But Quentin just laughed in response and drunkenly waved him away.

Harley left. I should've let him leave earlier. I don't know why I didn't. I supposed I felt emboldened in a way I wish I'd been in childhood, when other people had been aggressively dismissive of my existence. On reflection it was selfish on my part to make him endure it any further, even if I thought I was helping.

I followed Harley out of the house. He was already making his way down the street. When I stopped him he looked at me and said: 'Teddy, why did you do that? I said it was fine. I don't need you to defend me.'

'I'm sorry,' I said. 'It's just why should anyone get to talk to you like that. It's just—'

'I know,' he said. 'But I'm just not a very confrontational person. And it's really embarrassing standing there and taking that kind of abuse.' He sighed. 'If you think I'm some fragile baby with low self-esteem, I promise you I'm not. I don't need to be protected. I'm very much aware that it's his issue and not mine. That's why I just needed to remove myself from the situation. I've heard things like that before. And it would've been such an easy thing to get over if you hadn't had to escalate everything.'

'No, you're right,' I said. 'I just thought—' I stopped talking and looked at him. I didn't know what I wanted to say to him, other than to repeat that he was right.

He exhaled deeply and looked away. 'Can you do me a favour and let Kain know I'm going home?' he said. 'With all things considered, it's probably best I don't see him anymore. I'll call him later if he wants.'

By the time Kain had exited the house, Harley was gone. We were sitting in the van now. Neither of us had said anything for a while and the sky had darkened into a deep navy. Eventually I turned to him and said: 'Kain, why didn't you say anything?'

'I don't know,' he said. 'I fucked up. Again.'

'Yeah,' I said. 'You did.' He turned to look at me too. 'I don't get it,' I continued. 'It looked like he was making you so happy. For the last month you've been looking at your phone and giggling. I get that you don't like public displays of affection. But surely that doesn't extend to watching some absolute moron cut down someone you care about?'

His eyes were caught in the soft glow of a nearby street-lamp. They were glistening like he might cry, but no tears fell. He looked at me then in this wide-eyed way as if to extract some sense of sympathy from me. 'Oh, don't do that,' I said. 'Why is this so hard for you?'

After a brief pause he said: 'I'm just scared, innit. It's like you think it's a switch you can just turn off. I've never liked people I don't know knowing my business. I've never liked flaunting shit. I'm not like that. I thought I could be, innit. But I'm not. Why can't people just accept that I like my life private. Why do I have to tell people everything about myself. I mean fuck's sake, blud – *you* don't even do that.'

'But is it actually privacy you want,' I said, 'or do you just want everyone to be okay with you being embarrassed with who you are?' He didn't say anything. 'You know earlier, in the coffee shop, Harley asked me what I'd do if I was in his position?' I continued. 'If you and I were dating and you kept me a secret. And I literally didn't know what to tell him.'

'I wasn't keeping him a secret,' he said. 'Like I said—'

'I heard what you said,' I said. 'But I think you're pretending to be obtuse. And it's not cute. I mean, you had him saved in your phone as Hayley. But anyway. We're not the same. There used to be a time where I didn't want to know you. But I still would never have been okay with someone talking to you the way Quentin spoke to Harley.'

'But I wasn't okay with it.'

'Yeah, well,' I said. 'Here we still are.'

I looked down at his hands then. He kept shaking out his right fist and stretching his fingers, massaging them with his other hand. I asked him what was wrong and he just said: 'Don't worry about it.'

'What did you do?'

He shrugged. 'I told you, blud, it doesn't matter,' he said. 'Harley doesn't want anything to do with me anymore. So whatever I did, it doesn't matter.'

August 2001

Kain sits in the penthouse suite at the Dorchester. He's waiting for a meeting with Julian Blackwell, the head of the record label he's signed to. He's wearing a black oversized hoodie, a thick silver chain and a cap that's slightly off-centre, and his hands are plugged firmly in his pockets. The room is very airy and preposterously spacious, with a bright golden sheen that seems to make every ornament under its ceiling glow. His chair swivels, so he keeps swinging to the window and looking down into the bowels of London as he waits.

Julian is pouring a glass of brandy. He's in a dark-blue suit and the top three buttons of his shirt are undone. He keeps asking Kain if he wants anything to drink, and Kain keeps saying no, he's fine. To which Julian replies: 'Oh, go on, Kain. It's on the house.'

'Nah, I'm good,' Kain answers abruptly.

Julian walks over to Kain and holds the glass in front of him. 'At least just hold the bloody glass, eh?' he says. 'For me. C'mon, it's a sign of respect, isn't it? I've got you up here in this big fancy hotel, least you could do is not make me feel like a blimmin' alky.' And then in a somewhat mocking tone, Julian says: 'Don't make me drink alone, bruv.' Kain stares at him for a moment. 'My apologies,' Julian says now. 'I get a bit street, you know? A bit down-with-the-homies when I've downed a few. You know how it is.'

Kain wants to roll his eyes, but instead he tightens his lips and takes the glass.

'See,' Julian says, 'that weren't so hard, was it? Now, go on, have a sip.' Kain grips the glass tighter. 'Nah, I'm only joking. You see that, Kain? That's respect, that is. You don't wanna have a drink, so I don't make you drink. That's love. I told you, didn't I? We're a family here.'

Kain thought he knew why he was here. His A&R had told him yesterday that Julian wanted to have a meeting about the future of his career. He'd assumed it wasn't going to be a positive meeting, and that there was a strong possibility that he would be dropped from the label, so he had braced himself. He wasn't going to cry or beg or sell stories on how he can turn his fortunes around with the right song, because he understood what this was, what it had always been: under the scope of the label his dreams were entirely transactional. The label had invested hundreds of thousands of pounds in him and his group, before they had even released their first single, and it had performed terribly. And he couldn't muster up enough delusion to try and generate some optimism out of these events.

But when he got the invitation to the meeting and none of the other members of his group had, he thought he'd perhaps made the wrong assumption. That morning he'd called up a few of them and they'd all told him that Julian probably wanted him to go solo. And if the song hadn't performed so poorly on the charts, he might've entertained the idea. And now here he was waiting to hear what Julian had to say. Even as early as the call with his A&R, he could feel in the pit of his stomach that something was wrong. Why was the meeting taking place in his hotel room? And why had no one else been invited, not even his agent, or anyone that would've had some stake in the discussion of his future?

'You sure you don't wanna take that hoodie off?' Julian asks him now. 'It's bloody boiling in here.'

'Nah, man, I'm good,' Kain says. 'Eh, what are we here to talk about? I thought you were dropping me, innit. What's going on?'

Julian sits on the table and rests his foot on the seat of the chair. Kain looks up at him.

'Yeah,' Julian says. 'The numbers weren't great.' Julian's wrist is hanging off the edge of his knee and he's gently swishing the brandy around in his glass. The motion makes Kain feel uncomfortable as he watches the liquid rise closer and closer to the lip of the glass. He understands that this, however nonchalant, is intimidation of sorts but he doesn't understand why yet.

'But that's the thing with new talent,' Julian continues. 'It takes nurturing, doesn't it? And I think you can be nurtured. As a solo act, of course. How does that sound?'

'For real?'

Julian nods. 'For real, my son,' he says. 'You think we're gonna sink thousands and thousands into you and not make it work. That's what we do here, Kain. We find ways to make it work. Whatever it takes. Even if we have to break down the product and rebuild it – better, stronger.' He gives Kain a sharp look. 'And you've got what it takes, don't you?'

Kain nods.

Julian takes a sip of brandy and says: 'Oh, come on, give me a bit more than that. I'm giving you a bloody golden opportunity here.'

'Yeah,' Kain says. 'I've got what it takes, innit.'

'That's right,' Julian says, slurring slightly now and tapping Kain's lap. 'You've got what it takes, my boy.'

Kain notices that Julian's eyes are starting to narrow slightly. And that their eye contact is beginning to break. He also notices now that Julian's eyes are gliding down to his crotch and he keeps repeating that Kain has what it takes. He can see little globs of saliva forming at the corners of Julian's mouth.

Julian taps Kain's lap again and leaves his hand there this time. 'But you know how many artists I've come across that've all told me they've got what it takes. All very talented people. And I've just looked at them like: "Nah, I don't think you have. You say you do. But you're all talk, aren't you?" We all know how to talk. But only a good few of us can really back it up. Do you know what I mean? And I don't deal with talkers. I deal with doers. Go-getters.' Julian takes his hand off Kain's lap and takes another sip of brandy, then he gently tugs at his groin. 'Are you a go-getter, Kain?'

Kain stares at him. His face feels frozen and he has this sudden and curious hyper-awareness that life, down to its very microscopic detail, is moving around him, that there are invisible winds brushing against the windows, that there are little bugs wading through the soil of the topiary outside the hotel. And his body is the one thing, in this moment in time, that is entirely stagnant.

Julian puts his hand back on Kain's lap and slides his hand into his inner-thigh and says: 'Go on. Have a sip of that brandy. It's good stuff.'

Back in May, Element 23 filmed the video for their debut single on a quiet street in New Cross. When the video had been pitched to them, Kain had liked that it hadn't seemed terribly elaborate or expensive. It was just the seven of them, dressed in black sportswear, rapping in front of a rowdy crowd, primarily made up of their friends near his hometown.

But ever since the group So Solid Crew had released their song '21 Seconds', and Kain's label had seen its accompanying video and the traction it had garnered in music magazines and various radio stations, it boosted their interest in Element 23. Their grassroots cost-efficient video was scrapped for something filmed on a glossy soundstage with expensive post-effects that debuted on *The Lick with Trevor Nelson* on MTV Base. The original artwork for the single, which had been a candid shot of the group in the middle of the street, was scrapped for a proper photoshoot in a studio. And the song was re-recorded, so the chorus, which had originally been sung by Kain, was now sung by an unknown female vocalist who sounded a lot like Lisa Maffia, who the label had said had a more commercial voice than Kain's.

This influx of corporate interference had dulled Kain's aspirations. And nothing seemed to feel real anymore. But he realised that he'd really started to check out when every interview Element 23 did to promote the song seemed to be framed around some kind of rivalry with So Solid Crew, whom they had never even met. When he'd brought this up in one of the meetings with Julian, Julian had just said: 'Violence sells, my boy,' which Kain hadn't understood, because nothing about Element 23's lyrics were particularly violent. He mostly wrote songs about the desire to be rich and moving through life with the kind of arrogance and confidence he'd only seen in people who didn't look like him.

But a few weeks before the single was officially released, he was made aware of a review of the song in *Rush!* magazine. He didn't read *Rush!*. At the time, the only magazine he ever had any interest in was *Hip-Hop Connection*. But the group's publicist had been excited that they'd managed to get a piece in one of the country's biggest pop magazines without even having to pitch them the song. The reviewer seemed to understand the song – and Kain in particular – on a level that suggested that they'd known Kain personally. Kain read the review and noticed that there was a curious circumventing of the other members of the group – the song had seven verses, of which he'd only rapped one. And his vocals were no longer on the chorus. And there were other members who he considered to be more talented and who had more of a presence than he did.

But at the end of the review, he saw the name of its author: Teddy Asiedu. And he'd smiled at the text. The smile lasted so long that the publicist, as well as other members of the group, had asked him if he was okay, if he was having a stroke or something, for he so rarely smiled so openly.

He hadn't seen Teddy in over three years, since they'd left school, and he missed him. He felt lassoed by Teddy's words and yanked back to shore. This seemed to momentarily temper his disillusionment with the industry.

In the end, he'd asked if the publicist could find Teddy's phone number or his email address.

Now, Kain smashes the glass of brandy on the carpet and Julian flinches, cocking his head back. 'What are you doing, you silly twat?' Julian yells.

Kain hops off the chair and kneels by the little shards on the floor and watches the brown liquid weaving through them for a second. He selects the biggest piece of glass. Then he gets up and pins Julian down on the table with his forearm and holds the piece of glass against his neck.

Julian whimpers. 'I could have you done for this,' he says. 'You ungrateful little—'

'Eh, listen, yeah,' Kain says, his hand very steady by Julian's neck. 'You think I'm desperate, innit? And you think I'm stupid. You think you can sit there and chat shit to me about family and being a fuckin' go-getter like I won't understand. What – what do you wanna do? Make me suck your dick for a record deal? Are you dumb, blud?'

The first time Kain had ever met Julian, Julian had forced Kain to clasp his hand and then had placed his hand on Kain's back, leaving it there for a beat too long. Kain also thought he remembered Julian then gently moving his hand up and down but he couldn't tell if he was misremembering or not; if all the evidence of Julian's impropriety had metastasised, spreading to memories where there had been no malice.

'Oh, come on,' Julian says. 'I was just having a laugh with you. I'm a joker. I like to joke around. Make people laugh. You like to laugh, don't you?'

'Am I laughing, fam?'

'I guess you're not,' Julian says. 'Kain, put that thing down, eh? And we can just pretend this whole misunderstanding never happened.'

'I didn't misunderstand nothing,' Kain says. 'I know what you're doing. And it's fucked up. I'm not gonna suck your dick. Or anyone's dick for a contract. You get me?'

'Understood,' Julian says. 'I get you.'

As Kain lowers his hand, Julian shoves him. And then as Kain reflexively closes his palm, the glass slices through his skin and he starts to bleed all over the chair.

Julian watches the blood drip and says: 'Fuck's sake. All you do is cause me trouble. You know how much they charge for this kind of damage? This is the thanks I get for trying to help out someone like you. Lesson for next time, I guess.'

Outside the hotel, Kain takes out his phone and clicks through his contacts. He puts his mouth over the cut in his palm which is still bleeding. The doorman, in his long green coat and little black top hat, gestures irritably at him and asks him to move from the premises. Kain gives him a middle finger and then walks down the street. On his phone, he highlights Teddy's number.

He's trembling slightly now and taking very deep breaths. He doesn't feel particularly wounded by Julian's actions. What he is distressed by, however, is the aftermath and where his thoughts will go now. He doesn't like thinking about his sexuality. He knows he's bisexual but he's learned to navigate this identity with a kind of forced indifference. This detachment makes him feel a sense of normality without despising himself in the process. But sometimes even the effort of this indifference is too much. And then it no longer becomes about simply not thinking about men but not thinking about anyone. Of course, feigning ignorance rarely works. The landscape of his sexuality evolves and morphs into various shapes whether he's nourishing it with thought or pretending not to be a sexual being. It doesn't matter.

It's been this way since he was fifteen when, seemingly out of nowhere, he kissed Teddy in that empty classroom that one morning. It was only a tiny crush at the time. So minuscule that it should've been easily ignorable. He thought Teddy was cute. That was all. So why then did he feel compelled to keep talking to him despite being complicit in Teddy's misery? Even now, at nineteen years old, despite no longer having these violent, passionate outbursts – or at least they're much more sporadic now – he still feels as if there's something always giving him away. Maybe, he thinks, that's why Julian thought he could take advantage of him, because of this intangible thing that shows the world who he is without his permission.

He decides to call Teddy. Teddy picks up on the second ring. 'Hello?' he says. 'Who's this?' Kain stays silent for a while. 'Hello?' Teddy repeats.

'Hey,' Kain says finally. 'It's Kain.'

He hears Teddy gasp. 'Kain,' he says. 'Wow. Long time. How's it going?'

Another silence. 'Not good, fam,' Kain says. 'Not good.'

18

After my parents moved to Edinburgh my dad took up bird-watching. In addition to messaging me frequent enquiries about my apparent loneliness, he was also sending me photos of birds he'd taken in various parks. They were random and often I had no response other than a smiley-face emoji. But I liked that he had a hobby; I found it endearing. And it helped me find him less irritating whenever he asked if I was seeing anyone. So on my next visit later that August, when he asked if I wanted to birdwatch with him, I said I was happy to.

We were in Blackford Hill. It was a bright and slightly windy day. A pair of binoculars swung around his neck as we walked up wide steps caked in dirt. The foliage blew gently around us as we appeared in expansive grasslands overlooking the city. Oh, it was gorgeous. From this vantage point we could see the castle and the sea. I walked beside him as he raised his binoculars to his eyes and looked into the clear sky, towards the rocky outcrops and across the grass. He didn't keep a little book to note anything down. I don't even think he actually identified any birds. He just sort of pointed at them and nodded at me. And I nodded back encouragingly.

We walked around for about thirty minutes before we sat down on the grass. He put his arm around me and exhaled really loudly. I smiled and asked if this was how long he and Mr McAllister usually did this for. And he said that they usually walked around for longer and that they were part of a birdwatching group filled with people who were a lot more intelligent about birds than they were. But he just found the pastime relaxing.

My dad was a lot like Birch in some ways, in how he could become so impassioned by the things he loved that they influenced decisions he made in his real life. He had forged a kind of affinity with Scotland through various Scottish films he'd seen in the nineties. I remember once he took Birch and me to see *Rob Roy* and on the journey home from the cinema the two of them poorly mimicked the accents. And once during a stay in hospital, in an insane attempt to make me laugh, he smeared some chocolate over his face and said he was Ewan McGregor's character in that one scene from *Trainspotting*. I'd said: 'Dad, he didn't actually eat the poo in the toilet, he just crawled out of one.' And he replied that he had to work with what he had.

We sat in silence for a while, watching the sun casting long shadows across the meadows. Eventually he started asking about my life and I started to feel nervous. I'd never felt nervous around my dad before. The confidence I often had in deflecting his more intimate questions seemed to weaken in that moment. Even on the drive up I was thinking about explaining for the first time why he had never seen me with anyone. Aside from Nathan, Monty and now Harley, nobody had ever expected me to articulate my feelings on what I was sure was both asexuality and aromanticism; often their assumptions about me were enough to satisfy whatever curiosities they'd had. I frequently thought about the time Kain had kissed me when we were kids. And how

I could see now that it must've felt like a significant part of myself had become strangely irrelevant, even if I didn't entirely understand what that part was then. I always thought I could simply exist within my sexuality, much like I'd told Kain he could in his. But without acknowledging it, it was like that part of myself was this white space other people coloured in for me.

When my dad eventually said: 'So Theodore, is there a lover?' I laughed, shaking my head, and said it wasn't that long ago I was last here. And then he replied: 'You never know when love will strike, my son.' When I laughed again, he said: 'Look at you. You're smiling – who is he? Tell me.'

'Dad,' I said. 'I'm not gay. I'm—'

'Son,' he said with a slightly concerned expression. 'What is it?'

'I don't know how to explain it,' I said. 'It just really bothers me that you and Mum think I'm lonely. Or that I'm going to end up lonely, when that's not the case at all.'

He placed his hand on my back. Then he made an expression like: go on.

I exhaled. 'Dad,' I said. 'I feel like I have the capacity for love. Like, I really feel it. The kind of love you have for Mum and that Mum has for you. I know I have that. And it was wonderful growing up and seeing that between you two. But at the same time I feel like I've been wired to channel that love differently, you know? You're always saying you want me to find a lover. But I just think love is a lot more, I don't know, more expansive than you and Mum give it credit for. Recently I've been seeing it like a road or something, one that breaks off into hundreds of different lanes. You go down each of these lanes and each one is a completely different experience – the ground might feel different, the surroundings might look different, even the weather might be different – but, in the end, they're all leading to the same place, aren't they? Some place where we feel happy and content and fulfilled. And I think that's where we are now. You and Mum are on one lane and I'm just on another. And I think that's all there is to it really. And I think that should be fine.'

I felt him tighten his arm around me. I looked up at him and he smiled. I smiled back. 'So,' he said. 'What you're saying is that you're happy?'

'In the sense that I'm not looking for romantic fulfilment,' I said. 'Yes, I'm happy.'

'Okay, good.'

'Does this mean you'll stop asking me if I have a lover now?'

He looked up into the sky. Then he looked back at me and said: 'No.'

'Seriously?'

'I'll never stop asking if you have a lover,' he said. 'Maybe I don't understand this the way you want me to understand it. But you even just said it yourself: whether you're gay or straight or something else. You will still have love in your life and I want to know about it. Whatever it looks like.'

'I guess that's fair.'

He exhaled again. 'You know,' he said. 'This is not how I expected this conversation to go.'

'How do you mean?'

'I thought I would have to protect you,' he said. 'That I would console you and we would hug and I would say: son, it's okay to be gay. And then we would cry together. I've even been preparing. And now I'm even a little bit jealous of that gay child and his dad on that show with the songs. When I saw that I said: Ah. That's me and you.'

'That's quite an elaborate fantasy you've constructed there, Dad.'

He laughed. 'I thought we would have this conversation when you were fifteen. But then you had all these other problems. Then I thought we would have it when you were twenty, twenty-five. But you never came to me. So I decided I would—' He started prodding me gently with his finger. 'Start asking you questions.'

I laughed. 'Well, I'm sorry I deprived you of that.'

'Yeah, you should be,' he said. 'You're a thief.'

My dad shared everything I'd told him with my mother in a way that made me sound insidious and strange. I drove her to a garden centre just outside Edinburgh the next day; her garden show was two months away now, and she'd said that my father had told her I simply loved people 'differently', and she even did air quotes at me. When I told her what I'd actually said to him, that not being in a relationship had no bearing on my happiness, and that I experienced love regardless, she put her hand on her chest and gave a dramatic sigh of relief. 'Your father's not very good at talking,' she said. 'He said "differently" like you were casting spells on people. I don't care what you are, Teddy. But if you are participating in witchcraft then I will drown you in holy water. No son of mine will be a voodoo man.'

I laughed and told her I wasn't practising witchcraft and she said: 'Good.' Then after a slight pause she said: 'Your father also told me you didn't want us to ask if you have a lover anymore. So we will stop.'

'Great.'

'But only if you tell me, right now, if you are okay,' she said. 'Your life, your health, everything. You know I can tell when you're lying. If I believe you then I will never question you again.'

There was a brief silence. I looked at her. 'Yeah,' I said. 'I'm fine.' Another pause. Then, in an attempt at nonchalance, I asked her if she believed me. And she gave me a sighing look that suggested she didn't. But also that there was nothing she could do about this kind of dishonesty.

When we got to the store, I saw her inhale deeply and smile, as if she had stepped into a place so total in its serenity she needed to brace herself for its impact.

She looped her arm through mine and then we went up and down the aisles while I pushed a big green trolley. The store was sprawling. And every time we turned onto another aisle she almost shook with excitement. As we went up the exotic plant aisle, I asked her to tell me more about this show.

'The theme is tropical,' she said. 'So I'm looking for some banana plants. I want mine to look like a beautiful jungle. I want lots of colour.'

'Oh,' I said, 'so you'll want loads of orchids and hibiscus or something.'

She looked at me, surprised. 'How do you know that?'

I laughed. 'Every time you do something new in the garden, Dad sends a picture of it to me. And sometimes he explains what you've done exactly.'

She gave me a look, pretending to be annoyed by this, though I could tell she actually found it really endearing. She then took out her phone and began swiping through a string of photos. They were of a garden overloaded with tulips in a vibrant array of colours.

'That's beautiful,' I said. 'Whose garden is that?'

She hit my arm. 'No,' she said. 'It's ugly. Very, very ugly.'

'What are you talking about?' I said. 'Look at all the flow-ers. It's stunning.'

She scowled. 'Teddy, if you say it's beautiful one more time I'm going to rent your room to strangers when you leave.'

I laughed. 'Well, if you think it's so ugly, why do you have so many pictures of it on your phone?'

'It's Belinda's garden,' she said. 'She's one of our neigh-bours. She's doing the competition too. She's a show-off. I'm so sick of that woman.'

I sighed. 'Mum, why do you have beef with some lady called Belinda?'

'She has a big mouth,' she said. 'She talks too much. She thinks she's so much better than me at everything. She thinks her garden is better than mine. She thinks her opinion is better than mine. And she's always sending me pictures: "Oh, look at my garden. Oh, look at my children. Oh, look at the food I've cooked for my family." And, Theodore, I'm tired of looking.' She paused for a moment. 'And her children are ugly.'

I put my hand on her shoulder. 'Mum!'

'Theodore, you see?' she said. 'You see what she does to me? She makes me want to be a violent woman. And you know I'm a woman of the word.'

'You haven't seen the inside of a church since the nineties.'

She kissed her teeth. 'You don't know what I do or where I've been.' She then showed me the picture again and stared at me expectantly.

'Yeah, mum, it's fucking disgusting,' I said. 'Your garden is miles better.'

She whacked my arm again. 'You know I don't like that language,' she said. 'But thank you.'

As we were paying for everything, I saw a flyer stapled to

a noticeboard behind the counter. It had a picture of a ferret with little blue eyes on it. I asked the cashier if I could take a closer look. She handed it to me. The flyer said that the ferret was looking for a home and that she had something called Waardenburg Syndrome, a genetic condition that affected her hearing as well as the colour and patterns of her fur. At the bottom of the flyer was a number for the SPCA rescue and rehoming centre. I took a photo of the flyer and handed it back to the cashier.

In the car I told my mum that I was considering getting her for Birch. My mum squinted at the photo on my phone and said: 'Do you think he will want a deaf ferret?'

I smiled. 'I think he'd love one actually.'

When Birch loved something, however obscure, it was really important to him that the world knew about it too. It was the one thing I'd associated with his personality since the very first time I'd met him. I remembered a time in school when he'd found an injured squirrel on the field. It had fallen from a tree and broken its legs and one of its paws, and had been lying there unconscious. Birch had asked Nathan and I to get a teacher to come out. But the teacher didn't care and discarded the squirrel in one of the big wheelie bins outside the school gates. Birch had tried to hit the teacher after that and got suspended for a month.

A few days later I drove down to the SPCA centre outside of Edinburgh. The volunteer cheerfully showed me the ferret, who the team had temporarily named Cinnamon. She had a soft tan coat, bright-blue, wide-set eyes, a flat skull and a long white strip going down her back.

We talked a little about Waardenburg syndrome and he explained that beyond being deaf, it just meant she would need a bit of extra care. When he picked her up, she started rolling her head back, and then she started licking at his knuckles. He handed her to me. She felt so soft in my hands. She wiggled around a lot and made loud dooking noises. I slowly moved my thumb up and down her fur. The volunteer told me she responded to vibrations and that I could smack the floor to get her attention when she was preoccupied. I placed her on the floor and tried it. And she came shuffling towards me.

When I got home that afternoon, I went to my room and placed her on my desk. I watched her wiggle around in her carrier. I tried to think of a name for her; a name Birch would've come up with on his own. Eventually I knelt in front of her, resting my chin on the backs of my hands. She licked my nose through the slats. 'Oh, your dad is gonna love that you do that,' I told her. As she continued to lick me, I said: 'You would've had two brothers. Your dad might pretend that you still do, even though technically they don't belong to him anymore. And I suspect they never really did in the first place. Oh, and he's probably going to give you a ridiculous little name. I don't know if he'll love "Cinnamon". Your theoretical brothers were called White Magnum and Choc-Ice. You've got a bit of a tan on you, haven't you? So I bet he'll call you, I don't know, something like "Double Caramel" or something.' My eyebrows shot up. 'Yup. I think that'll be it. What do you think?'

I kept talking to her sporadically through the rest of the afternoon. I enjoyed doing it. She kept making noises that made me feel as if she was somehow responding to me. At one point during the evening I poured a little mound of kibble in her cage and watched her eat it. I was so excited to give her to Birch that I took out some of the old letters I'd written him during that ten-year period he wasn't in my life, which I'd never sent. I even walked idly around my room, reading various sections out loud, the bits about how much I'd missed him, the bits where I was desperate to know what he'd been up to, the bits where I'd hypothesised his reactions to various things that had happened in my life: going to university, graduating, moving to Scotland to live with my parents, moving back to London, being promoted to senior editor at *Rush!*.

I became acutely aware of how grateful I was that I no longer had to write him letters; that now he was always a phone call or a message away. I liked how now, being his friend meant never having to initiate a conversation; we'd been engaged in one continuous conversation since we'd been reunited. It also dawned on me then that during that period, these letters had become about more than just trying to check up on him. I'd considered him my first friend and I was desperate to not let his memory be lost to the past. Even if so much life had happened to us, I wanted some of what we used to be to remain. Like clawing through a dense forest years later and finding that a seed you'd planted was still there, still growing.

19

I got back to London the next day. It was the morning of the *Rush!* party. Kain was out with Nathan on an early job and Birch was in the shower. I placed Double Caramel on the living-room table and waited for Birch to come out of the bathroom. I could hear him singing the wrong words to 'You Gotta Be' by Des'ree and giggling to himself.

He was towelling himself dry when he walked out. When he saw me on the sofa he jumped and yelled: 'Fucking hell, Ted. When did you get back?'

I laughed and tried to distract him with idle talk so he would notice Double Caramel on the table on his own. 'How do you not know all the words to that song?' I said. 'You literally used to sing it all the time when we were kids.'

'Oh, I'm getting old, T-Bear,' he said, wrapping the towel around his waist. 'My brain's gonna be all crusty like the rest of you Neezes when I turn thirty.'

He kept talking to me as he walked over to the sofa and didn't seem to notice the carrier, so I repeatedly flicked my eyes towards the table. He was asking how Scotland was and how my parents were, until eventually I gestured dramatically at the carrier with my eyes widened. He made a face and turned around. He knelt down and looked inside.

Double Caramel was sleeping, curled up in what looked like a very uncomfortable position. Birch turned back to me with a confused expression and then back to the cage.

'Oh my god,' he said in a low voice. 'Who's this?' I told him she was his new pet and with this awed look in his eyes he said: 'You got me a new pet, Ted?' I nodded. He yelled again but then caught himself and said: 'Oh shit. She's sleeping—'

'Oh yeah,' I said. 'She's deaf. She's got something-something syndrome. I don't really remember—'

'You mean Waardenburg syndrome?' he said.

He reached into the cage and placed his hand near her for a moment before he actually stroked her.

'How do you know that?' I asked.

He turned to me with a raised eyebrow. 'What do you mean: how do I know? You think I don't know my ferrets, T-Bear? I'm a fuckin' ferret dad. See, I always suspected you thought I was dumb. Now it's all out in the open, innit?'

'Birch, I think I've made no secret of how dumb I think you are.'

He laughed. Then without turning back to look at me he asked if I'd named her yet. I told him that I had, and that I'd attempted to come up with something that he might've. I saw his cheeks puff into little balls as he smiled. He was still stroking her, lightly brushing his forefinger up and down her coat. He said he wanted to guess and suggested: Blue. Blue Eyes. Stripy. Stripes. Stripes with a z. I chuckled and said: 'I was thinking more along the lines of when you named Whitey and Choc-Ice.'

'Oh shit,' he said. 'She looks like a hazelnut Magnum. No. She looks more like double caramel, innit.'

In a high-pitched voice I said: ding ding. Then he

whispered: 'Oh, DC. It's so nice to meet you. You're gonna have a wonderful time with me.'

He tried to hug me after that but I said: 'No Birch, you're still all wet.'

He opened his arms wider and replied: 'No T-Bear, if anyone deserves a wet hug from me, it's you. Bring it in, you sexy generous bastard.'

In the evening Kain and Nathan got back from their last job and we changed into our outfits for the party. I'd thought Birch would still be annoyed we weren't being as flamboyant as we'd been in previous years. But every time he put on a piece of clothing he would run into the living room and watch DC sleeping in her carrier for a few minutes. We were all in the thick white cardigans Mya had made us with our names stitched onto the breast, bow ties, navy shorts and red baseball caps.

Kain and Nathan sat on the sofa and had a few beers before we left. I watched them fix each other's bow ties and adjust each other's hats. Then we watched Birch staring at DC and whispering things to her like: 'Please wake up before I get too drunk to remember that I have a new pet tonight,' and we laughed at him.

As we walked to the bus stop, Birch was still back at the flat placing a bowl of water and leftover ferret kibble by DC's carrier. Nathan had to ask the driver to wait as he ran down the pavement. At Aldgate two teenagers in pastel-coloured tracksuits got on. They looked at us and started covering their mouths and sniggering to each other. When one of them took out their phone and began taking pictures, Birch turned his cap around and posed for every shot, while Kain stood up with his eyes narrowed. But before he could yell at them,

Nathan pulled him back down and said: 'Eh, calm down, bruv. We're a bunch of grown men dressed like schoolboys, innit. People are gonna say shit. Let it go, fam.'

Nathan and Birch then looked at one another conspiratorially. They placed a finger each on the corners of Kain's mouth and pulled it upward. Kain laughed and shook their hands away. 'You know what, Kain,' Birch said. 'I think you'd be a lot less uptight if you just got your arse out like me.'

I looked across to Birch. 'What are you talking about?'

Birch stood up and wiggled his arse at us. He'd cut two big holes out the back of his shorts.

The party was on a rooftop in Shoreditch. The walls were strung with fairy lights and little triangular flags with the *Rush!* logo. We didn't have the budget for a real band, so Mya let Monty hire a few of the resident drag kings and queens from Passage. They were each dressed as a different member of the Spice Girls, pretending to play instruments and lip-syncing through a repertoire of various songs from the nineties.

Mya and Monty were already there. Mya had on a crochet top and leather trousers she'd modelled after an Aaliyah look. She also had a pair of sunglasses in her hair that she dramatically slid onto her eyes when she saw us. Monty was dressed like Vanilla Ice with baggy trousers and an oversized hoodie with the American flag on it.

When they came over to us, they said we looked cute. Then I put my hand on Birch's shoulder and said: 'Go on. Turn around. Show them what you've done, you absolute child.' He turned around. Monty spanked him and Mya screeched with laughter.

'Please don't encourage him,' I said. 'He might have other holes he hasn't shown us yet.'

A server with a plate of mini hot dogs passed us then. Nathan and Kain looked at each other and followed them into the crowd. Birch noticed the photobooth in the corner and grabbed Monty's arm and ran towards it. Mya and I then went over to the bar and ordered a few cocktails. When we sat down I thanked her for helping Monty out with the performers.

'He owes them big time,' she said. 'He actually agreed to be one of our Weekend Piggies at Passage as payment.'

'Stop it,' I said. 'And you explained to him what that meant?'

'Of course.'

'In detail? Naked on stage, ridden by a drag queen, spanked with a riding crop?'

'He didn't ask for details,' she said. 'He was just happy we didn't ask for money.'

I laughed. Then I noticed she kept fidgeting with her hair. She said her wig was making her scalp itch. Facetiously, I said: 'Ah, is it cheap like Birch said?' And she chuckled and hit me on my arm.

'I didn't even wanna wear a wig, you know,' she said. 'I really wanted to dye my hair silver. And I had this cute sleeveless jacket that I thought would be cool so I could be—'

'Sisqó?'

'Exactly.'

'What happened?'

She rolled her eyes. Then she flicked them over to Nathan, who was still with Kain, cornering the server with the hot dogs. She looked back at me with her eyelids lowered. 'I just couldn't be bothered to have the argument again,' she said. 'He's still being a little bitch about what I wear.'

'Seriously?' I said. 'Still?'

She nodded. 'He was all: I thought you only dressed

masculine on stage and blah blah blah. But I don't wanna talk about it anymore though,' she said. 'If I give it too much attention it's just gonna upset me. And I wanna have a nice time tonight.'

'Are you sure?'

She nodded again. The band started lip-syncing to 'My Love' by Kele Le Roc. We saw Nathan and Kain walking back to us. When they got to the bar, Nathan put his hand out for Mya to take. She exhaled and I seemed to be the only person who noticed how reluctantly she took it. Nathan then pulled her into the crowd and they slow danced.

I looked up at Kain then. He smiled at me with a mouthful of little hot dogs. He had one left in his palm that he offered me. I shook my head. But he kept it in front of me and flicked his eyebrows up. I took it and put it in my mouth.

As I chewed I asked him if he'd heard anything from Harley. He took his phone out of his pocket. 'Nah, fam,' he said. Then he showed me a large block of text he'd sent him. It'd been read about a week ago and not responded to. 'I'm still trying though, innit.'

Later that evening, during Groove Armada's 'I See You Baby', Birch got drunk and started showing people selfies he'd taken with DC on his phone, even people he didn't know. And they all nodded at him in this wide-eyed way like: get away from me please. I kept laughing and shaking my head. At one point he asked me what it was called when you were racist towards the deaf. And I said: 'I don't think people are being racist towards the deaf. They just don't want an inebriated man with his bum out shoving his phone in their face.'

And then he looked at me and said: 'Nah. That's not it.'

*

We saw Janice later. She was dressed like Gabrielle. She had on an eyepatch, long, beaded necklaces around her neck and a form-fitting black dress. She was already drunk. Birch pointed at her and yelled the lyrics to 'Dreams'. In her inebriation I imagined she'd forgotten that she had dismissed Birch from his role in the mailroom last year. She put her arm around him and joined him in singing. She hugged me after that. And when a Cleopatra song came on, Monty appeared and took Birch away to dance.

Janice sat at the bar with me. She was silent a moment. Then she sighed and said: 'It's over, Ted.'

I looked at her. 'What do you mean?'

'I mean it's over,' she said. '*Rush!* It's done. Finished.'

'Excuse me?' I said. 'But I thought you said—'

Drunkenly, she put her finger on my lips and said: 'Shh. I know what I said. I was just tryna keep everybody's raasclart hopes up, wasn't I?'

I took her finger away. 'Are you joking?' I said. But before she answered I put my face in my hands. Then I lifted my head back up and continued: 'I knew this would happen. I told you switching direction was a shit idea. I mean for fuck's sake, look at the sales. All we did was alienate our readership and just—'

'Eh, eh, eh,' she said. 'I'm gonna let this slide because I know you're angry. But I actually saved your job.'

'What?'

'Six years ago,' she said. 'When you were running your mouth about how I was tanking the magazine and about my poor decision making. Remember those conversations? When *Smash Hits* got shut down, we were next, you know. But no. I said we would re-brand. I said we would find a new bloodclart direction. And that's the only reason we weren't killed off.' I looked at her silently. 'Yeah, you're all quiet now, aren't you?' She told me that we had a few months left in business and the publisher was allowing us to publish a final issue.

'So what happens now?' I said. 'What are you gonna do?'

'Well, I got offered a likkle radio ting,' she said. 'Radio 1Xtra. As one of the music programmers. They said it would be right up my street. And I said to 'em: And what kind of street do you think I live on, darlin'? You think I'm gonna turn up at some bloodclart radio station? Have likkle meetings and tings? Me at my big age reporting to some likkle bwoy who's on the good side of twenty-five. Jumpin' around, tellin' me what to do and shit.'

'So you turned it down?'

She laughed. 'Unemployed? In this economy?' she said. 'Use your brain, love. Of course I didn't turn it down. I've got a second home in Spain to think about. I've got a Porsche and a Mercedes S-Class on finance. And it'll be a cold day in the hottest part of hell before I give those up.'

I made a face. 'Why do you have both?'

'Oi,' she said. 'You don't see me asking you silly questions like: why is your chunky little mate running around my party with his arse-cheeks hanging out, do you?'

I looked at her like: fair enough. I asked her if she'd told Monty. She slapped me on my back and said she was leaving that with me. We sat in silence for a moment. Then I looked at her with an earnestness that was almost embarrassing and said: 'What do I do now?'

'Ted,' she said. 'I've got nothing for you, okay? The industry is brutal – what can I say?'

'I've worked with you for nearly ten years and you can't say anything consoling?'

She sighed. 'And that's your problem right there,' she said. 'You don't get nowhere by being nice and consoling.'

'I don't know,' I said. 'I think those qualities can get you quite far.'

'Bollocks,' she said. 'There was no one consoling me when I first started out and couldn't get a pitch looked at; when I was shoved out of offices; when people were telling me: "We're not ready for someone like you," which was obviously code for: we're not checkin' for the likkle black gyal. Or that my voice was "too niche". Or my personal favourite: "You're not in line with the magazine's vision," when I was into the same bomboclart shit everyone else was. It was the eighties, Ted. I had on my likkle tutu and polka-dot tights like the rest of the gyal-dem. Where were you then, Ted? Huh? With your consoling raasclart words.'

'In my mum's uterus probably,' I said. She laughed at that. Then I said: 'But don't you think there's a breaking of the cycle that needs to be done here?'

'What you need to understand about me, Ted,' she said, 'is that I'm a bitter gyal. The bitterness keeps me warm at night. It's marbled in my skin like varicose veins. It sits in the passenger seat of my Merc – you get me? It goes—'

'For god's sake Janice,' I said, 'just say something encouraging to me.'

She laughed again, then tapped me on my back. 'You're a smart man, Teddy. You'll land on your feet. I don't doubt that. And that's all your getting from me, love.'

The band were miming to 'I Love You Always Forever' by Donna Lewis now. The others were dancing in a circle. I looked at them, all of them, and envisioned my life as this package bursting at the seams, and how everything I used to maintain my humanity felt as if it was emptying out of me. I knew I wouldn't tell them I was losing my job. And it was curious, even to me, how my hardships never seemed to bring my friends any closer to me, not like theirs brought me to them. Something always placed them just out of reach. The road that connected us only presented itself when I fed the delusion that there was something so trivial about my issues; that they could be shifted and rearranged to accommodate someone else's pain.

In the circle now, Birch smiled and held his hand out to me. When I took it he pulled me towards him and we began to sway. He then raised our arms and twirled me around and we laughed. He sang the lyrics of the song at me. I sang them back. We looked into each other's eyes. Then he arched an eyebrow like: remember this? And I nodded back at him, yes. This was one of the last songs we'd danced to at the last school disco we'd attended. On the morning of the disco he had got into a fight with Luke Williams and hadn't been allowed to attend. But he turned up anyway. I remembered sitting outside the assembly hall with him, with his head resting on my shoulder, saying how much he loved this song. I remembered laughing and showing him the list of songs I always kept with me, the one that documented everything he developed obsessions with. It was two sides long then. And I remembered him saying: 'Woah. What's this?' And when I explained he said: 'And you just keep this with you all the time?' And I replied: 'Of course. I don't want to miss anything about you.'

Now I looked at him. I saw him cough. It was so loud I heard it above the music. I mouthed: are you okay? And he kept nodding at me, smilingly, until he coughed again, raising a fist to his mouth.

I followed his fist as he pulled it away from his face. When he opened his palm it was streaked with blood.

December 2003

Birch boards the 436 at Vauxhall bus station. It's one of those long bendy buses so he doesn't pay. He sits at the back and gently lays his head against the window. He closes his eyes briefly and exhales when he feels the cold glass on his skin. As the bus pulls away, he watches the sequence of tall silver buildings trace across the soft peach-coloured sky. He smiles. It looks like a painting to him, as if someone's knocked over a glass of water on a sheet of craft paper.

But it hurts to smile. In fact, it hurts to breathe, so he only does so slowly. He tries to avoid his reflection in the window, but every time he catches it, he sees the purple bruising around his eyes and the discolouration on his lips where the skin has been split. He doesn't recognise himself. Or at least he doesn't want to, so he looks away again, upward, to the sky. There's a version of himself – a happier, healthier version – in his head that he likes to pretend he still resembles. The last time he had looked like this version was when he was in school, when he was fifteen. He's twenty-one now. And he finds it incredibly difficult to reconcile these two faces, so a lot of his life now is spent negotiating his own existence, navigating the delicate terrain of pretending this current version of himself simply doesn't exist.

The remainder of his life is spent living on the edge of some kind of existence. It's like his life has been filed down to the bare bones of what makes a person human, he often thinks. He accepted quite a long time ago that real evidence of his existence is now dictated by other people, like when he sits in front of a supermarket and some money is dropped in front of him or when fleeting eye contact is made with him or even when an enforcement officer asks him to move from wherever he's currently calling home.

When Birch left home several years ago, he eventually found himself a new home by total accident. He was walking aimlessly along Waterloo Bridge one night and happened to glance into this dark cavernous space beneath the round-about. He saw row after row of what seemed to be cardboard boxes, so many of them seemingly spotlit by little flickering lights of fire. When he eventually discovered that this wasn't a campsite but a settlement, he loitered around nervously and then ended up staying. There were people without homes everywhere living in various constructions made of wooden pallets and boxes and tarps. And the smell was something he knew he would struggle to get used to. But he tried and then eventually did. And it was better than park benches or alcoves or bus stations. And there were people here. People who could in one way or another make his loneliness feel less visceral.

He learned to beg for money in the early mornings and late afternoons by the taxi rank when the foot traffic was very high. And for the first few months he could still make himself look somewhat presentable by washing his face and hair in the toilets in the station. So in the late evenings, when he was hungry and hanging around by the railway arches, he could exchange oral sex for some money. In his desperation, he learned to navigate the subtlety of eye contact with men. When he was leaning against the brick with his hands in his pockets and men would glance at him and linger a beat too long, he would smile at them. When eventually it became increasingly difficult to maintain his appearance, his success dwindled significantly. But still he tried. The relative ease of the transaction was something he couldn't sacrifice.

Once Birch had made eye contact with a man in an expensive-looking navy suit and neat white-blonde hair and crystal-blue eyes. It was very early on a cold and rainy morning, and the man had looked really angry and tense. When Birch smiled at him, he didn't smile back. He just watched Birch for a moment and then approached him. He looked around suspiciously and then produced a twenty-pound note between his index and middle finger, silently waving it at Birch. Birch, despite looking the way he did, had assumed he'd only have to give him head or something to earn it. But the man started to walk and gestured for Birch to follow. And he did. All the way to a narrow alleyway beside the fire station.

He usually didn't have to walk very far. The last time someone had propositioned him he'd got in their car. And the time before that they had gone into the public toilets. This time he walked behind the man, wringing his hands, desperately wanting to know where they were going. But he just assumed there was a reason the man wasn't saying anything. And he didn't want to jeopardise the prospect of having some money for food that day.

In the alleyway, the man still had the note between his fingers. When Birch reached for it, the man pulled it back and laughed, shaking his head.

'Oh yeah, sorry,' Birch said. He lowered himself onto

his knees, put his hands on the man's waist and opened his mouth, looking up at him. He was waiting for him to unbuckle his belt, but instead the man laughed again.

The man then put his fingers beneath Birch's chin and said: 'No, no. Get up.'

Birch stood up. 'I'm sorry,' he said. 'Did I do something wrong? Isn't this what you want?'

The man didn't respond and instead grabbed Birch by his hair, snapping his head back, and hit him in his face, squaring his wet fist into Birch's eye.

When Birch yelled: 'Fuck!' The man shushed him gently, as if calming a baby. He put his finger on Birch's lips and held his face very close to Birch's and said: 'It's okay, it's okay.' The man showed him the twenty-pound note again. 'You want this, don't you?' Birch paused, the pain still sizzling around his eye, and eventually he nodded. 'Then we're all good, then.'

The man punched Birch in the face again, repeatedly and so ferociously, grunting with every hit, that it wasn't until he stopped to shake out his wrist that Birch could truly feel the pain cascading over him.

The man then tightened his grip on Birch's hair like he was trying to rip it out from his head and began hitting him again. Birch screamed and begged him to stop. 'Please,' he said. 'Enough. Please stop.'

'If you want this twenty quid, mate,' the man said in a low voice in Birch's ear, 'you'll shut the fuck up. Do you understand me?'

Birch was bent over now, shaking and guarding his face with his hands. The man then pulled Birch's hair tighter for a response. And when Birch eventually nodded, he spat at him and laughed and then put his hand around Birch's neck.

Birch knew then not to ask the man why he was doing this to him. Because he knew that his own comprehension of events wasn't the point, nor did it matter. He understood now that, just like sex, this wasn't something to understand but to endure. Life had continuously taught him that somehow his pain would be rewarded, however meagrely. And he knew life didn't always rearrange itself to offset his anguish, but it always seemed to give him something at least: so when the man eventually kneed him in the stomach and winded him so hard that he hit the pavement on the side of his face with a thud, he didn't register the malice as much as he did the inevitability of it. And then, at last – as the man placed the twenty-pound note in Birch's palm and walked away in the rain – he registered the reward.

The man came back, of course. Every few months, or sometimes every few weeks, Birch would see him. And sometimes the fear clung to him so tightly that he'd think about drifting from the settlement, from Waterloo entirely, and making himself harder to find. But then he'd had a good thing there. Even though it was difficult to maintain friend-ships in a space so transitory, he found a sense of normality in any fleeting connection that arose. He especially liked the residents who had been living there a while, who could fill his days with stories. He'd once met two Irish women who had been there intermittently since the late eighties and had told him about the time Princess Diana had visited the settlement and shaken their hands.

But then people disappeared or passed or were arrested. And eventually the high court granted an eviction notice against those who remained in the settlement, so he had to move, and could no longer anchor himself in friendship, however precariously, like he'd wanted. But he could anchor himself in routine and money. The man in the navy suit offered him a sense of purpose and income. It was difficult to feel useless if he had a function in someone else's life. So every day he found his way back to Waterloo and walked around. Sometimes he found the man, sometimes he didn't. But when he did, he would follow him into alleyways and he knew not to yell or complain or question. And eventually everything became administrative, the way things might if he worked a corporate job. His boss had asked something of him and he had simply performed the task and received money for it. But it was hard to maintain this level of delusion. Sometimes, when the man walked away and Birch was lying on the ground, trying as hard as he could to somehow distance himself from the pain, he'd be acutely aware that he was waiting to see if he would die first; if he would simply succumb to his injuries. And sometimes he'd feel as if his survival was an accomplishment and be proud of himself.

He's still smiling at the sky now as the bus drives over Vauxhall Bridge. He can sense other passengers covering their noses and moving away from him. But he's too exhausted to be embarrassed and just wants to sleep. It's not long before the bus reaches its destination at Paddington, and he doesn't want the driver to have to wake him up.

He'd secured shelter somewhere in Westminster the night before. But in the morning he'd got into a fight with a man who had accused him of stealing his shoes. He had lunged at Birch and they had hit each other repeatedly and had both got kicked out. He didn't even get a chance to use the showering facilities. It wasn't the first time something like this had happened, so when he was back on the street he was more disappointed than angry. And now it was onto the next thing.

Still, he often felt so claustrophobic with how circular his life was and how tightly it constricted itself around him.

As the bus passes through Victoria now, his smile fades as the sky turns murky. He looks past his reflection, at the people walking through the city, and sighs at how easily and beautifully the world seems to move without him. One of the last things his stepdad had ever told him was that he didn't matter. And while it was an easy thing for him to believe at the time, there was always a part of him that had hoped to be proven wrong. Thinking about this made him think of the man in the navy suit. The very existence of this man was something he could one day take back to his stepdad and say: look Dad, at one point in my life, I mattered to someone. Because that was the thing: he missed mattering. He missed being useful to someone. He missed being someone that someone else cared about.

20

Birch was in a hospital in Lambeth for two weeks. I'd put him on my private health insurance the week he'd moved in with me. He'd had various blood tests and X-rays and CT scans and now they had fixed an oxygen tube to his face. For the first two days he was very pale and periodically hot to the touch. When the doctor told us that Birch had experienced a recurrence of pulmonary tuberculosis, Birch crossed his arms and said: 'Oh, give it a rest. How many times do I need to get it? Isn't the once enough?'

The doctor laughed and said it wasn't uncommon for TB to lie dormant and then resurface. She told us that the good news was that they'd caught it before it progressed any further and that Birch's lesions were small so they could begin his treatment. I was confused by this diagnosis. I'd seen Birch cough up blood a further two times since the *Rush!* party, so how small could they be? When I brought this up with her, she explained that even with small lesions, irritation in the airways could cause mild haemoptysis, which was also common in TB patients.

I'd been trying to visit him every day after work. I had to co-ordinate my schedule with Kain so one of us would be home to look after DC. When I went into his hospital room one afternoon, he was watching television, a documentary on Channel 4 about a cannibal in Sheffield. I sat by his bedside watching him become increasingly obsessed with the subject matter. He kept aiming the remote at the television and saying: 'Oi Teddy, did you hear that? That's mental.' And I just nodded along smilingly.

When the documentary was over he said: 'Well, that was a bunch of bollocks.'

'Why?' I said. 'The guy was charged in the end.'

'But that's what I mean, Ted,' he said. 'They kept going: "Oh, he was a cannibal. Oh, he was a monster." Well, no he wasn't. He ate a *bit* of *one* person on a night out in Sheffield when he was high on MDMA.' I raised an eyebrow. 'You take a little nibble out of one sweaty raver in 1996 with Gina G going off in the club and suddenly they're callin' you a "cannibal" with "no regard for human life". And now you've got your own fuckin' documentary on Channel bloody 4.'

I laughed. 'Dare I ask why you feel so strongly about this?'

'It's an injustice, innit,' he said. 'It was the nineties. It was a different time, Ted. It was a bit of a laugh.'

'Birch, are you high?'

'No, I'm just bored, T-Bear,' he groaned. 'I don't wanna be here anymore. I'm going insane.'

'It's cute that you think your insanity has anything to do with you being in hospital for a few days.'

He laughed sarcastically and said: 'Very funny.' And then asked when they were releasing him.

'In a few days,' I said. 'They just wanna make sure all the medication they're giving you is being well tolerated.'

He then asked me how DC was and I said she was okay. Then I showed him a couple selfies I had taken with her. Even one we had taken with Kain where he was almost smiling. In some of the photos she was rolling her head back and I was looking at her with a confused expression. I'd managed to get one of her licking my face which made Birch smile. 'Oh, I can't wait to see her again,' he said. 'It's my face she should be licking. What is she like? I can't believe I don't know my own baby.'

'Well,' I said. 'She's very loud.'

'Really?' he said. 'But she's deaf.'

'Yeah,' I said. 'She's always screeching and making that little dooking sound. I think it's because she can't gauge how loud she's being. You have to slap the ground really hard to get her attention. And she's really rough – she literally destroys every toy she plays with. And she's really energetic for most of the day. Except for the mornings where she's really quiet and starts licking your face for no reason when you try and feed her. I think she would've gotten along really well with Whitey and Choc-Ice.'

'Oi,' he said. 'Ted, I don't wanna hear those names ever again. They're dead to me.'

'Stop it,' I said. 'They can't be dead to you. You love them.'

'Nah, Ted, I'm serious,' he said. 'Fuck those ferrets. And fuck Lucy and Charlie too. Look at this shit—' He reached for his phone on the bedside table and opened up Instagram. He went on to Charlie's profile. The grid was awash with a tranquil cerulean blue from all the photos he had taken at various beaches around the world. In many of them he was wearing swimming trunks with his arm around a blonde woman in a bikini. 'Is that Lucy?' I asked. And when he nodded I said: 'They're both fit.'

'Yeah, but don't let that distract you,' he said. 'They're evil.' He swiped down to a more cosy domestic photo of Lucy and Charlie in their massive living room, wearing Olympics merch, holding up Whitey and Choc-Ice to the camera and smiling. 'See—'

I narrowed my eyes. 'What am I looking at exactly?'

'They're smiling, Ted.'

'People tend to do that when they take pictures.'

'No,' he said. 'Whitey and Choc-Ice. Why aren't they miserable? They've been stolen from me and they're just cheesin' at the camera like they ain't been kidnapped.'

I took his phone out of his hand and put it back on the table. I gave him a hard look. 'Birch, be serious for a second,' I said. 'Why were you being so difficult about getting your cough checked out? Why didn't you just go to the GP like I asked?'

'I did,' he insisted. 'They really did just say it was a cough. And I knew it wasn't true but I just went with it 'cause I didn't wanna do all this shit again, man. All the antibiotics and people checking on me and stuff. I fucking hate it. That's why I didn't tell you. Because I knew you'd be all: Birch take your medicine. Birch stop movin' about. Birch why aren't you resting. And, Ted, you know I like to move about. I like to do shit. And you know me, I'm not one for the dramatics, being the quiet and reserved man I am. But I think I'll rest when I'm dead thank you very much.'

When Birch first moved in with me he was in a bad way. The day I brought him home was the first time he'd showered in a very long time. I felt an impossible kind of sadness looking at him. I even sat at the bathroom door while he showered. It was completely silent except for the water hitting the ceramic of the tub. When he was finished I laid out some clothes for him to wear. Then he joined me at the kitchen table. I made him some toast. He threw up after a few bites, a bright yellow liquescent gush that splashed across the table. He apologised profusely and cried, wailing into his hands.

I got up and held him tight and told him it was okay. I took him to my GP the next day. They said he had acid reflux and nausea from long periods of inconsistent nourishment. And that he had developed tuberculosis that had spread gastrointestinally.

The next time I saw Birch, we watched a lot of television together. We saw the Olympics closing ceremony. Throughout the show Birch seemed to get excited at every performance, and kept nudging me to say things like: 'Teddy, fuck, it's One Direction,' and 'Teddy, fuck, it's the bloke from Oasis. But where's the other one? And why's it say Beady Eye on that drum?' And then when the sparkly black cabs drove onto the stage he elbowed me, grinning, and said: 'Teddy, fuck, it's the fucking Spice Girls. All of 'em. Look, Ted. All five.'

And I kept responding: 'Yeah, Birch, I'm watching the exact same thing as you.'

Birch developed a new obsession with another show. This time it was a series about two comedians passionately exploring various scenic landscapes in Britain. In this episode they were in the Peak District. About halfway through the episode Birch turned to me and said: 'T-Bear, I just realised I've never left the country before.' He then dramatically put his hand on my chest and said: 'Oh my god, Teddy, I don't think I've ever left London.'

I looked at him contemplatively. 'Yeah you have,' I said.

'When?'

'You and Nate went to that rock-climbing place in Tunbridge Wells when we were in school.'

'We did?' he said. 'How the hell do you remember that? I swear you know more about my life than I do.'

'Well, I've spent a lot of time thinking about you.' I said. I had meant this to sound offhand and factual. But he looked at me with these wide eyes as if I'd just monologed my undying love for him.

Facetiously he glided his knuckles down my face and said: 'Have you been havin' impure thoughts about me, Ted?'

I took his hand off me and laughed. 'I just meant in the ten years I didn't see you. Before we saw each other on that train.'

'Oh,' he said. 'Well, do me a favour and never think about that again. I'd rather you think about me as the sexy hunk lying on a hospital bed before you today. Rather than the bloke who hadn't eaten in weeks and went around begging people for shit and getting his head slammed into a brick wall every day—'

My eyebrows shot up. 'What do you mean?'

His eyes twitched in this panicked, nervous way like he didn't mean to say what he just had. He looked down at his hands. 'Nothing,' he said.

'No,' I said. 'Birch, don't scare me like that. Was that a joke or what?'

He was silent a moment. Then he looked over at me and exhaled really hard. 'What do you want me to say, Ted?' he said. 'You can use your imagination. Really bad things happen when no one cares about you.'

He often referred to 'bad things' that had happened. And the implications behind this always seemed to go beyond what I already knew had happened to him in those ten years we'd been apart, which hadn't even been much. In truth I knew how difficult it would be for us to venture into that territory together. How could I make him show me things he didn't want to see again, things I didn't know if I could bear seeing for the first time. How could I have cradled him into my life, wiped away the dirt, and then led him back into the darkness? I sighed and ran my fingers through his hair with a mournful expression.

He told me then that he didn't want to talk about this anymore. Then he smiled as if this conversation had never happened and said: 'When I'm better I think I wanna go camping. In the Peak District.'

On the television now, the two comedians were standing on the summit of Mam Tor with their hands on their hips saying how beautiful the landscapes were. They then put their arms around each other as the camera panned upward unveiling the bucolic vastness of everything. I asked Birch if he was ever not easily influenced and he just shrugged and said: 'What can I say, T-Bear? I'm a sponge.'

I smiled and said: 'You know what Nate's gonna say if we ask him to go camping?'

He deepened his voice and mimicked Nathan. 'That niggas don't do that shit.'

I laughed and nodded. Then I said: 'Oh. That "nigga" is going to cost you. You're down to one letter now.'

'Just pretend I didn't say it,' he said. 'It's just the two of us here. And I was pretending to be Nate anyway. It shouldn't count.'

'No, Birchy,' I said, 'you know the rules.'

21

Over the next few weeks Birch had a nurse who frequently visited him at the flat. She was a Ghanaian woman called Helen who wore glasses and had a short black bob. She'd arrive with her blood pressure monitor and various documents and check his tolerance to his medication. Birch was sluggish during this time. It was as if someone had stuck a syringe in him and extracted the energy from his personality.

Kain had started cooking for him during these weeks too. It was the first time I'd seen Birch not go out of his way to irritate Kain. One morning before I left for work, I'd seen them having breakfast. They were talking and laughing about something. Instead of wondering what they could possibly have to laugh and talk about – outside of Birch's fleeting interest in sports – like I usually would, I just smiled at them and left. That evening Nathan and Bakari visited. *Dreamgirls* was on Film4 and Birch was making them watch it with him and sing the songs, tiredly holding his fist at their mouths like a microphone while DC crawled all over them.

One of the afternoons Helen had come over, when Birch seemed to be getting better, Birch and I sat in the living room with her while she drank a cup of tea I'd made her. 'So Birch, how have you been?' she asked. 'How's the medication been treating you?'

DC was curled up in his lap and he was absently stroking her head. 'Right, Helen,' Birch said. 'I'm mostly fine. But I just wanna know how long my pee is gonna be orange for?' Helen laughed. 'I was on this – what's it called? – Rifampin stuff before, like, five years ago. And my pee was clear as anything. Now it always looks like I'm pissing out Fanta. What's going on?'

She continued to giggle and said: 'Well, that happens sometimes. For all sorts of reasons. You're on a higher dosage now, aren't you? You could have variations in your metabolism, which could be influencing how your body is reacting to the medication. It's really not that uncommon.'

'So there's no reason for him to freak out?' I said. 'It's just if you give him an opportunity to be dramatic, even a little one, he'll take it.'

Birch laughed. 'He's right, Helen,' he said. 'I've been known to dabble in the dramatics.'

'Not at all,' she said. 'No dramatics needed. But if it does persist and you're concerned just let me know and we can re-evaluate your treatment plan.'

She asked him then if there was anything outside of that he wanted to discuss. And he said: 'This cough, Helen. It keeps coming and going. But when it's here it fuckin' hurts. Really does my chest in. And it really sucks because I wanna go camping—'

'You still wanna do that?' I asked. 'Have you told Nate and Kain yet?'

'They've been really nice to me lately,' he said. 'I don't think it will take that much convincing.'

'Right,' I said. 'But don't you think camping is quite a step above them cooking and singing *Dreamgirls* songs with you?'

'Not really, no.'

We looked back at Helen who laughed slightly. 'Birch,' she said, 'I think camping might be a bit ambitious at the moment. I'm really concerned with the pain you're experiencing with your coughs.' She took a sip of tea and looked through a stack of documents beside her. 'Your recent X-ray tests indicate—' She held some of the scans in front of her.

'Well, don't keep us in suspense, Helen,' said Birch.

I gently elbowed him. Then she told us the tuberculosis had left some impact on his respiratory system, that his airways were sensitive, and his treatments needed to be adjusted to manage his symptoms effectively. 'But it's not all doom and gloom—'

'Ah, I knew it,' Birch said, clicking his fingers. 'I knew you were havin' me on, Hel. You've got something special in your little bag, haven't you? Some special medicine. Something to take this cough away. What's it called, eh? I bet it's something dodgy like Rahimzaplin. But—'

I put my hand over his mouth and said: 'Sorry about that, Helen. Please continue.'

She laughed. 'What I was going to say was while I don't recommend a camping trip, at least not for now, there are ways we can work towards it. I know you've been stuck inside quite a bit. Maybe you and Teddy can do things with minimal physical strain—'

'Oh,' he said. 'I've tried, but Teddy doesn't want that kind of relationship with me.'

I widened my eyes. 'Birch, shut up—'

'No,' she said. 'I mean a walk, a picnic, some fresh air. Just to see how your body responds to being out for an extended period of time.' She laughed again and said to me: 'Is he always like this?'

'Well,' I said. 'He's sick right now so it's usually worse.'

'Oh please, T-Bear,' he said, putting his arm around me. 'I'm a gift to you.'

'Cling to your delusions if you wish,' I said. 'But please take this seriously.'

I thought looking after Birch could help delay engaging with my impending job loss in any meaningful way. I kept telling myself I had savings, that I had time, that I had connections to help alleviate the anxiety, that at worst I'd have to move back up to Edinburgh with my parents. But I found that when I came home from work and stepped out of my life and into Birch's, I was bringing with me residual anger that Birch seemingly had no context for.

One afternoon, during one of the weeks of Birch's recovery, I came home and he was sitting at the living-room table, silently looking at DC wiggling around on it. He was surrounded by various bits of shiny fabric and a little glue gun. When I shut the door he looked up at me, startled, and said: 'Oh, hey T-Bear.'

I was about to ask what he was doing. But then I noticed a strong musky odour in the flat. My nostrils flared and then I narrowed my eyes at him. 'Birch, DC stinks,' I said. 'You need to wash her.'

He sighed. 'I can't.'

I made a face and said: 'What do you mean you can't? Look, Birch, just look after her properly, okay? It's not that hard.'

'No,' he said. 'I mean I can't because a bit of her tail's glued to the table.'

'What?' I said. 'How did you manage that?'

'Trust me Ted,' he said. 'I wanna tell you. But you've got

this really annoyed look on your face and I'm scared you're not gonna find it funny.'

'Birch—'

'Okay,' he said. 'Mya's been bringing me little bits of scrap material she isn't using anymore because I've been bored. And she let me borrow one of her glue guns. So I decided to make DC a cute little outfit and now her tail's glued to the table.'

'What?' I said, looking at DC. 'Is she okay?' Then I looked at Birch: 'What the hell do you know about making clothes?'

'Well, nothing obviously,' he said. Then he held his phone up at me. 'That's why I've got a YouTube tutorial up. Do you remember that one Kylie Minogue video where she's jumpin' about in those little gold shorts? I saw it today and I got inspired to make DC a pair—' He flicked his eyes over to two poorly cut squares of shiny gold fabric. 'But look at all this stuff, Ted. It's so fiddly. And you know DC doesn't stay still.'

'Right, okay,' I said. 'But if she's glued to the table why are you just sitting there looking at her?'

He was quiet a moment. He sighed and then moved his eyes over to his left hand. 'Because I'm glued to the table too.'

I rolled my eyes.

'What?' He said. 'I was just waiting for the glue to harden or something so I could just pull us off.'

I looked at the packaging on the glue. 'It's water-soluble,' I said.

'I know—'

'So you just need some warm water.'

'What do you want me to tell you, Ted?' he said. 'It was just me here.'

*

After we unstuck DC, we went into the bathroom. We knelt at the side of the tub and Birch gently placed DC into lukewarm water. He then squirted some salmon oil on his forearm for DC to lick so she would be distracted while he lathered her in water. After the bath he laid a towel in the tub and placed DC in there to dry herself off. He then sat on the edge of the tub and watched her. We were both quiet for a while. It was just the sound of DC going berserk in the tub. Birch was smiling at her. Eventually he turned to me and said: 'Ted, why've you been so snippy tonight?'

I was sitting cross-legged on the floor. I looked up at him. 'Because you glued a ferret to my table?'

'Nah, you're extra snippy,' he said. 'You weren't nearly as snippy when I almost got arrested at Wetherspoons that one time.'

'I thought you told Mya that you just watched a bunch of people on a stag do get arrested.'

'You want me to tell Mya I got arrested while I was looking after Bakari. Are you insane?'

'Did you get arrested or not?'

'Ted, that is not the point,' he said. He looked at me for a second. The he asked if he could show me something. I shrugged like: sure. Then he retrieved his phone and showed me an article. I held it closer to my face. It was about *Rush!* shutting down. After I read the first few sentences I looked back him. Then he said: 'Ted, why didn't you say anything?'

I felt a kind of embarrassment I'd never really felt around Birch before. I couldn't look at his face. And I didn't know what to say. But eventually I said: 'I didn't realise you kept tabs on me like that.'

'I'm not keeping tabs on you,' he said. 'I saw it this morning but I was just waiting for you to say something. When did you find out?'

I sighed. 'Janice told me at the party,' I said. 'We were supposed to be working on an official statement this week. But someone else beat us to it apparently. I was going to say something eventually. But then you got your TB diagnosis—'

'Ah, Ted,' he said. 'Come on. Don't lie to me, man. It wasn't because of the TB. You never tell me shit that's going on with you. And I always feel like I can't ask, and I don't even know why. But I think it's because you think I won't be able to handle it and I'm telling you, Ted, I can.'

'Birch,' I said. 'I appreciate that, but the last thing you need is for me to burden you with my problems.'

'Ted,' he said. 'I can be just as empathetic as you. You just have to give me the chance. Come on – burden me a bit. How are you? You've worked at *Rush!* for what? Ten years?'

'Nine,' I said. 'Basically since I got out of uni. It was my dream job. Not even the senior editor job. But just constantly engaging with music in that capacity. It was really great.'

'So it probably feels like a break-up or something, innit?' he said.

'It does a little, yeah,' I said. 'And it sucks. But it's fine. I have a few months to figure out what I'm going to do.'

He opened his arms. 'Come on, T-Bear,' he said. 'Bring it in. Cry on me. Get me wet. It's fine. We're already in the bathroom.'

I laughed and said: 'I don't need to cry. But I guess I will take the hug.'

As we hugged I thought about how I should've told him that it was because of him that I enjoyed pop music so much. That in the beginning, a lot of the excitement of the job came from writing about music I knew he would've enjoyed too. But instead I just smiled into the base of his neck.

When we pulled ourselves apart, he said: 'Okay, now that we've talked about that, you can help me come up with ways to convince Nathan to go camping with us. I have, like, two different ways we can do it—'

'If either of those ideas include blindfolds or the general concept of kidnapping, I'm not helping you do anything.'

'Oh,' he said. 'Well, then I have nothing.'

22

In September the four of us drove up to the Peak District. The previous day Birch had watched *Tootsie* on Film4 and had got the song 'It Might Be You' by Stephen Bishop stuck in his head, so we had it on in the car. Birch was beside me in the passenger seat and Kain and Nathan were in the back. In the end, much to my and Birch's surprise, it hadn't taken much to convince Nathan to take the trip. Like Birch, he enjoyed the idea of leaving London for a while. Eventually Nathan reached out to the front and said: 'Okay, enough of that shit,' and disconnected my phone. He then turned on the radio. It was on Capital FM and 'We Found Love' by Rihanna and Calvin Harris was playing.

We had left London in the early morning and it was cold and bright by the time we'd arrived in Castleton. As we drove into the village, moving through all those rolling bucolic hills, I kept the brakes on and slowed as flocks of sheep cluttered the narrow road. Eventually we arrived at Rowter Farm Camp site. We were stood in the middle of vast plains of verdant countryside. Birch kept pointing out wildlife and then putting his hands on my shoulders and bouncing up and down like an over-enthusiastic child. We started taking things from the car to our spot. There were only a few other people set up near us. Birch waved at them and they waved back at us, but Kain and Nathan nodded at them awkwardly.

As we were setting up the tents I became irrationally pre-occupied with the whereabouts of Birch's medication. I had to stop myself from asking him if I could just look after it myself. A few weeks ago we'd gone to the hospital and he'd received a negative sputum test, which meant he was no longer contagious.

When the tents were up, I got into one and Kain and Nathan kicked a football back and forth in front of theirs. I was editing some articles for *Rush!*'s final issue. And Birch was walking around the field with his phone in the air trying to find some signal. Mya and Bakari were looking after DC and he wanted to remind them that DC didn't like drinking from a stagnant water source. 'Do you think if I tell Mya DC only likes fresh water she'll let her dehydrate just to spite me?'

For dinner that evening Nathan and I peeled, chopped and boiled some potatoes. Kain and Birch wrapped some pork fillets in tinfoil and placed them on the portable firepit that Kain had built. We then got some blocks of wood from the car boot and piled them on. We all sat around in foldable chairs around the pit. I looked down at the glowing embers, at the flames casting warm flickering light, at the fillets siz-zling. Kain and Nathan were discussing their plans for the handyman business after the council's rejection while they ate. They were talking about offering special rates to small businesses and homeowners and promoting themselves on the internet to try and drive up business. I heard Birch say: 'Oh, you should make little videos about all the work you do in a day and put 'em up on YouTube or something. And do it shirtless.' And they both said: 'Shut up.'

'Oh, come on boys,' Birch said. 'Every time I see a bloke

with his abs out on my phone I always pay attention. Sex sells, innit.'

Nathan laughed and looked at Kain as if he were considering it. Then they both asked him who would want to watch people doing something as mundane as handyman work on the internet. But Birch was still fixated on the shirtless thing. Eventually Kain kissed his teeth and said: 'Nah, allow it. I'm not taking anything off.'

'Fine, bruv,' Nathan said. 'Maybe I'll just do it. Everyone thinks I'm sexier than you anyway.'

Kain made a face. 'Who the fuck says that, blud?'

Nathan clicked his fingers at Birch and said: 'Oi.' And then pointed between himself and Kain. 'Which one?'

Birch threw his hands up. 'Nope,' he said. 'I'm not playing this game with you. You know *exactly* where I stand on this topic, I've got *two* holes for a—'

Nathan threw a bit of his food at him before he could finish the sentence. Then he noticed I hadn't been saying anything and said: 'Ted, you okay, fam?' I looked at him and told him I was. I'd had my food in my lap but I hadn't touched it. Since Birch had come home from the hospital I'd inadvertently masked my afflictions with his. I couldn't seem to outgrow the idea that if I didn't think about something, then that thing simply wasn't happening. And life seemed to take every opportunity it could to remind me of the inherent immaturity rooted in this mentality. It was as if it was punishing me for attempting to manipulate my distress; for daring to think this was no longer a subterranean force shuddering through the very ocean floor of who I was.

I felt like a character in a silent film while everyone else was aglow in loud technicolour. The only thing I could think about in that moment was making my food disappear. The longer it stayed in my lap the more tense my chest felt and the more disengaged I became from everyone. Birch started talking about that cannibal documentary he'd seen in the hospital again. So while Kain and Nathan were telling him how stupid he was, I took a big bite and chewed exaggeratedly and laughed alongside them. I had a little stack of tissues beneath my foil. I unloaded the bit of pork into my palm and then eventually into the tissue. Then I reached down and squashed it into the grass. I didn't look up for a while as they continued to talk to each other.

And then gradually everyone went silent. I looked up. Everyone was looking at me. 'What?' I said.

Nathan asked me again if I was okay and I said, in what I hoped was a relaxed tone of voice, that he'd already asked me that. He then looked at Kain and Birch. Then he sighed, looked back at me and said: 'Ted, bruv, we know you don't eat.'

Nobody said anything. I felt paralysed by his revelation. It was as if I was standing there watching someone force their way into my home and expose every piece of rot, while I silently pleaded that, in spite of this, everything was fine.

'What do you mean?' I said eventually. 'I eat.'

Nathan tutted. 'I just saw you, fam,' he said. 'You just spit your food out and stomped it into the grass like we wouldn't notice. I need you to talk to us 'cause I can't watch you do this shit to yourself anymore.'

'I'm not doing anything to myself,' I said.

'Are you serious, bruv?' said Nathan. 'Do you want me to come over there, pick it up and show you?'

Kain looked at Nathan and said: 'Eh Nate, chill, cuz.'

'Nah, fam,' Nathan said. 'How many times have we been like: we can't do this, we can't do that, we can't go to this place 'cause Ted won't come.' He looked at me fixedly now.

'I don't know, man. It's like you're always tryna make up for something, innit. It's weird, fam. I swear down. You buy shit and give us money, you do shit for Bakari at the drop of a hat—' He pointed at Birch and said: 'You give this fucking freeloader everything he wants. So then it's like: well okay, we can't pry into Ted's business because he's so nice, so generous, so caring. Let's all just mind our own business, innit. But that's not how this shit is supposed to work, you get me? I've tried to talk to you about this before. But you always twist the conversation so you don't have to. But you have to, bruv. You have to. You're collapsing in the club. We can't go out for food without shit gettin' all tense and weird. You always look like someone's told you that the world's about to fucking end.' He paused a moment. 'So what is it? You got one of them eating disorders, innit?' A lump hardened in my throat. My hands were shaking. I couldn't look at anyone. 'I don't wanna sound like a dickhead. But why do you get to care about me, about us? And I have to feel like an idiot when I try and care about you? Is that how it is, yeah? I'm supposed to just not give a shit?'

It went quiet again. In the silence I reran sections of his rant in my head to see if his perceptive reading of me would hurt as much as it did the first time. It did. The idea that every kind thing I'd ever done could've been misconstrued as some kind of fraudulent attempt to draw them to me, while simultaneously keeping them at bay, was particularly hurtful. So much of who I was had existed in a space in which they were everything to me. To have the integrity of this questioned made me want to hate him. The image of him pulling some kind of mask off me and effectively saying: 'Hey look, this is what we've really been in the presence of all this time,' had clouded any genuine concern his speech might've been laced with. But in the end the hatred failed to work its way to the forefront of my emotions.

'I'm so embarrassed,' I said. My voice trembled as I spoke. Tears filled my eyes and I put my face in my hands. I heard Birch say: 'Nate, you stupid bitch, look what you've done.' I didn't hear anyone respond. When I put my hands down I saw Birch approaching me to put his arms around me. He said: 'Let me get those tears for you, T-Bear,' and started rubbing his arms against my cheeks. I laughed and told him to stop because his arms were too hairy. And he replied: 'They're gonna soak up your tears, innit.'

I took his arm off me and looked at everyone. Birch sat cross-legged in front of me. 'I didn't mean to make anyone feel as if I was keeping them at arm's length,' I said. 'But at the same time doing that always made me feel safe and normal, I guess. Feeling like a normal person has always been really important to me. I do have an eating disorder, yes. And I've had issues with food for as long as I can remember, really.'

'Even when we were back in school?' Birch asked.

I nodded at him. 'That's why I was in hospital a lot that one year. I remember being so embarrassed I begged my dad to make up a reason for why I was out of school for so long. I don't even remember what the reason was now.' I paused a moment. 'But as I've got older I've been using this method of obsessively deflecting all my issues. And when you think you've found the cure to appearing normal, especially in front of your friends, I suppose you just cling on to that. Even if it's not particularly healthy and it actively hurts you in the process. All I know is the shame and the embarrassment and it makes me scared and feel disgusting and useless. And why on earth would I want to burden you guys with any of that? I mean, I didn't even want Kain to know—'

Nathan recoiled a little. 'What?' he said. 'Kain knew?'

We all looked at Kain and then he nodded. Then I said: 'He knows but we've never really talked about it.' Nathan asked how Kain could've known but we'd never discussed it and I just shrugged. I wanted to tell them that Kain's silent understanding was something that worked for me. But then I realised where I was emotionally and the conversation I was currently having, and didn't want to give Nathan the opportunity to say something like: 'That doesn't make any sense.' I looked at Kain then and somehow he seemed to get that even now I didn't want him to say anything either.

'Anyway,' Nathan said in a calmer voice now. 'It's actually breaking my heart that you didn't think you could say shit to me. We're supposed to be friends, innit. You said you wanted us to think you were normal. But what does that even mean, bruv? When did "normal" mean you had to pretend you're not dealing with really heavy shit?'

I didn't want to continue this conversation any longer. I smiled tightly at him and told everyone I was tired. I went back to the tent. Nobody followed me.

In the morning we had breakfast. Kain cooked some scrambled eggs on the pit and it was just as awkward as I imagined it would be. They were all quiet and kept stealing glances at me every time I went to eat. I wasn't feeling as loaded as I had the previous night so I laughed and said: 'Please don't make me feel like some kind of circus animal. I really wanna have a nice day today.'

We were walking up Mam Tor that morning. As Kain and Birch went to the car, Nathan fell behind and came up alongside me. He gently elbowed me and said: 'I just wanted to say sorry, innit.' I started to tell him it was fine but he stopped me and continued: 'Nah bruv. I shouldn't have come at you all crazy like that. I just wanted to know what was going on and I didn't know how to do it. You know much I love you, fam. And it was just killing me, innit.'

'It was probably good that it happened anyway,' I said.

'Why?'

'Well, my mum asked me recently if I was fine,' I told him. 'She even asked me not to lie to her when I answered the question. But I did anyway and I said I was fine. She didn't say anything but clearly she didn't believe me. And I guess since then I've been wondering who these lies are even for, really. I'm obviously not convincing anyone. And I suppose even I can see that trying to "convince" people should never have been the point. So I guess it's time to start talking to someone about it.'

He nodded and smiled at me like: good. Then he stopped walking and said: 'Can a brudda get a hug?'

I smiled too. Then he put his arm around me and pulled me close to his side.

When we arrived at Mam Tor the sky was thick with puffy grey clouds, and the land lay below us in a vast expanse of pale-green slopes. Kain and Nathan were in these little hiking shorts and brown worker boots. Birch and I were in sweaters and dark-grey trousers. We walked up the narrow muddy path until we got about halfway up the hill, where we watched the Dark Peak moorlands stretch out into the distance with all its heather fields and rugged peat-covered ridges. Birch asked a hiker passing by if he could take a picture of us by the Mam Tor sign. Birch put his arm around me and made devil horns with his fingers and stuck his tongue out; Nathan and Kain put their arms around each other and threw up peace signs.

As we continued walking up, we saw people paragliding against the murky sky. Birch and Nathan arched their hands around their mouths and yelled 'Go on!' as a few of them landed. When we reached the summit I felt lightheaded and a little nauseous; I could feel some saliva gathering on my tongue. Birch was breathing particularly hard and I asked him if he was okay. And he said: 'Ted, you only get one of those.' We all sat down at the edge of the stone-pitched surface and watched the layers of hills receding into the distance in purple and deep greens. Nathan and Kain leant forward and Birch rested his head on my shoulder.

I exhaled and said: 'It's really beautiful up here.'

After Mam Tor we walked down through farmlands, winding down past rocky outcrops, watching the terrain shift from green pastures to hedgerows as we approached Hope Village. We saw livestock grazing and wildflowers scattered along the edge of the meadows. The air smelt like damp earth as we followed each other through narrow footpaths in small fields, passing under low leafy trees. As we walked through Castleton and up to Winnats Pass, Kain and Nathan started enthusiastically initiating interactions with strangers instead of awkwardly responding. When we walked through the limestone cliffs towards Winnats Pass, Birch decided to become a jukebox and started singing 'Inner Smile' by Texas and tried to get Kain and Nathan to do the 'yeah yeah yeah' parts, which they actually did.

That evening Birch took that day's dose of his medication. We were in our tent lying on our sides facing each other. We were meant to be sleeping but he kept looking at me in this aggressively earnest way with his eyes wide and a little teary.

Eventually I said: 'What's up? Why do you keep looking at me like that?' He just pressed his eyes shut and shook his head. Then I said: 'Birch, don't be annoying. What is it?'

He kept quiet for another moment before he blurted out: 'I just feel really sad for you, okay?'

'Why?'

'I just can't believe you were going through that much shit and you didn't tell anyone.' I smiled then and tried to tell him it was okay but he continued: 'I'm just thinking about all the times we've gone out, all the places we've been to, and I'm just there tralala-ing along like a fuckin' idiot, like all is right with the world and you're just there suffering. I'm so fucking sorry. What kinda friend am I that I couldn't even see what you were going through? I mean, Kain knew? Even Nate cottoned on.'

'Birch, it's okay,' I said. 'Kain only knew because I was throwing up one night and he happened to walk in on me.'

'It doesn't matter,' he said. 'I should've seen something. Why am I so oblivious? Ted, I shit you not, you are literally my whole world. If you're struggling I should be able to tell, even if you don't say anything. Where the hell have I been, man?'

'Birch, listen,' I said. 'If I wanted you to know I would've told you. Until this year, it was just me and my parents that knew. It wasn't something for you to guess or sense. And it doesn't make you any less of a friend for not doing so.'

He sighed. Then he looked away from me thoughtfully. 'You know,' he said, 'sometimes when we're out, like at lunch or something, I'll see you and Kain give each other these weird little looks. I've never really thought about it but like – is that how he knows you're uncomfortable or something?' I paused for a moment. It wasn't something I would've banked on him catching. Not even because of his obliviousness but because I always thought Kain and I were very discreet. Eventually I nodded at him. Then earnestly he said: 'Does that help?'

I smiled. 'It does,' I said. 'It helps loosen the knots my thoughts get into when I'm in that kind of situation. I think what's usually scary is the fact that I don't know how my body will respond when a plate of food is put in front of me. If I'll get some kind of reprieve or if I'll embarrass myself.'

'Well,' he said. 'I'm glad you had someone. Even it wasn't me.' He smiled at me. Then he laid down with his hands behind his head and exhaled loudly. He said if there was anything else I needed to tell him then come on out with it. I laughed, then I told him I loved him and went to sleep.

23

After we got back from the Peak District, I managed to find a psychiatrist online called Matthew. His profile said he used to have a practice in Kent but now he was based in Stratford. I found that a lot of the psychiatrists I was scrolling through used the same keywords to describe their methods. Words like: empathy and understanding. But Matthew used words like 'cultural sensitivity' and 'trauma-informed care'. And the specificity of this approach seemed to quell the apprehension that kept rising within me.

After I booked that initial appointment, I told Kain and he said he would come with me. That afternoon we walked down Belgrave Street to the 339 bus stop. Kain was talking to me while I was reading an email from Monty about the letter we were writing our readers for the final issue of *Rush!*. But as we were about to cross the road, we ran into a little cluster of primary-school children. I felt Kain put his hand on my shoulder and say: 'Eh, Ted. Isn't that Birch?'

I looked up from my phone. Kain was looking at someone in a long hi-vis jacket and hat, standing in the middle of the road with his back to us. He was holding a lollipop stick and gesturing at the children to cross the road.

We could see strands of his curly hair peeking out from

the back of his hat. 'Oh,' I said. 'It is.' I called his name and he turned around. He smiled and waved at us excitedly. We asked him when he started doing this and he motioned to us like: one sec. Then he turned to the string of cars he'd been holding up. When they started beeping at him, he shouted: 'Eh! Calm down! I'm tryna get these bloody kids across the road.' Then he turned to the children and their parents and said: 'Pardon my language, folks,' and they laughed at him. We stood next to him while everyone crossed. Some cars kept beeping at him as they drove on, which made Birch angle the lollipop stick as if he were about to launch it at their cars and yell: 'Beep at me again and this is goin' straight through your window.'

I put my hand over his and said: 'Be careful with that.'

'Oh,' he said. 'Don't worry about it. I'm a professional, man.'

Kain made a face and said: 'You're a lollipop lady now?' Birch nodded at him. 'How long have you been doing this?'

'So this is my first day,' he said. He told us he'd been down to the job centre over the weekend. He said he'd been nervous when the advisor had asked for his CV and he'd told her that he didn't have one. But then she asked him to just go through his employment over the last few years. And he did, detailing the exhaustive list of various jobs he'd had and she helped him make a proper CV. 'Anyway, boys,' he said now, spinning around. 'Look at me. How sick do I look?'

Kain rolled his eyes and then tapped me on the shoulder. He said we needed to go and Birch asked us where. 'I have my first session with the psychiatrist today,' I said.

'That's today?' Birch said. 'Why didn't you remind me? I wanna come. I think I'm done for the day now anyway.'

'What?' Kain said. 'What about that big fucking stick?'

'I'll bring it with me.'

'You can't take that shit on a bus, blud.'

'Says who?' Birch said. He put his arm around me and said: 'Let's go.'

Birch and Kain sat in Stratford Park and waited for me while I went to see Matthew. His office was located on the fifth floor of a tall building, at the end of a long corridor lined with potted plants. When he opened the door he smiled and gestured me inside. He was wearing a black shirt and red checkered trousers. He had a very handsome face with an afro fade and these really expressive dark-brown eyes.

I couldn't place exactly what I was feeling at the time. But something about my demeanour must've suggested a kind of unease because he asked if I was okay as I sat down. I smiled at him a little tensely and said that I was. When he sat down too, he looked at me attentively and then at a clipboard on his lap. He said it was a pleasure to meet me and then asked if I preferred to be addressed as Theodore or Teddy.

'Teddy's fine,' I said.

'Well, Teddy,' he said. 'Thank you for coming in today. I just want you to know that this space is entirely yours, and you can share as much or as little as you feel comfortable with.'

At this, I smiled an involuntary smile that almost came out as a laugh. It made Matthew chuckle and say: 'What's up?'

'It's nothing,' I said. 'It's just – I didn't realise how nice it would feel to hear someone in your position say that to me.'

'Oh yes,' he said. 'I had a really thorough read of the background you provided. And I really appreciate your openness.' In the preliminary emails I'd told Matthew about the first time my dad and I had visited the GP to discuss what we had thought had been my disordered eating. 'I can only imagine how difficult it was to hear that kind of dismissive language the first time you decided to seek help, especially being so young.'

'Yeah, well,' I said. 'It was the early nineties, wasn't it?'

'Maybe so,' he said. 'But I think we can agree you probably deserved to be believed and taken seriously, didn't you?' I nodded at him like: I guess. 'And difficult relationships with food are something that's still so hard to talk about these days. So the fact that you even tried to do that back then, and even had support from your family, is pretty commendable.'

I couldn't disengage myself enough from the shame for his words to land as well as they should've, so I ended up not saying anything and looking at him awkwardly. He asked me then if I wanted to talk him through my experiences with food and I said: 'Honestly, I wouldn't even know where to start.'

'Well, how about we start with what brought you here today?'

I exhaled. 'I guess it started with this camping trip I took with my friends recently ...' I paused. But just before the silence became uncomfortable Matthew asked where we went. 'The Peak District,' I said. 'I basically told them everything there.'

'And what was everything?'

'Everything with food,' I said. 'I always thought I was protecting them by not burdening them with this. And I suppose on some level I knew it wasn't really working. That the walls I was putting up were essentially glass. And that this protection I thought I was giving them was actually creating distance. And me pretending as if I couldn't see it was creating a kind of resentment towards me.'

'And why did you feel like you had to protect them from something you were struggling with?'

I sighed. 'Because who wants to deal with something like this?' I said. 'If I know first-hand how difficult it is to stay above water with this thing tugging at you, trying to pull you beneath the surface, why wouldn't I try and save my friends from having to engage with it?'

He made a curious 'hmm' noise and wrote something down. 'If you're comfortable with it,' he said, 'I'd like to get a picture of what it looks like for you when you engage with food?'

'Well, I find it really difficult to eat in public,' I said. 'Or around other people. It's so bad that I will literally do anything I possibly can to avoid it. If I feel like I'm backed into a corner and being forced to be in that environment, I'll create any illusion I can so no one thinks I'm strange: I'll store food in my cheeks. I'll keep chewed food in my palm or in my pocket. Sometimes it feels as if my body knows I'm attempting to deceive people and starts working against me, so I'll have to excuse myself to the toilet or something and vomit.'

'And this is what you feel you need to protect your friends from?'

I nodded. And then he asked me if I remembered the first time I'd felt discomfort eating in public. I was silent a moment. I thought about my adolescence and then about my childhood. Often I felt so embarrassed by how deeply this illness had permeated my life that I was afraid to venture too close to any sort of root cause.

'I remember this one time in primary school,' I said. 'It was lunchtime. It's been like, what, twenty-something years, and I literally still remember everything on my plate at the time: those little smiley-face potatoes, some fish fingers and beans. The cakes with the white icing and sprinkles. The boy sitting next to me sneezed. It went all over my arm and then on my food. Everyone around the table laughed. And I remember laughing too but also feeling really embarrassed. Obviously I didn't want the food anymore but I was also fine skipping lunch that day. It just made me feel a bit sick – it didn't feel like such a big deal at the time. But everyone called the teacher over and started laughing at the boy and shaming him. The teacher even yelled at him and he started crying. And I felt so awful for him.' I trailed off and went quiet again. I hadn't thought about this in years and the story even felt a little alien coming out my mouth.

Eventually Matthew asked me what happened next and I continued: 'Well, the teacher replaced my food. Exactly how it was. By this time everyone had finished theirs and was in the playground, so she had to sit next to me and watch me eat. And I remember she said: 'You better make sure you eat all of that.' But all I was thinking was: I didn't ask for this. And the longer she looked at me, the more frozen I felt. But I also felt guilty because she really made it a point to let me know that she had gone to a lot of trouble to do this for me. But I just sat there. I think I was closing my eyes really tight, like that would somehow make her and my food disappear. But she became really irritated with me. She kept tutting and rolling her eyes and looking at her watch. At one point she even took my fork, stabbed it into the cake and held it at my lips and said: "For god's sake, it's just a bit of cake. Stop wasting our time. And stop wasting our food. You know there are people in bloody Africa, who look a bit like you, that would love to have a bit of this." And before that I just wanted to be left alone. But now I was looking at that piece of cake thinking if I put that in my mouth I think I'll throw up. But in the end she took my plate and just scraped everything into the disposal bin. She kept shaking her head and saying:

"What a waste. Just remember it's not our fault you're going home hungry today." I even remember her glancing over to the dinner ladies and gesturing at me like: get a load of him.'

Matthew put a hand on his chest and said: 'Oh, Teddy. No wonder that stuck with you. I'm so sorry. I can already see you've experienced a pattern of very dismissive responses in moments where you needed the most validation. I'd be intrigued to know how your relationship with food was before that moment?'

I shrugged and told him I didn't remember. 'At least I don't remember having any violent emotional reactions to food back then,' I said. 'I like to think I was pretty normal. I had foods I liked and foods I didn't, just like anyone else.'

'And these days?' He asked. 'How would you describe your relationship to food? I know you've expressed your aversion to public eating, but how about other moments?'

'It's still really complicated, I think,' I said. 'Even in private, I can't always predict what my body is going to do. And actually a lot of the time it's not even about private versus public. It's all weirdly intertwined—'

'How so?'

I told him about what had happened on my birthday with being unable to eat around my friends, about discarding the cupcakes Janice had given me, about the lunch I'd had with her and Monty and vomiting afterwards, about doing the same thing at my parents' house. I even told him about collapsing at Passage. 'I take these moments with me everywhere,' I said. 'So even when I'm eating by myself, I still feel that sense of embarrassment and failure around me. It doesn't go away, not really.'

'Thank you for sharing that with me, Teddy,' he said. 'I know how difficult it can be to put these things into words.

Right now what's standing out to me is that your experience with food seems quite nuanced. Before we go further, can I ask if you've ever been given a diagnosis? This could be a professional one or just a label you've considered for yourself.'

I looked away from him contemplatively and said: 'I'm pretty sure there's been a lot of misdiagnosing. I've been told quite a few different things. That GP I went to when I was eleven thought I was just suffering from academic pressure and depression. And then when I was about fifteen or sixteen I had to take quite a bit of time off school because I was hospitalised. They said I had gastroparesis. Because of that I went through this whole thing to change my eating habits: smaller meals, liquid nutrition, low-fibre diets, all of that stuff. But even still that whole physiological aspect of everything was still there. Every time I was diagnosed with something new I pretty much took it as gospel, even if deep down I knew it didn't quite fit. And I don't know. From then on I just found my own way to cope. But I guess I would like to know what it is actually is.'

He wrote some more things down. 'I think what's going to be important for our sessions,' he said, 'is that we don't rush to any conclusions or labels—'

'Rush?' I interrupted, laughing. 'It's already been a while, Matthew.'

He laughed too. 'What I'm saying is we'll be working together to try and make sense of your experience without immediately pinning it down. And you said yourself: you've had a few hasty diagnoses over the years. But as we said, this is your space, and if you want I can tell you what I *think* might be going on.'

'I'd like that,' I said.

'Well,' he said, 'it sounds like you're describing behaviour that doesn't fit into one specific category. But still clearly points to significant emotional struggles with food. And this is something that typically falls under what we call EDNOS – which stands for Eating Disorder Not Otherwise Specified. It basically categorises eating disorders that don't fit the exact criteria for bulimia or anorexia but still cause distress. Do you think this resonates at all with your experiences?'

I felt a strange kind of relief. Not so much in the label, but just in the idea that someone had come to this conclusion off the back of things I'd said. Sarcastically I said: 'Matthew, if you're sending me on another wild emotional goose chase, I'm not going to be very happy.'

He laughed and put his hands up. 'I promise you, Teddy,' he said. 'The last thing we want to do is have you out there chasing geese.' He put the lid on his pen. 'But like I said I'd like to learn a bit more about your experiences before we start applying labels. And we can come up with a plan and some concrete goals for you. What do you think?'

I nodded at him. He asked me then how I felt about keeping a food journal. 'Would you be open to giving that a try?' I nodded and asked him what exactly this would entail. 'I think for now we can just keep it simple. Just note down things you eat or drink and maybe a little about where you are emotionally during those times. That kind of thing. And bring it with you to our next session.'

When I left Matthew's office I felt as if parts of my cynicism had been chipped away at. I'd been so apprehensive and even scared to put myself in a position where I could be helped, that my life now felt physically different, as if I was stepping into it for the first time without this shame underpinning it. I thought about how I'd just told someone, in intricate detail, the things that plagued and haunted me. And they had looked at me and essentially said: yes, I believe you and there's a way out, if you're willing to try. It was difficult not to feel as if I'd just been poured out of a bottle and been allowed to spread across a surface and take up space.

Walking back to Stratford Park, where I'd left Birch and Kain, I found them talking to each other. Birch had his lolli-pop stick resting against the bench and I noticed people kept walking by, looking at him in his large fluorescent-green coat, and laughing. Surprisingly neither Kain and Birch seemed irritated with one another. In fact, they looked deep in con-versation. They didn't notice me until I was stood in front of them saying: 'I'm back.' Then they both glanced up at me with these surprised looks on their faces. 'How comes every time I walk in on you two you look like you've just been caught doing something you shouldn't?' I said. 'Do you guys hate each other or not?'

They looked each other conspiratorially. 'Don't worry about it, blud,' Kain said, laughing. 'How did it go?'

I looked at them suspiciously. Then I said: 'It was good. I really like him. I guess it was just nice to talk about this and be taken seriously.'

Kain looked at me with an expression that communicated that he was proud of me. I smiled back. Birch jumped up and hugged me. As he pulled away he said: 'How do you feel now?' He left both hands on my shoulders.

'I feel alright,' I said. 'He said he wanted me to start keep-ing a food journal to document everything I eat.'

'Oh?' Birch said. 'Should I get one too?'

I raised an eyebrow. 'Why?'

'Well, look how long you had to do this on your own,' he said. 'Why would we let you do this part on your own too?

That's insane. And, Ted, I've got a proper job now. I'm nearly on minimum wage. I don't do insane things anymore.' He snapped his fingers and looked at Kain. 'Oi – you. You get one of them journals too. Then Nate can get one and—'

I smiled at him. 'Birch, you don't have to do that.'

'Well, maybe I'll do one for DC anyway,' he said.

I was about to protest but then I said: 'I guess doing a food journal for a ferret does sound like something you'd do anyway.'

He laughed. 'Ah, Teddy Bear,' he said, putting his arm around me. 'You think I'm a pain in the arse now. But I'm gonna show you what annoying really is when you give me the chance to look after you for a change.' He coughed then. It sounded coarse and strained. I asked him if he was okay and he nodded. 'I'm freezing – let's go. I have to catch up with Mya about something.'

'Freezing?' said Kain. 'What are you talking about? It's not that cold, cuz.'

'And you've got that massive coat on,' I said.

He smirked at us. And Kain and I said: 'What?'

I looked at him questioningly for a moment. Then I opened his jacket. He had long red tassels stuck onto his nipples and he was in a pair of leather chaps and red speedos. I quickly closed his jacket and looked around. Then I looked back at him and said: 'Birch, if I said your insanity was worthy of close academic study, do you think that would be a fair assessment of who you are as a person?'

Kain opened Birch's coat again and laughed a squawking laugh I'd never heard from him before. Birch asked us what we thought and I said: 'I can't believe you're making me ask this. But why are you wearing nipple tassels in the middle of Stratford?'

'Why aren't you?' he said. I narrowed my eyes at him. 'Okay. Mya's gonna put me in one of her shows. And this is my outfit. Well, it's more of a prototype; she said she still has work to do on it. Anyway, I'm going to her rehearsals tonight. And I thought I might as well put it on in the morning to save time. Look at my thighs, Ted. Do you know how long it takes to squeeze into these chaps?'

'So much for not doing anything insane,' said Kain.

'There's nothing insane about this,' he said. 'What? I can't have two jobs now?'

24

In late September Nathan and I accompanied Birch to a respiratory centre in Queen Elizabeth Hospital. I had to remove him from my insurance to lower the premium now that I needed to save money. On the way there he'd kept coughing into a strip of toilet roll wrapped around his palm. He'd lost a lot of weight by then, and he'd been experiencing varying degrees of stomach pain in response to his medication. In the hospital room, Nathan and I watched him on the examination bed having a blood pressure cuff fitted round his arm, a small grey clip pinched onto his finger and a stethoscope placed on his back. Eventually Birch looked up at the respiratory therapist and said: 'Anything else you wanna hang off me? I feel like a bloody Christmas tree.' She laughed and then made him breathe into a contraption that looked like a jug with a little vacuum cleaner hose attached to it.

She told him his oxygen levels were low and that the sound of his lungs was concerning. Then she said she would have to adjust his medication again. Before we left, she asked him to schedule a pulmonary function test so we could have a more comprehensive look at the health of his lungs.

Back at the flat Birch was uncharacteristically quiet. He sat on the sofa and idly stroked DC, while he stared blankly into the carpet. Nathan was using my laptop to transfer new bookings for the handyman business, previously kept in a notebook, onto an Excel spreadsheet.

I'd had another appointment with Matthew that afternoon. It was a phone call this time, which I took in my room. I'd been updating him on my food journal task. I was telling him that the newness of the activity and how transparent I could be about it with my friends now was making it bearable. I realised then that I'd never used the words 'bearable' and 'food' in the same sentence before. I told him that I was finding myself eating during moments where I wouldn't ordinarily eat, just so I could have something to write down. 'Is this how it's supposed to work?' I asked. And he laughed and replied: 'Let's try and focus on what's happening rather than how things are supposed to work and go from there.'

After that we discussed various methods we could consider going forward to aid me, like mindful eating, breathing exercises and setting non-food-related goals for myself.

Mya came over later with a selection of clothes in a garment bag. She spoke to Birch about the show they were preparing at Passage, the one they had been rehearsing for. She'd had a change of heart about the outfit she had in mind for him, so she'd brought some different options. 'I don't think nipple tassels and chaps are right,' she said. And he replied: 'You mean I've been squeezing into those things for nothing?' She laid the materials on the floor and talked him through each one.

I felt annoyed listening to them talk about this. I was hoping Birch would say: 'You know what, Mya, look at me – this isn't a good idea.' But instead they laughed at various performance scenarios and talked about song choices. Birch said: 'I wanna dance to that song that goes: let the body groove. You remember that one?'

The frustration I felt seemed to shave itself down to a fine point and twist itself in my chest like a screw. I ended up interrupting and saying: 'You can't be serious?'

'What?' Birch said. 'You don't like that song? I think it's really fun.'

'You're not doing the show.' I said. Then I looked at Mya. 'I'm sorry but you'll have to find someone else. Maybe ask Monty?'

Birch looked at her too. 'Don't listen to him,' he said. 'I'm gonna do it. Ted's just being Ted. I'm fine.'

'You're literally the furthest thing from fine,' I said. 'The last place you need to be is on a stage in a smoky little club.'

Irritated, he placed DC on the floor and said: 'What's the point of all this shit I'm taking? And all these appointments I'm going to. And all this respiratory bollocks I'm doing, if I can't do anything else?'

I made a face. 'So you can get better?'

'And what if I never feel better?' he said. 'And what if I never feel as good as I used to? What – am I just gonna sit around doing fuck all? Just waiting until you give me permission to start living my life again?'

'Why are you making it seem like I'm the one doing this to you?' I said. 'Someone has to care about your health. And if it's not going to be you, then who is it going to be? Mya? Nate? Kain? No. It's me. It's always me.'

'Well, you might find this hard to believe, Teddy,' he said. 'But I'm capable of looking after myself. I did it for ten years without you. And I can do it for ten years more.'

There was a silence. I glared at him. 'Are you fucking joking?'

He was about to argue back. But then he fell into a cough-ing fit, during which he looked up at me with red watery eyes and said: 'You've done this. Getting me all agitated. Wasn't hacking my lungs up before you started having a go at me.' Mya sat by his side on the sofa. She put a hand on his shoulder and rubbed his chest with the other. I told him to stop blaming me for things that weren't my fault. Then I said I was just trying to look out for him. And he replied: 'Well, Ted, it feels like you're trying to control me.'

'Well, maybe you need to be controlled,' I said. 'Maybe you can't be trusted to make smart decisions about quite literally anything.'

Nathan, who had shut the laptop now, said: 'Ted—' And Mya gestured at me with her hands like: calm down. I said I didn't want to hear anything from them. 'You're not the one that has to look after him when he's sick,' I said. 'You don't have to make all those trips to the hospital with him. You're not the one paying to make sure he can get the best treatment he can. You're not the one not only making sure he takes his medication but also the right amount. You're not the ones that has to endure his tantrums. It's not your anxiety that's constantly being flared because he's so reckless. It's like he thinks he's a fucking cartoon character whose life can be reset with just—'

Birch stood up. 'Stop talking about me like I'm not here,' he interjected. 'I'm sorry my existence has been such a burden on you.'

'I'm not saying it's a burden,' I said. 'I'm saying sometimes it's very hard work. You're always doing foolish nonsense. And look where you always end up?'

I teared up though I didn't mean to. I wiped a palm over my eyes. Then we looked at each other for a moment. It was like we'd raced each other, jumping over hurdles, and now we were looking at the space we'd found ourselves in. Neither of us liked this space. But neither of us were willing to leave it.

'Well, T-Bear,' he said. 'It's not my fault you're boring. I don't care where I end up. I care about my experiences—'

'And what about my experiences?' I said. 'Do you think I enjoy watching you and your dismissive attitude towards your deteriorating health?'

He hardened his stare at me. 'Well, you won't have to anymore.' He stood up, briefly glanced around the room and left. Mya looked at me with a frustrated expression and followed him out.

Later that afternoon Mya sent me a text saying Birch was fine. She said they were at Passage having drinks and chatting shit about me. She punctuated the text with a smiley face. I showed Nathan the message and he gave me a shrugging laugh. It both upset and frightened me that no one seemed to care about Birch's health as much as I did. I'd always thought it was common knowledge among us that he masked and deflected his anguish with humour. But it seemed as if Birch had fooled them. They believed in his facade too much.

Nathan and I were on the sofa now. We were watching TV with DC asleep on our laps. Nathan stroked her chin while I slid my fingers across her stomach. We were flicking through the channels and landed on Kiss TV. They were airing a programme that *Rush!* had sponsored a few years ago, showcasing the nation's favourite black British musicians. I remembered pitching it to the network as this big fan-voted event. But in the end our editorial team just ended up choosing whoever they wanted. We watched videos from Estelle, Beverley Knight and Ms Dynamite before we switched over.

When DC started kicking her leg, Nathan turned to me and said: 'I can't believe Birch left her behind. He must be really pissed.' I looked at him and sighed. Then he said: 'Bruv, I've never seen you two argue like that before.'

'It was probably a long time coming.'

He gave me a hesitant look. I raised an eyebrow. 'I mean,' he said, 'sometimes you do baby him.'

I rolled my eyes. 'Oh, stop it,' I said. 'I'm not looking for any opinions about me and Birch—'

'I'm just sayin', innit,' he said. 'Sometimes—'

'Well, don't,' I said. 'I'm serious. You lot will throw around words like "babying" and "controlling" and "enabling" But if I suddenly said: fine. I'm done, and left him to deal with everything himself, you'd call me a bad friend. And I imagine we'd be having this exact same conversation but about how much I don't care and how heartless I am.'

'Fine,' he said. 'Nah you're right. Damn—'

We fell silent for a while. DC stopped kicking her leg and flipped over onto her stomach. Eventually Nathan said: 'Eh, can I ask you something, bruv?' I looked at him like: go on. Then he said: 'Did you know Kain's gay?'

I looked at him curiously. 'Is that what he told you?'

'Yeah,' he said. 'Actually, nah. He said he was bisexual.'

Casually I said: 'Good for him.' He asked again if I knew and then, chuckling, I said: 'I think you know I do or you wouldn't be asking.'

'See, this is what I'm always talking about,' he said. 'Why does no one ever tell me shit? You don't tell me shit. And Kain don't tell me shit. And who the fuck knows what I don't know about Birchy boy. You know, Kain only told me cause we were chillin' and he was on his phone, ignoring me, sending off this long text. So I finally asked who this Hayley gyal was.

Turns out there weren't no fuckin' Hayley gyal. Then he told me what was up. He got all emotional and shit. That lasted for, like, two seconds. Then he said he didn't wanna chat about it anymore. I don't get it, bruv.' He put his hand on my shoulder and shook me. 'Why are all you niggas so secretive? Are we not friends?'

I laughed. 'Nate, I don't know why Kain didn't tell you,' I said. 'But I'm assuming it's because he's really sensitive. And you're the only one out of the four of us that's pretty much a zero on the Kinsey scale. Even though you're friends I guess he just didn't wanna risk you rejecting him somehow, since he probably thought you'd be the only one to have a reason to.'

'But that's not fair,' he said. 'When have I ever been homophobic? That's some stereotyping shit, bruv.'

I raised my hands in defence. 'It's just my hypothesis.'

'So he even told Birch?'

'I don't think so,' I said. 'But that's probably because he doesn't particularly like Birch. But even then I'm not sure how true that is. I have this suspicion that they've had this secret extracurricular relationship that I don't know about.'

'You think Birch could keep that shit to himself?' I tilted my head like: that's true. 'Anyway,' he said, 'so how was this Harley bredrin?'

'He was lovely,' I said. 'Really nice guy. He's a writer too. I'm actually getting him published in the last issue of *Rush!*.' Then I told him that Harley and Kain had had quite a big argument a while ago but now Kain was trying to rectify things.

Slowly Nathan shook his head. 'My bro got his first boyfriend,' he said. 'And I didn't even get to meet him. That ain't it, cuz. That's fucked up.'

February 2006

Nathan stands beside the hospital bed holding Mya's hand after she has given birth to their son. The umbilical cord has been cut and the midwife is cradling the baby in her arms, checking his vital signs.

'You have a healthy baby boy,' she tells them.

Nathan feels his hand pulse even as Mya loosens her grip. Eventually she lets go completely and stretches her arms towards the nurse and says: 'Can I hold him now?'

Mya's face is damp with sweat and tears. When the nurse places the baby in her arms, she exhales hard and smiles, gliding her forefinger gently across his plump little cheek. Immediately she's flooded with this rush of anxiety and happiness. It makes her arms tremble slightly. It's only a slight tremor but still it feels strangely violent, and now she's scared she might hurt him.

She looks up at Nathan and says: 'Look—' And when she guides the baby over to him, she notices this blank look on his face. 'Hey babe,' she says. 'You okay?'

Nathan wants to feel happy, he really does. And on some level he knows that happiness is there. But it's clouded by this feeling of punishment. He feels as if his own life has conspired against him somehow; it's a life – or rather a moment in his life – that he feels unable to settle into. It's like he's been presented with a shape that he'll have to contort himself to fit, bending and sacrificing limbs to squeeze into the mould.

He still doesn't respond to Mya, so she clicks her fingers in front of his face. 'Nate, if you don't take this baby and start smiling, I swear down—'

He shakes his head. 'Sorry,' he says. 'I was just—' He doesn't know how to finish this sentence, so he just stops speaking. He can feel himself actively waiting for something to make sense, anything. Finally, he takes the baby and gazes at his soft face. But before he registers the love, he registers the fear. It sinks into him so deeply that it makes him want to cry. It's like the dark fragility of the world has suddenly clarified itself to him. And in all the spaces where he had once seen safety he now sees all kinds of horrors. He thinks about how much evil is built into the world. And how even though it won't be his baby's fault, his baby will still have to go through it all the same. It would be his own fault actually, he thinks now. He's willingly placed someone in a world that would sooner hate him before it got to know him.

But eventually he does register the love. He slides into the mould without deforming himself. 'Oh my days,' he says to Mya. 'We have a son.'

When Nathan told his parents that Mya was pregnant, his dad slapped him. And his mum sat on the sofa, staring blankly into the distance. His parents were always cordial in Mya's company. But Nathan knew this was only because they had expected the relationship to end; they wanted him to date a Christian woman who didn't pile on makeup and dress up as a man for a career. 'Do you know what people will say?' his mum had said eventually. 'Do you know what they would think?'

He'd told his parents he didn't care what people thought; that they had no bearing on his life and that he loved her. He liked defending Mya. He liked being someone she could seek validation from, someone who wouldn't allow her name to be defiled behind her back. But sometimes he felt his protection of her was performative in a way that genuinely frightened him. Because he knew his own private thoughts were not too dissimilar from his parents'. Would he prefer if Mya were less expressive? Less unconventional? Explicitly, he wouldn't admit the answer to himself. But he knew what he thought.

Still, he was excited by her talent. He was impressed by her craftmanship in all areas of drag. And if he could erase the judgement that came with being with someone who dressed up as the opposite sex, he liked to think he wouldn't be so self-conscious. When Mya told him she was pregnant, he wondered if she might abandon drag altogether. And then he wondered if this might make him feel better; if the idea of all these imaginary people calling him gay behind his back might stop and see how normal his life was now. He felt sickened by this desire for his girlfriend to abandon something that made her happy, just because it made him feel uncomfortable. But pregnancy did no such thing for Mya anyway. She even incorporated the bump into her various acts at Passage. If anything, her sets got more elaborate and dramatic and flamboyant.

Weeks after the pregnancy news, he felt himself oscillating between seemingly every emotion that could realistically exist inside him. He was in love with the idea of having his own family. He just wished the occasion had arrived at a time where he had been more financially stable. Not that he ever really had been. He'd stopped working various jobs at pubs and warehouses and consolidated all his time into one thing: retail. Though he wished it was as a manager and not as a sales assistant.

When Mya had told him to just ask for a promotion, he'd said: 'It's not that easy. It's really cliquey and shit.'

'Then why don't you find another branch?' she'd suggested.

'Another branch?' he'd said. 'Do you know hard it was just to even get this?'

He suspected Mya thought him unambitious and malcontent. And he didn't blame her. His existence had been persistently middling since secondary school; he'd never appeared at the top of anything, not with his grades, not with sports and so on. And his only real ambition in life was to move through it surrounded by friends and family with as little stress as possible

At the hospital now, all of Mya's friends from Passage are sitting in the hallway. They're dressed in dramatic, colourful outfits and talking very loudly. Nathan can hear them discussing something they've read about Britney Spears in the news.

Eventually the nurse allows them in the room. He stands to one side and watches them fawn over the baby. They call him adorable and ask to hold him and enquire about Mya's health. Then they ask if Nathan and Mya have a name.

'We were thinking of Bakari,' Mya says. 'After my dad.'

Nathan looks at Mya and they exchange soft smiles. Neither of them likes their fathers very much. But Mya enjoys the idea of repurposing the love she did, at one time, have for her father and giving it new life with her son.

Mya goes back to talking with her friends. And Nathan

watches them. He realises that, outside of his relationship with Mya, he's lonely. He's very jealous of her in that sense. He even suspects he wouldn't wade so deeply in his insecurities if he'd had friends like he did when he was in school. He would be surrounded by people who might've told him that wishing ill on your girlfriend's aspirations was probably a bad idea.

A few weeks after they bring Bakari home, Mya calls Nathan at work and tells him that an old university friend of hers is coming to visit. He closes his eyes and pinches the bridge of his nose in exhaustion. His parents have recently moved flats to another area of Deptford and have allowed them to stay, in spite of the prior animosity. But Nathan and Mya had been discussing moving out, so for the last few months he's been taking a lot of extra shifts. During these shifts, however, he's been having circular conversations with his colleagues about fatherhood. Initially it was nice to be included in conversations like these, to be found socially intriguing. But all they do now is prod him for cute anecdotes about Bakari that he's relayed time and time again. And he tries to be a good sport about it and perform for them. But he always ends the day exhausted.

On the phone Mya says: 'Babe, I know you've had a long day. But I haven't seen him in so long. And it'll be nice to see an old face again.'

'Fine,' he says. 'But when I get home, it's just gonna be a quick hi and bye ting, innit.'

When he gets home that evening, he hears Mya in conversation with someone in the living room. They're laughing, almost screeching. He walks down the corridor and looks inside. Then his eyes widen. 'Teddy?' he says.

Mya and Teddy are sitting in the middle of the room

surrounded by instruction manuals and disassembled parts of a new crib. Teddy, in his pressed white shirt with the sleeves rolled up to his elbows, jumps up and a bunch of little screws fall off his lap. 'Oh my god,' he says. 'Nate?'

It's been six years since they last saw each other. They look at one another for what feels like a long time. Then Nathan takes off his backpack, walks into the room and hugs him tight. Seeing Teddy like this, in his living room, feels like he's looking through a portal in which he can see another version of himself. A younger version who'd had his life and all its potential opened up before him.

'Wait,' Mya says, 'hold on a minute. How do you two know each other?'

Teddy looks at her now with his arm around Nathan. 'You're going out with Nate?' He says. 'Bakari's dad is Nate?'

'I'm freaking out,' Mya says. 'Someone better start giving me some answers.'

They tell her that they've known each other since secondary school, that they literally haven't seen each other since then, and they used to be very close friends. Nathan asks Teddy if he remembers Kain. And Teddy says: 'Yeah, he's actually renting a room from me now.' And then when Nathan asks about Birch, he sees a strange, resigned look in Teddy's face and he just shrugs and says: 'Oh, I don't know anything about him.'

As they laugh and squeeze each other's shoulders, Nathan looks around the living room and says: 'What's all this stuff?'

'Oh,' Teddy says. 'Mya and I went shopping today. She said you guys needed a new crib for Bakari because of all the splinters in the old one.'

Nathan looks at Mya. 'You told him about the splinters?' Mya doesn't respond and just looks at him sheepishly.

Nathan takes Teddy's hand off of him. 'You really bought this today?'

Excitedly, Teddy says: 'From Harrods.' He picks up one of the wooden pieces and shows Nathan. 'It's made from solid, FSC-certified oak. I don't even know what that means, but it's meant to be really good.'

Nathan asks how much it cost. But Teddy tells him not to worry about it. 'Nah, I'm serious,' Nathan says. 'I'll pay you back, innit.'

Teddy insists that it's fine. 'It wasn't that much,' he says. 'Just a couple hundred.'

Nathan makes a face. He wants to laugh and scream at the same time. 'A couple hundred, bruv?' he says. 'My nigga, what are you doing dropping a couple hundred on a fucking crib?'

Teddy paces back and looks at Mya, who says: 'Nate, he says it's fine—'

'So what the fuck am I doing then?' he yells. Nobody says anything. But the volume of his voice wakes up Bakari and he starts to wail from his old crib. Even as Mya goes to pick Bakari up, Nathan continues to shout about working extra hours and slaving away and breaking his back. He feels so heated that he pounds his fist on the dining table, which makes Bakari cry even louder and Mya shouts: 'Nate, stop it. Keep your voice down.'

'I'm tryna provide and shit,' Nathan goes on. 'And you just go and find someone to buy things I'm supposed to be buying for you. Shit I'm saving up for. What's the fucking point?'

He looks at Teddy now and starts several sentences he doesn't finish. He starts to say: 'You can't just come here and—' and then: 'Do you know how embarrassing it is to—' Then mostly to himself he says: 'I can't do this shit.'

They all stand in silence now. Teddy is staring at him uncomfortably. Mya is gently rocking Bakari back to sleep. Nathan realises Bakari isn't crying anymore. But *he* is. He's sobbing actually. He gradually lowers himself onto his knees with his head in his hands, his back against the wall. He's felt embarrassed before. But this level of it is entirely new to him. It almost feels like it's manifesting physically. The energy of it coursing through his bones. He's radiating it. He wants to make himself so small nobody can sense his existence. He tucks his head in between his knees now.

Eventually he feels two hands land on his back. He looks up and sees Teddy and Mya sitting on either side of him. They give him a gentle but concerned expression and sit there in the silence with him.

25

Birch and I didn't speak for several days after the argument. But it was difficult to feed into the hostility too much because we both could see how manufactured this was. Because we rarely argued, he was clearly enjoying the novelty and theatricality of it all. And admittedly, I was enjoying the performance. Whenever I came into the living room, he would pick up DC and look away, shutting his eyes dramatically, making a childish 'hmm' noise as he proceeded to leave. When I was in the bathroom I could hear him getting on his hands and knees to make the same noise through the little gap beneath the door.

I felt I could entertain this colour of foolishness because there had clearly been a silent admission on his part that I'd been right, and various steps had been taken to prioritise his health over random frivolous escapades. He was actually completing his drug regimen and I kept seeing empty blister packs in the bin. Then another step happened one day, when the four of us were at the tennis courts in Victoria Park. Birch was sitting against the fence, cradling DC and feeding her from a little bag of kibble. And Kain was playing against Nathan and me on the court. It was the first time we'd been there and Birch hadn't been narrating the game with inappropriate sexually explicit commentary.

After the game we all sat with Birch and DC by the fence. He showed us several illustrations on his phone that Mya had sent him. They were of outfits she was planning for him to wear for her show. It had evolved from nipple tassels and chaps to corsets and shoulder pads and elaborate head gear. He looked at all of us and said: 'I've decided not to do it.' I raised my eyebrows in surprise but I didn't say anything. Then dramatically he continued: 'Because of my ailment I don't think it would be right to partake in something so strenuous.' He glanced at me mischievously and I rolled my eyes. Then he looked at Nathan and said: 'I think you should do it.'

Nathan was idly bouncing a tennis ball. He caught it mid-bounce and said: 'What?'

'I said I think you should do it, man,' Birch repeated. 'I'm dropping out last minute because of you know—' He coughed forcibly into his fist. 'And Mya's gonna be looking for a replacement, isn't she? Now, Nate, I know you're not as sexy or as talented as me. And generally I don't think people like you as much as ol' Birchy here. But, still, I think you should do it.'

Nathan laughed. 'I'm not wearing nipple tassels, bruv,' he said. 'Are you dumb?' He looked at Kain and me like: can you believe him? Then Kain and I both gave him shrugging expressions and he said: 'Are you niggas serious?'

'Do it,' Kain said, smiling. 'Why not, innit?'

'Why's it gotta be me?' Nathan said. 'Why can't you do it? Or Ted? Or fucking Monty? Get him to do it. He loves that shit.'

'Oh, don't worry,' said Birch. 'Monty's gonna be there too. He's gonna be a little Weekend Piggie.'

'What the fuck is a Weekend Piggie?'

I explained what it was, about the nudity and the riding crop. Nathan exhaled hard and said: 'Nah. Miss me with that.'

'Oh, c'mon Nate,' Birch said. 'You've been such a dick to your girlfriend.'

'What, bruv?'

'Yeah,' Birch said, 'she told us all about you being a little bitch about her costumes and stuff. And you gotta put it right, man. Get those fuckin' nips out. Show her you love her. Show her you're not embarrassed.'

Immediately Nathan furrowed his eyebrows. 'Embarrassed?' he said.

'Yeah,' Birch said. 'She thinks you're embarrassed of her and what she does.'

At this, I thought Nathan would get irritated and maybe say he couldn't believe Mya had spoken this candidly about their relationship, and to Birch of all people. Even though this was something she did often. But instead he looked at us with this wounded, sincere expression and said: 'Shit. She said that?' Birch and I exchanged a brief look and nodded at him. 'I ain't embarrassed, I just—' he started to say. Then he said: 'You know what, fine. Fuck it. I'll do it. But Birch, I swear down, cuz. If this is just an excuse so you can see me naked—'

'Oh, Nate,' said Birch sarcastically, 'you crafty little handyman. You got me.'

Over the next few weeks Nathan came over to the flat almost every evening. Birch would sit in the living room with DC cradled in his lap, guiding Nathan through numerous routines and playing music from his phone. Sometimes, after work, I'd join them and pretend to be an audience member and cheer at him. It felt as if this new piece of Nathan was being unfolded for me. He exhibited the kind of infectious enthusiasm I'd only ever really experienced through interactions with Birch and my dad. Watching him dance and sing, I felt a compounded sense of happiness and excitement for him.

Even though Birch was still being playfully stubborn about letting our relationship revert to normal, it was still a precious few weeks. It was like we'd been insulated in this bubble that rejected our various adversities, all our illnesses, depressing job situations and so on. And encouraged us to take refuge in each other's company and sustain ourselves with laughter. I liked coming home and seeing Birch pumping his fist in the air at Nathan and yelling things like: 'More thrusting!' It was like a scene out of *The Full Monty*. When we told Mya that Nathan would be taking Birch's place in her show, she asked us what we were threatening him with. And when we said: no, he's doing it of his own accord, she looked bewildered, like there had been a door in their relationship that had until this very moment remained unopened, and now Nathan had finally taken a step inside, glanced around and nodded appreciatively at the interior.

On the night of the show Kain, Birch and I were backstage at Passage with Nathan and Mya. Mya had several pins in her mouth, adjusting Nathan's costume. He was in the leather chaps Birch had worn, only now Mya had altered them to feature long fringes down the sides. And now the crotch tore away to reveal Nathan in Union Jack underwear with Birch's name stitched across the back. Birch had expressed remorse in withdrawing from the show so Mya had suggested this to keep him involved somehow.

'I can't believe I'm fucking doing this,' Nathan said. 'I'm gonna look like a dickhead—'

'Nah, you've got this, bro,' Kain said, holding his fist out to him. But Nathan just looked at the fist and closed his eyes in frustration.

Birch put his hand on Nathan's shoulder and said: 'And so what if you look like a dickhead? You look like a dickhead most of the time and no one has a problem with it.'

Nathan opened his eyes and said: 'Fuck you.'

'There we go,' Birch said. 'Use that anger, my friend. Let it fuel you.'

I took Birch's hand off him and replaced it with mine. I smiled at him. 'You're gonna be great.'

Afterwards, Kain went to the bar and I stood by the stage. At one point a hand landed on my shoulder. It was Birch. He smiled at me and said: 'I'm so glad we're friends again, T-Bear.'

I made a face. 'Are we?'

'Yeah,' he said. 'And in good time too because, when the wounds were still fresh, I thought about torching your flat.'

'Excuse me?'

'Yeah, with both of us inside,' he said. 'But then I thought: no, Birch, don't do that. You're not a kid anymore. You'll get tried as an adult. And then you'll get sent to prison. And obviously I haven't read any updated legislature on whether ferrets are allowed in prison with you as travel companions.' I stared at him blankly for a long time. 'What?' he continued. 'You said all I do is foolish nonsense, so I thought what's more foolish than the charred remains of our bodies, lying side by side among the blackened rubble of the home we've shared for the last five years?'

After another pause I said: 'Do you think insanity is something they can test for these days?'

'I don't know why you're talking about testing me for

insanity,' he said. 'When you should be praising me for push-ing back on the voices that told me to kill us.'

Flatly I said: 'The voices told you to kill us?'

'And I didn't,' he said. 'Because you're my best friend. And I love you. Let's hug.'

'You know what,' I said, 'I'm just going to interpret all of that as Birch for: I'm sorry.'

'I mean, that's basically what I'm saying, Teddy Bear,' he said. 'Am I not being clear?'

In the end, we ended up not seeing very much of Nathan's performance. Birch kept coughing and clutching at his chest while insisting he was fine. Eventually the lights dimmed. When they came on again, Nathan walked onto the stage while 'Body Groove' by Architechs was playing. Other addi-tions to his costume were: a white cowboy hat, a Union Jack handkerchief wrapped around the bottom half of his face, and a corset that accentuated his pecs. Then as everyone cheered, Birch hacked up another cough that splattered bits of blood all over his hand. I looked at him. Then he looked back at me with this quiet helpless expression. Even under all the kaleidoscopic lighting, I could see reddened saliva around his mouth.

We went into the toilets. I told him I'd call Helen and ask about having his medication adjusted again. He didn't reply. He just clenched the edge of the basin and looked at his reflec-tion in the mirror. His eyes were red and watery. I watched him breathing slowly in the silence.

'Are you okay?' I asked.

Curtly he replied: 'Yeah. Of course.'

He turned on the tap and held his lips near the stream of water. He filled his mouth repeatedly and I watched him spit the water back out until it ran clear. Eventually the tears in his eyes started to fall. But then he looked at me and insisted he wasn't crying. 'Sometimes the coughs take a bit more effort to get out, that's all,' he said. 'But I don't wanna go on about it.' I asked him if he'd heard what I'd just said about Helen and his medicine and he gestured dismissively at me and said: 'Yeah, yeah—'

We could hear everyone cheering outside. I said it sounded like Nathan was doing a good job. But Birch just smiled and looked back into the mirror. We stood there for a while. People came in and glanced at us curiously. Some even asked if he was okay but Birch ignored them, and I nodded at them like: no, yeah, we're fine. His expression was so forlorn and introspective; it looked like he was trying to understand something about his life in that moment.

Eventually, almost as if nothing had happened, he looked at me and asked if I was feeling hungry because he was, suddenly. Then his eyes widened and he slid his hand into his pocket. He retrieved a crumpled-up piece of paper and showed it to me. It had his name on one side, DC on the other and a list of various foods underneath. 'What's this?' I asked.

'What do you mean: what's this?' he said. 'It's my food thingy. Well mine and DC's food's thingy.'

'You mean a food journal?'

'Yeah,' he said. 'Remember? I said I'd do it. In solidarity with you? I would've told you I'd started it but you were being really mean and controlling.' I pursed my lips and lifted an eyebrow and begrudgingly he continued: 'And I was being stubborn and didn't wanna talk to you.'

I rolled my eyes and took the paper from him. I scanned the list and eventually saw that he'd written down: Rifampin.

I looked at him and said: 'You put your medication on here?' He nodded. 'It's supposed to be a food journal.'

'Look, T-Bear,' he said. 'If it's going in my gob then it's food, alright? And anyway, look at me—' He stretched out his arm. 'There's not much of me left. If I didn't write down the pills, my side would be blank. I've had more capsules than grub these days. Even DC's had more meat in her than me.' I knew he wanted me to laugh at that, so I just stared at him. He stared back at me. Then eventually he put his fingers at the corners of my lips and pushed them upward repeatedly. 'There we go,' he said. 'That's better. That's what we like to see.'

I laughed and shook his hands off me.

September 1997

Birch is late home. He got detention again for being involved in yet another school fight, this time with another group of kids who seem to terrorise other kids without consequence. Ever since Luke Williams left for a grammar school in Kent a few months ago, he seems to have been replaced with students desperate to emulate him.

As Birch has got older, the fights have become more violent. These days he finds there's nothing to deter him from fighting anymore. He feels it's far too late to establish a reputation as a smart and studious person, so Mr McAllister's threats to his education and warnings about his future have lost their sting. His perception of good and bad has become so warped that he feels sorry for his younger, naive self who had shaped his morality through repeated viewings of the *Karate Kid* series.

His house is unusually quiet that evening. He can faintly hear the radio from the kitchen. 'You Might Need Somebody' by Shola Ama is playing.

'Hello?' he says when he's inside. 'Anyone home?'

He drops his bag and walks through to the kitchen where he finds his mother cowering on the floor. She is wearing a nightie, which is soaked in patches with blood. She has covered one eye with her hand, while the other eye has blackened.

'Mum!' he yells. His vision is swimming so profoundly he has to actively steady himself to absorb the situation. His mother doesn't say anything and refuses to look at him.

He begs her to tell him what's happened but she remains quiet. But he knows. He always knows. Once his mother had been crying as she prepared his breakfast. He wanted to ask why, even though he'd heard his stepdad Alan hit her repeatedly during the night. And another time he had been stood beside her in the kitchen as she was making this hummus recipe she liked. Alan had been yelling at her obnoxiously from the living room. But she continued submerging chickpeas in water, pretending it wasn't happening as her hands trembled. In any case, his relationship with his mother seems to collapse whenever he draws attention to the cruelty. And she gets very agitated with him, as if he has been the specific cause of her despair. So at some point, he decided that he too would try and prioritise the parts of their relationship that were pure over the abuse. If she could live not putting words to it, then perhaps he could too.

He hears Alan before he sees him. His footsteps thump against their wooden steps and then on the carpet through the corridor. Now Alan's resting against the kitchen door with an expression Birch can't quite decipher. It's a sort of mocking smile, or maybe a celebratory one, marvelling at his mother writhing on the floor. Birch is unfamiliar with the immediate aftermath of moments like these. He is usually only privy to these moments audibly, from the confines of his bedroom. Sometimes he imagines that Alan might be apologetic; that the blind rage dissipates and from beneath emerges a very sorry man. But looking at him now, all he can see is malice.

When Alan finally steps into the kitchen, Birch lunges at him. He hangs off Alan's large frame and starts punching him hard in the side of his head, while his mother screams in the background. His body is pulsing with adrenaline. His life feels so purposeful in this moment, so driven. Aside from Alan, no one has ever told Birch explicitly that he will never amount to much, but he can feel the sentiment in the air all the same, as if it's simply common knowledge. He finds that he's continuously grabbing for an easy sense of accomplishment, and that accomplishment comes the easiest when he fights.

He realises then that he has never punched anyone as hard or as fast or for as long. He used to view himself as a sort of comic-book hero, especially during the fights at school. He thought of himself as someone who could smile and make quirky little quips while he stomped out a perceived evil. He likes this aspect of his personality. But it's becoming harder to measure warmth and violence in equal parts and he feels that warmer side of himself slipping away.

Alan rubs at his at his face, sucking air through his gritted teeth. But then he laughs and knocks Birch onto the floor. Birch looks at his mother.

'Mum, let's go,' he says to her. 'It doesn't matter where. Let's just leave.'

But she still doesn't say anything, and now his stepdad has crouched beside them. Birch looks at Alan's knuckles and he can see they've reddened from where he's hit her so hard. Birch starts yanking at his mother's arm, trying to lift her off the floor, but she doesn't budge. In fact, she resists and shakes her arm loose.

Alan looks at his mother and laughs and then says: 'Right then, babe. I'm gonna give you a choice here. Cause I know that deep down you're a smart bird, aren't you?' He points at Birch but keeps his focus on her. 'I want that little runt outta here. It's me or him, love.'

Birch feels something collapse within him. He looks up at Alan with a teary, confused expression. He knows Alan has never liked him, not really. At the very least, Alan has been dismissive of him and has gone on to acknowledge his presence less and less. In the beginning, Birch had tried for his mother's sake. He tried to spark some kind of camaraderie through the shows Alan enjoyed, his football team, his music. And Alan often waved him away as if he were a persistent dog.

'Now, babe, don't piss me off,' Alan says now. 'Shouldn't even be a discussion, really. This is my house. And if you still want a roof over your fuckin' head I suggest you kick that lump out.'

There's a long silence then. His mother finally looks at him. 'Birchy, it's fine,' she says. 'You'll be fine.'

He tilts his head back. He feels as if he's viewing the world through dark, inverted colours, wading through the rubble with tape, uselessly trying to bandage the destruction back together. He can't bring himself to speak, but eventually he manages to say: 'Mum, how is this fine?'

She touches his face and tells him once again that everything is going to be okay. His tears start to fall then.

Alan grins at him. 'Well, there's your answer, mate,' he says. 'Even your old lady don't want you around. Now if you wanna do us all a favour and fuck off, that'd be lovely.'

Alan now forcibly ushers Birch out of the kitchen, gripping Birch's shoulders and Birch starts to shout and beg: 'Mum, please,' he says, 'I'm sorry. I won't get into fights anymore, I'll be good I promise. I'll change.'

But Alan has already brought him to the front door. He's still yelling for his mother, but she's now out of view.

Alan puts his hand on Birch's shoulder now and hangs his face directly in front of his. 'Look mate,' he says. 'I love your mum. And I've got a bloody good thing going here. I see a real future with me and her. And I'm gonna start treatin' her right, don't you worry. Today was just a bit of a blip, you know. Sometimes you just can't help yourself, can you? Some bird gets in your face and you just have to—' He makes a swift backhand motion with his hand. 'But yeah. We've had a chat and we're gonna start a proper family. A nice clean slate. And no offence, mate, you're just gettin' in the way, aren't you?'

Birch glares at him. He wants to hit Alan again but he knows Alan cares so little for his life that there's a chance that he'll fight back and hurt him worse than Birch could ever hurt him; maybe even kill him. He wonders then if even the threat of his death could trigger his mother into defending him.

'You're fifteen now or whatever,' Alan says. 'You're old enough to be on your own. Or you will be in a year or two – so why not get started early, eh? School ain't doin' you no good, is it? Gettin' in all those fights. And you're not learnin' much in that thick little head of yours, so go out and see the big wide world. If anything, it's an opportunity. Spread your wings.' Alan reaches into his pocket. 'And you know what, mate. Just so there's no bad blood, I'll even give you a tenner to get you started.'

Alan winks at him and waves the note in Birch's face. Birch looks back at him, silent.

That year in school, Nathan and Kain spent most of their time hanging out with the guys on their sports team, so eventually Birch stopped turning up to their matches or watching them play during break times. It had been more fun to do that with Teddy anyway. But since Teddy had been out of school for a while due to an unspecified illness, Birch had been on his own. He had been spending his lunch on the field watching squirrels climb trees and chase each other. He even started collecting acorns and cramming them into his pockets for no particular reason.

Where he used to impede his education by disrupting lessons with jokes, recently he'd been withdrawn and quiet. This shift in behaviour had been so jarring that it became a distraction in itself. Whenever a teacher asked if he was okay, he would just cross his arms and scowl. More recently he had a row with his English teacher, Mrs Clark, because she had asked a question and everyone had put their hand up apart from him. When she said to him: 'Don't you wanna give it a go?' And he'd replied: 'Does it look like I've got my fucking hand up? Why are you always picking on me?' He was sent to detention.

He used to spent a lot of time at Teddy's house so he didn't have to go home. But when he'd been over now no one would answer the door. The last he spoke to Teddy's father, it had been brief and curt.

He'd turned up at their house unannounced one Saturday morning. When Theodore opened the door, Birch had smiled and said: 'Is T-Bear in?'

And Theodore had replied: 'This isn't a good time.' And slowly closed the door. And that was that.

He felt divided then. On the one hand, he didn't know what was wrong with Teddy and at least wanted the opportunity to be there for him. But on the other he couldn't help but feel abandoned by both Teddy and his father. And he'd felt angry and embarrassed that he'd once considered Theodore

as a sort of surrogate father. Eventually he settled, very resolutely, into the anger and began to hate them a little bit. And
he started to wonder why people always found it so easy to
discard him; why his entire life seemed to be plagued with
this insidious idea that he didn't matter. If there had been
something inherently wrong with him, why hadn't he been
allowed a chance at redemption? But then, he thought, maybe
some people were irreparably bad. And he was one of those
people. How much more evidence did he need?

Life had been trying to tell him something for a very long
time and now, at last, he was ready to listen: he was something to escape.

He may not have known why, but he knew it was true.

Now he's standing outside his house. Alan wouldn't let him
get any of his things, instead he has indiscriminately picked
things from Birch's room and stuffed them into an old shopping bag and handed it to him.

Even as Alan closes the door for a final time Birch hopes
his mother will suddenly appear in his defence and leave
with him, that she'll apologise and hold him and say something like: this house doesn't matter, home is wherever we
are. Because she said something to that effect when he was
younger, when his father had left and he had cried in her
arms. But no one comes for him.

He doesn't cry for long this time. And he knows there's
no use in begging, so he turns around and looks across the
street, at the terraced houses, at the line-up of parked cars,
at the plane trees. He doesn't know what he's going to do or
what is going to happen to him.

But despite the fear, somehow he feels like the path to
the rest of his life has unfolded in all directions in front of

him. And all he needs to do is take a step towards that blank canvas, in the hopes that eventually whatever deity has deemed him worthless will forgive him.

26

During our last week in the *Rush!* office, Monty brought in a box of some of his old CDs he wanted to get rid of. He placed them on an empty desk in the middle of the office floor. I was in my office drafting an email to Harley, telling him the article he'd written would be featured in our final issue. He had reviewed the Weeknd's *Trilogy* compilation, which was being released next month. I'd also asked him to do some research and draft an obituary so he could have another byline for his portfolio. It was for a famous record-label exec called Julian Blackwell, who had been responsible for launching several bands at the beginning of the previous decade.

Eventually I went out and looked through the box. It was nearly empty. I retrieved an album by Liberty X called *Thinking It Over* and said to Monty: 'Are you sure you're not gay?' And he laughed and said: 'Fuck off, mate. Have you heard that title track? It's a banger.' Then he preceded to sing a portion of it.

'I'm sorry,' I said. 'I've had a lifetime of people making assumptions about me. I just wanted to know what it felt like.' He chuckled and then I continued looking and came across a Peter Cetera album.

'Ah yes,' Monty said. 'My old man was a big Chicago fan.'

I told him I wasn't a Chicago fan. But that Birch would abso-lutely love this.

As we left the building Monty told me that he'd joined a new band. He said he was only filling in because the previ-ous drummer had just had a kid. 'But I hope it turns out to be permanent,' he said. 'I think I really love these guys. We really click, you know. We're all into the same stuff.'

'They're really into Cleopatra too?'

'Oi,' he said. 'Told you that in confidence, mate.' We laughed. 'Nah. They're all rock heads. Anyway, after I'm done with this place, we've got quite a few gigs lined up all up and down the country. Gonna be back in my element.'

I smiled at him. 'So safe to say you're doing alright these days then?'

'Yeah, mate,' he said. 'I'm doin' alright.'

Outside it was raining and the sky was a dark leaden grey. I took out my umbrella and he joined me beneath it as we walked to the end of the road. 'So what about you then?' he said. 'You know what you're gonna do yet?'

'I don't know,' I said. 'But I'm sure I'll figure it out.'

When I got home that evening I gave Birch the Peter Cetera album. He was sitting on the sofa under a blanket watching the TV. He didn't say anything, he just held it in his hands and smiled at it. He looked like he might cry. With the blanket still wrapped around him, he got up and placed the disc in the stereo. When he walked back to me I noticed a gauntness in his face that frightened me slightly. He switched off the light. Then 'Glory of Love' started to play.

I felt him smile at me and put his hands on my shoulders. I asked him what he was doing, he just said: 'Dance with me.'

'What?'

He exhaled. 'Just dance with me, man.'

I didn't move. He then wrapped his arms around me. He nestled his head into my neck and started to sway. I kept my arms by my side, looking confused. But then he picked up my arms for me and placed them on his waist. 'There we go, T-Bear,' he said.

We were both quiet for a while. DC was energetically circling our feet and pawing at our shins. Eventually I asked Birch why we were dancing in the dark to Peter Cetera. I felt him inhale and then he said: 'I love this song so much, Ted.' He sounded a little wistful and distant. He held me a little tighter and then I placed my head by his neck too. He told me then that when he was living with Lucy and Charlie, the song had come on MTV Classic and that he'd taken Whitey and Choc-Ice out of their play area and glided around the living room with them.

'Yeah,' I said. 'That does sound like something you'd do.'

He sighed very hard. 'They were so happy with me,' he said. 'I could tell. They were rescue ferrets, you know. Lucy and Charlie wanted another pet. They wanted to go to a breeder. But then one day I saw Whitey and Choc-Ice at a rescue centre. And I knew I had to convince them not to get another dog or something. And to get these two ferrets instead. And, you know, it felt nice to do the saving for once.'

'The saving?'

'You know, man,' he said. 'Like you did for me.' I shook my head at him like: stop it. He sensed this motion in the dark and said: 'No, T-Bear. Let me say it. I really need to. You brought me into your home and you looked after me and made me feel like a human again. I know I can be a lot. But you're constantly saving and forgiving me. You really, really love me and I feel it every day. For as long as I've known you,

you've treated me like your brother or son or something. You keep choosing me, Teddy. And that's the thing, isn't it? You choose me every single time. Even my own parents didn't do that. I've had people tell me to my face that there was nothing about me worth caring about. I've literally been left for dead in the middle of the street. And I always thought I deserved it because I've never really had a reason to believe otherwise. But then you come along. You're like the superhero I was trying to be when we were kids. You always fight my corner, even when I'm being a twat or whatever. Teddy, I swear there is literally no one else in this world that makes me feel like I matter as much as you do.' He stopped talking for a moment and I felt him breathe. 'I guess what I'm saying is: I've always thought it would be nice to save something. And it is, man. It really is.'

I closed my eyes. I thought if I did this I could keep myself from crying but my face was already wet. I wiped my cheeks. I didn't know what to say. But before I could even think of anything, he coughed really violently. He apologised in a throaty, exhausted voice and I told him not to worry about it.

I made him some tea. We were lying on the sofa now and I had my arm around him. I kept gently threading strands of his hair through my fingers. We laid in the silence for a while. I couldn't stop thinking about what he'd said about me saving him. I was curious if he knew that he'd done that for me too.

'Birch,' I said eventually, 'you talk about me saving you, like you've never done the same for me.'

'Stop it, man,' he said. 'You don't have to say that. I've never done anything like that for you.'

I laughed. 'Of course you have.'

'You're only saying that because I'm sick.'

'No, I'm only saying it because it's true,' I said. 'Do you remember the first time we met?'

He went quiet then. I shook him as if to say: I can't believe you don't remember. Then he coughed and laughed and said: 'Give me a second. It was in detention, wasn't it? Mr McAllister's little club. What did he call it? His bad boys club or something.'

'Yeah,' I said. 'You and Nathan were arm-wrestling for sweets. And you kept going on about the *Karate Kid* and beating up Luke Williams and his friends.'

'Oh, that prick,' he said. 'I wonder what he's up to. You think he's still a prick?'

'I don't know,' I said. 'Probably. But anyway, I guess you didn't realise it, but you were so warm and welcoming and you didn't even know me. And at the time, I didn't even know you could make friends that way, that a stranger could just look at you and say: yeah, I like you. And that was that.'

'What?' he said. 'I saved you because I was nice to you? That's not the same, Ted. I didn't even do anything.'

I smiled. 'You did everything,' I said. 'I desperately needed something at that time in my life and you gave it to me. Now tell me, how is that any different from what I did for you?'

He smiled at me. Then he exhaled and closed his eyes. I was still running my fingers through his hair. I told him then that we could call Helen in the morning and schedule an appointment and get his medication adjusted again. And I felt him nod gently.

I couldn't sleep. I spent most of the night watching him. I kept thinking about our life together, and how there had been nothing perfect or even normal about it. But yet I'd found so much solace in our relationship. Every iteration of him made

me smile: his loud moments, his quiet moments; his belliger-
ent and irritating moments; his honest and sincere moments.
He brought such clarity to the very idea of love for me. He
made love make sense to me. He made it uncomplicated. He
made it accessible in a way in which I knew, after all these
years, I would still never be able to explain to him.

I woke up in the afternoon with soft rays of sunlight fil-
tering through the windows. Birch had fallen asleep on me.
I pulled myself from underneath him and stood up. I looked
at him; he was very still. I stretched, got up and went into the
kitchen. I asked him if he wanted breakfast or anything, as if
that would rouse him from his stillness. But he didn't reply.

I opened the fridge and said: 'I suppose I could fry up
some eggs and bacon. But the bacon is Kain's so I'll have to
replace that. I think the eggs are his too actually.' Birch still
didn't respond. 'Actually, just don't tell him. If you do I'll tell
him you're the one that keeps taking his Babybels. He keeps
thinking he's eaten one already when he hasn't. Honestly, I
don't know what's with you and cheese but—'

I looked at him on the sofa and walked back. For a moment
I wondered if he was playing a prank on me. It's something
he would've done.

'What are you doing?' I asked. 'Wake up.' I put my hand on
his stomach and shook him a little. 'Birch, wake up.'

Confused and frustrated expressions appeared on my face.
'This isn't funny,' I said. 'Stop messing around. Wake up.'

I shook him harder. I started to feel angry because tears
were forming in my eyes and gliding down my face. It was
as if my body had accepted something that my mind had not.

'Birch, please,' I pleaded. 'Wake up.'

A fiery panicked sensation tightened itself in my chest and
I felt as if I couldn't breathe. I was taking breaths faster than

I could speak. And in the panic, I felt so disappointed that I couldn't beg him to stay.

I rested the back of my hand against his face. 'Please,' I whispered desperately. 'Please – just wake up.'

It suddenly felt as if we'd been holding hands, running down this long hallway that had been so bright and vibrant with a party of colours. But somewhere along the way he had let go of my hand. And I'd been stood there trying to understand why. The further he got away from me, the more colour he took with him, stripping the walls, the floors, the ceilings, until he had disappeared so far down the way I could no longer see him. And then there was just me, standing alone, amid all this white space, trying to understand what had just happened.

But of course what had happened was very simple. He was gone. And the party was over.

November 2007

Bank station is closed, so after work Teddy walks to Fenchurch Street instead and boards a train for Limehouse. It's such a blisteringly cold day that he can see his breath waft through the air as he moves through the city.

On the train, he walks through to the first carriage and sits by himself in a section with six seats. Beside him there's a group of teenagers. One of them is playing the song 'Heartbroken' by T2 and Jodie Aysha very loudly. He has a headache, which has only grown more pronounced through-out the day, so he rests his head on the window as the train rattles along the tracks and he idly reads the graffiti etched into the glass, pretending he can't hear anything.

Moments before the train pulls into Limehouse, a foul odour fills the area, making his nose twitch. He looks up and sees a gaunt figure walking down from the other end of the carriage. The person has long brown hair, cinched by a dirty woolly hat, tracksuit bottoms that are too short and a green cardigan with holes all through the material. They walk through the gangway holding little bits of paper, mumbling things to passengers who forcibly bury their heads into their newspapers or press their noses behind their palms. They are continuously met with silence and promptly move on.

Teddy has no intention of reading what's written on their paper, but he readies a few coins to drop into their palm. When they finally appear beside him, the smell gets so intense that it makes Teddy squint. Their hands are shaking as they clutch two packets of tissues. Teddy looks up at them briefly before glancing back out the window. He can hear the teenagers laughing in the background. They've paused the music to shout profanities at this person.

'I'm supposed to leave these on the seats,' the person says weakly. 'But there were too many people on the train when I got on.'

Teddy's ears prick up and he looks back up at them intently. They have a very skeletal face and sad, dark eyes. It takes several tries before he can even speak. 'Birch?' he says eventually.

Birch jolts at the sound of his name. 'Oh my god,' he says, softly at first. But then his eyes brighten and he shouts: 'Oh my god, Teddy!'

Teddy wants to speak but he can't. He drops the coins onto the carriage floor and feels a wave of paralysis sweep over him. He's finding it difficult to reconcile this dishevelled man with the boy he'd known from school. This is the first time he's seen Birch in ten years and he's trying hard not to cry. But he knows he eventually will.

They get off at Limehouse and sit on a bench on the platform, beside a poster advertising a forthcoming Spice Girls reunion tour. They look at each other in silence for a moment. Teddy tries to keep calm, to not start weeping or yelling in frustration – not at Birch, but at the situation, at life, at what had happened to him to lead him here, like this.

Teddy looks down at the pack of tissues and the little note

in Birch's hand now. And then back up at Birch's face. He has a streak of spit slowly dripping down the side of his cheek, which Teddy points at in confusion.

'Oh,' Birch says, with a look of embarrassment, wiping at it with the sleeve of his cardigan. 'Some people don't like to be bothered in the afternoon. Or any time of day really.'

Teddy takes a tissue out of the packet and wipes the spit away properly. As he does this, his eyes begin to water as he notices the faded brown and purple bruising on Birch's cheeks, just beneath his eyes. The skin on his bottom lip has splintered and swollen too. He starts to feel so lightheaded from the effort of trying to suppress his anger, from the idea that someone could've inflicted this kind of pain on Birch.

As he continues wiping, Birch tells him that it's fine and gives Teddy a dismissive wave. 'I actually think it's better than being ignored, weirdly,' Birch says. 'Makes me feel like I still exist, you know? Why would anyone bother spitting at me if I wasn't still a part of the world, right?'

Teddy feels an impossible kind of sadness at this and finally he starts to cry. Birch laughs at him and asks what he's crying for and, through the tears, Teddy says: 'You know why I'm crying.'

He then asks Birch why he's carrying around packets of tissues anyway and Birch replies: 'Well, I saw this guy doing it a few days ago. And he made a couple quid every day, so I thought: why not, eh? I could use a couple quid. He's been nicking these from the Sainsbury's in Aldgate and gives me a pack whenever I see him around.'

Teddy can't stop looking at Birch's emaciated face. His thoughts are being infiltrated with images of the plump, mischievously cheerful face he had known in adolescence.

When he asks Birch where he's been staying all these years,

Birch says: 'You know, man, just here and there. I can't always get into a shelter, so I just find my way around, see where the day takes me.' He pauses for a moment and looks away contemplatively. 'Well, actually, there was that bit outside Waterloo station – you know, the tunnel bits – that was quite good. I liked it there. Found a good group of people. But you got moved on a lot. But then in a few weeks, you'd just wander back and see people setting up again. They've got that big new cinema there now, haven't they?'

Teddy takes a hard breath. 'How long have you been living like this?'

Birch shrugs. 'A while,' he says. He looks at Teddy now with this sudden desperate look in his eyes. 'Ted,' he says now. 'I know I look like *this*. But can I hug you, please, man?'

Teddy immediately cages his arms around him and Birch collapses into him, his arms flopping behind Teddy's back. Teddy holds him so tight that he can feel the ridges of Birch's spine.

Birch tucks his face into Teddy's neck and whispers: 'Thank you.'

27

I used to believe that there was something immortal about a friend's presence in your life, in a way that wasn't true for biological family. It wasn't hard to accept that someday my parents would pass away. There was a kind of inevitability about their deaths that didn't seem so apparent when I thought of Kain and Nathan and, yes, Birch. I even questioned whether I was naive in believing so resolutely in the enduring power of friendship. I decided that yes, yes I was. And concluded that in the end, life weighed all relationships equally – eventually they all came to an end.

I didn't sleep properly for several weeks after Birch died. I would lay in bed trying desperately to delay the pain of his memory for as long as I could. Sometimes I felt myself tense up when tears fell down my cheeks, in an effort to delude myself into thinking I was crying about something else. And sometimes it wasn't even about pretending to think about something else, but instead trying to think of nothing, which was always superior because thinking of 'something' inevitably led me back to Birch.

In those weeks I needed the world to feel very distant. And the only way I could accomplish this was if I stayed still. In my flat, in my bed, flattened beneath my sheets, the world felt far enough away that I could pretend I was no longer a part of it. I know I was visited by various people, that my phone was called and texted relentlessly. But I wanted to suspend myself within this numbness and hold no thoughts and denounce any sense of being. I didn't want to be a person anymore.

One morning during those weeks I went into the bathroom and reached for my toothbrush. It was the first morning since Birch's passing that I'd spent more than two or three minutes in the bathroom. It was also the first time since then that I'd looked at my reflection in the mirror. I narrowed my eyes struggling to reconcile my sunken eyes and cheeks with the face I was familiar with.

My hands shook as I held the toothbrush. I looked at it for a moment, idly brushing my thumb across the bristles. Then I slowly rotated the toothbrush until its tapered end was upright. I walked to the other end of the bathroom and fell to my knees at the toilet. I inhaled hard and guided the toothbrush into my mouth and rested it on my tongue. I began to retch. Over and over again. And when nothing came out of me, I jammed the toothbrush repeatedly into the back of my throat, gagging and screaming, pressing my eyes shut so tight that they became sore and hot with tears. I vomited in long stringy bands, in soft cubed chunks, in dark acidic brown gushes. Every time I forced the toothbrush deeper inside me I wondered if this was the moment I would feel better; if this was the moment where making the effort to integrate myself back into the world would feel worth it. But I could feel myself moving further and further away from touching this reprieve I craved. I felt so far removed that I could no longer describe myself as human. I felt as if I was floating above myself, watching this husk of a person beg its body for something it could no longer give him.

I heard someone yell my name then. It was Kain standing at the door holding two shopping bags. I hadn't even heard him open the front door. He dropped the bags. He face was overwrought with horror. I could feel how wet and gluey my face was with spit and sick and tears. But I no longer had the capacity to be embarrassed. I turned away from him. He appeared behind me, grabbing my arm, trying to pull the toothbrush out of my mouth. I resisted. 'Please, Kain,' I yelled. 'Please just leave me alone.'

He clamped his hand around my arm and said: 'Ted, what the fuck are you doing, blud. Stop it.'

I used my elbow to jab him away, nudging him in his stomach. But he still overpowered me. When he managed to dislodge the toothbrush from my grip, he slung both arms around me and held me tight. I was coughing and wailing as my tears continued to plink onto the porcelain of the toilet. I felt like an animal, severely wounded, further disengaging me from everything I'd thought had made me human. I felt as if my life had collapsed into rubble around me. The world almost seemed to present itself to me in a different hue, now that the facade and pretence and the desire to cling on to some semblance of normality had faded. And all this time, behind everything, was just this: a naked, shivering man, buried beneath the dusty relics of his failure: failure to better himself, failure to convince the world of his humanity, failure to keep his best friend alive. I understood then that there would be no coming back from this. If so much of who I was had been tied up in protecting the people I loved, then what was left of me now?

I sobbed into Kain's arms. 'I can't do this,' I said. 'I can't do this anymore. I can't—'

He made gentle hushing noises. We sat there on the cold tiles for a long time while I calmed down. My breathing slowed and I shut my eyes while Kain cleaned my face with a towel. We were resting against the bathtub now. I was sitting between his legs, resting the back of my head against his chest. And he had his arms around me. Eventually Kain said: 'You okay now?'

My throat was burning. 'No,' I said. 'I don't know if I'm ever going to be.' I swallowed despite the pain. 'Life just hurts too much.'

After another long silence he said: 'I wish I knew what to do to help you.'

I sighed. 'Me too.'

We fell silent again. Eventually he started to hum 'Dreams' by Gabrielle. My skin prickled with goosebumps and I started to cry again. I tried to hum along too but I stopped and let him continue on his own. I told him that I'd become frightened of Birch's memory; that allowing myself to allocate space for him in my head felt like I was placing my hand in fire and leaving it there to burn. Kain told me that Birch would hate that. 'You know the brudda liked the attention,' he said.

'That he did,' I said. And then after a pause continued: 'I don't know how I'm going to do this, Kain. I mean, do I have to try and get in contact with his stepdad and his mother? You know for years I tried to find them. I wrote them god knows how many letters until I realised they probably moved ages ago.'

'Nah, fuck them,' he said. 'If they gave a shit about him they would've been in his life, innit? They wouldn't have kicked him out and abandoned him. We're his real family. And that's all that matters.'

I looked up at him and smiled. 'I think this is the first time you've called him family.'

'Nah, I swear I've called him family before.'

'Kain,' I said. 'You've never called him that.'

'Me and Birch were like this, you know,' he lifted his hand and crossed his fingers.

'No you weren't,' I said. 'You pretty much hated him.'

'That's what you think, innit.'

'What?' I said. 'You thought he was annoying and he always ate all your food. One time he pulled your shorts down when we were playing tennis and you said you were gonna stab him.'

'But did I stab him, though?'

'I guess you didn't.'

He smiled at me coyly. 'Not with a knife at least.'

I jolted my head back. 'Excuse me?' I said. He giggled to himself. Then he stared at me as his eyes gradually widened with this mischievous smirk. I narrowed my eyes. He then flicked his eyebrows upward repeatedly. 'Bullshit,' I said.

'Nah, it's true, blud.'

'Bollocks,' I said. 'You want me to believe you and Birch were secretly having sex. And you just pretended to not like him. And you just let him throw every verbal perversion at you for years.'

He shrugged. 'Yeah.'

'How long for?' I said 'Like – for the last five years? Did you do it in your room or on his pull-out bed? Was this before or after Harley?'

'On and off,' he said. 'And obviously in my room, innit. And before Harley. Yeah, Birch was annoying. But he was actually pretty chill when he had my cock in his mouth.'

I tore myself away from him. 'Enough of that,' I said. 'Now

I have to process this grief as well as this betrayal. So thank you for that.'

I took this distraction and clung to it. That evening he cooked us dinner. He made spaghetti carbonara. It was the first time I'd even attempted to eat properly in weeks. At the table we tried to talk about Birch's cremation and the various administrative tasks that kept arising. But I kept bringing it back to their secret relationship. I kept going over certain events in my head and blurting out: 'I fucking knew it. I knew something was going on. Didn't I always say? You both always looked so suspicious when it was just you two in a room.' And he just laughed. He could tell I needed this, to bask in the shock and surprise of it all.

'Wait a minute,' I said at one point. 'So that time we were on the courts and Birch said – and I'm gonna quote verbatim here – that you had the kind of penis that would make some-one need anal-reconstruction surgery afterwards. And you were all pissed like: "Shut up, blud." That was – what? Birch actually bragging.'

He just cackled and wound more spaghetti around the tines of his fork.

We watched TV together that evening with DC energetic-ally crawling all over our laps. We clicked through the music channels in silence. There was a career retrospective for the girl group Honeyz on Flava TV, playing all seven of their singles that we stayed for, and then we watched one for Shola Ama that aired next.

Later that night he told me that he'd seen Harley's articles in the final issue of *Rush!*. He had a copy in his room which he retrieved. I asked him if Harley was happy with the finished print. And he nodded and said Harley had texted me to say thank you, but I still hadn't been looking at my messages. I sensed a strange shift in atmosphere then as he opened the magazine and turned to Harley's article. I thought he was going to show me Harley's review of the new the Weeknd release and maybe say he'd listened to and really liked it. But instead he showed me the obituary I'd asked Harley to write for the deceased record-label executive Julian Blackwell.

I started to ramble about how I didn't know much about him, but his passing seemed to have had everyone in the industry quite shaken; that I'd asked Harley to write the obituary to simply expand his writing portfolio. I began to trail off when Kain started to look a little saddened. I asked him what was wrong. He went quiet for a moment. Then he took a deep breath and glanced at me in this hesitant way as if he wanted to tell me something he couldn't. I put my hand on his back. And eventually he started to tell me the things Julian had done to him. He turned his head away from me as he relayed the events. His hands were clasped very tightly on his knees. He even told me that the night he'd first called me, all those years ago, was when the worst of it had happened. His voice seemed to shake with every word that came out of his mouth. There was no doubt that these sentences carried the weight of someone who once had tried to bury their memory. It hit me sharply in my chest and I swelled in a rush of rage so searing I wanted to punch several holes in something.

Somehow I felt sympathy and hugs would be an insufficient response. So I took the magazine from him, tore out the page and went into the kitchen. I turned on the stove and held the page at the flame until the page started to curl and brown and distort and then finally disintegrate. He stood behind me laughing, saying: 'What are you doing, blud?'

I shook my head. 'I don't know,' I said. 'It just felt like the right thing.'

Still laughing he said: 'Wait a minute. I've got another copy, innit. I'm gonna do it too.'

When he came back and held the page to the fire, he said: 'Fuck him.' And I repeated the sentiment.

The following week I decided to resume my sessions with Matthew. I'd amassed several missed calls from him over the last month and I was beginning to feel guilty for ignoring him. It was guilt that remained even when I thought mean things like: well, he only wants my money. The world at large still seemed too much to engage with. In any case we agreed to conduct the rest of our sessions over the phone.

He said it was nice to hear my voice again. I let the comment sit there awkwardly between us and didn't say anything. 'So tell me,' he said. 'What's been going on? How have you been?'

I was in the living room. DC ran in from seemingly nowhere and jumped into my lap. I smiled and ran my fingers through her fur. I only started to feel sad when I remembered how often I used to do this to Birch's hair. She nuzzled my palm then and started sniffing my skin. 'My best friend died,' I told Matthew. 'A few weeks ago.'

In a sobering tone of voice he said: 'I'm so sorry to hear that.'

'Yeah, well,' I said. 'I'm sorry to have to say it.' He asked what his name was and I said: 'Birch. Well, actually Billy. But everyone called him Birch.' He asked how I'd been coping and a nervous laugh leapt out of me. DC started licking at my fingers, then buried herself in my lap. 'I haven't been,' I answered. 'I haven't been eating, at all really. Even when I feel hungry I think I'll just throw it back up, so what's the point? Essentially I don't know what normal is supposed to look like for me anymore. And now I'm currently unemployed so I don't even have that to distract me.'

He said he could understand how overwhelming this was, that there was no easy way through this, and that I didn't have to have everything figured out now. He asked me then if I was okay to continue with the session and I said I was. 'You mentioned what normal is supposed to look like,' he said. 'I'm curious what you think that looked like for you?'

I went quiet. Then I sighed and said: 'The opposite of this, I guess. I felt like a bit of a weight had been lifted when I finally told people about my eating disorder. I felt like I could navigate it in the open now and not have it feel like this dirty secret. But now it feels like none of that progress, however minuscule, matters.' He asked me what else and I said: 'I guess normal was having one of the most important people in my life still here. Still having a job. And I didn't even really realise it at the time but I was also kind of mentoring this guy. That felt pretty normal.'

'I do have to say that even minuscule progress is something to be proud of,' he said. 'It's work you've done. And it's work no one can take away from you. Not even yourself. It's always going to matter.'

I said okay even though I didn't really believe it. Then he said: 'You mentioned something about mentoring. Can you tell me more about that?'

'It was one of my friend's boyfriends,' I said. 'He's a writer and I helped him get published in *Rush!*. I think I'd been falling out of love with writing. Well, writing in that particular industry anyway. And helping him kind of reignited a little bit of passion. Not necessarily for being an editor or even for writing, really. But for helping someone else out. It meant a lot to him. But do you see what I mean? Look how normal all of this was.'

'Why do you think normal is such a prominent topic of concern for you?'

'Well it's important, isn't it?'

'To who?'

'To me?' I said. 'To everyone? If normal wasn't important then I wouldn't have started seeing you in the first place. I wouldn't be doing things like journalling and mindful eating and breathing exercises if normal wasn't what I was striving for.'

'I think it's very difficult to strive for something as, let's say, subjective as the idea of normal.'

I laughed. 'I hear what you're saying, Matthew,' I said. 'I'm not being obtuse, I swear. And I know it's your job to get me to disentangle preconceived notions about pretty much everything. But I just don't think you're gonna get me to suddenly believe that there's no threshold for normal. I had normal. And now I don't. And that's how my life makes sense to me now.'

'I'm not saying there's no threshold, per se—'

'Well, it sounds like that's what you're saying.'

He laughed too. 'Okay, let me try it this way, Teddy: If I said I think the idea of normal changes over time and is shaped by circumstance. You would say—?'

I didn't say anything for a while. Then eventually I said: 'I'd say it's maybe something to think about.'

Facetiously he replied: 'You know, it's okay to admit I'm right sometimes.'

DC looked up at me. I made a childish face at her, rolling my eyes. I heard Matthew say: 'You're making faces aren't you?'

'No,' I said. 'Not at all. I'm actually nodding agreeably. My pet ferret can corroborate if you'd like.'

'Well done Teddy,' he said. 'You've fulfilled the time-honoured tradition of telling barefaced lies to your psychiatrist.'

Later, after I told him how much I'd languished throughout the last several weeks, he said we needed to work on restoring some control in my life. 'I think we need to discuss ways we can get you back to managing your food properly,' he said. 'But I also think there's something there about what you mentioned about mentoring someone. If this grief has taken away a sense of normalcy from you, then perhaps this could be an option to restore it?'

'Mentoring someone?'

'Yeah,' he said. 'I mean, tell me if I was just hearing things, but I'm pretty sure your voice lit up a bit when you were talking about it.' I smiled down into DC's fur. 'If losing Birch took away some stability in your life, then maybe actively helping someone might provide you with a different kind of stability.'

Before we ended the call, Matthew said: 'Have you thought about writing a letter?'

'What do you mean?' I said. 'A letter to who?'

'To your friend that passed away,' he said. 'To Birch.'

I raised an eyebrow. 'Why would I do that?'

He said writing to him could be a valid way to process my emotions. 'It wouldn't have to be anything formal,' he said. 'Just a way for you to release and maybe make sense of what you're going through.'

I didn't tell him that I'd been here before: writing to Birch knowing he wouldn't reply. Still I said: 'That's nice in theory. But I'm sorry. I can't imagine I'll be doing that any time soon.'

'That's fine,' he said. 'No apologies needed. But maybe something to think about?'

28

It was understood between Kain, Nathan and I that there would be no discussion on how we would lay Birch to rest. I still felt disengaged from the world, and interacting with it, even on a very basic level, felt very threatening to me. I didn't want to take on the effort of forming fully realised thoughts and ideas and presenting them in proper sentences. My brain seemed to generate things in very fragmented ways now and I wanted to engage with these thoughts as they came to me. So when I said to Kain and Nathan that I wanted to scatter Birch's ashes somewhere in the Peak District, the only thing they asked was what date we would be driving up.

A week before we went, I received Birch's death certificate in the mail. Under cause of death it said: respiratory failure due to complications from acute bronchitis and tuberculosis. I glanced at the words, then I closed my eyes. When I opened them I tried to read the words again to see if I could accommodate his loss into my life as easily as the loss of hair, or something. I became obsessed with trying to bypass the forthcoming pain. I was even thinking about it the night he passed away, when the paramedics came over, when I was in the hospital with Helen. I thought about it as they were asking me about his medical history and his pre-existing conditions and the circumstances of his death. I even thought about it as the doctor relayed the details of his passing. Eventually it was me and Helen in the hallway. I had my face in my hands and she'd put a hand on my back as she simplified the doctor's language for me. She told me he had contracted bronchitis which had placed a lot of strain on his respiratory system. 'The TB and bronchitis ended up triggering something called acute respiratory syndrome and it led to respiratory failure.'

I wanted to yell at something, at someone. Instead I left my head in my hands, and let my tears puddle inside my palms.

The day before we drove up to the Peak District I got a call from Lucy and Charlie. I was on speaker to both of them. They asked if this was Teddy speaking and when I said yes, they offered their condolences about Birch and asked if they could have my address. They then asked if I would consider taking custody of Whitey and Choc-Ice. They figured Birch would probably want me to have them.

On the drive I told this to Nathan and Kain. We had Gabrielle's greatest hits in the CD player then. 'When a Woman', was playing. They asked me how they even got my number and I said: 'For some reason Birch gave it to them. They're in Thailand at the minute. They said they'd drop them off when they got back.'

Nathan laughed and said: 'How did he even meet them anyway? I've always wanted to know.'

'I think it was when he was doing that statue thing in Hyde Park last year, when he painted himself silver and tried to be a tourist attraction. Lucy and Charlie were out and they saw him and I'm guessing he started flirting with Lucy. And Charlie was into it and things went from there, I suppose.' They asked me what they were like. 'Posh,' I said. 'They sound like people off of *Made in Chelsea* or something.'

'How did they even know he died?' Kain asked. 'I swear he stopped talking to them after they took Whitey and Choc-Ice away from him?'

'Monty left his condolences in the comments under one of his pictures on Facebook,' I said. 'They must've been stalking him for some reason.'

I decided to scatter Birch's ashes at Stanage Edge. I thought about how much he would've loved to return to the Peak District when he wasn't sick. Though he probably would have wanted to visit a different spot this time.

We parked at Hollin Bank. When we got out the car I held his urn tightly. Over our t-shirts and black trousers, we wore the cardigans Mya had made us for the *Rush!* party. It was also her idea to cut little holes in the chest as tribute. We didn't climb up to Stanage Edge; we hiked an artificial route. The wind was loud and brisk and made our eyes water. At the top, we walked along the ridge. I smiled at the vast expanse of rolling hills and winding country roads and the farmlands in the valleys below. Beneath the pale, cloud-streaked sky, the world felt immeasurable and endless. Eventually we stopped walking and stood there in silence for a long time, looking out into the horizon.

Kain and Nathan put their hands on my shoulders. Then I opened the urn. The first time I tried to tip out Birch's ashes they blew back into our faces which made me and Kain laugh and Nathan say: 'Eh, Birch, fuck you, bruv.'

In the end, as Birch's ashes slowly faded into the distance, Kain sang a rendition of Quindon Tarver's 'Everybody's Free', which was somehow even more emotional than the original. He took his time and sustained certain notes. Then his deep voice drifted up into a falsetto so sad and delicate it was like he had his hand in my chest, clutching my heart. Without turning to look at me, Nathan held my hand. From my periphery I could see he was crying. I was too. Then eventually Kain's voice cracked and then he cried too.

We stayed in a little bed and breakfast in Hathersage. It was an old, converted farmhouse with veins of ivy creeping up the stone walls. After Stanage Edge, we had dinner in the cafe. We ordered a ploughman's lunch. I still couldn't bring myself to talk about Birch in any emotional capacity but I was happy to listen. Kain and Nathan went back and forth with stories, stories from school, stories from five years ago, stories from as recently as a few months ago, stories I had never heard before, stories that I had. His life was a vast tapestry of stories. He was like a funhouse with spinning tunnels and moving floors and wacky stairs and those mirrors that warped your reflection. I smiled as they spoke. More tears were falling from my eyes. I treated it like a performance they were putting on for me.

Eventually I realised I was eating without my mind racing. I ate the eggs, the cheeses, the meats. I even slathered some butter on a piece of bread and finished it and reached for another. I wanted to protect the moment somehow by not acknowledging it. But I also wanted to know what various factors had led to this. I thought about what I would write in my journal; about how I would tell this to Matthew. I wondered how important it was to understand the moment or if I could just accept it had happened. Would I be trading in one batch of obsessive thoughts for another? It was as if a door had been cracked open to a dark room I'd been standing in.

And despite everything, this version of normal – or what I wanted to be my normal – was still possible.

On the way up to our room, Kain told us that he and Harley were going out again, that they had a date in a few days. Nathan nudged him with his elbow and said: 'Why haven't I met the brudda yet?' And Kain laughed and said he would set something up. In the room they showed me videos they'd been making and uploading to YouTube for their handyman business. Each of them had about a thousand views. They looked like they were having fun. In one video Kain was recording Nathan taking a break after installing some fresh paving stones. He was wiping his face with his shirt and Kain was narrating to the camera in this animated way I hadn't seen since I'd first seen him in a music video. 'You're both shirtless in this,' I said. 'You took Birch's advice?' They exchanged conspiratorial looks and then Kain said: 'It's what he would've wanted, innit.'

I knew I wouldn't be able to sleep that night so Nathan and Kain shared the bed and I stayed up watching music videos on the TV with the volume low. On one of the channels there was an *X Factor* retrospective that featured videos from Leona Lewis and Alexandra Burke. Then I switched to Clubland TV where they played DJ Sammy's 'Heaven', and LMC's 'Take Me to the Clouds Above,' back to back. It was so pointed that I actually looked out the window and into the sky. I shook my head and laughed quietly to myself.

A few days after I got back to London I went on a video call with my parents. My mum had got my dad a new laptop and he was excited by its features. So far he'd just used it to discover the 'Gangnam Style' video. And at various points during the call, he kept yelling: 'Hey sexy lady' at me. And at other points he even got up to show me the dance, crossing his wrists and pretending to ride a horse. But he also said the reason for the upgrade from calls to video calls was because he didn't trust me to tell the truth about whether I was fine or not. He said he wanted to see my face and judge for himself.

They were having dinner at the time with Mr McAllister. They'd placed the laptop at the top of the dining table so I could see them all. I was eating leftover lasagne Kain had made. My parents had cooked Mr McAllister banku and okro soup and I watched him pinching awkwardly at the white dough, which made me laugh. They said they were trying to teach him about Ghanaian food.

'Last time we had jollof rice and he said it was too spicy,' my mum said.

'Aye,' Mr McAllister said. 'It was.'

My mum kissed her teeth. 'That wasn't spice,' she said. 'You don't know spice.'

'And before that you had me eatin' that brown gloop with "shite" in the title,' he said. 'I like a wee bit of spice. But not a bloody inferno in my gob.'

'Is he talking about shitto?' I said. 'Why would you even let him have that?'

My dad laughed. 'It wasn't that bad.'

I'd told my parents I didn't want to talk about Birch. But they hadn't communicated that to Mr McAllister. So when he eventually offered his condolences and started recalling various memories he'd had of Birch and me in school, I had a false smile frozen on my face and tears were filling my eyes. Then he finished by saying: 'He was a good kid.' And I nodded at him, tight-lipped. When my dad saw my face he tried to change the subject. Excitedly, he said he'd forgot to tell me that my mum had come second place in another gardening show she'd participated in. Then he went to fetch a little plastic trophy they'd given her and held it up to screen.

'Take it away,' my mum said. 'I don't want to see it.'

'Why?' I said. 'Did you come second place to Belinda or something?'

'Theodore,' she said. 'I don't want to hear that woman's name in his house.'

'Then it's a good thing I'm not there,' I said.

After the dinner, when Mr McAllister had left, my parents went into their bathroom and placed the laptop on the edge of the bathtub as they brushed their teeth together, preparing for bed. I decided to tell them then that I was in therapy for my eating disorder. They both stopped brushing at the same time and looked into the camera. But before they could say anything I explained that I'd relapsed a few months ago. I told them not to be mad that I hadn't told them before, but that the help I was receiving now felt substantial and that despite everything, I could see a way out for myself, even if I wasn't quite there yet. 'I'll be okay,' I said. 'Obviously I can't stop you from worrying about me but, yeah, I really think I'll be fine.'

My dad picked up the laptop and held it at face level and said: 'Son, you keep stealing my shine. You're a thief. You don't let me comfort you. You don't let me say: it's going to be okay. You keep doing everything for yourself as if you're an adult. And I don't like it. I don't like it all.'

My mum hit him on his arm and laughed. I laughed too. 'Okay,' I said. 'Go on – say it.'

I went to bed after the call. Kain texted, asking if I was okay and I said I was. He was out with Harley at an Emeli Sandé concert at the Royal Albert Hall. At some point during the evening he sent me a selfie he'd taken with him. He was kissing Harley on the cheek while the row of people behind them watched. I saw it on the way to bathroom when I woke up in the morning. I balanced my phone against the window and continued to look at it as I washed my face. I felt a deep appreciation then for the different ways in which I could extract some sense of warmth and happiness. It was like I was watching little bulbs on a switchboard light up every time I welcomed a bit of that warmth into my life: watching my friends fall in love, be given second chances, having their businesses succeed, explore things that genuinely made them happy. Life – and all the things that made it both terrible and brilliant – somehow, despite absolutely everything, went on.

29

I was on the phone to Mya when Charlie and Lucy came over with Whitey and Choc-Ice. She was asking if I could pick up Bakari from school on Friday because she and Nathan were going to be looking at properties in Lewisham and Blackheath.

'Congratulations,' I said.

'Yeah,' she replied, 'we finally have enough for a deposit.'

She said she'd always imagined she'd be looking for a place with three bedrooms when the time came.

'Because you wanna have another kid?' I asked.

She laughed. 'No,' she said. 'Because of Birch.'

'Seriously?'

'I mean how many Lucy and Charlies was he gonna meet?' she said. 'And he couldn't stay on your pull-out sofa or in your bed forever. And I just didn't see him ever getting a job with a salary high enough for him to get a mortgage. And even if he did, how long was he gonna keep that for before he just moved around again?'

Wistfully I said: 'Yeah, he did like to, quote: move about a lot.'

'Wow,' she said. 'A direct quote. You're getting better at this, babe.'

'I'm really not,' I said. 'I don't know why I even said yes to taking in two more ferrets. Sometimes I can't even bring myself to interact with DC because I know how much he loved her. She feels like a part of his memory I shouldn't be touching, you know? It feels like every time I play around with her we're moving further away from this specific relationship he had with her. I mean, I'm never gonna make her gold booty shorts or subject her to my nonsensical ramblings, am I? And I know it sounds stupid but it makes me feel like I'm killing another part of him.'

'No, I get what you mean,' she said. 'I used to feel that way. When my mum died she left behind all these wonderful clothes and makeup and stuff. Ah Ted, I was obsessed with her. When she was at work I remember I would always sneak into her room and just rub my face raw with literally every bit of makeup she had. I was on some proper clown shit. And then I would put on her clothes. But when she died, doing all of that kinda scared me. And then I didn't know how to make her stay. Do you know what I mean? Like, I didn't know how to keep her memory alive. Because my dad wasn't speaking to me so I couldn't talk to him about her. And I felt touching her things would ruin her memory somehow. But in the end I had to stop looking at it like I was moving away from her memory. But stepping into it. And I think that's how you get people to stay. I know it's really hard, my love. And his memory will hurt you and make you angry and burst into tears. But despite that I think you also have to give his memory a chance to comfort you.'

There was a knock at the door then. I told Mya to hang on. I held the phone to my chest and opened the door. Lucy and Charlie were a young-looking couple, probably the same age as me if not a little older. Lucy was in a polka-dot blazer, black tights and heels. And Charlie was wearing jeans and a shirt with a V-neck so deep you could see little tufts of his chest hair. Lucy was holding a blue carrier that contained Whitey and Choc-Ice. I could hear them tussling around inside.

When I said hello, Lucy smiled with a sort of forced giddiness and said: 'We've never been this far east before. It's very uh, very urban. Very up and coming. Very ghetto but like, in a good way. Do you know what I mean? There's so much culture here.' Then without breaking eye contact with me, she tapped Charlie on his chest repeatedly and said: 'Babe, isn't it all very urban and up-and-coming?'

Charlie glanced around non-committally with his hands in his pockets and said: 'Yeah – very urban.'

I shrugged casually and said: 'Yeah, that's Limehouse. Very urban. Do you guys wanna come inside?'

She laughed. 'Oh no,' she said. 'We can't stay. Elsbeth has Ashtanga yoga for puppies at eleven.' I stared at her. 'Oh, it's like an elevated form of mindfulness that—'

'Lucy,' I said. 'I promise you I'm not even a little bit curious. I'm sure it's wonderful.' I looked down at the carrier. 'Can I take them?'

'Oh yes, of course,' she said. When she handed them to me she said: 'We're so sorry to hear about Birch. We had a very nice time when he was living with us. It's a shame it didn't work out like we wanted. I'm sure his passing has affected the community. I truly believe that when one of you dies, it elicits a little bit of a death within all of us.'

She put a hand on her chest. Then put the other on Charlie's and closed her eyes briefly. There was a very long silence.

'Right,' I said eventually. 'And what community is that exactly?'

'You know,' she said. 'The, uh, urban community and such things like that—'

I laughed awkwardly and replied: 'Yeah, it's hit us all really hard. We're not even turning up to the meetings anymore.' She and Charlie looked at me with this earnestly mournful expression. Then I felt compelled to tell them I was only joking. 'Anyway,' I said, 'thank you for bringing the ferrets over. Have a lovely day. You too, Charlie.'

I closed the door. I could already hear Mya laughing before I put my phone back to my ear. But still I said: 'Did you get any of that?' And she just screeched and said: 'Yeah. Sounded very urban.'

I ordered several things for Whitey and Choc-Ice that arrived a few days later. I'd got some chew toys, an additional litter box and some climbing shelves. I'd spent the morning trying to balance both of them on my shoulders like Birch used to do. They were just as energetic as I remembered them being. They raced around me as if they'd missed me; I coaxed them up with little chunks of meat I'd defrosted, waving them above my shoulder. They ran up my arms and licked my neck and then criss-crossed down my back.

A letter addressed to Birch arrived that morning too. After I piled all the ferret gear in the living room, I sat on the sofa and held it in my hands. For some reason I felt this sudden rush of nervousness. It seemed to hit me somewhere in the pit of my stomach and travel upward to my chest in this fiery surge. I'd assumed I was done with the administrative aspect of his passing and thought: what now? I opened it. It was from the Tower Hamlets Council, the Highways and

Transport department. It said they had noticed that he hadn't been attending his scheduled shifts as a school crossing patrol officer for the past few weeks and wanted to check if everything was okay. They wanted to know if anything was affecting his ability to work and if so to let them know as soon as possible. They said if they didn't hear from him by the end of the week they would assume he no longer wished to continue with the role.

A laugh leapt out of me. It was so shrill that I put my hand over my mouth in surprise. It also made Whitey and Choc-Ice look at me, which made DC look at me too. I started laughing hysterically then. It lasted a long time and I couldn't seem to control it. The laughter echoed throughout the flat and poured out of me even as tears emerged in my eyes. I couldn't tell if the tears were because of the laughing or the sadness. I nestled my elbow into my thigh and rested my head in my hands, shaking my head, feeling very out of breath. Whitey, Choc-Ice and DC circled my feet then, doing some kind of war dance, folding around and crashing into each other. Then they ran up my legs and up my arms, making that clicky dooking sound, licking and nudging at my face.

Eventually I slid onto the floor and stared at the ceiling as the laughter died away. I was breathing hard. My face was wet. I rotated my head to the side and saw Whitey and Choc-Ice running towards my face, then, after some hesitation DC joined them, pouncing on me. I tried to catch one of them but they all evaded my grasp as they ran in zigzags across my body. When they settled down DC rested on my chest, I ran my hand across her fur and quietly said: 'Look at that. The one time your dad gets fired and it's not even his fault.'

That afternoon, I tried to call the council but the number on the letter wasn't working and no email address had been provided. I decided to charge and then switch on Birch's phone to see if he'd already had any prior correspondence. His wallpaper was that photo the four of us had taken on Mam Tor, where he had his fingers in devil horns and his tongue out. And the only apps he had were the social media ones and various augmented-reality apps, like the one where you could pretend you were drinking a pint of beer. His missed call log was very extensive. But it was comprised of mainly one number that hadn't been saved. I had so much of his life in my hands, I thought. It felt like having access to behind-the-scenes footage long after a television show had been cancelled.

The phone started to ring just as I went into his emails. I was so preoccupied with the mystery of who it might be that I let it ring out.

After a few seconds they called again. 'Hello?' I said cautiously.

'Alright mate,' the voice replied. It was a man with a deep gruff voice. 'Finally decided to pick up the phone, did you?'

'Who is this?'

'Oh, pull the other one, Birchy,' he said. 'You tryna give your old man a hard time, are you?'

Curiously I repeated: 'Old man?' And then he said: 'What are you, a bloody parrot?' There was a brief pause before he continued: 'Anyway, it's good to hear your voice, mate. I know there's been a bit of bad blood between us. And I don't blame you for ignoring me when I sent you those text messages. Or for ignoring my Facebook request. I know I weren't the nicest to you when you got in contact all that time ago. But I was just a bit embarrassed about everything, wasn't I? But it did make me pretty bloody happy when you reached out. I just weren't ready to be in your life again. I know I was a bit of a shitty stepdad to you. All the things I said to you, all the things I did – knockin' your mum about and whatnot. Throwing you out when you were just a little'un. Leavin' you on your own. It weren't right. I haven't seen your mother either to be honest. Not for years. Anyway, I'm doing a twelve-step thing. I'm supposed to call up people I'm meant to have hurt and try and make amends. So what do you say? Wanna go and have a coffee or something?'

I didn't say anything.

'You still there?' He asked.

Coldly I replied: 'This isn't Birch. This is his friend Teddy.'

'What are you doin' with his phone then?' He said. 'Where's Birch?'

'He's dead.'

Neither of us said anything for a moment. Then in a flat tone he said: 'Oh. How'd that happen then?'

I told him the cause of Birch's death was beside the point; that he had long missed the many windows of opportunity he had to reconnect with him. Even in this attempt to disengage from my feelings, I felt tears sliding down my face as I spoke and my eyes began to sting. I told him that he was irrelevant to both Birch and his memory. And then emotionlessly I said: 'Alan, I'm sorry but you don't matter.' And hung up.

On Friday I picked up Bakari after school and took him to Deptford Park. It was a cold, wintery day and the sky was a milky white. Bakari and I sat on a bench and looked into the distance. He was wearing a little puffy winter coat and eating a Mars bar I'd bought him on the way there. He unwrapped it and kept reaching up to offer me a bite. Every time I took one, he would smile to himself, which made me laugh.

With chocolate smeared all around his mouth, he looked up at me and said: 'Uncle Ted. You're laughing.'

'I am.'

'Does that mean you're not sad about Uncle B anymore?'

I looked at him. 'No,' I sighed. 'I still am.'

He looked confused. 'But you've got a smile on your face.'

'Sometimes people can look fine on the outside,' I said. 'But on the inside, not so much.'

The confused expression turned into a sad one. 'So you're not fine on the inside?' I smiled again and shook my head at him. Just then an elderly man walked by with his dog. As they got farther away, Bakari pointed at them and said: 'What about him? He looks like he's fine. Do you think he's not fine on the inside?'

'Maybe,' I said. 'I think eventually you'll find that we're all dealing with something.'

'Oh,' he said. He paused for a moment and then said: 'What about me?'

'Well how do you feel?'

'I was sad about Uncle B too,' he said. 'But every time I think about him he makes me laugh. Like when he got arrested by the police and told me not to tell Mum. Then I don't feel sad anymore. So I think I feel fine. I hope I look fine.'

'Well then, I guess you're fine, aren't you?' I said, ruffling his hair.

I couldn't stop thinking about what Mya had said about memory earlier that week; about stepping into it. I even brought it up in my next session with Matthew. When I told him he said: 'Well, you've got a smart friend there.' Then he told me that in his own experience memory wasn't something you simply preserved but also found little ways to interact with. 'I think letting them change as we change is what keeps them alive,' he said. 'Sometimes it's not so much about holding on to the past but finding some way to bring them into the present. Does that make sense?'

I said it did.

During that session I told him I'd thought about the mentoring thing.

'Oh yeah?' He said.

'I think it's a good idea,' I said. 'I have the experience and the contacts and in this – what I'm calling – downtime, I could maybe set up some kind of workshop. I don't know, partner with schools or something. I haven't worked out the details yet. But you were right. I think there's something there.'

Finally, at the end of the call Matthew asked if I'd given anymore thought to writing that letter to Birch. I let the question linger for a while. 'Teddy?' He said. 'You still there?'

I took a breath. 'Fine,' I said. 'I'll do it.'

December 2012

Dear Birch. Or should I for the first time in my life call you by your real name: Billy. Billy Birchall. I've always thought it was funny that Mr McAllister introduced you to me as Birch and not Billy. I mean, we were only a few months into our first year of school. But I guess there was something about you that made the teachers or whoever pull you out of your government name and say: no, you're Birch.

It's funny. We've been out of contact for so long it feels like I'm speaking to you for the first time. Anyway, I've been putting off writing this for a while. Ever since you went away (I'm sorry I still can't say the word) I've been trying really hard to keep things from feeling too real. So obviously, for a while, that meant trying not to think about you. But I think about you now. It's not hard. I do it pretty easily. But now the issue is how long I do it for. I always think if I approach your memory in this specific and methodical way, then I can cheat the system somehow. That I can bypass the emotion that comes with engaging with you like this. Maybe if I recall a memory in the morning and then distract myself for the rest of the day for example, then I manage everything that way. But it doesn't work. I'm sad all the time. I cry whether I think about you for two minutes or two hours.

So anyway, I think I'll start here because I know you'll want to know: we have custody of Whitey and Choc-Ice again. Lucy and Charlie dropped them off when they came over to give me their condolences. First of all, I wish I could ask you what it was you saw in them. Was it just the big house and how admittedly attractive they are? Anyway, I can't believe you gave them my number. Whitey and Choc-Ice are doing great by the way. They get on really well with DC. Everyone has a turn taking care of them now – even Kain. He's actually the only one of us who's managed to get them to balance on each of his shoulders at the same time. I can kind of do it with Choc-Ice, barely.

You know, ever since I stopped being angry that you left, I started looking at the world with a lot less scepticism. I've become a little obsessed with the idea that when you left us, you left something behind, you know? The things you loved, the things that would bring you joy, the way you seemed to move through life as if the obstacles that presented themselves simply weren't there, had to have meant something. And I don't know if I've ever actually said or actively believed in the words: life *has* to have meaning. But it has to, right? And not in a metaphorical way but in a very real way. The idea of life having meaning can't just be this abstract ideology we use to exaggerate the importance of our lives. I need to believe it's true. So I've decided it's true. The things you did while you were here mattered. And every ounce of love you made me feel is still here somehow.

And I guess now I often catch myself thinking: what exactly does life mean now without you? The other day I was thinking about that saying: you'll always remember how someone made you feel, even if you don't remember everything they did and said. I don't think this is true for us.

I think twenty years from now I'll still remember everything about you in forensic encyclopaedic detail. Because, Birch, you took my hand and you ran, pulling me across a spectrum of emotions. You made me feel everything. I've hated you as much as I've loved you. And that's one of the many things I'm grateful for. I feel like I lived, truly lived, with you. In our little life together, in our corner of east London, with your eccentricity, your grandiosity, your sheer ridiculousness – you brought the world to me.

So now I let myself bask in your memory. I'm not afraid of it. I go to sleep every night knowing there's a chance that you'll come to me. And you do. Often. In fleeting images. You don't do much; I'll see your chirpy little face and you'll grin at me and then you're gone. So now, even if it hurts, I keep trying to find ways to make you stay. Sometimes I'll force myself back to sleep. Sometimes I'll just replay what I saw in the dream over and over again. Embracing your memory in this way made me realise how stupid I was for thinking that I could've ever continued my life without it. So, Birch, rest assured: I'm never going to let you go. Another saying I haven't quite come to grips with is setting someone free if you really love them. And I don't think I want to. I'm keeping you with me forever, my friend.

So speaking of desperately finding ways to get you to stay, I guess the last thing I should tell you is the dream I had about you. I recently found the copy of Gabrielle's greatest hits album that I got you. I ripped it and put it on my iPod and went to sleep listening to it. In the dream, we were in my car driving to the south coast. We were the only ones on the road and you had your head out the window with your tongue out like a dog and 'Don't Need the Sun to Shine' was playing on the radio.

At the beach we took off our clothes and stood there watching the sea shimmering brightly. A squabble of gulls soared across the pale cloudless sky. Surfers in dark wetsuits returned to shore on their boards. We looked across to each other and smiled. Then we took each other's hands and ran towards the wide open space before us, our feet quickening across the sand, faster and faster until we were submerged in water.

In that moment all I heard was our laughter. All I felt was our happiness. I floated on my back and looked up into the sky as you splashed around me.

But then suddenly you stopped and looked up at all that white space with me. After a moment you turned back to me and said: 'I have to go, Teddy Bear.'

When you looked at me your eyes were so wide and bright.

'Can't you stay with me?' I asked. 'Please? It's such a beautiful day.'

You touched my face. 'Teddy,' you said. 'You know I can't.'

I started to cry. 'Isn't there anything I can do?' I pleaded. 'Let me help you. Just this one last time. Please, just tell me what I can do to help—'

You smiled at me. 'Teddy,' you said. 'You're gonna be absolutely fine. Thank you for caring about me.' Then you turned back to the sky. 'You know, you're right. It really is a beautiful day. Do me a favour and enjoy it, yeah? You deserve it.'

I smiled back and nodded. I closed my eyes and reached for you. But my arms passed through you and I sensed you were gone.

Then I woke up and smiled into the flares of sunlight pouring through my bedroom window.

Acknowledgements

Thanks to: Juliet Mushens, Rachel Neely, Wilhelmina Asaam and Chris "Corporate Daddy" White.

Thanks to: Aimee Tutchener, Oliver Williams and Pim Wangtechawat.

And thanks to: Gulcan "GP" Akbal, Andrew Huddleston and Terry Miller.